EIRIK THE R...

AND OTHER ICELA... ...S

The Icelandic sagas relate th... ...ives of individuals and families between 930 and ... ...n as oral tales, but were so skilfully refined and res... ...when ...ritten down in the thirteenth and early fourteenth ce... ...t ...ney must be regarded as written literature. Some are preci... ...storical; others have been proved to be imaginative creations. All deal with battles, bloodfeuds, perilous journeys, and the demands or conflicts of loyalty. They are rooted in the Germanic heroic tradition, and rank with *Beowulf*, *Maldon*, the story of the Nibelungs, Waltharius, and the Eddic lays of Helgi and Sigrun.

GWYN JONES, Professor of English Language and Literature at the University College of Wales, Aberystwyth, 1941–64, and at University College, Cardiff, 1965–76, is the author of *Kings, Beasts and Heroes*, 1972, *A History of the Vikings*, 1984, and *The Norse Atlantic Saga*, 1986; translator of many Icelandic sagas, including *Egils Saga*, 1960, and (with Thomas Jones) of the Welsh classic, the *Mabinogion*; and editor of *The Oxford Book of Welsh Verse in English*, 1977. He has translated the nine sagas in this volume with rare eloquence and verve, allowing the modern reader to appreciate these full-blooded stories from medieval Iceland.

In 1963 he was made a Knight of the Icelandic Order of the Falcon; in 1987 the President of Iceland conferred on him the Commander's Cross of the Order for his services to Old Norse scholarship.

OXFORD WORLD'S CLASSICS

For over 100 years Oxford World's Classics have brought readers closer to the world's great literature. Now with over 700 titles—from the 4,000-year-old myths of Mesopotamia to the twentieth century's greatest novels—the series makes available lesser-known as well as celebrated writing.

The pocket-sized hardbacks of the early years contained introductions by Virginia Woolf, T. S. Eliot, Graham Greene, and other literary figures which enriched the experience of reading. Today the series is recognized for its fine scholarship and reliability in texts that span world literature, drama and poetry, religion, philosophy and politics. Each edition includes perceptive commentary and essential background information to meet the changing needs of readers.

OXFORD WORLD'S CLASSICS

Eirik the Red
and other Icelandic Sagas

Translated with an Introduction by
GWYN JONES

OXFORD
UNIVERSITY PRESS

OXFORD
UNIVERSITY PRESS

Great Clarendon Street, Oxford OX2 6DP

Oxford University Press is a department of the University of Oxford.
It furthers the University's objective of excellence in research, scholarship,
and education by publishing worldwide in

Oxford New York

Athens Auckland Bangkok Bogotá Buenos Aires Calcutta
Cape Town Chennai Dar es Salaam Delhi Florence Hong Kong Istanbul
Karachi Kuala Lumpur Madrid Melbourne Mexico City Mumbai
Nairobi Paris São Paulo Singapore Taipei Tokyo Toronto Warsaw

with associated companies in Berlin Ibadan

Oxford is a registered trade mark of Oxford University Press
in the UK and in certain other countries

Published in the United States
by Oxford University Press Inc., New York

Selection, Translation, and Introduction © Oxford University Press 1961

The moral rights of the author have been asserted

Database right Oxford University Press (maker)

First published by Oxford University Press 1961
First issued as a World's Classics paperback 1980
Reissued as an Oxford World's Classics paperback 1999

All rights reserved. No part of this publication may be reproduced,
stored in a retrieval system, or transmitted, in any form or by any means,
without the prior permission in writing of Oxford University Press,
or as expressly permitted by law, or under terms agreed with the appropriate
reprographics rights organizations. Enquiries concerning reproduction
outside the scope of the above should be sent to the Rights Department,
Oxford University Press, at the address above

You must not circulate this book in any other binding or cover
and you must impose this same condition on any acquirer

British Library Cataloguing in Publication Data

Data available

Library of Congress Cataloging in Publication Data

Data available

ISBN–13: 978–0–19–283530–7

8

Printed in Great Britain by
Clays Ltd, St Ives plc

CONTENTS

INTRODUCTION

THE word *saga* means 'a saw', 'something said', something recorded in words, and hence by easy extension a prose story or narrative. Specifically it is the term used to describe, or rather distinguish, the prose narratives of medieval Iceland. These were of many kinds, but closest to our present purpose are the *Íslendingasögur* or Sagas of Icelanders, which relate the lives and feuds of individuals and families during the so-called Saga Age, A.D. 930–1030. They were first written down during the thirteenth and early fourteenth centuries. The Family Sagas, as they are also called, are the very heart-strand of the native literature of medieval Iceland; they are also part of the heroic literature of the Germanic peoples. '*Þú ert Grettir, þjóðin mín !*' cries the poet: 'You are Grettir, O my people!'—and no people has ever more closely identified itself with, or owed more to, its written records than the Icelanders; yet the tales that tell of the star-crossed outlaws Grettir and Gisli, of Gunnar of Hlidarendi and Burnt-Njal, and the men and women of Laxardal, stand ranked in their prose kind alongside *Beowulf* and *Maldon*, the story of the Nibelungs, Waltharius, and the Eddic lays of Helgi and Sigrun. This twofold significance, native and Germanic, reinforcing their high literary merit and strong human interest, has made the Sagas of Icelanders a priceless legacy of medieval European literature.

Iceland was discovered by the continental Norsemen about the year 860, and permanent settlement began in earnest with Ingolf Arnarson at Reykjavik some fourteen years later. The first settlers found a few Irish priests at Papey in the south-east, but otherwise inherited a land so empty and remote that, as *Egils Saga* tells us, 'all living creatures were then at their ease in the hunting-grounds, for men were unknown to them'. By 930 the coastal fringe and habitable valleys (together hardly one-sixth of this formidable fire- and ice-tormented island) were filled with chieftains from western Norway, in flight from the conquering Harald Fairhair,[1] and with men of Norse or mixed Norse and Celtic blood from earlier Norse settlements in Ireland and the Western Isles. The precise degree of Celtic influence upon the subsequent course of Icelandic literature has yet to be defined; but the quality of the settlers was demonstrably high, and among them was a notable percentage of well-born lordly men, restless of constraint, vigorous, and self-reliant, the inheritors, sustainers, and transmitters of a strong and distinctive culture. No country was ever happier in its founding families.

Limitations were at once imposed upon that culture. The visual arts had flourished in both Ireland and Scandinavia, but in Iceland there was no stone to hew, no wood to carve, no metal to mould; architecture and illumination were in the nature of things beyond their reach; and there is little evidence that they were a musical people. Their artistic expression

---

[1] Harald's long reign covered roughly the last quarter of the ninth century and the first third of the tenth, and thus coincided with the *Landnámatíð*, or Period of Settlement. He was the first to subjugate the petty kings and lordlings of Norway and make the kingdom one. His victories in Norway, especially that at Hafrsfjord (*c.* 885), and his later punitive expedition to the Western Isles were thought by the saga-writers and historians to be the main cause of the colonization of Iceland.

must be in words, and by a singular stroke of fortune many of these words could be preserved. The long dark winters provided all the time in the world, the need to kill off most of their cattle ensured a large supply of week-old calves' skins for vellum, and the coming of Christianity in the year 1000 provided a practicable alphabet and a conventional format. Beginning on the estates of the wealthy chieftains and bishops, and in the monasteries south and north, but spreading later among the farmers over the whole island, transcription took place on an unprecedented scale. There still exist some 700 Icelandic manuscripts or fragments of manuscript on vellum, and these, in Sigurður Nordal's words, are 'like the poor wreckage from a proud fleet', which on a cautious estimate must have been ten times as numerous.

The substance of some of them is known to all. There are those precious repositories which contain the Eddic poems (for the mere fact of migration seems to have made the Icelanders jealous guardians of Scandinavian heroic and mythological poetry); there are the undisputed works of Snorri Sturluson, the prose Edda, and *Heimskringla* or 'The Lives of the Kings of Norway'; there are the family sagas and *þættir* or short interpolated stories, roughly 120 of them, with all the skaldic verses they preserve; and there are the *Fornaldarsögur*, or tales of times and heroes past, of which *Völsunga Saga* is the most famous exemplar. Less familiar, but still blessed with English readers, are such foundations of Icelandic history as *Landnámabók*, the 'Book of the Settlements'; the *Libellus Islandorum* of Ari the Learned, 'the Father of Icelandic history' and the first man, according to Snorri, to write scholarly works in his native Icelandic; the Bishops' Sagas, and that dramatic sequence of twelfth- and thirteenth-century history whose title is *Sturlunga Saga*. But there is an immense literature besides, much of it hardly to be discerned in the shadow of these works of native, national impulse. The Icelanders were earnest translators and adaptors of foreign works. They rendered into their own tongue histories from Sallust to Geoffrey of Monmouth; there exist voluminous collections of story and lore concerning Our Lady, the Saints (including Thomas à Becket), and the Apostles; there is a full homiletic literature in Icelandic; and the treasuries of southern Romance were ransacked for 'sagas' of Gawain and Owain, Flores and Blanchiflor. The general impression is one of intense and unending activity, a broad, strong river of words—creative, informative, derivative—flowing from eager and acquisitive minds to the haven of the vellums.

The sagas, then, are written literature. For various reasons the point is worth emphasizing. Conditions in medieval Iceland, it is true, were remarkably favourable for the development of story-telling and oral tradition, and we hear a good deal about the practice of reciting stories before kings abroad and at entertainments, marriages, and assemblies at home. But the sagas, as we have them, are written. It is certain that oral tales, oral tradition, form no inconsiderable part of the raw material of the saga-writers; but it is no longer possible to regard the Icelandic saga as the mere transcription of an oral tale or tales. In Björn M. Ólsen's famous and decisive words: 'The more closely we read our sagas and conduct research into them, the clearer it becomes that they are works of art, that an artist's quill inscribed them on vellum, and that behind him was no unified oral tradition enshrining a completely shaped saga, but only a mass of separate oral tales which the author must bring together, and from which he selected the material to make his integrated whole.' Further, we grow increasingly aware of the importance of written sources, both native and foreign, historical, legendary, homiletic, and exemplary, for the sagas. Thus the ultimate source of information about unipeds in *Eirik the Red* is as remote as Isidore of Seville, and Thorstein's dream in *Gunnlaug Wormtongue* and the episode in *The Vapnfjord Men* whereby Spike-Helgi wins his nickname both derive from *Trójumanna Saga*, the Icelandic Tale of Troy. On the other hand, considerable portions of some sagas are in exact accord with *Landnámabók* and Ari's *Libellus Islandorum*, and can often be shown to have been based on these sure historical foundations.

The third main source of material for the saga-writers consisted of poems and verses, whose highly disciplined form in general kept them from corruption. Often a single verse meant an anecdote or story, and in *Gunnlaug Wormtongue* a succession of verses means a saga. But we must remember here too that the saga-writer aimed to master as well as use his sources, and he would be an innocent reader who assumed that every verse in every saga was authentic and of the tenth century. Thus the dream-verses of *Gunnlaug Wormtongue*, whoever composed them, were not composed by Gunnlaug and Hrafn, who at the time were dead; and in his prose our author is silent about such apparently important verse-matter as that Thorstein married Helga to Hrafn for his money's sake.

It follows that the sagas cannot be regarded as strict historical documents. At times their material is historical, precisely and exactly; more often it is a reworking of history (if we allow that to include both oral and written sources), with an eye at once to entertainment and instruction; at times it is a more or less complete departure from history as we find it recorded in reliable sources. There are, of course, obvious non-historical sagas, fictitious sagas, *lygisögur*, which need not be taken into account at all here. One of the most striking features of recent saga scholarship has been the dispassionate assessment of their historicity; many cherished beliefs have been ruthlessly overthrown, and many a fond prejudice painfully discarded. Thus, *Hrafnkel the Priest of Frey*, long celebrated as a record of fact, has been shown to be quite unhistorical—to be, in fact, a brilliantly realistic novella, the work of a creative writer. *Hen-Thorir* now appears a work in which the author has allowed himself both historical freedom and geographical licence. *Gunnlaug Wormtongue* is an elaborate and romantic reworking of an old story, and its author has clearly been much influenced by southern chivalric and courtly patterns of behaviour. In brief, we no longer assume the truth of a saga. Rather we must ask ourselves the question: Is this history, though freely and perhaps not impartially presented, or is it a work of the imagination based upon oral and written sources? We get one kind of answer for the sagas of Hrafnkel and Gunnlaug, quite another for that of Eirik the Red. For there, the more hostilely the records are sifted and probed, the more securely the voyages of Eirik, Leif, and Karlsefni are seen to belong to European and American history. And with each answer nothing of lasting value is lost.

The sagas, we have said, are part of the heroic
literature of Germania. They are the prose (and
sometimes homespun) counterparts of Germanic
heroic poetry. This is because the Icelandic con-
ception of character and action was heroic. The men
and women of the sagas had a comparatively un-
complicated view of human destiny, and of the part
they were called upon to play in face of it. They had,
it is not too much to say, an aesthetic appreciation of
conduct. There was a right way to act: the consequences might be dreadful, hateful; but the conduct
was more important than its consequences. In
Burnt-Njal's Saga Flosi burns Njal and his sons
(and incidentally an old woman and child) alive, not
because he wants to; he loathes the task, but fate has
put him in a position where it is the only thing he
can do. So he does it. In part, this is the familiar
tragic dilemma of the Germanic hero: he has a
choice not between right and wrong, but between
wrongs, and cannot renegue. In part, it is a saga
reading of character and destiny: to see one's fate
and embrace it, with this curious aesthetic appreciation of what one is doing—it was this that made one
a saga personage, a person worthy to be told about.
The principal characters of *The Vapnfjord Men*
carry out their deadly manoeuvres like partners in a
ballet: that arrogant, unhappy, and hell-bent Brodd-
Helgi slaughtered like the doomed ox he was by the
unforgiving, supple, and far-sighted Geitir; then
Bjarni, for all his noble instincts (amply revealed
at the end of the saga and in *Thorstein Staff-Struck*),
brought inexorably, almost like a sleep-walker, to
his bitter vengeance; and Geitir's son Thorkel
stalking and snaring his prey in turn. Even Skald-
Hrafn's betrayal of Gunnlaug when he brought him

water to drink was well done, because it was what he had to do. We know the name of Bjarni Grimolfsson not so much because he sailed to America as because he gave up his place in a boat to a man more concerned to live than he. Certain death was the price of his gesture, but the name of the survivor was not worth remembrance. He was merely the occasion of Bjarni's moment of destiny. Death, it is true, was not to be sought, but it was not to be avoided either, if by avoidance a man lessened his own stature. For that reason, and not for false pride or folly, Eyvind Bjarnason would not ride away to safety from the pursuing Hrafnkel. Hrafnkel, an altogether tougher exponent of the heroic ideal, could bide his time because he knew his time would come. He knows both himself and the old proverb: 'A slave takes vengeance at once, a coward never.' The Saga Age in Iceland was a last flowering of the Germanic Heroic Age; it was wedded to the blood-feud, and the sagas mirror it in every detail. That is why, for all their realism and sobriety, the family sagas are heroic literature.

The sagas of the present volume have been chosen for their excellence and variety from among the shorter Icelandic sagas. There is a general critical agreement that *Hrafnkels Saga Freysgoða* stands first among these, by virtue of its construction, style, narrative strength, characterization, and persuasive realism. Not that it has ever rivalled *Gunnlaugs Saga Ormstungu* in the affection or number of its foreign readers; all the world loves a lover—especially a foredoomed one—and during the nineteenth century at least the classical virtues were less admired than the romantic. *Hœnsna-Þóris Saga* is an admirable example of one kind of historical fiction, in which everything leads to or follows from one central incident, the burning of Blund-Ketil (though according to Ari the Learned it was not Blund-Ketil but his son Thorkel who was burned to death); while *Vapnfirðinga Saga* supplies in reasonably short space an example of a saga covering a family feud through two generations. *Þorsteins Þáttr Stangarhöggs* is an admirable little tale in itself, homely and vivid, and skilful in its use of native and knightly convention; it is also a sequel or tailpiece to *Vapnfirðinga Saga*. *Eiríks Saga Rauða* (sometimes called *Þorfinns Saga Karlsefnis*) with its account of the Greenland and American voyages, and such extras as the Little Sibyl, has a most eloquent claim on our attention. *Þiðranda Þáttr Síðu-Hallssonar* serves to represent the many legends of the early Church; and *Auðunar Þáttr Vestfirzka*, so seeming-simple, is the best of all Icelandic *þættir* and one of the most flawless short stories ever written. Finally, *Hrólfs Saga Kraka*, which probably approximates closer to popular notions of a saga than any family saga can hope to do, has been translated as representative of the heroic sagas, the Sagas of Times Past, a genre neglected not so much by choice as for lack of opportunity by the English reader. It is deservedly among the best-esteemed of its episodic, savage, and legend- and folklore-laden kind.

The history of the first Icelandic Republic, from 860 to 1264, with its literary aftermath for another seventy years, consider it how we will, is a remarkable record of human endeavour. We end in admiration and wonder that a people so small (never more than 70,000 in number during the creative centuries), inhabiting an island so stern and remote, in conditions so apparently daunting, could bring forth from its scanty soil so rich and continuous a harvest of poetry, history, and saga. *Inopiam ingenio pensant.* Saxo's adage of seven and a half centuries ago carries less than a full freight of truth, yet what lover of Iceland and the sagas ever found himself disposed to contradict it? 'They make good their impoverishment with the imagination.' What the Normans gave to statecraft and war, their northern brothers gave to the blood-feud and literature, and their greatest victories are on the vellums.

GWYN JONES

University College of South Wales
and Monmouthshire, Cardiff

TRANSLATOR'S NOTE

THE sagas in this volume have been newly translated in their entirety, except that I have omitted from *Thidrandi* one of the dreariest short sermons yet penned against the Devil, and from various of the Family Sagas genealogical information of neither use nor interest (it seems to me) to the general reader. I began by aiming at a consistent convention for the spelling of proper names, but the forms Authun, Bothvar, and Athils (rather than Audun, Bodvar, and Adils) seemed so established for English readers, that in their two sagas I have followed common usage. I am happy to acknowledge an obligation to two friends: my colleague Dr. Desmond Slay was generous enough to put at my disposal, in advance of its publication in the Editiones Arnamagnæanæ, his researches into the text and interpretation of *Hrólfs Saga Kraka*; while the scholarship of Mr. Hermann Pálsson has resolved some notorious difficulties in *Vapnfirðinga Saga* and *Eiríks Saga Rauða*. Whatever errors remain are entirely my own.   G. J.

SAGAS OF
ICELANDERS

HEN-THORIR

I

THERE was a man by the name of Odd Onundarson living in Borgarfjord, at Breidabolstad in Reykjardal. He was married to a lady called Jorunn, a shrewd woman of fine breeding, and they had four children, two fine sons and two daughters. One of their sons was called Thorodd and the other Thorvald, and their daughters were called Thurid and Jofrid. Odd was known as Tungu-Odd, and had no great reputation for fair dealing.

A man by the name of Torfi Valbrandsson had married Odd's daughter Thurid, and they were living at a second farm called Breidabolstad.

Living at Nordtunga was a man by the name of Arngrim Helgason. He was known as Arngrim the Priest, and had a son called Helgi.

There was yet another man, Blund-Ketil by name (he was the son of Geir the Rich, and grandson of that Ketil-Blund after whom Blundsvatn gets its name), living in Ornolfsdal. This was somewhat above where the farm stands now, and there were quite a lot of farms still higher up the valley. He had a son named Herstein. Blund-Ketil was the richest and most righteous-hearted of all men of the old faith. He owned thirty tenant-farms, and was the best-loved man in the entire country-side.

Living out beyond Nordra at Svignaskard was a man known as Thorkel Trefil, the son of Rauda-Bjorn. There was a brother of his, called Helgi, living at Hvamm in Nordrardal. Thorkel Trefil was a good, sensible man, well blest with friends, and very well-to-do.

Finally, there was a man by the name of Thorir, hard-up for cash, and not much liked by people in general. He made it his practice to go travelling round, district by district, with his summer's wages, selling in one place what he bought in another, and soon made a lot of money by his peddling. On one occasion when he set off from the south over the heath, he took poultry with him on his trip to the north country, and sold it along with his other wares, by recson of which he got nicknamed Hen-Thorir. And now he made so much money that he bought himself the place known as Vatn, up from Nord-tunga; and he had not been keeping house many winters before he became so rich a man that he had large sums out on loan with practically everyone. Yet though he had made so much money, his un-popularity remained unchanged, for there could hardly be a more detestable creature alive than Hen-Thorir was known to be.

One day Thorir set off from home and rode to Nordtunga, where he saw Arngrim the Priest and offered to stand foster-father to one of his children. 'I will take your son Helgi and give him the best deal I can; but in return I require your friendship and backing, so that I get my rights from people.'

'As I see it,' replied Arngrim, 'I shall hardly hold my head higher for this kind of fosterage.'

'Rather than lose the fostering of him,' said Thorir, 'I will give the boy half my money. But you must make things right for me, and bind yourself to do so, whoever I have to deal with.'

'I hold it a sound rule,' said Arngrim to that, 'never to say no to a good offer.'

So Helgi went home with Thorir, and from that day on his farm has been known as Helgavatn. Arngrim kept a protecting eye on Thorir, and it was soon apparent that he was now even more awkward to deal with than before. He exacted his dues from everybody, and whatever he touched turned to money. He became a very wealthy man, but with it all was none the better liked.

One summer it happened that a ship put into Borgarfjord from the open sea. She was not berthed in the estuary itself, but lay outside in the haven. Her skipper's name was Orn, a popular man and a sound trader. Odd heard tell of the ship's arrival. It was his practice to get down to the market among the very first and set a price on the merchants' goods, for he held rule over the district, and no one presumed to buy or sell till they were clear as to his intentions. So now he met the merchants and asked them their business, and how soon they wanted to get their goods on sale, explaining that it was the practice there for him to fix the price of men's merchandise.

'We mean to dispose of our goods ourselves, without you,' Orn informed him. 'You have not so much as a penny stake in our wares, and, say what you like, you are not going to run things your way this time.'

'Something tells me,' replied Odd, 'that this is going to turn out worse for you than for me. But very well, so be it then! I now proclaim that I forbid all men to buy or sell with you, and I am likewise banning all movement of goods. By the same token I shall levy fines upon any who give you the slightest help. And, finally, I know that you cannot get out of the haven here till the next spring-tide.'

'You can lay down the law to your heart's content,' Orn assured him, 'but we'll not let ourselves be any the more put upon for that.'

So with that Odd rode off home, while the Norwegians lay there in the haven and could not get away.

The following day Herstein Blund-Ketilsson had ridden out to Akranes and came across the Norwegians as he was riding back. He struck up an acquaintance with their skipper and liked him. Orn told Herstein how very unjustly Odd had treated them. 'We simply do not know how to get on with our business.' They talked the matter over that day, and in the evening Herstein rode home and told his father about the merchants and what a plight they were in.

'I recall this man by your account of him,' said Blund-Ketil, 'for I stayed with his father when I was a child, and have never met a more helpful man. It is a bad thing he should be in such a tight corner, and it would certainly be his father's intention that I should keep an eye on his affairs were he in need of it. Now early tomorrow morning you must ride down to the haven and invite him out here with as many men as he likes; though if he prefers it, I will bring him on his way north or south, wherever he likes, and set myself to help him with all my heart.'

Herstein agreed that this was a good and manly resolve. 'Yet it is more likely than not that we are going to win the displeasure of certain others in return for it.'

'In so far as our case is no weaker than Odd's,' answered Blund-Ketil, 'that probably won't affect us too badly.'

The night went by, and bright and early in the

morning Blund-Ketil had horses driven in from the pastures and made ready for the journey. Herstein drove a hundred and twenty horses down to meet the merchants, and there was no need to seek outside help. When he got there he told Orn of his father's offer. Orn said he was only too happy to accept, but guessed the father and son would win the hatred of certain others for this. Herstein assured him they would not be put off by that. 'Still, my crew must be off to other districts,' said Orn, 'for the risk is big enough though we are not all in the one locality.' Herstein now took Orn home with him, together with his cargo, nor did he leave till all the traders were away from there, and the ship laid up, and everything in good order. Blund-Ketil gave Orn a right royal welcome, and he stayed there on the most hospitable terms.

News of what Blund-Ketil had done reached Odd's ears, and there were some to comment that he had shown himself no friend to Odd. 'Say so if you like,' responded Odd, 'but this is a man well-blest with friends and brave as they make them, so for the present I am letting it lie.'

And so all was quiet.

2

That summer there was a thin, miserable crop of grass, for there was little opportunity to dry it, and men's store of hay was poor indeed. Blund-Ketil went round his tenants in the autumn to tell them that he wanted his hay-rents paid over on all his land. 'We have a lot of stock to feed, and precious little hay. Also I want to settle for all my tenants how many beasts are to be slaughtered on each farm this autumn, and then we should get by nicely.'

Now the summer passed and winter drew on, and
was soon very severe north around Thverarhlid.
Supplies ran short, and men felt it cruelly. Such was
the state of affairs till after Yule; and by the time
January came in people were in sore straits, and
many of them at the end of their tether. One day one
of Blund-Ketil's tenants came to him of an evening
to tell him that he was right out of hay, and ask him
for some relief.

'How is this?' Blund-Ketil asked. 'I thought I had
so arranged matters in the autumn that I might
assume we would get by none too badly.' The tenant
admitted that he had killed fewer of his beasts than
he was told to. 'Well,' said Blund-Ketil, 'we will
make a bargain, you and I. I will help you out of the
fix you are in this once, but don't tell a soul, for I do
not want folk to get the habit of running to me, and
all the more so since you went contrary to my ruling.'

Home he went, to tell his friend how Blund-Ketil
was a paragon of men in his dealings, and how he
had helped him out of the fix he was in; and this
friend told his friend, and in this fashion the affair
became known all over the country-side.

Time wore on, and now February came in, and
with that along came two of his tenants to tell him
they were out of hay. 'You did wrong to disobey my
orders,' Blund-Ketil told them, 'for it so happens
that though I have a good deal of hay, I have likewise
far more stock, and if I now go sharing it with you,
I shall have nothing for my own beasts. And that is
the choice before me!' But they kept on pleading
their case and rehearsing their sad plight till he
thought it pitiful to hear their complaints, so he had
a hundred and sixty horses driven in, slaughtered
the forty that were in worst shape, and gave his

tenants the fodder which was intended for these horses, and home they went rejoicing. But the winter grew worse the longer it lasted, and many saw their hopes turn to ashes.

Now March came in, and along came two of Blund-Ketil's tenants. These were somewhat better placed with regard to money, but by now were right out of hay. They asked for some relief, but by way of answer he told them he had nothing to spare and was certainly not proposing to kill any more stock. They then asked if he knew of anyone who had hay to sell, and he answered no, he thought not. But they kept pressing him, and now put it to him that their beasts must die if they got no help from him. They had brought it on themselves, he maintained. 'Yet I am told that Hen-Thorir has hay for sale.'

'We shall get nothing out of him,' they said, 'unless you go along with us. But he will sell in a minute if you stand surety for us in the deal.'

'I can do that,' he agreed, 'and go with you. And right enough, those who have should sell.'

They set off early in the morning. There was a wind blowing from the north, and a bitter cold one at that. Just then farmer Thorir was standing out-of-doors. He spotted the men riding towards the yard, walked back in, closed the door and had it bolted, and sat down to breakfast. There was a knock at the door, and the lad Helgi spoke up, saying: 'Go out, foster-father, do, for there are men wanting to see you.' Thorir said he must eat first, but the boy jumped up from table and went to the door, and offered a courteous greeting to their callers.

Blund-Ketil asked whether Thorir was at home, and the boy said he was.

'Ask him to come out,' said Blund-Ketil.

The boy did this, saying how Blund-Ketil had arrived outside and wanted to see him.

'What is he so nosy about now?' asked Thorir. 'It would surprise me if he were up to any good. I have no business with him.'

The boy went and told them that Thorir would not be coming out.

'Ah well,' said Blund-Ketil, 'in that case we'll be coming in.'

They walked into the living-room and got a greeting there, but never a word out of Thorir.

'It has come to this,' said Blund-Ketil, 'we want to buy hay from you, Thorir.'

'Your money is nothing to me,' replied Thorir. 'I prefer my own.'

'There can be two opinions about that,' suggested Blund-Ketil.

'How comes a money-bags like you to be out of hay?' asked Thorir.

'I am not actually out of it myself,' Blund-Ketil told him, 'but I am trying to buy for my tenants, who find themselves in need of relief. I would gladly get them some, were it possible.'

'You have all the right in the world,' said Thorir, 'to help people with what is yours, but not with what is mine.'

'We are not asking for a gift. Let Odd and Arngrim settle a price on your behalf, and I will make you a present over and above.'

To this Thorir replied that he had no hay to sell. 'Besides, I don't want to sell.'

Then Blund-Ketil went outside with his companions, and the boy with them. 'Which is it?' Blund-Ketil asked him. 'Has your foster-father no hay for sale, or is it that he is unwilling to sell?'

'Of course he has,' replied the boy, 'if only he was willing.'

'Then lead us to where the hay is.'

He did so. Blund-Ketil now checked the fodder for Thorir's livestock, and calculated that even if it was all stall-fed to the time of the Assembly there would still be five stacks over. After that they went back indoors, and Blund-Ketil had this to say: 'I calculate from your store of hay, Thorir, that there will be a good surplus left over even if all your livestock requires indoor-feeding to the time of the Assembly—and that surplus I should like to buy.'

'And what shall I have next winter,' asked Thorir, 'should it turn out like this, or worse?'

'I will make you this offer,' said Blund-Ketil, 'to provide you with the same quantity of hay, and of no worse quality, this coming summer. I will even carry it into your yard for you.'

'But if you have no supply of hay now,' countered Thorir, 'what better off will you be in the summer? However, I realize that there is such a difference of strength between us that you can carry off my hay if you want to.'

'That is no way to take it,' Blund-Ketil told him. 'You know well enough that silver is good tender in all transactions throughout the land, and that is what I will give you for it.'

'I don't want your silver,' said Thorir.

'Then take such goods as Odd and Arngrim shall decide on for you.'

'There are few workmen here,' said Thorir, 'and I have no taste for getting about. I cannot be bothered with such things.'

'Then I will have it carried home for you,' promised Blund-Ketil.

'I haven't the house-room for it,' objected Thorir, 'so it is sure to be spoilt.'

'I will supply coverings of hide, and in that way arrange for its safety,' said Blund-Ketil.

'I will not have strange men tramping about my house,' said Thorir.

'Then it can remain with me over the winter,' said Blund-Ketil, 'and I will have the care of it.'

'I know this fancy talk of yours,' replied Thorir, 'and I want no truck with you.'

'So much the worse then,' said Blund-Ketil, 'for even if you forbid it, we intend to have your hay just the same, and put down the money here and now, and take advantage of our being the more strongly placed.'

At this Thorir held his tongue. He was as mad as can be. But Blund-Ketil had ropes fetched to truss up the hay; they hoisted the loads on horseback and carried off the hay, having made full provision for all Thorir's stock.

3

Thorir's actions are now to be told of. He made ready to leave home, and Helgi, his foster-son, with him. They rode to Nordtunga, and got a warm welcome there. Arngrim asked the news.

Said Thorir, 'I have heard of nothing newer than the robbery.'

'What robbery was that?' asked Arngrim.

'Blund-Ketil has robbed me of all my hay,' Thorir replied, 'so that I can't count on a thing to throw to my beasts in the cold weather.'

'Is this so, Helgi?' asked Arngrim.

'Certainly not,' the boy replied. 'Blund-Ketil behaved very well in the matter.' And he went on to tell him the whole story of what had happened between them.

'That sounds more likely,' Arngrim agreed, 'and it is better use for the hay that he should have it than that it should lie rotting on your hands.'

'It was an ill hour for me,' complained Thorir, 'when I offered to foster a son of yours. Let there be any outrage whatsoever heaped upon me, I find no comfort here with you, nor any redress for my wrongs, and what a shame that is.'

'It was a piece of folly from the start,' said Arngrim, 'for I have a bad one to help in you.'

'Hard words break no bones,' replied Thorir, 'but I am sadly disappointed that this is how you repay all I have done for you, aye, even to letting men rob me, for it comes out of your pocket just as much as mine.'

On that note they parted. Thorir rode off and came to Breidabolstad, where Odd gave him a good welcome and asked him his news.

'I have heard of nothing newer than the robbery,' said Thorir.

'What robbery was that?' asked Odd.

'Blund-Ketil has taken all my hay,' said Thorir, 'so that I am now clean out of it. I would gladly have your help in this; besides, it concerns you too, in that you are the legal head of the district, to set right all wrongdoing here; and you might remember while you are at it that he is an open enemy of yours.'

'Is this so, Helgi?' asked Odd.

He said that Thorir had told the whole thing upside-down, and went through the story exactly as it happened. 'I want no part of it,' concluded Odd. 'I should have done the same, had I the same need.'

'Well, it is true what they say,' said Thorir;
' "Best know bad by hearsay only", and "A man's
worst company comes from home".'

Thorir rode off with this for his pains, and Helgi
with him, to make his way home very disgruntled
indeed.

4

Thorvald Tungu-Oddsson had sailed from abroad
to the north of Iceland the previous summer, and
found lodging there over the winter. When summer
was just round the corner again he left the north to
come home to his father, and spent a night at
Nordtunga with the best of welcomes. There was
already one man there for the night, whose nickname
was Widefarer, a vagrant loping from one end of the
land to the other. He was Thorir's close kinsman,
and just as close to him in disposition. That same
evening Widefarer took to his heels and went bolting
off, and he hardly stopped to draw breath before he
reached Thorir's. Thorir welcomed him with open
arms. 'For I know something good comes my way
when you do!'

'It may well be so,' agreed Widefarer, 'for Thorvald Oddsson has just arrived at Nordtunga and is
staying there for the night.'

'I knew,' said Thorir, 'that something good would
befall me, I felt so happy when I saw you.'

The night went by, and first thing in the morning
Thorir and his foster-son rode to Nordtunga. A
great many men had congregated there; a seat was
found for the boy, but Thorir was pacing the floor.
Thorvald caught sight of him from where he and
Arngrim were seated on the dais, talking together.

'Who is he,' asked Thorvald, 'the man pacing up and down the floor?'

'He is my son's foster-father,' Arngrim informed him.

'So!' said Thorvald. 'Then why not give him a seat?'

It was of no consequence to him, according to Arngrim.

'That is not so,' said Thorvald, and had him called over and found him a place to sit alongside himself. The next thing, he was asking him what was the important news.

'It was quite a business,' Thorir told him, 'when Blund-Ketil robbed me.'

'Oh, and has that been settled?'

'Far from it,' said Thorir.

'How comes it, Arngrim,' asked Thorvald, 'that you chieftains let such shameful things take place?'

'Most of what he says is lies,' said Arngrim. 'There is very little in it.'

'Yet it is true that he took the hay?'

'Of course he took it!'

'Everyone has a right to his own,' maintained Thorvald, 'and he gets small benefit from being a friend of yours if he can be trodden under foot just the same.'

'Thorvald,' said Thorir, 'you are a man after my own heart. Yes, and my heart tells me that maybe you can right my case for me.'

'There is little help in me,' demurred Thorvald.

'I will give you half of all I own,' said Thorir, 'for righting my case and winning me a verdict of out-lawry or an award on my own terms, so that my enemies are not left in possession of my goods.'

'Have nothing to do with it, Thorvald,' Arngrim

warned him, 'for he is a bad one to back, while in Blund-Ketil you will find an adversary at once wise and noble-hearted and befriended by all.'

'I see that you are jealous lest I get his money,' said Thorvald, 'and that you begrudge it me too.'

'There is also this to think of, Thorvald,' put in Thorir, 'how my livestock is famed for its high quality, and others besides myself know how my dues are withheld from me far and wide.'

'I will try once again to dissuade you from taking on this case,' said Arngrim. 'Still, you will do as you please. I can't help feeling something bad will come of it.'

'I am not going to say no to an offer of money,' said Thorvald. And there and then Thorir made a conveyance to him of half his property, and his law-suit against Blund-Ketil along with it.

Arngrim spoke again. 'How do you intend to proceed with this suit, Thorvald?'

'First I am going to see my father, and will think up a plan for later.'

'That's no good to me,' said Thorir. 'I am not in the mood for dawdling. I have put down a big stake, and I want to go first thing in the morning and summon Blund-Ketil.'

'We may well find that you and good luck don't go together,' Thorvald replied, 'and that some great mishap will arise because of you. But so be it now!' And he and Thorir pledged themselves to meet at an appointed place the following morning.

In the morning bright and early Thorvald rode off with Arngrim and thirty men. They met Thorir, who had only two with him, Helgi Arngrimsson and Thorir's kinsman Widefarer.

'Why so few, Thorir?' asked Thorvald.

'Ah,' he answered, 'I knew you'd not be short of men.'

They now rode up over Thverarhlid. Their riding was noticed from the farms, and everyone came rushing out of his house; he reckoned himself happiest who reached Blund-Ketil's first with the news, and there was a host of men waiting for them there. Thorvald and his men rode as far as the yard, where they dismounted and walked up to the house. The minute Blund-Ketil saw this, he walked out to meet them, inviting them to stay there and enjoy his hospitality.

'We have other business here than eating food,' said Thorvald. 'I want to know what answer you can make to a charge of carrying off Thorir's hay.'

'The same to you as to him,' replied Blund-Ketil. 'Fix your own price, as high as you like, and I will give you gifts over and above, as much better and bigger as your worth exceeds Thorir's, and so amply will I show my esteem for you that the whole world will say you have gained much honour.'

Thorvald stood silent, thinking this a most handsome offer, but Thorir had his answer all ready. 'This is not acceptable, and there is no need to debate it. I had this offer long ago, and I don't call this giving me help though I now get it again. It was a lot of use my giving you money!'

'What are you prepared to do then,' Thorvald asked Blund-Ketil, 'in respect of the legal issue?'

'Only this, that you go ahead and make your own award, just as you please.'

'Then it seems to me,' replied Thorvald, 'that there is nothing else for it but to get on with the summoning.' And he summoned Blund-Ketil for theft, naming his witnesses, and using the strongest words and expressions he could find.

Blund-Ketil turned back to the house and met Orn the Norwegian as he was attending to his wares. 'Are you wounded, franklin,' asked Orn, 'for your face is as red as blood?'

'Not wounded,' he replied, 'but it could be no worse if I were. Such words have been spoken to me now as have never been spoken before: I am dubbed thief and robber.'

Orn caught up his bow and set an arrow to the string, and came out of doors just as they were getting to horse. He shot, and found a mark, and a man fell down off his horse—it was Helgi the son of Arngrim the Priest. They ran to him, but Thorir pushed forward between them, shoving everyone out of his way and ordering them to make room—'For this concerns me more than any.' He bent down to Helgi, who by this time was dead. 'Are you so weak, my foster-son?' Then he stood up from him, saying, 'The lad spoke to me. He said the same thing twice. It was this: "Burn Blund-Ketil. Burn him in his house!"'

'Now things go the way I feared,' answered Arngrim, 'so that evil grows from evil; and I always knew, Thorir, that some great disaster would overtake us because of you. And how do I know what my boy was saying, though you jabber this, that, and the other? And yet it is only too likely that something of the kind will now take place. This business had a bad beginning, and such may be its ending too.'

'I should have thought,' said Thorir, 'you had something more pressing to do than stand there abusing me.'

Arngrim and his men now rode off to a piece of woodland, where they dismounted and waited for nightfall. But Blund-Ketil thanked men warmly for their help and told everyone to ride back home at his best convenience.

The story goes on to tell how as soon as it was night Thorvald rode with his men to the farmstead in Ornolfsdal, where everyone was now asleep. They hauled a stack of firewood to the house and set it alight, and Blund-Ketil and his people did not wake till the house was in flames over their heads. Blund-Ketil asked who was lighting so hot a fire, and Thorir told him. He asked whether there was any hope of terms, but Thorir replied, 'There is nothing for it but to burn!'

Nor did they leave till every living soul was burnt to death inside the house.

5

That same evening Herstein Blund-Ketilsson had gone to Thorbjorn his foster-father's (he who was nicknamed the Strider, and was rumoured to be more of a warlock than appeared on the surface). Herstein woke up in the morning and asked whether his foster-father was awake. He said that he was— 'And what do you want?' 'I dreamt that my father came walking into the room here, and all his clothes were ablaze on him, and it looked to me as though he was nothing but flames.'

They got up and walked outside and saw the light of the fire at once. They took their weapons and moved fast, but the attackers had all made off by the time they got there.

'This is a terrible thing to happen,' said Herstein. 'And what is to be done now?'

'It seems a good time to make use of an offer often in Tungu-Odd's mouth, that I should have recourse to him in case of need,' said Thorbjorn.

'I cannot think that very promising,' replied Herstein, but off they went even so till they reached Breidabolstad and called Odd outside. He came out, gave them a welcome, and asked the news. They told him what had happened, and he had some strong things to say about it. Then it was Thorbjorn's turn. 'It is this way, master Odd,' he told him. 'You have promised me your assistance, and I now want to accept this much of it, that you give us some good advice and come along with us.'

Odd agreed to do so, they rode for Ornolfsdal, and got there before it was day. The house had now fallen in and the fire was mostly reduced to ashes. Odd rode to the only one of the buildings which was not entirely consumed, reached for a birch rafter and pulled it off the house, and then rode widdershins round the house with the burning brand, crying out: 'I take this land here for my own, for I see no inhabited dwelling here. Let those witnesses who are hereby pay heed to it.' And finally he spurred his horse and galloped off.

'What do we do now?' asked Herstein. 'This turned out far from well.'

'Keep quiet, if you can, whatever happens,' was Thorbjorn's advice.

Herstein retorted that all he had said so far was hardly to be judged excessive.

The storehouse was unburnt in which lay the Norwegian's goods and a lot of valuables besides. And now, in this nick of time, old Thorbjorn vanished. Herstein now looked in the direction of the farm, and he could see the storehouse opened up and the goods being carried out, yet there was never a soul in sight. Then they were trussed up to form loads, and immediately after this he heard a great hullabaloo in the home-field and could see all the horses his father had owned driven in, with the sheep and the cows from the byre, and all the livestock. Then the loads were hoisted up, and straightaway they all moved off, with everything of value borne clean away. Herstein followed after them and could see that it was old Thorbjorn driving the animals. They moved off down through the country-side, to Staf-holtstunga, and so out across Nordra.

The shepherd of Thorkel Trefil of Svignaskard was going to his sheep this same morning, and he saw where they were on the move, driving animals of every kind. He told Thorkel of this, who answered, 'I know what this will be: it must be my friends, the men of Thverarhlid. They have suffered badly this winter, and will be driving their beasts this way, and right enough too, for I have hay in plenty and ample pasture for winter-grazers.' Out he went just as they came to the home-field, to give them a welcome and offer them all the hospitality they cared to receive. They could hardly dismount unaided, so warm was the master in welcoming them.

'Your welcome is a heart-warming thing,' said Thorbjorn, 'and a great deal depends on your stand-ing by all you have promised us.'

'I know the business you are on,' said Thorkel, 'and how the stock is to be left behind here. And indeed there is no lack of good pasture enough.'

'We will accept that,' said Thorbjorn.

He then took Thorkel aside by the house, saying: 'There are great things to tell of.'

'And what might they be?' asked Thorkel.

'Franklin Blund-Ketil was burned to death in his house last night.'

'Who did so monstrous a deed?' asked Thorkel.

Thorbjorn told him the whole story, just as it had happened. 'And now Herstein needs your good offices.'

'I doubt I should have been so quick with my offer,' said Thorkel, 'had I known this beforehand. However, I shall go ahead with it now, so for a start let us go and eat.'

They agreed to this. Thorkel Trefil had not a lot to say and was looking very thoughtful, and as soon as they finished eating he had their horses brought round. They took their weapons and mounted. Thorkel rode in front for the day, but first gave orders that the beasts should be well looked after in the pastures and those in the stalls well fed.

They now rode out to Skogarstrand, to Gunnarsstadir, far inward on the Strand, where lived a man named Gunnar Hlifarson, a big, strong, gallant fellow, married to a sister of Thord Bellow, Helga by name. Gunnar had two daughters, one called Jofrid and the other Thurid. They arrived there late in the day and dismounted up above the house. There was a very cold wind blowing from the north. Thorkel walked to the door and knocked, whereupon a servant answered it, greeted them, and asked who could it be. Thorkel said he would be none the wiser if he told him—'But ask Gunnar to step outside.' Gunnar had gone to bed, he said. Thorkel said to tell him that there was a man wanting to see him. The servant did so; he went indoors and told Gunnar that there was a man wanting to see him. Gunnar asked who could it be. The servant said he had no idea—'Except that he's a big one.' 'Then go and tell him to stop the night,' said Gunnar.

The servant went and did as he was ordered, but Thorkel said he would not accept this invitation from a thrall, but only from the master himself. The servant said that might well be so—'But Gunnar is not in the habit of getting up at night. So do one thing or the other: either clear off, or come inside and stay the night.'

'No', said Thorkel, '*you* do one thing or the other: either run my errand like a civil fellow or I lay my swordhilt to your nose!'

The servant shot back inside and slammed the door behind him. Gunnar asked what was his hurry. He said he had no desire to talk with the new-comer any longer—'His words are altogether too rough.'

At this Gunnar got up and walked out into the home-field. He was wearing his shirt and linen breeches, with a cloak over him, black shoes on his feet, and a sword in his hand. He had a warm welcome for Thorkel and asked him to come in. There were still more of them, Thorkel explained. Gunnar walked out into the home-field, but Thorkel reached swiftly for the door-ring and pulled the door to. They walked round to the back of the house, where Gunnar greeted them. 'Let us sit down,' invited Thorkel, 'for we have a lot to talk over with you, Gunnar.'

So that is what they did; they sat down on either side of him, and so close that they were sitting on the very skirts of the cloak Gunnar was wearing.

'Well,' began Thorkel, 'this is how it is, franklin Gunnar. There is a man in my party named Herstein Blund-Ketilsson, and there is no hiding the fact that he wants to ask you for your daughter Thurid in marriage. I have come along with him for this reason—I don't want you sending him about his business, for it looks to me the happiest match, and it is a matter of deep concern to me that his proposal, backed as it is by me, shall neither be treated lightly nor wait long for an answer.'

'The answer to his proposal,' said Gunnar, 'does not lie with me alone. I must talk it over with the girl's mother, and with my daughter too, and above all with her kinsman Thord Bellow. I have heard nothing but good of this man, and his father too, so it is an offer worth considering.'

'You had better get one thing clear,' replied Thorkel Trefil. 'We are not going to hang about hat in hand for the lady, and we think this match no less an honour to you than to us. I am puzzled at a man of your common sense, that you should be humming and hahing when the offer is such a good one. We have not made this journey from home for nothing— so, Herstein, I will back you any way you like to drive on with this affair, if he cannot so much as see where his honour lies.'

'What I cannot understand,' said Gunnar, 'is why you are in such a great hurry, or why you should be using these threats; for it looks to me a very fair match. However, I can see you will stick at nothing, so I think I had better decide to shake hands on it.'

And so he did, and Herstein named his witnesses and betrothed himself to the woman. After that they rose to their feet and walked indoors, where they were well entertained. And now Gunnar asked the news. Thorkel told him they had heard nothing newer than the burning to death of Blund-Ketil. Gunnar asked who had done it, and Thorkel said Thorvald Oddson was the chief offender together with Arngrim the Priest. Gunnar's answer was a brief one: he blamed little, and commended nothing.

First thing the next morning Gunnar was up and doing. He came to Thorkel and said they should get their clothes on, and so they did and went to breakfast. The horses were now ready, they mounted, and Gunnar led them in along the fjord, which had a lot of ice on it. They made no break in their journey till they reached Thord Bellow's farm at Hvamm. He gave them a good welcome and asked the news, and they told him only what suited them. Gunnar drew Thord aside to talk with him, explaining that Herstein Blund-Ketilsson and Thorkel Trefil had come along with him—'And their errand is that Herstein wants to join the family and marry my daughter Thurid. What do you think of it? He is handsome and able, and does not lack for money, for his father has said he is prepared to give up the farm and let Herstein take it over.'

'I like Blund-Ketil,' was Thord's answer to this, 'for once when Tungu-Odd and I had a dispute at the Assembly over the price of a thrall, which I was duly awarded against him, I went to collect the money with a couple of my men in the most abominable weather, and got as far as Blund-Ketil's by nightfall. We received a warm welcome there, and stayed with him a whole week. He changed horses with us, and presented me with a fine stallion. That was how I fared at his hands, and yet I cannot help thinking it would be no bad thing not to close with this bargain.'

'You might as well understand,' said Gunnar, 'that she will not be bestowed on anyone else, even should she be asked for; for this one looks to me a fine fellow with a fine offer, and there is a real risk as to the consequences if he is sent packing.'

Next Gunnar went to see his daughter, for she was being fostered there with Thord, and asked what she thought about it all. She answered that she was

not so eager for a husband that she would not find it
just as attractive to stay single at home. 'For I am in
the best of keeping here with Thord my kinsman.
Still, I should like to please you both, in this or anything else.'

Gunnar now urged the matter hard with Thord,
reckoning that this match appeared to him in every
respect a suitable one.

'Then why not give him your daughter, if you
want to?' said Thord.

'Because I will give her only if it meets with your
approval as much as my own.'

Then that was what they would settle on, the two
of them, said Thord.

'But I want you, Thord, to pledge this woman to
Herstein.'

'But that is for you to do,' said Thord, 'to pledge
your own daughter!'

'I think it a more honourable course,' replied
Gunnar, 'if you pledge her. It will be more becoming
too.'

So now Thord let himself be talked over, and the
betrothal took place. 'One other thing,' said Gunnar,
'I want you to let the wedding be held here at
Hvamm, for then it will go off in all honour.'

Thord agreed he should have his way in this too,
if he thought it better so.

'Then we will settle to hold it in a week's time,'
said Gunnar.

After that they got on horseback and moved off.
Thord saw them part of the way and again asked
whether there was any news to tell.

'We have not heard of anything newer,' Gunnar
told him, 'than the burning to death of farmer Blund-
Ketil.'

Thord asked how that had come about, whereupon Gunnar gave him a full account of the burning,
who was the prime mover in it, and likewise who
were the men who carried it out.

'This match would not have been settled so fast,'
said Thord, 'had I known of this. You will now be
thinking you have been altogether too smart for me
and fooled me to the top of my bent, whereas I am
by no means sure you could trust yourselves to handle
this case alone.'

'We are safe in relying on a man like you,' Gunnar
told him. 'Besides, you are now bound to help your
son-in-law, just as we are bound to help you, for
plenty of people heard how you betrothed the woman,
and the whole thing was carried through by your
advice. And it is as well if you now try out once and
for all which of you chieftains is top dog, for you
have long torn at each other like wolves.'

With that they parted, and Thord was as angry
as could be, feeling that they had made a complete
fool of him. But for their part they rode first to
Gunnarsstadir, complimenting themselves on how
well they had played their hand, so that Thord had
been drawn into this lawsuit with them. They were
in fine spirits now. They did not ride south as yet,
but invited people to the wedding, and returned to
Hvamm at the appointed time. Thord had a lot of
guests there, and he marshalled them to their seats
in the evening. He himself sat on the one bench
along with Gunnar his brother-in-law and his men;
and Thorkel Trefil alongside the bridegroom on the
other bench, together with their invited guests. The
bride and her attendants occupied the dais.

And now when the tables were set up and everybody in their seats, Herstein the bridegroom strode

clear over the table and went to where there was a stone standing, and setting one foot on the stone he said: 'I swear this oath, that before the Assembly is over this summer I shall have Arngrim the Priest fully outlawed or the right to make my own award.' This said, he strode back to his seat.

Then Gunnar sprang to his feet, saying: 'I swear this oath, that before the Assembly is over this summer I shall have brought Thorvald Oddsson into outlawry or have the right to make my own award.'

Then he strode back to seat himself at table, and said to Thord, 'Why sit there, Thord, without a word to say for yourself? We know you have the same cause at heart as we.'

'It can lie quiet for now,' said Thord.

'If you want us to say it for you, that can be done. We know you have set your heart on Tungu-Odd.'

'You settle your own pronouncements,' Thord advised him, 'and I'll rule my own tongue. Just see to it that you make a good job of what you have vowed to do.'

Nothing else worth telling of happened at the wedding. It went off splendidly, and once it was over everyone departed about his business, and winter wore away. Then in the spring they gathered their men together and proceeded south to Borgarfjord, and arrived at Nordtunga, where they summoned Arngrim and Hen-Thorir to the Law-meeting on Thingnes. Thereupon Herstein parted company from them with thirty men, towards where he maintained Thorvald Oddsson had had his latest lodgings, for he had finished with his winter quarters. And now the whole country-side was in a turmoil, with great debate, and a drawing together of men on one side or the other.

6

The next thing that happened was that the moment he heard tell who had enlisted in the case, Hen-Thorir vanished from the country-side with a dozen men, and nothing could be learned about him. But Odd assembled a force from the Dales, from the two Reykjadals and Skorradal, and from the entire country-side south of Hvita, and had a lot of reinforcements from other places too; while Arngrim the Priest collected men right through Thverarhlid and part of Nordrardal. Thorkel Trefil mustered men from the lower Myrar and Stafholtstunga, and had some of the Nordrardal men with him too, because Helgi his brother lived in Hvamm and took Thorkel's side. Thord Bellow gathered men from the west country, but had no very big force. All those who were leagued in the lawsuit met together: they had two hundred and forty men all told. They rode down the west bank of Nordra and through the river at Eyjavad above Stafholt, meaning to ford the Hvita at a place called Thrælastraum. But now they could see a big body of men on the move south of the river—Tungu-Odd, no other, with almost four hundred and eighty men. They pressed on in the hope of reaching the ford first, but there was a head-on meeting at the river, where Odd's men sprang from their horses and guarded the crossing, so that Thord's party could make no headway, anxious though they were to get to the Law-meeting. They now started fighting, wounds quickly followed, and four of Thord's men fell, including Thorolf Fox, the brother of Alf o' Dales, a man of the first importance. With matters so they parted, and one man of Odd's had fallen and three were badly wounded. Thord now committed his case to the National Assembly itself, and rode back west, and the pride of the westerners was thought to have taken a good thrashing.

Odd rode on to the Law-meeting, but sent his thralls back home with the horses. When they rode in, his wife Jorunn asked what news. They knew nothing to report, they said—except that there was a man come out of the west country, from Breida-fjord, who of all men knew how to answer Tungu-Odd, and whose voice and outcry were as the bellow-ing of a bull. That was no news, she commented, though Odd got a rejoinder like other men. Even so, she added that what they said had happened was not very likely. 'There was a fight too,' they explained then, 'and a total of five men fell, and many were wounded'—yet they had not said a word of this before.

The Law-meeting came to an end without any-thing remarkable happening. But when that father and son-in-law came back west they exchanged dwellings, Gunnar moving to Ornolfsdal and Her-stein taking over Gunnarsstadir. After that Gunnar had all the timber Orn the Norwegian had owned brought to him from the west and shifted home to Ornolfsdal. Then he set to and rebuilt the farm, for Gunnar was the handiest man alive, and gifted in every way besides, the best man at arms, and most gallant in everything.

The time went by till men rode to the Assembly. There were great preparations in the country-side, and the two parties rode out in force. But when Thord Bellow and his men reached Gunnarsstadir, Herstein was sick and unable to go to the Assembly, so he handed over his lawsuits to the others. Thirty men stayed behind with him, but Thord rode on to the

Assembly. He gathered his friends and kinsmen about him and reached the Assembly early. At this time the Assembly was held under Armannsfell; and as the companies rode in Thord had a very strong body of men. Then Tungu-Odd's coming was observed, and Thord rode out to meet him, for he wanted to deny him the sanctuary of the Assembly. Odd was riding with three hundred and sixty men when Thord and his following barred their way in, and they started fighting at once. Soon men began to fall, and a great many were wounded. Six of Odd's men fell there, for Thord had by far the bigger following.

Right-thinking men could see now what great troubles would arise if the whole Assembly came to blows, and what slow work it would be to amend them, so they intervened and parted them, and the suit was set to arbitration. Odd was overborne by numbers and forced to yield, both because he knew he had the worse case to propound and must, in any case, give way for lack of strength. It was proclaimed that Odd must pitch his booths outside the sanctuary of the Assembly, but go to the courts and attend to his business, yet behave quietly, and neither he nor his men do anything to make trouble. Then men debated the case and tried for a settlement between them, but Odd got the heavy end of the stick, because there was a greater strength arrayed against him.

Meantime there is something to tell about Herstein. His sickness left him soon after they rode off to the Assembly, and he went over to Ornolfsdal. It happened that early one morning he was in the smithy, for he was a highly skilled worker in iron, when a farmer by the name of Ornolf came in and spoke to him after this fashion. 'My cow is sick,' he

said, 'and I beg you, Herstein, to come and see her.
And how happy we are that you have come back to
us, for that way we get some recompense for your
father, who was so very helpful to us.'

'I can't be bothered with your cow,' replied Herstein, 'nor have I the skill to tell what is the matter
with her.'

'What a difference between you and your father,'
exclaimed the farmer, 'for he gave me the cow, and
you will not so much as look at her!'

'I'll give you another cow,' replied Herstein, 'if
this one dies.'

'The first gift I want from you,' said the farmer,
'is for you to come and see the one I have.'

Then Herstein sprang to his feet, he was so an-
noyed by this, and walked out of the smithy and the
farmer with him. They turned into a path towards
the wood, where there is a winding path with trees
on both sides of it; but as Herstein was climbing the
cliff-path, he came to a halt. He had the keenest eyes
of any man alive. 'A shield showed,' he said, 'in the
wood.' And when the farmer said nothing—'Have
you betrayed me, you dog? Now if you are under
oath to keep it from me, lie down in the path and
don't utter a word—for if you do, I'll kill you!'

The farmer lay down, but Herstein hurried home
and called out his men. They took their weapons
and went hot-foot to the wood and found Ornolf
still in the path. They ordered him forward with
them to the place where it had been arranged that
he and the others should meet. They kept moving
till they reached a clearing, when Herstein told
Ornolf, 'I shall not force you to talk, but now get on
with what you were instructed to do.'

The farmer ran up on to a hillock and whistled

shrilly, whereupon a dozen men came rushing out, with Hen-Thorir in the lead. Herstein and his troop took them all prisoner and killed them, and it was Herstein himself who struck off Thorir's head and carried it away with him. They then rode south to the Assembly and told their news there. Herstein won great honour for this deed of his, and warm commendation, as was only to be expected.

They now set to debating these same cases, and the end of it was that Arngrim the Priest should be made a full outlaw, and all those who were present at the burning, except for Thorvald Oddsson. He must go abroad for three years and then be free to come back. Money was paid down for him, and for the passage overseas of other men too. Thorvald went abroad this same summer and was taken prisoner in Scotland, and made a slave.

And after this the Assembly was dissolved, and men reckoned that Thord had pursued the case both bravely and well. Arngrim the Priest went abroad this same summer, but there is no record of how much money was paid over.

Such was the end of this case. Men rode home from the Assembly, and those who were outlawed went abroad, even as had been stipulated.

7

Gunnar Hlifarson was now settled in at Ornolfs-dal, and had built a fine homestead there. He made great use of his shielings in the mountains, and usually there were few men home on the farm. His daughter Jofrid had a tent pitched for her out of doors, finding this less dull, and one day it happened that as Thorodd Tungu-Oddsson was riding to

Thverarhlid, he passed Ornolfsdal on his way, and walked into Jofrid's tent and had a kind greeting from her. He sat down beside her and they were talking together the two of them when in came a boy from the shieling and asked Jofrid to help him unload the horses. Thorodd went with him to unload them, and then the boy took himself off and arrived back at the shieling.

Gunnar asked him how he had been so quick about it, but he made no answer.

'Did you see anything to tell of?' asked Gunnar.

'Not a thing,' said the boy.

'No, no,' said Gunnar, 'it is written all over you that you saw something worth telling of. So tell me, did anybody come to the house?'

'I saw no one come,' said the boy.

'You will tell me, never fear,' Gunnar promised, and laying hold of a big switch he set to and beat the boy. Yet for all that he got nothing more out of him than before. Next he caught hold of a horse, jumped on its back, and rode at top speed down to his main farm in Thverarhlid. Jofrid caught sight of her father on his way, informed Thorodd of it, and begged him to ride away. 'I had rather no trouble should arise because of me.' Thorodd said he would be off all in good time. Gunnar came pelting along, jumped off his horse, and rushed into the tent. Thorodd greeted him courteously, and Gunnar took this well enough, but then asked him what he had come there for. He just happened to be passing by, said Thorodd—'And certainly I would not be doing this out of ill will to you. But what I really want to know is how you will answer me if I ask for Jofrid your daughter.'

'I shall not give you daughter of mine for this sort

of conduct,' replied Gunnar. 'Besides, we have been in opposite camps of late.' And with that for an answer Thorodd rode home.

One day Odd happened to announce that it would not be a bad notion to get some use out of the land in Ornolfsdal, 'where those others, contrary to all right, have settled on what is mine.' The women agreed that this was a good idea—'For the sheep yield hardly anything, and will milk much better for the change.'

'Then that is where they shall go,' said Odd, 'for there are fine pastures there.'

'I think I will offer to go along with the sheep,' said Thorodd, 'for then those others will think it less safe to interfere.'

Good enough, said Odd, and off they went with the sheep; but once they had gone a good long way Thorodd directed them to keep the sheep where they would get the worst grazing and the barrenest ground. The night passed, and next morning they drove the sheep in, and when the women had milked them they vowed they had never yielded so little as now, so the thing was not tried again.

In ways like this the time wore on, till early one morning Odd said to his son Thorodd: 'You must get down through the district and collect men, for I am now going to drive those people clean off my land. Torfi shall go up Hals way and let them know of our mustering, and we will all meet together at Steinsvad.'

They did this and assembled their forces. Thorodd and the others raised ninety men and rode to the ford. Thorodd's party was the first to arrive there, so he ordered them to ride on—'But I shall wait for my father.' When they reached the farmyard at

Ornolfsdal, Gunnar was loading a cart, and a boy who was with him called out to him: 'There are men riding up to the farm, and no small crowd of them!' 'Aye,' said Gunnar, 'so there are.' He went back to the house and took his bow, for he was the best shot of any man, and only Gunnar of Hlidarendi was reckoned his equal. By this time he had a fine home built there. In his outer door there was a window through which a man could put out his head, and it was there, by this door, that he took his stand, bow in hand. At this same moment Thorodd arrived at the farm, walked to the door, and asked whether Gunnar would make them any offer of atonement.

'I don't know,' he replied, 'that I have anything to make an offer for. On the other hand, I believe that before you work your will on me, these arrow-maids of mine will have stung some of your comrades with a sleep-thorn ere I sink on the grass.'

'True,' agreed Thorodd, 'you are beyond most men of our time, yet so strong a force may be deployed against you that you simply cannot withstand it, for my father is riding to the farm with a big troop of men, intending to kill you.'

'Very well then,' said Gunnar. 'Yet I rather fancied taking a man with me when I fell on the field. And I very much fear your father will shy away from this atonement.'

'On the contrary,' Thorodd assured him, 'we are most anxious to make the peace, so give me your hand now with all your heart and promise me Jofrid your daughter for my wife.'

'You will not get daughter of mine by threatening me,' replied Gunnar. 'Yet it would be by no means a bad match where you are concerned, for you are not such a bad fellow after all.'

'No right-thinking man would take that view of it,' said Thorodd, 'and I owe you a world of thanks if you accept my offer with all such conditions attached as are right and proper.'

So now by the persuasion of his friends, and this besides, that he thought Thorodd had acted very well in the affair, it came about that Gunnar held out his hand, and that was the end of it.

At the same moment Odd reached the home-field. Thorodd turned instantly to meet his father and asked him what he thought he was doing. He meant to burn the house, said Odd, and everybody in it. 'But the case has taken a new turn,' Thorodd told him, 'for Gunnar and I are now reconciled.' And he explained how it had all come about. 'Listen to the fool!' cried Odd. 'Would you be any worse off marrying the girl if Gunnar was killed first—the very head and front of our enemies? I did a bad day's work raising you!'

'Well, you must now fight with me first,' replied Thorodd, 'if nothing else will serve your turn.'

Now men intervened between them and brought father and son together again, and the end of it was that Jofrid was promised to Thorodd—to Odd's intense displeasure. With so much settled they rode home. In due course men sat to the wedding feast, and Thorodd was well pleased with his match. But at the end of the winter he went abroad, for he had heard how Thorvald his brother was in captivity and wanted to ransom him with money. He reached Norway, but never returned to Iceland again, neither he nor his brother.

Odd now began to age greatly, and once he learned that neither of his sons would be coming back, he fell very ill. When he felt he was past recovery he requested his friends to carry him up to Skaneyarfjall once he was dead, saying he wished to look out from there over the whole tongue of land from which he got his name. And this was done.

As for Jofrid Gunnarsdottir, she was married later to Thorstein Egilsson of Borg, and proved a most remarkable lady. And that is the end of Hen-Thorir's saga.

THE VAPNFJORD MEN

I

WE begin this story at a point where there was a man
by the name of Helgi living at Hof in Vapnfjord.
He was the son of Thorgils, who was in turn the
son of Thorstein the White. Thorstein the White
was the first of his stock to come out to Iceland, and
lived at Toftavoll away beyond Sireksstadir. It was
Steinbjorn, Ref the Red's son, who then lived at
Hof, but after he had got rid of his money for sheer
munificence Thorstein bought Hofsland and lived
there for sixty years. He married Ingibjorg, Hrod-
geir the White's daughter. Thorstein's son Thorgils
was the father of Brodd-Helgi, and he took over
Thorstein's farm. Thorkel and Hedin killed Thorgils, Brodd-Helgi's father, so once again Thorstein
the White took over the farm, and reared his grandson Helgi.[1] Helgi developed early into a tall, strong
man, handsome and imposing, not much of a talker
in his youth, but overbearing and headstrong from
his early years, tricky and capricious. Regarding
this there is a tale of how one day at Hof, when the
cows were at the milking-pen, there was a bull
belonging to the kinsmen there at the pen, and a
second bull came along, and the bulls started butting
at each other. The lad Helgi was outside and saw

[1] These events are recounted in full in the saga of *Thorstein
the White*. Unlike his grandson Brodd-Helgi, Thorstein the
White was a noble and magnanimous man, and the scene
of his reconciliation with the brother of his son's slayers a
moving one.

how their bull was getting the worst of it and backing away. He took an iron spike and fastened it to
the bull's forehead, and from there on their bull got
on the better. For this deed he was nicknamed
Brodd- or Spike-Helgi. He towered head and shoulders in ability over all the men who grew up there in
the district.

There was a man by the name of Svart who came
out here to Iceland and made his home in Vapnfjord. Next to him lived a man named Skidi, who
was not very well off. Svart was a big, powerful
fellow, very handy with his weapons—indeed, too
handy. Svart and Skidi fell out over the grazing, and
it ended so that Svart killed him; whereupon Brodd-
Helgi took up the bloodsuit and had Svart outlawed.
Brodd-Helgi was twelve years old at the time. After
that Svart lay out on the heath we call Smjorvatnsheid, a short way from Sunnudal, and made inroads
on the Hof dwellers' stock, doing altogether more
damage than he need.

A shepherd at Hof came home one evening and
went indoors to old Thorstein's bed-closet, where
he lay sightless.

'How have things gone today, friend?' asked
Thorstein.

'As bad as can be,' reckoned the shepherd. 'Your
best wether has disappeared, and three others
with it.'

'They will have made off after someone else's
sheep,' said Thorstein. 'They'll come back.'

'No, no,' replied the shepherd, 'these will never
come back.'

'Say anything you like to me,' warned Thorstein,
'but tell nothing of the kind to Brodd-Helgi.'

The following day Brodd-Helgi asked the shepherd how he had been getting along, and he had exactly the same answer for him as for Thorstein. Helgi made as though he had not heard and went to bed in the evening, but once the rest of them were asleep he got up, took his shield and went outside. The story goes that he picked up a big, thin, flat stone, putting its one end in his breeches and the other in front of his chest, while in his hand he carried a huge pole-axe with a long haft. He made his way to the sheep-pen, and from there followed the tracks, because there was snow on the ground, and came up out of Sunnudal on to Smjorvatnsheid.

Svart came out of doors and saw a brisk-looking fellow coming towards him. He asked who was there. Brodd-Helgi said it was he.

'Then you are thinking to get in touch with me, and not for nothing at that,' said Svart.

He ran towards him and thrust at him with a big broad-bladed spear, but Brodd-Helgi warded it off with his shield. The spear struck the outer face of the shield and then the flat stone, to glance off so sharply that Svart fell forward after his thrust, and Brodd-Helgi cut at his leg so that it was taken right off.

'This shows how different are our fortunes,' said Svart; 'that you will be my executioner, while such kin-hurt shall persist in your family from now on that it will be remembered for ever, as long as the land is lived in.'

After that Helgi struck him his death-blow.

Now old Thorstein woke up back at Hof. He left his bed and felt in Brodd-Helgi's place, and it had grown cold. He routed out his housecarles, bidding them go and seek Brodd-Helgi, and once they had come outside they followed his tracks the whole way,

and found him where Svart lay dead. Later they
buried the corpse, and carried away with them everything of value there. Brodd-Helgi's fame spread far
and wide, and he was highly praised by all for this
brave deed he had done, such a youngster as he still
was at the time.

2

At the time when Thorstein was living at Hof and
Brodd-Helgi grew up in his care, a man called Lyting
Asbjarnarson lived at the outer Krossavik. He was
a wise man and well off for money, and was married
to a woman by the name of Thordis, the daughter of
Herlu-Bjarni Arnfinnsson. They had two sons who
appear in this saga, one named Geitir, and the other
Blæng. One of Lyting's daughters was called Halla,
and the other Rannveig. They were much of an age,
Brodd-Helgi and these brothers; there was the
closest friendship between them, and Helgi married
Halla their sister. Their daughter was that Thordis
Todda whom Helgi Asbjarnarson married, while
Bjarni was their youngest son and Lyting the elder.
Bjarni was fostered at Krossavik by Geitir. Blæng
was a powerful man but somewhat limping in his
gait. Geitir married Thidrandi's daughter Hallkatla,
an aunt of the sons of Droplaug. Such loving friendship was between Brodd-Helgi and Geitir that they
shared all their amusements and business together,
and met almost every day, and it was the talk of
everyone how great their friendship was.

At this same time there lived in Sunnudal a man
by the name of Thormod, nicknamed Stickgazer,
the son of Stubby-Steinbjorn, and brother of Ref of
Refsstadir and Egil of Egilsstadir. Egil's children
were Thorarin, Hallbjorn, and Throst, and that Hall-

frid whom Geitir's son Thorkel eventually married. Thormod's sons were Thorstein and Eyvind, and the sons of Ref, Stein and Hreidar. These were all Geitir's retainers. He was a man of great wisdom and good judgement. Halla and Brodd-Helgi were happy in their marriage. Lyting was fostered in Oxarfjord by Thorgils Skinni. Brodd-Helgi was a very wealthy man.

The story goes on to tell how one summer a ship came out to Vapnfjord. The man who skippered this ship bore the name Thorleif; he was nicknamed the Christian. He had a farm at Krossavik in Reydarfjord and was stepson to Asbjorn Shaghead. The other partner, Hrafn by name, was a Norwegian by birth, rich and fabulous for his treasures, but a miserly man, taciturn and self-contained. It is said that he possessed a gold ring which he wore constantly on his arm, and a small strongbox which he never let out of his sight and was reputed to be full of gold and silver. Thorleif went off home to his farm at Krossavik, and the Norwegians got themselves lodgings. Brodd-Helgi rode to the ship and invited Hrafn to come and stay with him.

The Norwegian replied that he would not be going to him for a lodging. 'You are described to me as both lordly and greedy for money,' said he, 'whereas I am humble and soon content, and the two things cannot mix.'

Brodd-Helgi asked to buy some valuables from him, for he was a great man for show, but Hrafn replied that he had not much fondness for selling goods on credit.

'A fine way you have treated my journey here,' was Brodd-Helgi's answer to this, 'spurning my hospitality and refusing my trade!'

Geitir too came to the ship and met the skipper. It had not been very wise of him, he said, to put up the back of the most notable man in the countryside.

'What I had in mind was to lodge with some honest farmer,' replied the Norwegian. 'Now, will you take me in, Geitir?'

Geitir hung back rather, but the end of it was that he took the skipper into his house. The crew got themselves lodgings, and the ship was drawn ashore. The Norwegian was furnished with a storehouse to keep his wares in, and he sold them in driblets only.

When it came to the first nights of winter, the sons of Egil held their autumn feast, and both Brodd-Helgi and Geitir attended. Helgi walked in front and had the innermost seat, for he was a great one for appearances. It was a matter for comment that Helgi and Geitir appeared to be so engrossed in talk at this feast that the assembly could get neither talk nor entertainment from them. Then the feast came to an end, and everyone left for his own home.

During the winter there was a well-attended games at a farm called Hagi, a short way from Hof, at which Brodd-Helgi was present. Geitir strongly urged the Norwegian to attend this gathering, explaining that he would meet a lot of the people who owed him money there. So in the end they went, and the Norwegian harped and harped on his outstanding debts. When the games were over and men were making ready to leave, Helgi was sitting in the best room, talking with his retainers, when a man came in and told them that Hrafn the Norwegian had been killed and that they had no clue to the killer. Helgi went outside at once and had some strong words to say of this deed that had been done there. Hrafn's funeral was duly carried out after the fashion of the time.

There was a man living at Gudmundarstadir by the name of Tjorvi, a big, powerful fellow, and the friend of Brodd-Helgi and Geitir. He had been missing the whole day the Norwegian was killed. It was some men's version of the death of Hrafn that he had been steered into some dangerous place and met his end there. Messages passed between Brodd-Helgi and Geitir that they should each take half of Hrafn's riches, but not share them out till after the spring Assembly for law, and Geitir took possession of his goods in the spring and secured them in his storehouse.

In the spring too Thorleif the Christian overhauled his ship for a voyage abroad, and was fully in readiness by the time of the spring Assembly. When the time came, men proceeded to the Assembly in Sunnudal, including both Brodd-Helgi and Geitir, and in many places there were only a few men left at home. Then, when the Assembly was well under way, Thorleif woke early one morning and roused his shipmates; they got into their ship's boat and rowed to Krossavik, where they put ashore and made for Geitir's storehouse, opened it up and carried out the entire stock which had belonged to Hrafn, then transferred it back to the ship. Halla Lytingsdottir was there, but she did not interfere. Brodd-Helgi now set off home from the Assembly along with Geitir, but before they arrived there they were told how Thorleif had seized all Hrafn's goods and intended to carry them clean out of the country. Helgi took it that Thorleif would be mistaken as to the point of law here, and would at once release the goods if he was called on; so with that they made their way out to the ship. They had a lot of boats, yet small ones, and when they were within hailing distance Brodd-Helgi demanded that Thorleif should release the goods. Thorleif replied that he knew little law, but he understood, he said, that it was the duty of one partner to convey his money to the other's heirs.

'We have no intention of running a fool's errand,' said Brodd-Helgi to this.

'Before you get so much as a penny,' warned Thorleif, 'we shall all have a fight on our hands.'

'Just listen to what he is saying, the good-for-nothing backslider,' cried Brodd-Helgi. 'Let us raise a storm will make some of them smart for sure!'

But Geitir now broke in, saying, 'I think it a mistake to attack them from small boats, nor do we know but that a head wind will spring up and drive them ashore, and we can then still deal with this on our own terms.'

This was approved by all, and this was the plan adopted. They put back to land, and Brodd-Helgi went home with Geitir and spent a few nights there with him. But Thorleif got a fair wind immediately, crossed without delay, and transferred the wealth which Hrafn had owned to his heirs. They were grateful to him for this, and presented him with their share of the ship, and later they parted the best of friends.

Brodd-Helgi was particularly bad tempered that summer, and could hardly wait for Thorleif's return. At every gathering Brodd-Helgi and Geitir used to meet and talk over their losses. Brodd-Helgi asked Geitir what had become of the little strongbox which Hrafn owned, but Geitir maintained he did not know whether Thorleif had taken it abroad with the rest of the goods—or, indeed, would the Norwegian have had it with him?

'I am more inclined to think,' said Helgi, 'you have it in your own possession.'

'And where is the ring he had on his arm when he was killed?' retorted Geitir.

'That I don't know,' said Helgi. 'But I do know he did not have it in the grave with him.'

At every gathering where they met, Helgi would ask about the box and Geitir in return about the gold ring, and they were now plainly at loggerheads over this. It followed that each thought he was not getting his due from the other, and a coolness began to develop between them.

The following summer a ship came out to Reydarfjord which was owned by Thorleif the Christian and two Germans in partnership with him. Thorleif sold his share in the ship and afterwards went to his farm. Brodd-Helgi was glad to hear this news, but once he learned that Thorleif had made over the entire property to Hrafn's heirs he thought it not much to the purpose to bring this particular lawsuit against him. However, he was still determined to sink his claws into him. There was a woman named Steinvor who was a temple-priestess and kept the head temple to which every householder must pay temple-tax, and this Steinvor came to see Brodd-Helgi because she was related to him, and told him her troubles, how Thorleif the Christian would not pay temple-tax like other men. Brodd-Helgi promised to look after the matter and pay her what she was due, and he took over from her her case against Thorleif.

Living in Fljotsdal was a man called Ketil, known

as Stout-Ketil, a most worthy and gallant person.
There is this to report of a journey of Helgi's that
he came for a night's lodge to Ketil, who made him
most welcome. They made a firm pact of friendship
between them.

'There is just one thing,' said Helgi, 'which I
want to ask you to do for me—to prosecute Thorleif
the Christian for his temple-tax. You summon him
for a start, but I will come to the Assembly, and we
can then take care of things together.'

'I would not have made a pact with you had I
known this lay behind it,' said Ketil, 'for Thorleif
is a man with a host of friends. Still, I won't put you
off this first time.'

With that they parted and Helgi went his way.
When he judged the time ripe Ketil prepared to
leave home; they set off a party of ten and reached
Krossavik early in the day. Thorleif was standing
outside; he hailed Ketil and offered them all lodging
for the night, but Ketil said it was early in the day
to accept lodging, what with the weather being so
good. He asked whether Thorleif had paid his
temple-tax, and Thorleif said it was paid as far as
he was concerned.

'Well, that is my business here—to claim the
temple-tax,' said Ketil. 'And it would be unwise of
you to withhold this trifle.'

'There is a lot more to this than mere stinginess,'
Thorleif assured him. 'For to my way of thinking
what is paid to a temple is put to very bad use.'

'This is very conceited of you,' chided Ketil,
'reckoning to know better than all other men put
together, and refusing to pay such lawful dues.'

'I could not care less what you say about the
matter,' replied Thorleif.

At that Ketil named his witnesses and summoned Thorleif the Christian, but once the summons was over Thorleif again invited them to stay there, warning them that the weather was not to be relied on. Ketil insisted that he must be off, but Thorleif urged them to turn back if the weather began to worsen. Off they went, had but a short time to wait for bad weather, and had to turn back. They reached Thorleif's very late and were utterly spent. He gave them a warm welcome, and they spent two nights there weatherbound, and the longer their stay the better became the hospitality. So when Ketil and his men were ready to leave, he said this: 'We have had good treatment here, and Thorleif has proved himself one of the best. I am going to repay you, in that this charge against you shall fall through, and I will be your friend from this day forth.'

'I prize your friendship highly,' replied Thorleif, 'but as for the charge, it is all one to me whether it falls through or not. I can call on a Partner who will not have me hauled to account for such.'

After that they parted, and that was the state of things till the spring Assembly. It is told that Brodd-Helgi had a strong force of men at the Assembly and was full of confidence as to the outcome. Towards the end of the Assembly he asked Ketil how the case stood against Thorleif the Christian, and Ketil told him the truth.

'You have deceived me greatly over this lawsuit, Ketil,' Helgi told him, 'and our pact of friendship must end.'

He got no hold on Thorleif, and he is now out of our story. Brodd-Helgi and Geitir met soon after the Assembly, and Helgi reproached Geitir bitterly, maintaining that he had got this humiliation through him, when he might well have righted it. And now their friendship was greatly on the wane.

3

The story goes on to tell that Halla Lytingsdottir spoke one day with Brodd-Helgi, saying: 'Our life together has long been a happy one, but I feel my health failing badly, and brief now will be my management of your household.'

'I reckon my marriage a good one,' Helgi answered, 'and for my part I should like it to last as long as we live.'

For it was the custom in those days that a married woman could offer to give up her place in the home.

There was a woman named Thorgerd, nicknamed Silver, the daughter of Thorvard the Tall, young but even so a widow, living in Fljotsdal at the farm known nowadays as Thorgerdarstadir, with a brother of hers by the name of Kolfinn to look after the place. Thorgerd invited Brodd-Helgi to visit her with a couple of his men; he went along, and she gave him the warmest of welcomes, set him in the high-seat, and sat herself down beside him. They had a great deal to tell each other, and to cut a long story short, before Helgi left for home he had become engaged to Thorgerd Silver. Nothing is told concerning Helgi before he got back home to Hof, where he was asked his news.

There was a woman engaged to a man, he said.

'Is that Thorgerd Silver ?' asked Halla.

'Yes.'

To whom was she engaged ? she asked.

He told her.

'It seems to you none too soon,' said Halla.

Helgi said that he would go and see Geitir about this. Meantime he asked that she should stay on at Hof, and she let herself be talked into not leaving before Thorgerd came. This news was soon learned throughout the district, and received much hostile comment, for Halla was well-liked by everyone. The brothers sent men to fetch Halla, and once Helgi returned home she went away, taking with her her personal valuables. Helgi stood outside in the doorway and acted as though unaware that Halla was leaving. Hardly was Halla on horseback when her brother Geitir came riding up. The messenger said they should be riding on, but Geitir turned to have the matter out with Helgi, and asked when he would be paying over the property which Halla had in his keeping.

'It would suit me,' replied Helgi, 'if Halla is not too anxious to remain at Krossavik once she gets there. She will be returning here to Hof yet.'

With so much for his trouble Geitir rode for home, and neither he nor Helgi thought things better than before. And when he overtook them, Halla asked what he and Helgi had been discussing, and he told her exactly how things stood. 'You have been too hasty in the matter,' she replied. 'Maybe Helgi feels his loss even before you make him part with the property too. We have a safe investment in Helgi, and my property will not grow any less in his keeping if it stands there at interest.'

'I see the way the wind is blowing,' said Geitir. 'It seems to me the greatest possible insult is intended if you ride from his yard without your property.'

The winter passed and in the spring Geitir went to Hof to claim Halla's money a second time, but

Helgi would not pay. Next, Geitir summoned
Brodd-Helgi to the Sunnudal Assembly over Halla's
property; they each rode to the Assembly with a big
following, Geitir having the choicer men and Helgi
the greater number. When the case should have gone
into court, Geitir was forcibly overborne, and Helgi
won the day. Geitir now committed his case to the
National Assembly itself, but Brodd-Helgi again
voided it for him, mostly because of Gudmund the
Mighty's backing, and now open enmity arose
between Brodd-Helgi and Geitir.

Living in Sunnudal at a farm known as Tunga,
on the same side of the river as Hof stands, was a
retainer of Helgi's called Thord. He and Thormod
owned some forest land in common, and made
division of the tree-felling and the grazing too. Thord
felt that he was getting far less than his due from
Thormod, so he went to see Brodd-Helgi and told
him of Thormod's encroachments. Brodd-Helgi
declared he had no intention of quarrelling over
property of Thord's, and would have nothing to do
with it unless he transferred the property to him,
Helgi, and moved over to Hof with everything he
had. He chose to do so, and surrendered the property
to Helgi in return for a berth for life.

One day Brodd-Helgi called on Thord to ride to
the common pasture and look over the barren beasts
he had there. So with that off they went and came
to the pasture. 'Well,' said Brodd-Helgi, 'we have
now looked over the stock which you and Thormod
owned.' He then set about collecting the oxen belonging to Thormod, cut off their heads and let them lie
there, and then went home and sent messengers to
Thormod, advising him to check up on his oxen. He
did so, and the slaughtered cattle were carried home.

Later, Thormod rode to Krossavik to inform
Geitir; he asked him to right his wrongs, but Geitir
said he had no intention of quarrelling with Brodd-
Helgi over this.

'It is shabby of you not to back my case,' said
Thormod.

'Your nagging leaves me unmoved,' said Geitir.
'But fetch the meat over here, and I will buy it, so
that you are none the worse off.'

Thormod returned home no better off than he had
come there, and Brodd-Helgi was informed that he
had been to tell Geitir his troubles. 'I only wish,'
said Helgi, 'that he need not run such errands much
oftener.' A little later Brodd-Helgi called up his
tenants and ordered them to go along with him, and
his housecarles and guests in addition. They went
to the forest which Thord and Thormod had held in
common, cut down all the timber, and hauled every
tree back to Hof. As soon as Thormod discovered
what injury had been done him, he went a second
time to see Geitir and reported what injustice had
been offered him. 'I think there is much more excuse for your taking this injury amiss, rather than
the earlier one,' agreed Geitir, 'for I thought that of
little account. So now not only am I not going to help
Helgi in this matter, but I am even going to give you
some advice. Go and see your nephews Stein and
Hreidar, the sons of Ref the Red, and ask them to go
summoning with you to Hof. Go to Gudmundarstadir too, and ask Tjorvi to go with you, but don't
be more than eight in all. You must summon Thord
for tree-felling, and so contrive matters that Brodd-
Helgi is not at home. Otherwise you will achieve
nothing.'

Thormod went away with this for his pains, and

called to see the men Geitir had named. They all promised to go with him, and fixed when they should set about it. Then Thormod rode back and told Geitir where matters stood. But true is the old proverb, that 'Word carries, though mouth stands still', and this came to Brodd-Helgi's ears, so that he did not leave home as had been arranged.

The morning they were expected, Brodd-Helgi had a word with his housecarles, that they should on no account leave the house that day. 'You must cut yourselves great switches of wood,' he ordered, 'and lots of cudgels. There are men expected here today, and you must then use your cudgels and beat the horses under them, and so drive the whole pack of them off the premises.'

Thormod and his companions now left home as had been arranged and came to Hof. They saw no one about, so rode at once to the farmyard, where Thormod named his witnesses and summoned Thord for tree-felling. Helgi was indoors and heard the summoning. He rushed out and thrust at Thormod, shouting, 'Drive away this rabble, and let them have that for their errand to Hof today!' With that out dashed the housecarles and beat the horses under them, and they all gave way from the yard, and that and no better was the end of their lawsuit. Geitir's men got away in sorry plight, both wounded and beaten, and some fell dead there. Everyone was convinced that Brodd-Helgi had been the death of the men that perished. He had the bodies carried to a roofless hut and covered over with brushwood.

Geitir's men were profoundly dissatisfied with their lot, and nothing hurt them worse than that they might not bury their kinsmen and dear friends. They often came to talk the matter over with Geitir, whose answer was to bid them wait a while. 'It is said that "He with a short knife must try, try again", and so it must be in respect of us and Brodd-Helgi.'

Then in due course Geitir sent word to his followers, and later they set out from Krossavik and took the road to Hof. 'We have not assembled this company so secretly that Brodd-Helgi will not have heard of it,' Geitir told them, 'so I expect there will be a lot of men waiting for us there. What we have to do is to ride into the home-field, dismount and tether our horses, remove our cloaks, and thereafter keep moving at a good steady pace. I expect Brodd-Helgi and his men to come out and meet us, but I do not expect him to make an armed attack on us. Now you must be on your guard against giving anyone injury or offence first: just drag everything out as long as can be. Egil's sons must now leave our company, together with Big Tjorvi, up this side of the river to Gudmundarstadir, and so into the forest behind Hof. They must have big coal-baskets on their horses, emptied of all their dust, and as soon as they reach the wall of the home-field go in hiding along to the hut, take the bodies and lay them in the baskets, and so go back the same way to meet with me.'

They broke up, and each party did according to Geitir's instructions. When Geitir's own party had come almost as far as the homestead they dismounted and went along in their own good time. Helgi had a lot of men with him, and at once turned out to meet Geitir. Greetings were far from cordial. Brodd-Helgi asked Geitir where he thought he was going, and he answered that he had little comment to make, and that he thought their errand would be obvious to everyone. 'We are offering no violence this time,' he said, 'though we have cause enough, and are anxious to make one further attempt before abandoning our plans entirely.'

In this fashion they hung about the whole day, the crowd of them rambling now this way, now that, about the fields. Then one of Helgi's men broke in: 'There are men over there, and not so few either, moving about with pack-horses.'

'They are only charcoal-burners,' answered a second, 'coming from the forest. Those are baskets on the horses. I noticed them today as they were going to the forest.' So their talk fell through.

'Well,' said Geitir, 'it will be the case now as so often that we get the worst end of the stick, since we cannot carry away the bodies of our kinsmen.'

'Why do you carry on this way?' asked Helgi. 'It is only to be expected that the weaker must shrink in his horns. And yet it seems likely that neither of us will suffer any dishonour from the other at this meeting. Anyhow, I am now willing to make an end of this tedious wrangling, if you think fit—but what I am not willing for is for you to come any nearer to the house than you have come now.'

With that their gathering broke up. Geitir and his men went to their horses, but Helgi and his men stayed behind in the fields. Geitir's party joined up with that of Egil's sons, at once dismounted and called a halt. Helgi's men were now standing by the yard back at Hof and saw that they had come to a halt. 'Aye,' said Helgi, 'a fool grows wise after the event. We have spent the whole day milling around here, and now, when it is all over, I see that none of Geitir's best men were with him. They will have carried off the bodies in the coal-baskets. Well, it has always been the case that Geitir is the wiser

of us, though he has time and again been borne
down by force.'

There was no bloodsuit for the slaying of Thormod, and in no case did Geitir get justice from
Helgi. Thorkel Geitisson went abroad, and from
land to land continually, from the day he was old
enough, and was not much involved in the disputes
between Brodd-Helgi and Geitir his father.

Over at Krossavik the sickness of Halla Lytingsdottir grew great and dangerous. It is told that
Geitir left home on a visit to Eyvindara in Fljotsdalsherad, and was away for more than a week; and
when he had gone Halla sent a man to fetch Helgi,
begging him to come and see her. He went to Krossavik without delay. Halla greeted him, and he took
her greeting kindly. She asked him to look at the
tumour she had. He did so, and said his heart mis-
gave him because of it. He pressed a lot of water out
of her tumour and she grew very weak thereafter.
She asked him to stay there overnight, but he was
not prepared for that. And because she was so weak
and downhearted about him too, she said, 'No need
now to offer you a lodging here. You have now
made an end of the business. But I think this—not
many men will finish with their wives as you now
with me.'

Brodd-Helgi went back home and was greatly up-
set. Halla lived but a short while after this, and was
dead when Geitir reached home. He was told the
whole story, just as it had happened. And now for
a while there was quiet.

After this bitter enmity sprang up between Brodd-
Helgi and Geitir. One summer it happened that
Helgi found himself short of backing at the Assem-
bly, and asked Gudmund the Mighty for help, but

Gudmund said he was not disposed to grant him help at this or any other Assembly, and so win himself the dislike of other chieftains, and get no profit from him in return; so they reached this understanding over the case, that Gudmund promised his help and Helgi should pay him a half-hundred of silver. When the hearing was concluded, and Helgi's case had proved successful, he and Gudmund met by the booths, and Gudmund claimed his price from Helgi; but Helgi maintained he had nothing to pay him—he did not see, he said, that he need pay money between friends such as they.

'It is very shabby of you,' answered Gudmund, 'always to have need of others, but not pay what you are pledged to. I think your friendship of little worth. I shall not claim this money a second time, and will never help you after this.'

On those terms they parted, and their friendship came to an end. Geitir learned of this. He went to see Gudmund and asked him to accept money in exchange for his friendship; but Gudmund told him he did not want his money, adding that he was little inclined to help people who were for ever willing to bow and scrape to Helgi in all matters whatsoever. Men now returned home from the Assembly, and for a while there was quiet.

The story goes on to tell how a ship came out to Vapnfjord, with Thorarin Egilsson on board. He had the reputation of being a very good trader and an accomplished man. Brodd-Helgi rode to the ship and invited Thorarin to come and stay with him, together with such men as he chose. He said he would accept, so Brodd-Helgi went back to announce that they might expect skipper Thorarin as their guest. Geitir too rode to the ship and met

Thorarin, and asked whether he was thinking to go
to Hof. It had been mentioned, he replied, but not
settled. Geitir said it would be more advisable for
him to come to Krossavik—'Because few men of
mine, I fancy, do themselves much good by accepting hospitality from Helgi.'

What emerged was that Thorarin was going to
Krossavik. Brodd-Helgi heard this and immediately
rode to the ship with saddled horses, intending to
take Thorarin back with him, but Thorarin said
there had been a change of plan. 'I want to make it
clear,' said Helgi, 'that my invitation has no hidden
motive at the back of it, for I shall have no hard
feelings though you go to Krossavik.' The following
day Helgi rode to the ship and gave Thorarin a stud
of five horses together for his friendship, and they
were all dandelion-yellow. Next, Geitir went to
fetch Thorarin, and asked him whether he had
accepted these horses from Brodd-Helgi. That was
so, he said. 'Then I advise you to send them back,'
said Geitir. He did so, and Brodd-Helgi took back
the horses.

Thorarin spent the winter with Geitir, but went
abroad the following summer. By the time he
returned to Iceland, Geitir had moved house and
was living at a place called Fagradal, so Thorarin
went to lodge at Egilsstadir. Geitir's followers now
took counsel together and, feeling that they could no
longer endure Brodd-Helgi's oppression, they went
to see Geitir. Thorarin was spokesman for them.
'How long must this continue?' he demanded.
'Until everything is at an end? A lot of men are now
leaving you, and are all drawn to Brodd-Helgi, and
we reckon your timidity the only reason why you
fail to tackle him. You are the sharper-witted of the

two, and besides, you have no worse fighters on your side than he on his. There is now the choice of two things at our hands: that you go back to Krossavik to your farm and never move from there again, but take action against Helgi if he does you any dishonour from now on, or else we will sell our holdings and clear out, some from the neighbourhood, and some from Iceland itself.'

So now Geitir made ready for a journey from home, and went north to Ljosavatnsskard to Ofeig Jarngerdarson's. Gudmund the Mighty came to see Geitir, and they sat talking a whole day. Afterwards they parted, and Geitir enjoyed a night's hospitality at Myvatn with Olvir the Wise. He inquired closely about Brodd-Helgi, and Geitir spoke well of him. He was an outstanding man, he said, quarrelsome and headstrong, but with it all a good fellow in many respects.

'But is he not a very unjust man?' asked Olvir.

'I have felt this much in particular of Helgi's injustice,' answered Geitir, 'that he grudges me the same sky over my head as he has over his.'

'Must all this be borne from him?' asked Olvir.

'It has been so far,' said Geitir.

They now left off talking, Geitir returned home, and all was quiet over the winter.

4

The following spring Geitir moved house back to Krossavik, and kept a lot of men there. There was a severe famine that year. As time drew on towards the spring Assembly, Brodd-Helgi and Geitir met, and Helgi asked with how many men he would be riding to the Assembly.

'Why ride with an army?' asked Geitir. 'I have nothing on hand there. I shall ride to the beginning of the meeting, and with a few men only.'

'Then when I go we will meet,' said Helgi, 'and ride together. I too shall be riding with only a few men.'

'Very well,' said Geitir.

Brodd-Helgi's son Bjarni rode from home for the beginning of the Assembly with his own and Helgi's retainers, but Lyting waited for his father, because Helgi loved him much more. Geitir had watch kept for Brodd-Helgi's setting out. Helgi rode from home once he was ready, and his son Lyting with him, together with Thorgils Skinni, Lyting's foster-father, Eyjolf the Fat, Kol the Norwegian, Thorgerd Silver and her daughter by Brodd-Helgi, Hallbera by name. Geitir too rode from home, and with him the three sons of Egil, Thorarin, Hallbjorn and Throst, Tjorvi the Big, and seven other men.

It is some men's say that Helgi had a foster-mother who could see into the future, and that he used always to go and see her before he travelled from home. He did so this time again. When he came to her, she was sitting with her face buried in her hands, and weeping, so he asked her why she wept and was so low-hearted. She said that she was weeping at her dream.

'I dreamed,' she said, 'that I saw a fawn-coloured ox rise up here at Hof, big and handsome, with his horns carried high, and he set off for the gravel-banks there by Sunnudalsmynni. And I saw cattle come roaming through the country-side, big and far from few, and at their head moved an ox flecked with red. Neither big nor handsome, but mighty strong was he. These cattle gored the first ox to

death. Then here at Hof arose a red ox, the hand-
somest-looking of all beasts, his horns of ebon hue.
He gored the red-flecked ox to death. Then there
rose up in Krossavik a certain young bull, with the
hue of a sea-cow on him, and marched bellowing
through the whole country-side and all the heaths,
and sought always the red ox. And with that,' said
she, 'I awoke.'

'You must mean,' said Helgi, 'that I and the fawn
ox are one, and Geitir and he flecked with red, and
he will be my bane.'

'I mean that, indeed,' she replied.

'You must mean,' he continued, 'that Lyting is
the red ox, and will avenge me.'

'No,' she answered. 'Bjarni will avenge you.'

'Then you know nothing about it,' he retorted,
and flung out in a temper.

[The next part of the saga is missing. From the
dream, various words and phrases following the
missing section, and the twelfth-century Islendinga-
drápa, it can be deduced that Brodd-Helgi's party
was brought to battle at Sunnudalsmynni, and that
Helgi himself, his son Lyting, and certain other men
fell there. Geitir appears to have ridden on to the
Sunnudal Assembly, where a preliminary agreement
was reached, whereby Bjarni should award himself
such money-fines as he pleased against Geitir, while
the nature and extent of the banishment accepted
by various of Geitir's followers was defined. The
three sons of Egil may well have been banished
overseas for three years, and Tjorvi the Big was
pronounced a district outlaw and was to move house
the following spring. During the summer this agreement was formally confirmed at the National

Assembly, with the connivance and help of Gudmund the Mighty, with whom Geitir must have dis-
cussed his plans on his visit north. Bjarni awarded
himself a hundred of silver for his father's death,
with an extra thirty for the ambush.]

After that they returned home from the Assembly,
and everything was now quiet. Bjarni lived at Hof
with Thorgerd Silver his stepmother, and it was
there that those brothers and sisters grew up, Bjarni
and Thorgerd's own children. The kinsmen Bjarni
and Geitir often met. . . . Time wore on to the days
for moving house, and Tjorvi the Big had disposed
of his land. His entire household and stock had
taken its departure on the Saturday morning, but
Tjorvi's horse was tethered to the fence, for he
planned to leave secretly a little later and ride un-
hampered. At that moment a shepherd walked
indoors at Hof, and Bjarni asked what had he to
report. 'That Tjorvi's goods are now on the move,'
he answered. Bjarni rose to his feet, took his shield
and spear, and jumped on the shepherd's horse and
came to Gudmundarstadir. Tjorvi had gone to fetch
his horse. He could see Bjarni coming, and turned
quickly for home, and such was the difference
between their speeds that as Tjorvi got inside the
home-field Bjarni reached its fence. He lunged for
him and drove his spear through him, and afterwards
rode back home and told Thorgerd of Tjorvi's
slaying.

'It is better than nothing,' she said.

Geitir heard about Tjorvi's violent end and had
him buried, nor did he make any claim on Bjarni
for it. The two of them attended feasts together, and
Bjarni paid a visit to Krossavik, and he seemed of

the same mind as Geitir concerning everything. And so it went for a long time, that all was quiet the while. Bjarni married, taking to wife a woman by the name of Rannveig, the daughter of Thorgeir Eiriksson from Guddal. She was a good-looking and able woman, and had the management of his household.

The next thing to tell of is that Bjarni attended a feast at Krossavik, and men were sitting by the fireside. Those kinsmen Bjarni and Geitir. . . . There was a partition down the room, with a couple of apertures in it. Geitir was staring through one of these, and Bjarni asked what was it he could see.

'Strange, most strange,' said Geitir, 'is what appears before me. It looks to me as though the clothes are red of hue, and so great a redness is reflected from the clothes that it seems to me to fill the whole room.'

'I can see nothing,' said Bjarni. 'It must be too much drink affecting your eyes, or it's because of the fire.'

'Maybe so,' said Geitir.

They went in after that. . . . Later men went home, and now everything was quiet for a while.

It was a custom of the district that men used to hold a meeting at the beginning of the last month of winter at a farm called Thorbrandsstadir, where they would talk over any business that was thought necessary. . . . Geitir enjoyed a general trust, and many had business there with him. . . . There was a heavy snowstorm out of doors, and Bjarni asked what he should wear. Thorgerd Silver brought out a bundle and handed it to Bjarni. He took it and unrolled it, and it was Helgi's cloak, all bedabbled with blood. Bjarni struck her. 'Take it, you wicked woman, you!' . . . and was going out hurriedly.

'You need not ask why I do this,' she said. 'My loss was no less than yours. . . .'

He made as if he paid no heed to her words. He had a small axe in his hand . . . he came to the meeting, and there were a lot of men present. Geitir was sitting by the door. . . . Bjarni acknowledged their greetings, but rather coldly.

'You look to me,' said Geitir, 'as though you will have felt before you left home that you had some cause for anger against me. Now I cannot have that.'

Bjarni was very silent. Kolfinn had left home with Bjarni, and now by ill luck he broke in, looking up at the sky, and saying, 'The weather is all shapes these days. I thought it looked rather stormy and cold, but now it seems to be turning to a thaw.'

'It will thaw at any time if this turns to a thaw,' said Bjarni. And then he stood up, saying: 'My foot has gone to sleep.'

'Take it easy then,' advised Geitir.

There and then Bjarni struck at Geitir's head, and he was killed outright. And as soon as he had struck Geitir, he repented of it and sat himself down under Geitir's head, and he died on Bjarni's knees. Geitir was buried later. After this they went away, and no one looked for reparation.

This deed was strongly condemned and held most base in its execution. Bjarni returned to Hof, and when he got there he drove Thorgerd Silver away, telling her never to come into his sight again. Geitir's son Thorkel was absent from Iceland when his father was killed, but Blæng kept the farm going at Krossavik with the assistance of the sons of Egil, who were Thorkel Geitisson's brothers-in-law. In the spring the householders did away with the local Assembly; they were not prepared to hold it, judging it hopeless to intervene between men who were involved in such great feuds. It is said that Bjarni set a man named Birning to keep watch whether any open hostilities were to be looked for, and keep Bjarni informed, so that they might not come on him unawares.

We must here introduce a man by the name of Thorvard. He was well thought of, and it was the general opinion that he was the best physician anywhere in the district. His home was at Sireksstadir.

Thorkel Geitisson now returned to Iceland, and went at once to his home at Krossavik, and acted as though he was not much concerned. Bjarni sent men who were friends of them both to meet Thorkel, to offer him atonement, honourable redress, and the right to award his own damages, but when they delivered their message to Thorkel he acted as though he had not heard, and did not turn from what he was talking about before. So the messengers went back to inform Bjarni how matters stood, and everyone assumed that Thorkel was determined on revenge.

Bjarni used to go up to the mountain pastures every autumn, just as his father had done, and at such a time no one ventured to injure his fellow. But Thorvard Leech came to know that Thorkel was getting ready for a trip into the mountains, and had some picked men with him by way of reinforcement. He let Bjarni know of this, and Bjarni stayed home, getting others to go in his place. So now, when men went up into the mountains, there was no such meeting with Bjarni as Thorkel had intended, and they stayed peaceful over the winter.

5

The next thing to tell of is that Thorkel sent a man one day from Krossavik up to Egilsstadir, to have some talk with Thorarin. The name of the messenger was Kol, and it was Kol's errand to find out how many men there were at Hof. When he got to Egilsstadir he met Thorarin outside, and told him his errand. 'You will not think much of my hospitality,' said Thorarin. 'You must get back home as fast as you can, and let no one know of your journey, but I will find out what Thorkel wants to know.' He added that he would pass the news on to him. So Kol now turned back, and had to travel late. But this same evening it so happened that a man broke his leg at the farm next to Sireksstadir, and Thorvard Leech was sent for, and came to bind up the leg. He was invited to put up there, but preferred to ride home that night, and met Kol on the way. They had a chat together, and asked each other the news. Thorvard inquired where Kol might be coming from, while Kol in his turn asked why he was travelling by night. That was neither here nor there, replied Thorvard—'But tell me now, what was your business, Kol ?'

'I have been up through the district looking for sheep, but did not find them,' replied Kol.

They parted, and Kol reached home that night. Thorvard too reached home that night, but the next morning he caught his horse and rode up to Hof, where he was made most welcome. He was asked for news, and reported that a man had broken his leg. He had a private talk with Bjarni and told him how he had met Kol, and that he must have been coming from Egilsstadir. He was convinced, he said, that he had not told him the truth about his movements.

'I see now,' said Bjarni, 'that you want nothing to happen out and around the district that I am not informed of. Accept my sincere thanks for that. Now go back home and call at the farm at Faskrudsbakki in the heart of the district. There are men of Thorkel's there, and if there are any questions as to how many men are here, then say that some of my men rode in this morning, and that horses were driven in in no small numbers, but you have no notion what they are for.'

So off went Thorvard and called at Bakki, where he was asked how many men would be at Hof. He repeated what he had been told, and then rode on home. The minute he left they sent men to Egilsstadir and reported that there was a strong body of men at Hof. In turn Thorarin sent word to Thorkel that it would not be easy to attack Hof just now; and this winter passed off again.

The following spring Bjarni had to go down to the sea-shore at Vapnfjardarstrond. He had to take the upper route over the high ground because the inlets were all in flood. There were shielings up on the heaths, and Bjarni was riding past one of these with a couple of men and noticed nothing at all till there ahead of him was Thorkel and eight men, for he had been posted as to Bjarni's movements.

In front of the shieling stood a big, three-legged chopping-block. 'Now we must take the block,' said Bjarni, 'drape it with my cloak, and set it in my saddle. Ride one on each side and prop it on the horse's back, and ride off to that rise of ground nearest to the shieling, but I will go inside the shieling. If they ride after you, and away from the shieling, then I shall make for the forest and save my skin. But if they turn this way to the shieling—well, I must defend myself as stoutly as I can.'

They did as they were told. Thorkel was not a sharp-sighted man, but all the same he was shrewd and sharp witted, and as they closed in on them he asked whether they could see for certain that there were three men riding from the shieling—'For it would be a good move to go inside the shieling, and then to the forest, if once we ride on past it.'

They insisted they could see that there were three men riding away.

'I saw that there were three horses,' said Thorkel, 'but I have my doubts whether there was a man on the back of each one of them.'

The more certain was it that there was a man on the back of each, they persisted, in that he was the biggest of them who rode in the middle.

'Well,' said Thorkel, 'we will trust to how it looks to you, but I think it a mistake not to search the shieling.'

Thorkel and his men now gave chase, and when they had been in pursuit a long way, Bjarni's companions let fall the block, and then rode off. Bjarni got away to the forest, and was saved from Thorkel and his men this time again. But Thorkel turned back and betook himself home, disgusted with the way things had turned out for him. As soon as they thought it safe, Bjarni's companions went to find him; they proceeded on their way, and once again Bjarni and Thorkel steered clear of each other for the time being.

Not long after this Thorkel sent men into Fljotsdalsherad for his cousins-in-law Helgi and Grim, the sons of Droplaug, with a request that they should come to Krossavik. They set off immediately with Thorkel's messengers, and when they reached Krossavik were given a warm welcome. Helgi asked what was to do, that he had sent for them.

'A short while ago,' Thorkel confessed, 'I went on an outing by which, as things stand, I am deeply mortified. I showed plainly that I wanted Bjarni dead, yet I got nowhere. I now want to go to Hof without delay and attack Bjarni in his home, and get at him with fire if we cannot manage it with weapons.'

Helgi warmly approved this resolve of his, but first they went to sleep for the night. Thorkel's health was rather delicate and he was often taken ill without warning. Helgi was awake promptly at break of day. He dressed himself, went to Thorkel's bed-closet, and said, 'Time to get up, if you are still of the same mind as yesterday. For sleepers are seldom conquerors.'

'Little work shall I carry through today,' answered Thorkel, 'by reason of my sickness.'

Helgi put himself forward for the expedition, to do what had been determined on already.

'I think no man other than myself should be leader on this expedition,' replied Thorkel.

Then Helgi began to lose his temper. 'You need not send for me again,' he said, 'if you play the coward now, when I have come to help you, and you are not even willing for others to get on with it.'

With that they parted in anger. The brothers went home and there was quiet for a while, and Bjarni and Thorkel did not clash this time either.

6

The following spring both these chieftains, Bjarni and Thorkel, went to the spring Assembly in Fljots-dalsherad. Accompanying Thorkel were Blæng and the sons of Egil, Thorarin, Hallbjorn and Throst, and Eyjolf who lived at Vidivellir; they were fifteen all told. They went to Eyvindara to Groa, who furnished them with whatever they needed. But with Bjarni there travelled Thorvard Leech from Sireks-stadir, Bruni from Thorbrandsstadir, Eilif Torfason from Torfastadir, the two brothers from Buastadir, Berg and Brand, the sons of Gliru-Halli, Skidi, Bjarni's foster-father, and Hauk Loptsson; they were eighteen all told. Helgi Asbjarnarson and Thordis Brodd-Helgadottir gave them a good welcome when they reached Mjovanes. When the Assembly came to an end, Thorkel was ready to leave first, which suited Bjarni very well. When he was all set to return, Thordis Todda, his sister, gave him a fine necklace, vowing that she would take nothing in exchange, and arranged it so that it was fastened—and fastened strongly—about his neck.

Thorkel was meanwhile making his way across the heath together with his comrades. They were late coming down into Bodvarsdal, where they found lodging for the night with a householder called Kari, one of Thorkel's followers. When they went to sleep Thorkel bade Kari keep watch whether anyone came down off the heath, and let him know of it immediately.

Bjarni was crossing the heath in his own good time, and was well satisfied that Thorkel had left a trail there, for the going was bad. They came for the night to a woman named Freygerd, and after-

wards pushed on across the heath, and early in the
morning came down into Bodvarsdal past Kari's
farm. And since the tracks made by Thorkel's men
led off to the farm, Bjarni ordered that three men
should go in a row, three others after them, then a
third three, and so with the rest of them. 'It will
then look like three men's tracks,' said he.

They did so. Kari was outside when they went
past the home-field, but he did not raise the alarm.
He thought it a ticklish situation between the kinsmen, and had no wish to get involved in it.

Thorkel woke in his bed and roused his fellow
travellers, reckoning they had slept their fill. They
armed themselves and afterwards went outside.
Thorkel ordered some of them to walk back along
the trail and see whether any footprints branched
away from the tracks they had made, and they saw
how the tracks of three men went branching off. He
went to the tracks himself. 'These were heavy men,'
said Thorkel. 'I believe Bjarni and his men have
gone this way. Let's get after them, and fast!' When
they came some distance from the farm they could
see that the tracks had scattered. They pressed on
now as hard as they could, until they came almost to
the opening of the valley. A small farm stands there,
Eyvindarstadir by name, and Eyvind was the name
of the man living there. When Bjarni and his men
were only a short way from this farm's home-field,
they stopped to rest.

'I shall run from Thorkel no longer,' said Bjarni.
'This is where we must take whatever is coming
to us.'

With that they saw Thorkel's men approaching.
As they drew near, 'Have at them now like men!'
ordered Thorkel. 'You and I, kinsman Bjarni, will

take each other on, Blæng and Birning, Thorvard and Throst, and so with each of the rest as best he can.'

The fighting started, and Bjarni's men put up a brave resistance. It happened for a while that there were no men wounded. 'Feeble is our onset now,' cried Thorkel, 'and not worth the telling.'

'You have spirit all right,' commented Bjarni.

At Eyvindarstadir a woman went out of doors and saw men fighting. She went hurrying back inside, and, 'Eyvind,' she cried, 'I think those kinsmen, Thorkel and Bjarni, will have come to blows here, a short way from the house. And I saw a man lying under the fence, and he seemed to me to be frightened out of his wits.'

'Let us get a move on as fast as we can,' returned Eyvind, 'and take clothes with us, and fling them over the weapons.'

Eyvind took a partition-beam and hoisted it on to his shoulder, and crossed the fence at the point where the man was lying. It was Thorvard. He jumped up and was quite panic stricken. As soon as Eyvind arrived on the scene, men began to fall in battle. Thorvard had cast himself down under the fence for sheer exhaustion. First Birning fell before Blæng. Then Blæng cut at Bjarni and got home on his neck. There was a loud crack, for the necklace was shattered. Bjarni got a slight wound, and the whole necklace fell down into the snow. Bjarni reached full-stretch for the necklace and tucked it inside his corslet.

'You are still greedy for money, kinsman,' said Thorkel.

'You are so fixing things today, we shall have need of our money,' retorted Bjarni.

Thorkel then sat down, but Blæng attacked Bjarni with the utmost fury. The end of their clash was that Blæng fell. Then Thorkel rose to his feet and attacked Bjarni hotly, but got such a wound in the arm that he was unfit to carry on. Both of Gliru-Halli's sons fell there; and Eilif too fell before Hallbjorn, yet kept alive after a fashion. Then Eyvind arrived and went forward so strongly with his beam in between the men that they fell back on both sides. There were women there with him too, flinging clothes over the weapons, and the fighting died down. Four men had fallen from among Bjarni's company, and there were many wounded who yet lived to tell the tale. Four men had likewise fallen on Thorkel's side. Eyvind asked whether Thorkel was willing for him to convey Bjarni and his men home. He could see, he said, that Thorkel and his men would prefer to make shift for themselves. Thorkel said nothing to stop it; whereupon the bodies of those who had fallen were seen to, and after that each party went its way. Thorkel and his following went home to Krossavik, but Eyvind escorted Bjarni and his men in along Vapnfjord till they reached Hof. Thorvard Leech came to Hof and bound up their wounds. Eilif Torfason was laid up for a long time with his wounds; still, he was cured at last.

Without delay Bjarni went to see Gliru-Halli, and told him of the death of his sons. He invited him into his own home, promising to be as a son to him.

'I think it a great pity about my sons,' Halli answered, 'and yet I think it better to lose them than that they incur a charge of cowardice like some of your comrades. I shall rest content with my own home, and not shift to Hof, but I am grateful to you for the offer,' he said.

It happened one day that Bjarni said to Thorvard Leech, 'It has now come to a point with our wounds here at Hof that, what with your care, we can look after ourselves. But I know that Thorkel is wounded and has no one to heal him, and he is growing very weak. I want you to go and cure him.'

Thorvard agreed to do what Bjarni wanted. He set off and reached Krossavik towards midday. There was a game of chess in progress, and Thorkel was sitting up and looking on at the game. He was very pale. No one gave Thorvard a greeting, but he walked up to Thorkel, saying, 'I should like to see your wound, for I have had a bad report of it.'

Thorkel bade him please himself; he spent seven nights there, and the goodman grew better day by day. Thorvard then left Krossavik, and Thorkel made a handsome return for his cure; he gave him a horse and a silver bracelet, and afterwards spoke to him with friendly words. Thorvard then set off for Hóf to tell Bjarni all about it; and Bjarni thought things had turned out well since Thorkel had grown better.

That summer there was little haymaking, because Thorkel was unfit for much work at Krossavik, and the outlook was so unpromising that it appeared that the stock would have to be killed off. He was by this time married to Jorunn Einarsdottir from Thvera. A housecarle of Thorkel's had a journey up into the district, and took a night's lodging at Hof, where he was made most welcome. Bjarni asked him about the health of men and beasts. 'All goes well with the health of men,' said the housecarle; but the cattle, he added, were in a very bad way. In the morning the housecarle left, and Bjarni saw him off. 'Ask Thorkel if he would like to move his household over here,' he said, 'or if he so prefers I will provide him with meat and hay, so that there need be no question of killing off the stock. Be a trusty messenger now!'

The housecarle made off and arrived home just as men had sat down to table. Jorunn was carrying in the food. He walked up to Thorkel and told him the whole of Bjarni's message. Jorunn had stayed in the room and was listening to what he said. Thorkel made no answer.

'How can you be silent about this,' said Jorunn, 'when it is such a noble offer?'

'I am not going to give a hasty answer in this matter,' said Thorkel, 'for so handsome an offer would catch most men off balance.'

'What I should like,' Jorunn told him, 'is for us to take ourselves off to Hof in the morning and meet Bjarni, for such an offer seems to me in every respect honourable from a man of his character.'

'You shall have your way,' agreed Thorkel, 'for I have found, aye, and many a time, that you are both wise and kind.'

The next morning they left home, twelve of them together, and when their coming was seen from Hof, Bjarni was informed of it. He was overjoyed the moment he heard of it; he went out to meet them, and had a warm greeting for Thorkel. And once the kinsmen had a good talk together, they went into all their problems well and truly; and then Bjarni offered Thorkel atonement and the right to make his own award, declaring that he was anxious to meet Thorkel's wishes in everything from that day forth, for as long as the two of them lived. Thorkel accepted this offer, and they came together now in whole-hearted reconciliation. Thorkel awarded himself a hundred of silver for the slaying of Geitir his father, and each granted the other peace and kept it faithfully ever after.

Bjarni was a brave and resolute man. The Hof folk have not been great sages, yet in most things they have proved to be successful. Thorkel was a great chieftain, the most dauntless of men, and a great participator in lawsuits. His means gave out in his old age, and when he gave up his farm Bjarni invited him over to Hof, and he grew old there till his end.

And so we end the saga of the Vapnfjord men.

THORSTEIN STAFF-STRUCK

THERE was a man living in Sunnudal by the name of Thorarin, an old man of ailing sight. He had been a stark red viking in his youth, and was no easy person to deal with now that he was old. He had an only son, whose name was Thorstein, a big man, strong and calm tempered, who worked so hard on his father's farm that the labour of three other men would not have stood them in better stead. Thorarin was on the poor side rather, yet he owned a fine assortment of weapons. They owned stud-horses too, this father and son, and selling horses was their main source of wealth, for never a one of them fell short in heart or performance.

There was a man called Thord, a housecarle of Bjarni of Hof, who had charge of Bjarni's riding-horses, for he had the name of one who really knew horses. Thord was a very overbearing sort of person; he also made many aware that he was a great man's servant, yet he was none the better man for that, and became no better liked. There were other men too staying at Bjarni's, one named Thorhall and the other Thorvald, great mouthers-over of everything they heard in the district. Thorstein and Thord arranged a horse-fight for the young stallions, and when they drove them at one another Thord's horse showed the less heart for biting. Once he saw his horse getting the worst of it, Thord struck Thorstein's horse a great blow over the nose, but Thorstein saw this and struck Thord's horse a far greater blow in return, whereupon Thord's horse took to its heels, and everyone raised a loud hullabaloo of derision. With that Thord struck at Thorstein with his horse-staff and caught him on the eyebrow, so that the skin hung down over the eye. Thorstein tore a strip from his shirt and tied up his forehead, acting as though nothing in particular had happened. He asked them to keep this from his father, and there the matter ended for the time being. But Thorvald and Thorhall made it a subject of ill-natured jest and nicknamed him Thorstein Staff-struck.

That winter, a short while before Yule, the women rose for their work at Sunnudal. At the same time Thorstein rose; he carried in hay, and afterwards lay down on a bench. The next thing, in came old Thorarin his father, and asked who was lying there. Thorstein said it was he.

'Why are you afoot so early, son?' asked old Thorarin.

'There are few, I fancy, to leave any of the work to that I am responsible for here,' replied Thorstein.

'There is nothing wrong with your head-bones, son?' asked old Thorarin.

'Not that I know of,' said Thorstein.

'Have you nothing to tell me, son, of the horsefighting that was held last summer? Were you not knocked dizzy as a dog there, kinsman?'

'I saw no gain in honour,' Thorstein told him, 'by reckoning it a blow rather than an accident.'

'I would never have thought,' said Thorarin, 'that I could have a coward for a son.'

'Speak only those words now, father,' Thorstein advised him, 'which you will not consider overmuch in the days to come.'

'I will not speak about it as much as my heart would have me,' Thorarin agreed.

At these words Thorstein rose to his feet, took his weapons, and left the house. He walked on till he came to the stables where Thord looked after Bjarni's horses, and where he happened then to be. He met Thord face to face and had this to say to him: 'I want to know, friend Thord, whether it was by accident that I got a blow from you last summer at the horse-fight, or did it come about intentionally— in which case are you willing to pay reparation for it?'

'If you have two cheeks,' retorted Thord, 'then stick your tongue into each in turn, and, if you like, call it accident in one and intention in the other. And that is all the reparation you are going to get from me.'

'Then rest assured,' said Thorstein, 'it may well be I shall not come claiming payment a second time.'

Then Thorstein ran at Thord and dealt him his death-blow, after which he walked to the house at Hof and met a woman outside and said to her, 'Tell Bjarni that an ox has gored his groom Thord, and that he will be waiting for him there till he comes, alongside the stables.'

'Get off home, man,' said she. 'I will report this when I think fit.'

So now Thorstein went off home and the woman went about her work. Bjarni rose during the morning, and when he was seated to his food he asked where was Thord, and men answered that he must have gone off to the horses. 'All the same,' said Bjarni, 'I think he would have come home by now if he was all right.' Then the woman whom Thorstein had met started on her piece. 'True it is what they often say of us women, how there is little sense to draw on where we she-creatures are concerned.

Thorstein Staff-struck came here only this morning
to report that an ox had so gored Thord that he was
past helping himself; but I lacked the heart to wake
you at the time, and it has slipped my mind ever
since.'

Bjarni got up from table. He went to the stables
where he found Thord dead, and later he was buried.
Bjarni now set on foot a lawsuit and had Thorstein
outlawed for the killing. But Thorstein went on
living at home in Sunnudal and working for his
father, and Bjarni let things lie just the same.

That autumn there were men sitting by the
singeing-fires at Hof, while Bjarni lay out of doors
by the kitchen wall and listened from there to their
conversation. And now the brothers Thorhall and
Thorvald began to hold forth. 'We did not expect
when first we came to live with Killer-Bjarni that
we would be singeing lambs' heads here, while
Thorstein, his forest outlaw, should singe the heads
of wethers. It would be no bad thing to have been
more sparing of his kinsmen in Bodvarsdal,[1] and
his outlaw not sit as high as he now in Sunnudal.
But, "E'en doers are done for once wounds befall
them", and we have no idea when he proposes to
wipe this stain from his honour.'

Some man or other answered: 'Such words are
better swallowed than spoken, and it sounds as
though trolls must have plucked at your tongues.
For our part, we believe that he has no mind to
take the food out of the mouth of Thorstein's blind
father or those other poor creatures who live at
Sunnudal. And I shall be very surprised if you are

---

[1] The references here and on pp. 85–86 to Bjarni's dealings
with his kinsmen at the fight in Bodvarsdal are explained in
The Vapnfjord Men, pp. 71–74 above.

singeing lambs' heads here much oftener, or gloating over what happened in Bodvarsdal.'

Men now went to their meal and afterwards to sleep, and Bjarni gave no indication of knowing what had been talked about. In the morning he routed out Thorhall and Thorvald, bidding them ride to Sunnudal and bring him Thorstein's head, divorced from his trunk, by breakfast-time. 'For you appear to me the likeliest to remove this stain from my honour, considering I have not the courage for it myself.' They now felt they had opened their mouths too wide for sure, but made off even so until they came to Sunnudal. Thorstein was standing in the doorway, whetting a short-sword, and when they came up he asked them what they were up to.

They said they had the job of looking for stray horses.

Then they had only a short way to look, Thorstein told them—'Here they are, by the home-fence.'

'It is not certain,' they said, 'that we shall find them, unless you show us the way more clearly.'

So Thorstein came outside, and when they had come down into the home-field Thorvald hoisted up his axe and ran at him, but Thorstein gave him such a shove with his arm that he fell headlong forward, and Thorstein drove the short-sword through him. Then Thorhall would have attacked him, but he too went the same road as Thorvald. Thorstein then bound them both on horseback, fixed the reins on the horses' necks, got the whole outfit headed in the right direction, and the horses made their way home to Hof.

There were housecarles out of doors at Hof, and they went inside and told Bjarni that Thorvald and his brother had returned home, adding that they had not run their errand to no purpose. Bjarni went outside and saw how things had turned out. In the main he had no comment to make, but had them buried, and everything now stayed quiet till Yule was past.

Then one evening when she and Bjarni had gone to bed, his wife Rannveig began to hold forth. 'What do you imagine is now the most talked-about thing in the district?' she asked.

'I have no idea,' said Bjarni. 'There are plenty whose chatter strikes me as not worth bothering about.'

'Well, the most frequent subject of gossip is this,' she told him. 'Men just cannot imagine what Thorstein Staff-struck must do for you to decide you need take vengeance on him. He has now killed three of your housecarles, and it seems to your followers that there is no hope of support where you are concerned if this is left unavenged. You do all the wrong things and leave the right undone.'

'It comes to this, here again,' replied Bjarni, 'just as the proverb has it: "None takes warning from his fellow's warming." So I will see that you get what you are asking for. And yet Thorstein has killed few without good reason.'

They gave over talking and slept the night through. In the morning Rannveig woke up as Bjarni was taking down his shield. She asked him what he was proposing to do.

'Thorstein and I,' he replied, 'must now settle a point of honour in Sunnudal.'

'How many men are you taking with you?' she asked.

'I shall not lead an army against him,' said Bjarni. 'I am going alone.'

'Don't do it,' she begged. 'Don't expose yourself all alone to the weapons of that fiend!'

'Aye,' said Bjarni, 'and are you now not carrying on like a true woman, crying one minute over the very thing you provoked the minute before? For a long while now I have suffered only too often the jeers both of you and of others, and it is useless to try and stop me now that I am settled to go.'

Bjarni now made his way to Sunnudal, where Thorstein was standing in the doorway. They exchanged a few words.

'You must come and fight with me today, Thorstein,' said Bjarni, 'in single combat on this same mound which stands here in the home-field.'

'It is quite hopeless for me to fight with you,' maintained Thorstein, 'but I will get abroad by the first ship that sails, for I know the manliness of your nature, how you will get all the work I see to done for my father, if I must be off and leave him.'

'It is useless to cry off,' warned Bjarni.

'Then let me go in and see my father first,' said Thorstein.

'Do that,' said Bjarni.

Thorstein went into the house and told his father that Bjarni had come there and challenged him to single combat. Old Thorarin answered him thus: 'Any one, if he contends with a man higher in rank than himself, and lives in the same district with him, and does him some dishonour too, can expect to find that he will not wear out many shirts. Nor can I make outcry for you, for you seem to me richly to have deserved it. Now take your weapons and defend yourself like a man, for I have known the day when I would not have bowed my back for such as Bjarni, great champion though he is. And I would rather lose you than have a coward for a son.'

Out again went Thorstein, and he and Bjarni went off to the mound, where they began fighting in deadly earnest, and cut away most of each other's shield. And when they had been fighting for a very long time, Bjarni said to Thorstein, 'Now I grow thirsty, for I am less used to the work than you.'

'Then go to the brook,' said Thorstein, 'and drink.'

Bjarni did so, laying his sword down beside him. Thorstein picked it up, looked at it, and said: 'You will not have had this sword in Bodvarsdal.'

Bjarni made no reply. They went back up on to the mound and fought for a while again, and Bjarni found his opponent skilled with his weapons and altogether tougher than he had expected. 'A lot goes wrong for me today,' he complained. 'Now my shoe-string is loose.'

'Tie it up then,' said Thorstein.

Bjarni bent down, but Thorstein went indoors to fetch out two shields and a sword; he went back to Bjarni on the mound, saying to him, 'Here is a shield and sword which my father sends you. The sword will not prove blunter in the stroke than the one you have owned so far. Besides, I have no heart to stand defenceless under your blows any longer. Indeed, I would gladly give over this game, for I fear that your good fortune will show better results than my ill luck. And if I could have the say here—well, in the last resort, every man loves his life.'

'It is useless to beg off,' said Bjarni. 'We must fight on.'

'I'll not be the one to strike first,' said Thorstein.

Then Bjarni cut away Thorstein's entire shield, whereupon Thorstein cut away Bjarni's too.

'A great stroke that!' cried Bjarni.

'You struck one no less,' replied Thorstein.

'That same weapon you have had all day so far is biting better for you now,' said Bjarni.

'I would spare myself disaster, if I might,' Thorstein told him. 'For I fight with you in fear and trembling. I should like to commit the whole thing to your verdict.'

It was now Bjarni's turn to strike, and they were both quite defenceless. Said Bjarni: 'It would be a bad bargain to choose a foul deed in place of good hap. I shall count myself fully repaid for my three housecarles by you alone, if only you will be true to me.'

'I have had opportunity enough today to betray you, if my weak fortune was to prove stronger than your good luck. No, I will not betray you.'

'I see,' said Bjarni, 'that you are past question a man. Will you now give me leave to go inside to your father, to tell him just what I like?'

'Go how you will, for all I care,' warned Thorstein. 'But watch your step!'

Bjarni then went inside to the bed-closet where old Thorarin was lying. Thorarin asked who came there, and Bjarni told him it was he.

'What news have you to tell me, Bjarni mine?'

'The slaying of Thorstein your son.'

'Did he show fight?' asked Thorarin.

'In my opinion, no man was ever brisker in battle than your son Thorstein.'

'It is not surprising then,' said the old man, 'that you were hard to handle in Bodvarsdal, if you have now got the better of my son.'

'I want to invite you to Hof,' said Bjarni, 'where you shall sit in the second high-seat for as long as you live, and I will be to you in place of a son.'

'My state,' said the old man, 'is like any other man's whose say goes for nothing—and a fool dotes on a promise. And such are the promises of you chieftains, when you wish to comfort a man after any such mishap, that nothing is too good for us for a month, but then our worth is fixed at that of other paupers, and with that our sorrows drop but slowly out of mind. And yet anyone who shakes hands on a deal with a man like you can rest well satisfied with his lot, whatever the verdict given. So I will take your offer after all. Now come over here to where I am in bed—you will have to come close, for the old fellow is all a-tremble in his legs for age and sickness, and never believe that my son's death has not pierced my old heart!'

Bjarni now went up to the bed and took old Thorarin by the hand, and found him fumbling for a big knife which he wanted to stick into Bjarni. 'Why, you old stinkard!' cried Bjarni. 'Any settlement between us now must be hitched to your deserts. Your son Thorstein is alive and shall come home with me to Hof, but you shall be provided with thralls to do your work, and shall lack for nothing for the rest of your days.'

Thorstein went home with Bjarni to Hof and followed him till his death-day, and was reckoned pretty well any man's match for valour and prowess. Bjarni fully maintained his reputation, and was the more beloved and magnanimous the older he grew. He was the most undaunted of men, and became a firm believer in Christ in the last years of his life. He went abroad and made a pilgrimage south, and on that journey he died. He rests in a town called Sutri, a short way this side of Rome. Bjarni was a man blest in his offspring. His son was Skegg-Broddi, a man widely known to story and in his day unrivalled.

And that is the end of what there is to tell about Thorstein Staff-struck.

HRAFNKEL THE PRIEST
OF FREY

IT was in the days of king Harald Fairhair, son of Halfdan the Black, son of Gudrod the Hunting King, son of Halfdan the Freehanded but Food-stingy, son of Eystein Fret, son of Olaf Woodcutter the Swedish king, that a man by the name of Hallfred brought his ship out to Iceland, to Breiddal, which lies east of Fljotsdalsherad. On board were his wife and a son by the name of Hrafnkel, who was fifteen years old at the time, handsome and enterprising. Hallfred built himself a house to live in; then, during the winter, a foreign bondwoman died whose name was Arnthrud, which is why the place has been known as Arnthrudarstadir ever since.

In the spring Hallfred moved house northwards over the heath, and built himself a new home at a place called Geitdal. One night he dreamt how a man appeared to him, saying: 'There you lie, Hallfred—and rashly, to be sure! Move your home away from here, west across Lagarfljot. All your good luck lies there.' After this he awoke and moved house out over the Ranga river into Tunga, to the place now known as Hallfredarstadir, where he lived till he was an old man. But a goat and she-goat got left behind him, and the very day Hallfred moved out a landslide crashed on to the farm, and those fine animals perished there—which is why the place has been called Geitdal ever since.

2

Hrafnkel made it his practice to go riding over the heath in summer. By this time Jokulsdal had been fully settled right up to the rock-bridges. Hrafnkel went riding up along Fljotsdalsheid and saw where an empty valley branched off from Jokulsdal, which looked to him a better place to settle in than any other valley he had seen up to then; so when he got back home he asked his father for what was due to him of their property, and announced that he had a mind to make his home there. His father gave him his head over this, and he built himself a home in the valley and called it Adalbol, or Manor. Hrafnkel married Oddbjorg, Skjaldulf's daughter from Lax-ardal, and they had two sons, the elder called Thorir and the younger Asbjorn.

Once Hrafnkel had taken possession of the land at Adalbol he went in a lot for sacrifices and had a big temple built. Hrafnkel loved no other god more than Frey, on whom he bestowed a half share in all his best treasures. He occupied the entire valley and apportioned men their land, but was determined to be their master even so, and took the priesthood over them, for which reason his name was length-ened and he was called Frey's Priest. He was a very overbearing, if talented, man, and compelled the Jokulsdalers to become his retainers. To his own people Hrafnkel was kindly and pleasant, but to-wards those of Jokulsdal he proved harsh and hard-headed, and they had a rough time of it at his hands. Hrafnkel took part in numerous single combats, and paid no one so much as a penny, so that nobody got any redress from him, whatever it was he did.

Fljotsdalsheid is a hard place to get about in,

being very stony and boggy, but despite this father
and son were always riding on visits one to the other,
for their relationship was very real to them. Hallfred
found the road troublesome, and cast about for a
route over the high ground which stands in Fljotsdalsheid, where he found a drier if longer road, the
one known as Hallfredargata. They alone use this
road who really know their way about in Fljotsdalsheid.

3

Living at a farm called Laugarhus, in Hrafnkelsdal, was a man by the name of Bjarni. He was married, and had two sons by his wife, the one called
Sam and the other Eyvind—handsome, promising
men. Eyvind lived at home with his father, but Sam
was married and living in the northern end of the
valley at a farm by the name of Leikskalar. He was
quite well-to-do. Sam was a highly contentious man
and clever at the law, but Eyvind became a merchant
and returned to Norway, where he spent the winter.
From there he travelled into foreign parts, coming
to a halt at Constantinople, where he won the favour
of the Greek king and stayed on for a while.

Hrafnkel had one particular treasure in his possession which he prized higher than anything else.
This was a stallion, dark mouse-grey in colour and
with a black stripe the length of his spine, which he
called his Freyfaxi. He gave his friend Frey a half
share in this stallion. He was so besotted with this
stallion that he swore a great oath that he would
be the death of any man who rode him without his
express permission.

Bjarni's brother Thorbjorn was living in Hrafnkelsdal, at a farm called Holar, opposite Adalbol to the east. Thorbjorn had few assets and many dependants. His eldest son was a big, handy lad by the name of Einar, and it happened one spring that Thorbjorn had a word with Einar, how he should be looking round for some employment—'For I cannot use more labour than this household here can provide, while you are such a handy man you will easily get a good place. This is not a case of lack of affection making me get rid of you, for you mean much more to me than my other children. No, it is rather my lack of means that causes it, and my poverty. My other children are growing into workmen, but you will find a good job more easily than they.'

'You have told me about this too late,' replied Einar, 'for by now every one will have his hands on the best jobs, and I don't much fancy having the leavings.'

One day Einar caught his horse and rode to Adalbol. Hrafnkel was sitting in the living-room and gave him a warm and cheerful welcome. He asked Hrafnkel for a job.

'Why are you so late asking this,' was his reply, 'for I would have taken you on the very first? But by now I have engaged all my hands, except for the one job you will not care to have.'

Einar asked what this might be. Hrafnkel explained that he had not yet engaged anyone for sheep-tending, and admitted he needed a good man for this. Einar said that he was not much concerned what he did, whether it was that or anything else. He stressed that what he needed was a job with full keep both winter and summer.

'Then I will give you a quick choice,' said Hrafnkel. 'You shall drive home the fifty ewes at the

shieling and fetch in all the summer firewood, and
that shall be your work for the two seasons. But I
must get one thing straight with you as with my
other shepherds. Freyfaxi roams the upper end of
the valley with his stud. You must look after him
winter and summer, and I warn you against one
thing: it is my will that you never get on his back,
however great may be your need, for I have sworn
a great oath about this, how I would be the death of
any man who rides him. Twelve mares run with him,
and whichever of these you want to ride, night or
day, shall be at your disposal. Now do as I tell you,
for it is an old saying: "His hands are clean who
warns another." Bear in mind now what I have been
talking about.'

Einar said he would not be so bent on trouble as to
ride this horse which was forbidden him—all the
more so since there were plenty of others. With that
he went home for his clothes, removed back to
Adalbol, and later off they went to the shieling in
the upper reaches of Hrafnkelsdal at the place called
Grjotteigssel. Everything went well for Einar that
summer, so that there was never a sheep lost right
up till midsummer, but then there were nearly thirty
ewes missing in a single night. He searched all over
the pastures without finding them, and the sheep
were missing nearly a week. One morning it happened that Einar went out early, and all the southern
mist and drizzle had cleared away. He took a staff
in his hand, a bridle, and saddle-cloth, and walked
up across the river Grjotteigsa, which falls away
there from the shieling, and there on the tongue of
land lay the sheep which had been at home overnight. He headed these back to the shieling and
went to look for those others which had been lost

earlier. He could see the mares farther out on the tongue and wondered about catching a horse to ride, feeling that he would get along faster if he rode than if he walked. When he reached the mares he stalked them, but these, which never used to run away from man, were now hard to approach—except for Freyfaxi alone. He was as still as if he had taken root.

Einar realized that the morning was wearing on, and judged that Hrafnkel would not know even if he did ride the stallion. He now laid hold of him and bridled him, fixed the saddle-cloth under him on the horse's back, and rode up beside Grjotargil, so up to the glaciers and west alongside the glaciers where the river Jokulsa falls away, and so down along the river to Reykjasel. He asked all the shepherds at the Reykjasel shieling whether any of them had seen the sheep, but nobody could say that he had. Einar rode Freyfaxi from dawn right to mid-evening, the stallion covering a lot of ground with him in a short time, he was such a fine horse. It now occurred to Einar that it would be time for him to get back and drive in the sheep that were at home, even if he failed to find the others, so he rode east over the ridges into Hrafnkelsdal. As he came down to Grjotteig he heard the bleating of sheep from higher up the very ravine he had ridden by before. He turned that way and saw thirty ewes running towards him, the very ones he had lost the week before, and he headed for home with the sheep.

The stallion was all running with sweat, so that it dripped from every hair he had. He was caked with mud and utterly spent. He went rolling over and over a dozen times, and after that set up a loud neighing; then away he went at a great gallop down along the pathway. Einar turned after him, meaning to head him off, catch him, and lead him back to his mares, but this time he was so shy that Einar could get nowhere near him. He went tearing down the valley without halt or pause till he reached Adalbol, where Hrafnkel was sitting at table. As soon as the horse came in front of the door he neighed shrilly. Hrafnkel spoke to a woman who was serving at table, telling her to go to the door—'Because a horse neighed, and it sounded to me like the neighing of Freyfaxi.' She walked out into the doorway, where she saw Freyfaxi in sorry plight, and told Hrafnkel that it was indeed Freyfaxi outside the door, as filthy as could be.

'What can my brave lad want, that he has come home?' asked Hrafnkel. 'This can bode no good.'

With that he went outside and took a look at Freyfaxi. 'I do not like it,' he told him, 'that they are treating you this way, foster-son, but you had your wits about you when you told me of it. It shall be avenged, so off with you to your stud!'

With no more ado he trotted back up the valley to his mares.

Hrafnkel went to bed that evening and slept through the night. In the morning he had his horse caught and saddled and rode up to the shieling. He rode in blue clothes, had an axe in his hand, but no further weapon. Einar had just driven the sheep into the fold. He was lying on the fold wall, counting the sheep, and the women were busy milking. They greeted Hrafnkel. He asked how they were getting on.

'I have had a bad time of it,' confessed Einar, 'for there were thirty sheep missing the best part of a week. They are found now though.'

Hrafnkel said he had no quarrel with this or its like. 'But has not something worse taken place? It has not happened as often as one would expect that the sheep have got lost, but did you not maybe ride my Freyfaxi yesterday?'

Einar said he could not deny it.

'But why did you ride this horse which was forbidden you, when there were any number of others at your disposal? I would have forgiven you a first offence, had I not sworn so great an oath in the matter. And yet you have owned up to it like a man.'

But in the belief that nothing goes right for those men who draw down on themselves the curse for a broken oath, he dismounted, ran at him, and struck him his death-blow. After this he rode back to Adalbol without more ado, told his news, and later sent another man to the sheep at the shieling. He had Einar carried west from the shieling to the hillside, and raised a cairn there to mark his grave. The place is called Einarsvarda, and is mid-eve mark from the shieling.

Thorbjorn heard tell over at Holar of the killing of Einar his son, and took the news hard. He caught his horse, rode over to Adalbol, and asked Hrafnkel to make redress for killing his son.

Hrafnkel retorted that he had killed more men than this one. 'And it can be no news to you that I am unwilling to make anyone reparation, and folk have to put up with it just the same. Even so, I admit that this deed of mine strikes me as among the very worst killings I have committed. You have been my neighbour a long while now, I have liked you, and each of us the other. No small matter would have made trouble between me and Einar, had he not ridden the stallion. Well, we must often regret opening our mouths too wide—and seldom repent speaking too little rather than too much. I am now going to make it clear that I regard this deed of mine as worse than anything else I have done. I shall provide your household with milch cows in summer and with meat in the autumn, and I shall do this for you season by season as long as you want to keep on your farm. Under my management your sons and daughters shall be taken off your hands, and so endowed that they can make good matches as a result; while anything at all you know to be in my possession that you have need of from now on, you must tell me and never again go short of whatever it is you need. You shall keep on your farm as long as you please, but come here to me as soon as you grow tired of it, whereupon I will look after you to the day of your death; and we shall then be atoned. I shall expect this too, that most people are going to say the man was pretty dear.'

'I'll not take this offer,' said Thorbjorn.

'What do you want then?' Hrafnkel asked him.

'I want us to appoint men to arbitrate between us.'

'Then you consider yourself my equal,' replied Hrafnkel, 'and we shall never be atoned on those terms.'

At this Thorbjorn rode away and down along Hrafnkelsdal until he reached Laugarhus and met Bjarni his brother, to whom he told his news, with a request that he should play some part in the affair. But Bjarni held that it was no fair match if Hrafnkel came into it. 'For while we have lots of money we cannot possibly tackle Hrafnkel. It's a good saying too that a wise man knows his limits. He has tied up plenty in lawsuits who have more bone in their fists than we. As I see it, you behaved like a fool in refusing so good an offer. I want neither part nor parcel of it.'

At this Thorbjorn spoke many bitter words to
Bjarni his brother, maintaining that the more there
lay at stake the more gutless he proved. Then he
rode away, and they parted with little kindness. He
made no stay till he came down to Leikskalar,
where he knocked and they answered the door.
Thorbjorn asked Sam to step outside. Sam had a
warm welcome for his kinsman and invited him to
put up there, an offer which Thorbjorn accepted
without much eagerness. Sam could see that Thorbjorn was heavy-hearted; he asked what had happened, and Thorbjorn told him of the killing of
Einar his son.

'It is no great news,' commented Sam, 'though
Hrafnkel kills a man.'

Thorbjorn asked whether Sam was prepared to
help him in any way. 'The case stands thus, that
though the dead man is closest to me, the blow has
landed not so very far from you either.'

'Have you by any chance tried for redress from
Hrafnkel?' asked Sam.

Thorbjorn told him the whole truth, how things
had gone between the two of them.

'I have never heard tell before,' said Sam, 'that
Hrafnkel has made such offers to anyone as to you
now. So I am prepared to ride with you up to Adalbol, and let us approach him humbly and see if he
will stand by the same offer. He is sure to behave
well one way or another.'

'For one thing,' answered Thorbjorn, 'he will no
longer be willing for it; and for another, it is no
more to my liking now than when I rode away.'

'It is heavy work,' said Sam, 'I fancy, to bring a
lawsuit against Hrafnkel.'

'You young men,' scolded Thorbjorn, 'you will

never get anywhere, the way you make mountains out of molehills. I cannot believe anybody has such wretches for kinsmen as I. This strikes me as the height of meanness in a man like you, who consider yourself so smart at law and go falling over yourself in petty suits, but are unwilling to take on this case which is so glaringly clear. It will be a reproach to you, right enough, for you are the biggest boaster in the whole of our family. Well, I see now how the affair will turn out.'

'What better off are you than before,' asked Sam, 'though I do take on the case, and we are both of us thrown out of court ?'

'Just the same,' said Thorbjorn, 'it will be a great comfort to me if you take it on, come of it what may.'

'I shall be going into this against my will,' Sam warned him. 'It is mainly for our kinship's sake that I am doing it. And you may as well know, I think I am helping a fool in helping you.'

Then Sam reached out his hand and took over the case from Thorbjorn.

Next Sam had his horse caught and rode up along the valley to a farm where (he had already enlisted men for the purpose) he gave notice of the killing against Hrafnkel. This reached Hrafnkel's ears, and he thought it a great joke that Sam had started a law-suit against him. The winter wore away, and in the spring, when the summons-days came round, Sam rode from home up to Adalbol and summoned Hrafnkel for killing Einar. Afterwards Sam rode down through the valley and summoned the neighbours to ride to the Assembly, and thereafter kept quiet till men made ready for their journey there.

At this point Hrafnkel sent down through the valley to summon his men together. He set off from his territory with seventy men. With this troop he rode east across Fljotsdalsheid, and so past the head of the lake, and across the pass to Skridudal, up along Skridudal and south to Oxarheid, to Berufjord, where he took the direct road of all riders to the Assembly to Sida. South from Fljotsdal it is a seventeen days' journey to the Assembly at Thingvellir.

Once he had ridden away from the district Sam assembled his men. For the most part he got masterless men to ride with him, in addition to those he had called up before. All these too he provided with weapons, clothes, and victuals. Sam left the valley by a different route, proceeding north to the rockbridges, where he made his crossing, and from there over Modrudalsheid, to spend the night in Modrudal. From there they rode to Herdibreidstunga, and so inland of Blafjoll, on again to Kroksdal, and so south to Sprengisand, making down for Sandafell, and from there to Thingvellir, where Hrafnkel had not yet arrived. He was making slower time because he had the longer road. Sam pitched a booth for his men well away from where the Eastfirthers usually encamp, and somewhat later Hrafnkel reached the Assembly, to pitch his booth where he normally did. He heard that Sam was at the Assembly and thought the whole thing a great joke.

This Assembly was very crowded. Almost all the chieftains who were in Iceland were present there. Sam approached all these chieftains and asked them for help and assistance, but all answered the same way; not one of them could say he was under such obligation to Sam that he was prepared to get into a fight with Hrafnkel the Priest and so imperil his good name; they added further that it had gone one way for most of those who had dealings with Hrafnkel at the Assembly, in that he had driven everyone who had tackled him headlong from their lawsuits. Sam returned to his booth, and the kinsmen were heavy-hearted indeed, fearing that their case would so fall through that they would win nothing but shame and dishonour, and such great dismay filled uncle and nephew that they could neither eat nor sleep; for all the chieftains hung back from helping them, including those they had fully expected to lend them a hand.

4

Early one morning old Thorbjorn awoke. He roused Sam and told him to get up.

'I can't sleep.'

Sam rose and got into his clothes. They went outside, down to the Oxara river below the bridge, where they washed themselves.

'It is my counsel,' said Thorbjorn to Sam, 'that you have our horses driven in, and let us make ready for home. It is clear by now that nothing lies ahead of us except humiliation.'

'And fair enough too,' replied Sam, 'for you wanted nothing in the world except to fight this out with Hrafnkel, and were unwilling to accept an offer which so many would have been glad to accept who had to claim redress for a near kinsman. You cast a great slur on my courage and everybody else's who didn't want to get into this lawsuit with you, and now I will never give up till I think it beyond all hope that I get something or other to show for it.'

At this Thorbjorn was so moved that he wept.

It was then that they saw how, a little lower down than where they were seated, five men came walking together from a booth and east towards the river. He was a tallish man, not very thickly built, who walked at their head, in a leaf-green kirtle and with a mounted sword in his hand, his features regular, and his colouring ruddy, of distinguished appearance, and with a fine head of chestnut hair on him. He was a man easy to recognize, for he had a whitish lock of hair on the left side.

'Up we get,' said Sam, 'and let us cross west of the river to meet these men.'

They walked down alongside the river, and this man who was walking in front got in first with a greeting. He asked who they might be, and they told him.

Sam asked the man his name. He said his name was Thorkel, adding that he was the son of Thjostar.

Sam asked what might his origins be, and where was his home.

He was a Westfirther, he said, by birth and descent, and had a home in Thorskafjord.

'Are you a man with a priesthood?' Sam asked him.

'Far from it,' he replied.

'Are you a farmer then?'

No, he said, he was not.

'What sort of man are you then?'

'I am a footloose sort of man. I came out to Iceland last winter. I have spent seven years abroad, and went out to Constantinople, where I became a liegeman of the emperor; but at the moment I am lodging with a brother of mine named Thorgeir.'

'Is he a man with a priesthood?' asked Sam.

'To be sure he is, with a priesthood the length and breadth of Thorskafjord, and wider still throughout the Westfirths.'

'Is he here at the Assembly?' asked Sam.

'To be sure he is.'

'And how is he off for men?'

'He has seventy,' said Thorkel.

'Have you any more brothers?' asked Sam.

'There is a third,' Thorkel admitted.

'And who is he?'

'His name is Thormod. He lives at Gardar on Alptanes. He married Thordis, Thorolf Skallagrimsson's daughter, from Borg.'

'Would you care to lend us a hand?' asked Sam.

'Why, what do you need?'

'The help and strength of chieftains,' replied Sam, 'for we have a lawsuit to thrash out with Hrafnkel the Priest for the killing of Einar Thorbjorn's son. And we could safely trust to our pleading with support from you.'

'It's as I said,' Thorkel pointed out. 'I hold no priesthood.'

'But why are you pushed aside so,' demanded Sam, 'since you are as much a chieftain's son as your brothers are?'

'I did not tell you,' said Thorkel, 'that I had no stake in such, but I handed over my authority to Thorgeir my brother before I went abroad. Nor have I taken it back since, for it strikes me as being in very good keeping however long he looks after it. Go and have a word with him, and ask him to help you. He is a man in a thousand, a splendid fellow and in every respect outstanding, youngish still and eager to distinguish himself. In short, the likeliest kind of man to lend you a hand.'

'We shall get nothing out of him,' said Sam, 'unless you put in a word for us.'

'I will promise this much,' said Thorkel, 'to be

for you rather than against, for it seems to me a man's plain duty to take up the bloodsuit for his close kinsman. Now get along to the booth, and make your way inside. The men are still asleep there. You will see where two hammocks extend across the innermost side of the booth. I got up from one of them, and in the other Thorgeir my brother lies resting. He has had a big boil on his foot ever since he came to the Assembly, and as a result has had little sleep of nights, but last night the foot broke and the core is out of the boil. He has been sleeping since, and has stuck his foot out from under the bedclothes on to the foot-board, because of the excessive heat which is in the foot. Let the old man lead the way on into the booth. He seems to me very infirm both in sight and years. And, friend,' Thorkel went on, 'when you reach the hammock you must stumble heavily, and fall on to the foot-board, catch hold of the toe which is tied up, wrench it towards you—and find out how he takes it.'

'You are going to be a great help to us,' said Sam, 'but this does not sound a good plan to me.'

'You can do one or the other,' replied Thorkel. 'Do as I suggest or seek no advice of mine.'

'Then what he advises,' announced Sam, 'shall be done.'

Thorkel said he would be coming along later. 'For I am waiting for my men.'

So now Sam and Thorbjorn set off and arrived inside the booth. All the men there were asleep. They soon saw where Thorgeir was lying. Old Thorbjorn went in front, stumbling awkwardly, and when he reached the hammock he went sprawling on to the foot-board, grabbed at the afflicted toe, and wrenched it towards him. This roused Thorgeir, who shot up in bed, demanding to know who could be dashing about the place so headlong as to go falling over people's feet, which were bad enough before. But Sam and Thorbjorn had nothing really to say for themselves.

Then Thorkel stepped briskly into the booth to speak to Thorgeir his brother. 'Don't be in such a flurry and panic over this, brother. It won't hurt you. Many a man acts worse than he intends, and it happens every day that a man cannot attend with equal care to everything when he has a great deal on his mind. Yet it is your excuse, kinsman, that your foot is painful, and, indeed, has suffered great affliction; and you yourself will be the one to feel it most. Now it may also be the case that to this old man his son's death is no less painful, yet he can obtain no cure or redress, and nothing goes right for him. He will be the one to feel this most, and it is only to be expected that a man with so much on his mind will not pay due heed to everything.'

'I had no idea he could quarrel with me over it,' Thorgeir retorted. 'For I didn't kill his son, and by the same token he cannot avenge it on me.'

'He didn't mean to avenge it on you,' said Thorkel. 'He came at you harder than he intended, and paid the penalty for his failing sight. In fact he was looking for some help from you, and what a fine thing it would be now to help a man so old and needy! For this is duty in him, not greed, when he takes up the bloodsuit after his son. But now all the chieftains hang back from helping these men, and in so doing show great cowardice.'

'Whom are they accusing, these men?' Thorgeir asked.

'Hrafnkel the Priest has killed Thorbjorn's son

without cause,' explained Thorkel. 'He commits crime after crime, and will pay recompense to nobody.'

'I must stand with the rest,' said Thorgeir. 'I do not find myself so obligated to these men that I want a fight with Hrafnkel on my hands. It seems to me he sets to work in such a way every summer against those men who have lawsuits to settle with him that most of them win little or no honour before it ends, and as I see it, it goes one and the same way with the lot of them. That, I fancy, is why most men who have no duty in the matter feel no desire to meddle with it.'

'It may be,' Thorkel replied, 'that if I were a chieftain myself I should act the same way, and think it a bad business to clash with Hrafnkel. But the way things are, I just do not see it in that light, for I should think it best to pit myself against the very man from whom all took a tumble before; and I believe that mine or any other chieftain's fame would increase greatly who could out-row Hrafnkel, yet not grow less though I went the same road as the others, because what happens to the rest can happen to me, and, "Nothing venture, nothing gain".'

'I see how you are inclined,' said Thorgeir. 'You would like to help these men. I am now going to hand over to you my priesthood and authority; you hold it on just such terms as I have held it before, and from there on let us share it equally—and then you help anybody you want to.'

'It appears to me,' said Thorkel, 'that our priesthood is in the safest keeping the longer you hold on to it. I should not care for anyone to hold it as I do you, for you have many talents beyond all us brothers. Nor am I just now settled what I intend

to do with myself. Besides you know, kinsman, how
I have kept very much to myself since I came to
Iceland. However, I can see now what my advice
is worth. I have pleaded as much as I will for the
present. Maybe Thorkel Lock will come where his
word has more weight!'

'I see now the way the wind blows, brother,'
replied Thorgeir. 'You are offended, and I cannot
have that, so we will help these men, come of it
what may, if you want to.'

'I ask only such things,' said Thorkel, 'as I think
will be better granted.'

'What do these two reckon themselves capable
of,' asked Thorgeir, 'so that their case may have
a happy ending?'

'Even as I said today' (this was Sam speaking),
'our need is for the strength of chieftains, but I can
manage the pleading of the suit myself.'

Thorgeir told him that in that case he was easy to
help. 'And what is now necessary is to prepare the
case as accurately as can be. I fancy too that Thorkel
would like you to let him know before the courts go
into procession. You will then get some return for
your pains, some comfort or shame even greater
than before, and anguish and humiliation. Now, go
home and be cheerful, for if you are proposing to
tackle Hrafnkel the Priest you need to bear up well
in the meantime. But let no one know we have promised you aid.'

They now returned to their booth and were in
high spirits. Everyone was astonished at this, why
they had so quickly changed their mood, for they
were quite downcast when they left their booth.

They waited there till the courts went into procession, when Sam called out his men and marched

to the Lawhill, where the court was by this time in session. Sam went boldly into court, at once began naming his witnesses, and presented his case against Hrafnkel the Priest according to the true law of the land, without error and with distinguished pleading. Hot on his heels came the sons of Thjostar with a strong force of men. Everybody from the west country stood behind them, and it was clear that the sons of Thjostar were well off for friends. Sam prosecuted his case in court to the point where Hrafnkel was called on for the defence, unless some man was present there who desired to put forward a defence on his behalf. There was loud applause for Sam's case, and no one offered to produce any legal defence for Hrafnkel. Men ran to his booth to tell him what was happening. He was quickly on the move, collected his men, and marched towards the court, expecting to find the coast all clear. It was his intention to give such small fry their bellyful of bringing lawsuits against him: he meant to wreck the court for Sam and drive him from his case. But by now there was no chance of this. There was such a press of men in front of him that he could get nowhere near the place. He was crowded away by sheer force, so that he might not hear his prosecutors' case, which made it rather a problem for him to bring forward his defence. So Sam drove his suit to the full limit of the law, till Hrafnkel was declared an outlaw at this Assembly.

Hrafnkel returned to his booth at once, had his horses caught, and rode away from the Assembly, profoundly dissatisfied with his end of the case, for nothing of the kind had ever happened to him before. He rode east to Lyngdalsheid, and so eastwards to Sida, and made no stay till he arrived in

Hrafnkelsdal and settled in at Adalbol, where he acted as though nothing had happened. But Sam stayed on at the Assembly, strutting about with his tail up. A lot of people were well pleased that it had turned out this way, that Hrafnkel had suffered this blow to his self-esteem; and they now called to mind how he had shown injustice to many.

Sam waited till the Assembly was dissolved and men made ready for home. He thanked the brothers for all they had done, and Thorgeir, laughing, asked Sam how he thought things were going.

It had gone off very well, he maintained.

'You think yourself any better off now than before?' asked Thorgeir.

'I think Hrafnkel has suffered a humiliation which will be remembered for a long time,' replied Sam, 'and that is worth a lot of money.'

'The man is not outlawed so long as the court of execution is not held,' quoted Thorgeir, 'and that must needs be done at his own domicile, and take place fourteen nights after the weapontake.' They call it the weapontake, or recovery of weapons, when the gathering rides from the Assembly. 'Now it is my guess,' Thorgeir went on, 'that Hrafnkel will have arrived home, intending to sit firm in the saddle at Adalbol. It is my further guess that, for anything you can do, he will maintain his position there. So you will be reckoning to ride home and at best remain on your farm—always supposing you can manage it. I guess you have this much from your lawsuit that you can call him a forest outlaw, but he will hold the same old helm of terror over most as before, with the exception (so I guess) that you must needs crawl somewhat lower.'

'I have never been frightened of that,' said Sam.

'You are a bold fellow,' Thorgeir assured him, 'but I fancy brother Thorkel is not thinking to leave you in the lurch. He now wants to go on backing you till all is concluded between you and Hrafnkel, and you can rest easy. You must feel that we are bound to stand by you, for we have taken the biggest part in this so far, so we are going to help you this once in the Eastfirths. Do you know any road to the Eastfirths which is not a frequented way?'

Sam said he would follow the same route he had travelled from the east, and was all cock-a-hoop at this.

Thorgeir picked his following and had forty men ride with him. Sam too had forty men, and the entire company was well equipped with weapons and horses.

After this they all followed the same route till they reached Jokulsdal just before dawn. They crossed the river at the bridge; and it was the very morning they had to hold the court of execution. Thorgeir asked how they might best take them by surprise. Sam reckoned he would know a plan for this, and without more ado turned from the path up to the bluff, and so along the ridge between Hrafnkelsdal and Jokulsdal, till they came out from under the mountain beneath which stands the farmstead at Adalbol. Grassy clefts ran up on to the heath there, and there was a steep slope down to the valley, and there below stood the farmstead.

Here Sam dismounted. 'Let us leave our horses here, with twenty men to watch them,' he suggested, 'and the other sixty of us will make a dash for the farm. I feel sure there will be few up and doing there.'

They did this, and the place has been called

Hrossageilar, Horselanes, ever since. They raced swiftly for the farmstead. The hour for rising was past, but the people had not got up. They dashed a beam against the door and rushed inside. Hrafnkel was lying in his bed. They dragged him out of it, together with every man of his household who could use arms. The women and children were driven into a building on their own. In the home-field stood a storehouse, and from this back to the wall of the main building there extended a beam for the washing. They led Hrafnkel that way along with his men. He made many offers for himself and his followers, and when these served no purpose pleaded for the lives of his men.

'For they have done nothing to offend against you, while it is no discredit to me though you kill me. I am not asking to be spared that, but I do ask to be spared humiliation. There is no credit to you in that.'

'We have heard tell,' said Thorkel, 'that you have proved hard-mouthed in harness for your enemies. It is just as well that you are today made to feel this in your turn.'

They laid hold of Hrafnkel and his men and tied their hands behind their backs. After that they broke into a storehouse and took a rope down off the hooks. They next took their knives and pierced holes through their hough sinews, threaded the rope through, swung them up so over the beam, and secured them so, eight together.

'So it has come to this, Hrafnkel,' said Thorgeir, 'that you have got your deserts at last. And how unlikely you must have thought it that you would come by such shame at anyone's hands as is now the case. Which will you do now, Thorkel: stay here with Hrafnkel and keep an eye on them, or will you go with Sam away out of the yard, yet within arrow-shot of the house, and hold the court of execution on some rocky mound where there is neither meadow nor furrow?'

This should be done at the time when the sun is full south.

'I'll stay here with Hrafnkel,' replied Thorkel. 'That looks to me the less bothersome.'

Thorgeir and Sam then went and held the court of execution, after which they walked back, took down Hrafnkel and his men, and laid them out in the home-field. By this time the blood had started into their eyes.

Thorgeir told Sam that he could do just as he pleased with Hrafnkel. 'He seems to me to present no problem now.'

'I am offering you a choice of two things, Hrafnkel,' said Sam to that. 'One is that you shall be led away from the house with such men as I please and be killed. However, because you have so many dependent on you, I am prepared to let you go on looking after them. But if you choose to live, then leave Adalbol with all your household, and have only those assets I assign you—which will be precious little. For I shall take over this homestead and all your authority too. You shall never lay claim to these, you nor your heirs; nor shall you ever again live nearer than east of Fljotsdalsheid. You can now strike hands on our bargain, if you can bring yourself to accept it.'

'To many,' said Hrafnkel, 'a quick death would seem better than such disgrace. But I shall take the same course as most others: my choice is life, if choice there be. I do it mainly for my sons' sake, for theirs is a poor prospect if I die and leave them.'

Hrafnkel was then loosed, and he gave Sam the right to make his own award. He allotted Hrafnkel such goods as he pleased, and this was painfully little. Hrafnkel had his spear with him but no further weapon. That same day Hrafnkel took himself off from Adalbol, and all his people with him.

'I cannot think why you are doing this,' Thorgeir told Sam. 'You will live to regret it more than anyone that you are giving Hrafnkel his life.'

That was how it would have to be then, said Sam.

Hrafnkel now removed to a home east of Fljotsdalsheid and across Fljotsdal to eastwards of Lagarfljot. At the end of the lake stood a little farm, Lokhilla by name, where he bought land on credit, for he had no money beyond what he needed for his farm things. There was a lot of talk about this, how his haughtiness had been humbled, and there were many to call to mind the old proverb—'Pride goes before a fall'. This was fine, extensive forest-land, but sadly off for buildings, and that was why he bought the land cheap. Hrafnkel spared no expense; he felled the timber because it was big, and raised a stately farm there which has ever since been called Hrafnkelsstadir, and from that day to this reputed a good farm. He lived there in great hardship that first winter. He had a lavish yield from the fisheries. He went hard at work while the farm was building. That first year he kept calf and kid for feeding through the winter, and all the animals he took that risk with he looked after so well that nearly all of them lived; so that it could just about be said that there were two heads to each of his beasts. That same summer there was a big run of fish in Lagarfljot, which proved a great help towards housekeeping in the district, and that held good every summer.

6

Sam started housekeeping at Adalbol after Hrafnkel, and later held a splendid feast, to which he
invited all those who had been retainers of Hrafnkel,
offering himself to be their leader in his place. They
agreed to this, but were not without misgivings all
the same.

The sons of Thjostar advised him to be cheerful,
liberal, and kindly to his men, a helper to everyone
who had need of him. 'Then they are no men if
they do not stand firmly by you, whatever your
need. We give you this advice because we would
like you to make a success of things, for we take you
to be a gallant sort of fellow. Now, keep your eyes
open and look out for yourself, for "It is warm work
watching out for the wicked".'

The sons of Thjostar sent after Freyfaxi and his
stud, saying that they wanted to see these precious
creatures about whom there had been such great
tales told. The horses were fetched in and the
brothers looked them over.

'These mares appear to me useful for farmwork,'
said Thorgeir. 'It is my advice that they perform
such useful tasks as they may, till they can no longer
keep going for old age. As for the stallion, he strikes
me as no better than other stallions—indeed, rather
worse, in that so much evil has come about because
of him. I have no desire that further killings come
about through him than have arisen already. It is
only right that he who owns him should now
take him.'

They led the stallion down along the level ground.
A crag stands below by the river, and underneath
it a deep pool. They led the stallion out on to the

crag there. The sons of Thjostar drew a bag over
his head, tied a stone round his neck, then took long
poles and pushed the horse over the edge, so making
an end of him. Since then the place has been known
as Freyfaxahamar.

Lower down stood the temple which had belonged
to Hrafnkel. Thorkel wanted to have a look at it.
He had all the gods plundered, and then set fire
to the temple, and burnt the whole lot together.
Later the guests made ready to leave. Sam chose
splendid treasures by way of gifts for both the
brothers. They vowed everlasting friendship between
them and parted on the most cordial terms. They
rode the quickest road west to the Firths and came
home to Thorskafjord with honour. Sam established
old Thorbjorn at Leikskalar (he was to live there),
but Sam's wife went to live with him at Adalbol,
and Sam dwelt there for a while.

7

East in Fljotsdal Hrafnkel heard how the sons of
Thjostar had destroyed Freyfaxi and burnt the
temple. 'I think it folly,' he said, 'to believe in gods,'
and announced that from then on he never would
believe in gods, and he kept to what he said, so that
he never again offered up a sacrifice.

Hrafnkel sat tight at Hrafnkelsstadir and raked
money together. He quickly won great honour in
the district, and everyone showed willingness to sit
or stand as he decided for them. At this time ship
after ship came sailing from Norway to Iceland
(most of the land in the district was settled in
Hrafnkel's day), but no one was allowed to settle
there in peace unless he asked Hrafnkel's permis-

sion. They all had to promise him their backing, and he promised his support in return. He brought under his authority the whole country-side east of Lagarfljot. This territory was soon much bigger and better blessed with men than the one he had ruled before, reaching up around Skridudal, and the whole way along Lagarfljot. And now a change had come over his temper. He was much more popular than before. He had the same mind to be helpful and hospitable, but was now altogether more reasonable than before and gentler in every way. Sam and Hrafnkel often met at various gatherings, but they never made mention of their dealings together. In this fashion six years went by. Sam was well liked by his followers, for he was quiet and easy-going and always ready to help in time of trouble, and bore in mind what those brothers had advised him. Sam was a great man for show.

8

The story goes on to tell how a ship put into Reydarfjord from the open sea whose skipper was Eyvind Bjarnason. He had been abroad for seven years. Eyvind was a much improved man in style and breeding, and had grown into the gallantest person. He was soon informed of what had happened, but he made little or no comment on it. He was a rather reserved sort of man.

As soon as Sam heard the news he rode to the ship, and there was now a great and joyful meeting between the brothers. Sam invited him home out west, and Eyvind accepted eagerly, requesting Sam to ride on home and send horses for his cargo, while he hauled his ship ashore and made it ready for the

winter. Sam did as he was asked, went home, and
had horses driven to meet Eyvind; and once Eyvind
had made arrangements about his cargo he made
ready for his journey to Hrafnkelsdal and started up
along Reydarfjord. There were five men in the
party. The sixth was Eyvind's servant lad, an Icelander by birth, and related to him. Eyvind had
plucked this lad from destitution, and carried him
abroad with him, and looked after him as himself.
This deed of his had become quite famous, and it
was the general opinion that there were few to
equal him.

They now rode up Thorisdalsheid and were
driving sixteen pack-horses in front of them. There
were two of Sam's housecarles there and three
sailors. They were all dressed in coloured clothes
and rode with gay shields. They rode across Skridudal and over the ridge to Fljotsdal, at a place called
Bulungarvellir, then down to Gilsareyr, where the
gravel bank runs west to the river between Hallorms-
stadir and Hrafnkelsstadir. Then they rode up along
Lagarfljot, below the meadow at Hrafnkelsstadir, so
past the head of the lake, and forded the Jokulsa at
Skalavad. The time was about 7.30 in the morning.

There was a woman by the lake doing her day's
wash, and she saw the men passing. The servant
woman swept her linen together and ran home,
where she flung it down outside near the woodpile
and went scurrying indoors. Hrafnkel had not yet
got up. Some of the more favoured men were lying
about the hall, but the workmen had departed about
their tasks. It was haymaking time.

The woman burst into speech the moment she
came inside. 'Aye, true it is,' she cried, 'that old
proverb—"Grow old and grow afraid". Small grows

that honour which is acquired early, if later a man grows shamefully slack and wants for courage ever to exact his dues—and such is very strange in a man who in his day showed spirit. How different is their way of life who grow up in their fathers' homes and seem to you mere nobodies compared with yourselves; but no sooner are they out of their childhood than they go travelling from land to land and are thought of great weight wherever they come, and so they return home again, counting themselves greater than chieftains. Eyvind Bjarnason has just ridden through the river here at Skalavad with so gay a shield that the light came sparkling off it. He is a good enough man to reap a good vengeance on.'

The servant woman really let herself go. Hrafnkel got up and gave her this answer. 'No doubt you are babbling what is only too true, yet not out of any good will either. It is just as well then for you to bear some of the load. Hurry south to Vidivellir for Sighvat and Snorri, the sons of Hallstein. Tell them to come to me instantly with any men there who can use arms.'

He sent a second woman servant out to Hrolfsstadir for Thord and Halli, the sons of Hrolf, and any there who could use arms. Both sets of brothers were able and worthy men. Hrafnkel also sent after his housecarles, so that they were eighteen all told. They took up their weapons in earnest, and rode through the river as the others had done before.

By now Eyvind and his men had got up on to the heath. He kept riding west till he reached Bersagotur in the middle of the heath. There is a turfless swamp there—it is like riding through nothing but ooze, and one is sinking all the time to the knee or thigh, and on occasion to the horse's belly, while below the surface it is as hard as a slab of rock. Next comes a great waste of stony ground to the west of it, and as they reached this waste the boy looked back and said to Eyvind: 'There are men riding after us, no fewer than eighteen of them, with a big man riding in blue clothes. He looks to me like Hrafnkel the Priest, though it is a long time since last I saw him.'

'What business is that of ours?' replied Eyvind. 'I cannot imagine I have anything to fear from a gallop of Hrafnkel's. I have done nothing against him. He must have an errand west to the Dale to meet his friends.'

'I have a feeling it is you he wants to meet,' the lad replied.

'I am not aware,' said Eyvind, 'that anything has happened between him and Sam my brother since they came to terms.'

'I should like you to ride off west to the Dale,' replied the lad. 'Then you will be safe. I know Hrafnkel's temper, how he will do nothing to us if he fails to get at you. Everything is taken care of so long as you are all right. The game is not in the toils then, so all is well, whatever happens to us.'

Eyvind said he would not ride off quite so fast. 'I don't know who they are, and there would be plenty to laugh at me if I took to my heels with nothing proved.'

They now rode west from the stony ground. Ahead of them lay a second swamp, called Oxamyr. This one is very grassy. There are soft patches, so that it is wellnigh impassable, which was why old Hallfred established the higher way round, even though it proved longer.

Eyvind now rode west into the swamp. Their

horses sank deep into the mire and they were
seriously delayed. The others, who rode unham-
pered, were overhauling them fast. Hrafnkel and
his men were now riding up to the swamp while
Eyvind's company were just coming out of it. They
recognized Hrafnkel and both his sons, and begged
Eyvind to make his escape.

'All the bad places are now past. You will get to
Adalbol while the swamp stands between you.'

'I'll not run from men to whom I have done no
wrong,' replied Eyvind.

They then rode up on to the ridge. Hillocks stand
on the ridge, and on the slope of the mountain is
a turf knoll much denuded by the wind, with high
banks surrounding it. Eyvind rode to this knoll,
where he dismounted and awaited them.

'We shall soon know their errand now,' said
Eyvind.

After that they climbed up on to the knoll and
tore up some stones for missiles.

At the same time Hrafnkel turned from the path
and south to the knoll. He had never a word for
Eyvind, but instantly made the assault. Eyvind
defended himself skilfully and like a brave man.
Eyvind's lad judged himself not strong enough for
the fray, got hold of his horse and rode westward
over the ridge to Adalbol to tell Sam what game was
afoot. Sam moved quickly and sent for his men.
They were twenty all told, and a well equipped
company, and with these he rode east to the heath
to the scene of action. But by this time the battle
was over. Hrafnkel was riding eastward from his
work, while Eyvind had fallen and all his men with
him. The first thing Sam did was to look for life
in his brother, but the job had been thoroughly

done: they were all dead, the five of them together. Twelve of Hrafnkel's men had fallen too, and six were riding away.

Sam made short stay there, but bade his men instantly give chase. They rode off after them, but their horses were flagging.

'We may be able to catch them,' said Sam, 'for their horses are tired, while ours are all fresh. Still, it will be a close thing whether we catch them or not before they get down off the heath.'

Hrafnkel had by now put himself east of Oxamyr. Pursued and pursuers kept riding till Sam reached the brow of the heath, where he saw how Hrafnkel had come a long way down the slope. He saw too that he would escape away down into his own territory.

'This is where we turn back,' he told his men. 'It will be easy now for Hrafnkel to collect all the men he wants.'

So Sam turned back with that for his pains. He came to where Eyvind was lying, and threw up a mound over him and his mates. The place-names there are now Eyvindartorfa, Eyvindarfjoll, and Eyvindardal.

Then Sam returned to Adalbol with all Eyvind's goods. When he reached home he sent word to his retainers that they should muster there in the morning before breakfast. He had made up his mind to ride east over the heath—'Be our outing as it may,' said he. In the evening he went to bed, and a lot of men had gathered there.

9

Hrafnkel rode home and told what had happened. He ate his food and after that gathered a force together, so that he set out with seventy men, and riding with that band westward over the heath, came unawares to Adalbol, seized Sam in his bed, and led him out.

'Now, Sam,' said Hrafnkel, 'your plight has become such as must have seemed unlikely to you even a short while since, in that I have your life in my hands. I must not now prove a worse fellow to you than you were to me, so I am giving you your choice of two things: to be killed, or the other, that I alone shall shear and shape between us.'

Sam said he would rather choose to live, adding that he thought even so either way would be hard.

Hrafnkel said he could expect that. 'For we have that to repay you; whereas I would have treated you twice as well, had you deserved it. You shall move away from Adalbol down to Leikskalar and settle there on your own farm. You shall take with you the goods that Eyvind owned. But you shall not carry away any more in the way of property than what you brought here—all that, though, you shall carry away in full. I shall take back my priesthood, the farm, and homestead likewise. I see that there has been a big increase in my holdings, but you shall not benefit by that. No payment shall be made for Eyvind your brother, because you followed up the bloodsuit too ruthlessly for your former kinsman; while for your kinsman Einar you have had redress enough in that you have enjoyed power and wealth these six winters. Not that, in any case, I consider the killing of Eyvind and his comrades worth more than the maiming of me and my men. You made me a fugitive from my own country-side, but I am content for you to remain at Leikskalar. At the same time it will prove as well for you if you do not puff yourself up to your own hurt. You shall stay my underling as long as we live; and you can count on this too, that the worse we get on together, the worse you will find things.'

Sam now went away with his household down to Leikskalar, and there he stayed, on his farm.

10

Hrafnkel organized the household at Adalbol with his men, and put his son Thorir in charge at Hrafnkelsstadir. He now held the priesthood over the entire country-side. Asbjorn stayed with his father, because he was the younger son.

Sam remained at Leikskalar that winter. He was taciturn and kept much to himself, and it was obvious to many that he was disgruntled with his lot. But the winter over, once the days grew longer, Sam with one other man and three horses set out over the bridge, and from there across Modrudalsheid, so over the Jokulsa river (the one up on the mountain), and on to Myvatn, and from there over Fljotsheid and Ljosavatnsskard, making no real break in his journey till he arrived west in Thorskafjord, where he was made most welcome. Thorkel had just got home after a sea-voyage, and had been abroad for four years. Sam spent a week there, resting himself, and then he told them what had now happened between him and Hrafnkel, and asked the brothers for help and backing this time as before.

Thorgeir did more of the answering for the brothers this time. He would be keeping out of it, he said. 'There is a great distance between us. We thought we had put things right for you before we came away, so that it would be easy for you to hold on to; but things have turned out as I felt sure they would when you gave Hrafnkel his life, that you would live to regret it most. We begged you to take his life, but, no, you had to have your own way. And how obvious it has become what a difference of judgement lay between you, when he let you live in peace and made his attack only when he had removed from his path him who, in his opinion, was a better man than you. We cannot burden ourselves with this lucklessness of yours, nor have we such great eagerness to quarrel with Hrafnkel that we feel tempted to endanger our good name all over again. But we should like to invite you here in under our lee with all your household, if you consider it less galling here than alongside Hrafnkel.'

Sam said he had no wish for that. He told them he wanted to get back home, and asked them to change horses with him, a thing that was quickly put right. The brothers wanted to give him fine gifts, but he would accept nothing, arguing that it would show a mean spirit. With so much for his pains Sam rode back home, and there he remained till old age. He never achieved anything against Hrafnkel to the end of his days.

But Hrafnkel lived on his farm and kept his honours. He died of a sickness, and his burial mound stands in Hrafnkelsdal, down the valley from Adalbol. Great riches were laid in the mound alongside him, all his armour and that good spear of his. His sons succeeded to his authority, Thorir living at Hrafnkelsstadir and Asbjorn at Adalbol. They shared the priesthood between them, and were reckoned very able men.

And that is the end of Hrafnkel's Saga.

EIRIK THE RED[1]

I

THERE was a warrior-king named Olaf who was known as Olaf the White. Olaf went raiding in the west and conquered Dublin in Ireland along with the territory that went with it, and made himself king there. He married Aud the Deep-minded, the daughter of Ketil Flatnose, son of Bjorn Buna, a man of rank from Norway; and the name of their son was Thorstein the Red. Olaf fell in battle there in Ireland, whereupon Aud and Thorstein made their way to the Hebrides, where Thorstein married Thurid the daughter of Eyvind the Norwegian and sister of Helgi the Lean. They had many children.

Thorstein became a warrior-king and allied himself with Earl Sigurd the Mighty, the son of Eystein Glumra, and they conquered Caithness and Sutherland, Ross and Moray, and more than half Scotland. Thorstein made himself its king, till the Scots betrayed him and he fell there in battle. Aud was in Caithness when she heard tell of Thorstein's fall. She had a merchant ship built secretly in the forest, and once she was ready she hoisted sail for the Orkneys and found a husband there for Thorstein the Red's daughter Gro, the mother of that Grealada whom Earl Thorfinn Skull-splitter married. After

[1] There are two sagas which deal with the Norse voyages of discovery and settlement to América (Vinland): the Saga of Eirik the Red (*Eiriks Saga Rauða*) written *c.* 1265, and the Greenlanders' Saga (*Grænlendinga Saga*) written *c.* 1200. They do not agree in all respects, and probably represent differing local versions of the common Icelandic traditions of the Greenland and American voyages of the period *c.* 980–1020.

that she set off to seek Iceland and had twenty free-
men on board her ship. She reached Iceland and
spent the first winter in Bjarnarhofn with her
brother Bjorn. Later Aud took in settlement all
Dalelands between Dogurdara and Skraumuhlaupsa.
She made her home at Hvamm and had a chapel at
Krossholar, where she had crosses set up, for she
had been baptized and held the Christian faith.

Many notable men accompanied her to Iceland
who had been taken prisoner on the western raids
and were, in a manner of speaking, slaves. One of
these was called Vifil. He was a man of good family
who had been taken prisoner over the western sea
and was, nominally at least, a slave till Aud set him
free. When Aud gave homes to her ship's crew,
Vifil asked why she did not give him one like the rest
of them, but Aud said it hardly mattered, maintaining that he would be held a fine man as he was.
However, she gave him Vifilsdal and he made his
home there. He married a wife, and their sons were
Thorbjorn and Thorgeir. These were promising
men and grew up with their father.

2

There was a man by the name of Thorvald who
was the son of Asvald Ulfsson. Thorvald's son was
called Eirik the Red, and both father and son left
Jadri in Norway for Iceland because of some killings.
They settled in the Hornstrandir and made a home
at Drangar, where Thorvald died. Eirik then married Thjodhild, the daughter of Jorund Ulfsson and
Thorbjorg Ship-bosom, who was by this time
married to Thorbjorn the Haukadaler. Eirik now
left the north and cleared land in Haukadal and made
his home at Eiriksstadir alongside Vatnshorn. In

time Eirik's thralls caused a landslide to crash down upon the farm of Valthjof at Valthjofsstadir, whereupon Valthjof's kinsman Eyjolf Saur killed the thralls by Skeidsbrekka above Vatnshorn. For this Eirik killed Eyjolf Saur. He killed Holmgang-Hrafn too at Leikskalar. Gerstein and Odd of Jorvi, both kinsmen of Eyjolf's, took up his case, and Eirik was driven out of Haukadal. He then settled Brokey and Oxney, and lived at Tradi in Sudrey for the first winter. It was now that he lent Thorgest his hall-beams. Later Eirik moved to Oxney and made his home at Eiriksstadir. He asked for his beams but could not get them. Eirik went to Breidabolstad after the beams, but Thorgest gave chase, and they came to blows a short way from the house at Drangar. Two of Thorgest's sons fell there as well as certain other men.

From now on both parties kept a large body of men under arms. Styr and Eyjolf from Sviney, Thorbjorn Vifilsson and the sons of Thorbrand from Alftafjord backed Eirik, but backing Thorgest were the sons of Thord Bellow together with Thorgeir from Hitardal, Aslak from Langadal, and Illugi his son.

Eirik and his following were outlawed at the assembly for law at Thorsnes. He put his ship all ready in Eiriksvag, while Eyjolf kept him in hiding in Dimunarvag for as long as Thorgest and his men were combing the islands for him. Thorbjorn, Eyjolf, and Styr escorted Eirik on his way out through the islands, and they parted on warm terms of friendship, Eirik promising that they should receive just such help themselves if it lay in his power to provide it and he knew they had need of him. He told them he meant to look for that land Gunnbjorn

Ulf-Krakuson sighted the time he was storm-driven into the western ocean and discovered Gunnbjorn's Skerries. He would be coming back, he said, to make contact with his friends should he discover that land.

Eirik sailed to the open sea by way of Snæfells-jokul and made a landfall in Greenland at the glacier which is called Blaserk, or Bluesark. From there he headed south, to discover whether the land was habitable there. He spent his first winter at Eiriksey, near the middle of the Eastern Settlement, and the following spring went on to Eiriksfjord where he sited his house. In the summer he made his way into the western wilderness and gave place-names there far and wide. He spent his second winter at Eiriks-holm off Hvarfsgnipa, but during the third summer pressed on north the whole way to Snæfell and on into Hrafnsfjord. He now thought he must have got as far as the head of Eiriksfjord, so retraced his steps to spend the third winter at Eiriksey off the mouth of Eiriksfjord.

The following summer he returned to Iceland and reached Breidafjord. He spent the winter with Ingolf at Holmlat. In the spring he came to blows with Thorgest and his men, and Eirik got the worst of it, but later they reached peace terms between them. This same summer Eirik sailed away to colonize the land he had discovered, calling it Green-land, for he maintained that men would be much more eager to go there if the land had an attractive name.

Ari Thorgilsson tells us that twenty-five ships set sail this summer for Greenland from Breidafjord and Borgarfjord, but only fourteen of them arrived there. Some were forced back and some perished. This was fifteen years before the Christian faith

became law in Iceland. Eirik afterwards took Eiriksfjord by right of settlement and lived at Brattahlid.

3

Thorgeir Vifilsson took to himself a wife, marrying
Arnora the daughter of Einar of Laugarbrekka, the
son of Sigmund, himself the son of that Ketil who
settled Thistilfjord. Another of Einar's daughters
was called Hallveig, whom Thorbjorn Vifilsson
married, getting land at Laugarbrekka, at Hellis-
vellir, along with her. Thorbjorn moved house there
and became a man of great note. He was a good
farmer and had a splendid estate. His daughter's
name was Gudrid, who was a most beautiful woman
and distinguished in everything she did.

Living at Arnarstapi was a man by the name of
Orm, who had a wife named Halldis. Orm was a
substantial farmer and a great friend of Thorbjorn's,
and Gudrid spent a long time there with him as his
foster-child.

Living at Thorgeirsfell was a man by the name of
Thorgeir. He was very well-to-do and in his day
had been freed from bondage. He had a son named
Einar, a man both handsome and accomplished, and
also a great one for show. He was engaged in foreign
trade, and had done very well for himself. He always
spent his winters in Iceland and Norway alternately.
It must now be told how one autumn when Einar
was in Iceland he set off with his wares out along
Snæfellstrand, proposing to sell them there. He
came to Arnarstapi, where Orm invited him to put
up, and Einar accepted, for they were on friendly
terms together. The wares were carried into a storehouse. Einar then opened up his goods and displayed

them before Orm and his household, inviting him to take anything he liked. Orm accepted, and maintained that Einar was both a good trader and a very lucky fellow.

As they were busying themselves with the wares a woman walked past the storehouse door. Einar asked Orm who that lovely woman could be who walked past the door there. 'I've not seen her here before.'

'Oh,' replied Orm, 'that is Gudrid my foster-child, the daughter of Thorbjorn of Laugarbrekka.'

'She would make a fine match,' commented Einar. 'Have not quite a lot of men come asking for her?'

'Yes, she has been asked for, naturally,' Orm told him, 'but she is not just for the picking up. It looks as though she will be pretty particular in her choice of a husband, and her father the same.'

'For all that,' said Einar, 'she is the woman I intend to ask for in marriage, and I want you to handle my bid with Thorbjorn her father, and bend all your efforts to seeing that it succeeds. If I get my way, I shall repay you with the full weight of my friendship. Master Thorbjorn must surely see that these family ties would suit us both admirably, for he is a man of high reputation and great estate, yet his wealth, I am told, is waning fast. But I, and my father with me, lack neither land nor money, and it would do Thorbjorn a power of good if this match could be arranged.'

'To be sure,' said Orm, 'I consider myself your friend. But even so I am slow to advise that we undertake this, for Thorbjorn is a proud man and nothing if not high-stomached.'

Einar's answer was that he would agree to nothing but that his marriage offer be put before Thorbjorn, and Orm agreed that he should have his way. Einar then travelled back south until he reached home again.

Some time later Thorbjorn gave a harvest-feast, just as he was used to do, for he was a most open-handed man. Orm came there from Arnarstapi, and a good many other friends of Thorbjorn's. Orm found an opportunity to talk with Thorbjorn, and told him how Einar from Thorgeirsfell had visited him recently, and that he was developing into a most promising sort of man. Then Orm broached his offer of marriage on Einar's behalf, claiming that it would be a good thing for more reasons than one. 'It could well prove of great assistance to you, franklin, from the money point of view.'

'I did not look for such words from you,' replied Thorbjorn, 'as that I should bestow my daughter on the son of a slave. You must be very convinced my affairs are in low water when you put forward an offer of this kind. And she shall not stay in your house a day longer, since you think her deserving of so miserable a match.'

After this Orm returned home, and each and every one of the guests to his proper abode. But Gudrid stayed behind with her father and spent the winter in her own home.

Then in the spring Thorbjorn gave a feast for his friends; a lot of people attended, and the entertainment was of the best. During the feast Thorbjorn asked for silence and spoke as follows: 'I have lived here a long time and have experienced men's goodwill and love towards me. And I believe we have got on well together. But now my affairs are taking a turn for the worse on account of my means, though till now my estate has been held an honourable one. Now I prefer to uproot my home rather than destroy my good name, and will sooner depart the country than bring shame on my family. I plan to take advantage of the promise of my friend Eirik the Red, which he made when we parted in Breida-fjord, and if things go as I wish, I mean to go to Greenland this summer.'

This resolve of his dumbfounded them all, for Thorbjorn was a man most dear to his friends, but they felt quite sure that Thorbjorn had committed himself so far by his words only because there was no possibility of stopping him. Thorbjorn gave presents to his guests, the feast came to an end, and with that everyone returned home. Thorbjorn sold his lands and bought a ship which had been drawn ashore at the mouth of Hraunhafn. Thirty men addressed themselves to this voyage with him, among whom were Orm from Arnarstapi, together with his wife, and other of Thorbjorn's friends who were unwilling to part from him. In due time they put to sea, but once they were out at sea the fair wind dropped, they lost their course, and made slow progress the whole summer through. Next, sickness broke out among their company, and Orm died, as did Halldis his wife, and half their party. A big sea got up, and they suffered great hardship and misery of all kinds, yet with it all reached Herjolfsnes in Greenland at the very beginning of winter. Living there at Herjolfsnes was a man by the name of Thorkel, and an excellent man he was. He took Thorbjorn into his house with all his crew for the winter, and right royally he entertained them.

At this same time there was a great famine in Greenland; men who had gone out fishing caught poor catches, and some never came back. There was a woman there in the Settlement whose name was Thorbjorg; she was a seeress and was called the Little Sibyl. She had had nine sisters, all of them seeresses, but now only she was left alive. It was Thorbjorg's practice of a winter to attend feasts, and those men in particular invited her to their homes who were curious to know their fate or the season's prospects. Because Thorkel was the leading householder there it was thought to be his responsibility to find out when these hard times which now troubled them would cease, so he invited her to his home, and a good reception was prepared for her, as was the custom when a woman of this kind should be received. A high-seat was made ready for her, and a cushion laid down, in which there must be hen's feathers.

When she arrived in the evening, together with the man who had been sent to escort her, this is how she was attired: she was wearing a blue cloak with straps which was set with stones right down to the hem; she had glass beads about her neck, and on her head a black lambskin hood lined inside with white catskin. She had a staff in her hand, with a knob on it; it was ornamented with brass and set around with stones just below the knob. Round her middle she wore a belt made of touchwood, and on it was a big skin pouch in which she kept those charms of hers which she needed for her magic. On her feet she had hairy calf-skin shoes with long thongs, and on the thong-ends big knobs of lateen. She had on her hands catskin gloves which were white inside and hairy.

Now when she came inside every one felt bound to offer her fit and proper greetings, which she received according as their donors found favour with her. Master Thorkel took her by the hand and led her to the seat which had been made ready for her. Thorkel then asked her to run her eyes over the household and herd and likewise the home. She had little comment to make upon anything. During the evening tables were brought in, and what food was prepared for the seeress must now be told of. There was porridge made for her of goat's beestings, and for her meat the hearts of all living creatures that were available there. She had a brass spoon and an ivory-handled knife mounted with a double ring of copper, and with its point broken off. Then when the tables were cleared away farmer Thorkel walked up to Thorbjorg and asked what she thought of what she had seen there, and how satisfactory she found the house and the manners of its people, and how soon she would feel sure of what he had asked her and men were so anxious to know. She replied that she would have nothing to announce till the following morning, when she had first slept through the night.

But on the morrow, towards the end of day, she was fitted out with the apparatus she needed to perform her spells. She asked too to procure her such women as knew the lore which was necessary for the spell, and bore the name Varðlokur or Spirit-locks. But no such women were to be found, so there was a search right through the house to find whether anyone was versed in these matters.

'I am unversed in magic, neither am I a prophetess,' said Gudrid then, 'but Halldis my foster-mother taught me in Iceland the chant which she called Varðlokur.'

'Then you are wise in good time,' said Thorbjorg.

'This is a kind of proceeding I feel I can play no part in,' said Gudrid, 'for I am a Christian woman.'

'Yet it might happen,' said Thorbjorg, 'that you could prove helpful to folk in this affair, and still be no worse a woman than before. But it is Thorkel I must look to to procure me the things I need.'

Thorkel now pressed Gudrid hard, till she said she would do as he wished. The women now formed a circle round the platform on which Thorbjorg was seated. Gudrid recited the chant so beautifully and well that no one who was present could say he had heard a chant recited by a lovelier voice. The seeress thanked her for the chant, adding that many spirits had been drawn there now who thought it lovely to lend ear, the chant had been so admirably delivered—spirits 'who before wished to keep their distance from us and give us no hearing. And now many things are apparent to me which earlier were hidden from me as from many others. And I can tell you, Thorkel, that this famine will not last longer than this winter, and that the season will mend when spring comes. The sickness which has afflicted us, that too will mend sooner than was expected. As for you, Gudrid, I will repay you here and now for the help we have derived from you, for your fate is now all clear to me. You will make a match here in Greenland, the most distinguished there is, yet it will not be of long duration; for your ways lie out to Iceland, where there will spring from you a great and goodly progeny, and over the branches of your family will shine beams brighter than I have power to see precisely as they are. And so, my daughter, farewell now, and happiness go with you.'

After this men approached the prophetess and inquired, each of them, about what they were most concerned to know. She was free with her information, and little indeed of what she said failed to come about. Next she was sent for from another house, and off she went, and then Thorbjorn was sent after, for he would not stay in the house while such heathendom was practised. The weather quickly improved, just as Thorbjorg had announced. Thorbjorn made his ship ready and journeyed on till he reached Brattahlid. Eirik welcomed him with open arms, expressing warm satisfaction that he had come there. Thorbjorn spent the winter with him together with his family, but they found lodgings for the crew among the farmers. Later in the spring Eirik gave Thorbjorn land at Stokkaness, a stately house was built there, and he lived there from this time onwards.

4

Eirik had a wife whose name was Thjodhild, by whom he had two sons, one called Thorstein and the other Leif, both of them promising men. Thorstein was living at home with his father, and no man in Greenland was held as promising as he. Leif, though, had sailed to Norway, where he was staying with king Olaf Tryggvason.

But when Leif sailed from Greenland in the summer, they were driven off course to the Hebrides. They had a long wait for a fair wind thence, and had to remain there for much of the summer. Leif took a fancy to a woman by the name of Thorgunna. She was a woman of good birth, and Leif had an idea that she saw further into things than most. As he made ready to sail away Thorgunna asked to come with him. Leif asked whether her people were likely to approve of this, to which she answered she did not care. Leif replied that he didn't see how he could just carry off so high-born a lady while in foreign parts—'For I am short of men for that.'

'It is not certain,' said Thorgunna, 'that you think you have chosen the wiser course.'

'That is a chance I must take,' said Leif.

'Then I am telling you,' said Thorgunna, 'that this is no longer a question of just me alone, for I am with child, and the child, I tell you, is yours. I believe that when this child is born it will be a boy, and though you wash your hands of us now, still I shall raise the boy and send him to you in Greenland once he can travel with other men. I believe, too, that having this son will prove just such a pleasure to you as your desertion of me now merits. And I am thinking I may come to Greenland myself before the game is played out.'

Leif gave her a gold ring for her finger, a cloak of Greenland woollen, and an ivory belt. This boy came to Greenland, declaring that his name was Thorgils, and Leif admitted his paternity. It is some men's tale that this same Thorgils came to Iceland before the Froda-marvels in the summer.[1] He was certainly in Greenland thereafter, where it was thought that there was something uncanny about him before the finish.

Leif and his men set sail from the Hebrides and reached Norway in the autumn, where he proceeded into the court of the king Olaf Tryggvason. The king paid him many honours, feeling certain he would be a man of parts.

[1] An account of the hauntings at Froda, one of the best stories of the supernatural in the sagas, may be read in *The Eyre-Biders' Saga* (*Eyrbyggja Saga*), chapters 50–54.

There came a day when the king found occasion to speak with Leif. 'Are you counting on Greenland this summer?' he asked him.

'I am,' said Leif, 'with your permission.'

'I think all will be well,' replied the king. 'You shall go there with my commission and preach Christianity there.'

Leif said it was for the king to command, but added that he thought this mission would be a hard one to carry out in Greenland.

The king said he had not seen a man better fitted for this than he. 'You will bring it good luck!'

'That will be so,' said Leif, 'only if I enjoy luck from you too.'

Leif put to sea, and was at sea a long time, and lighted on those lands whose existence he had not so much as dreamt of before. There were wheat-fields growing wild there and grown vines. There were also those trees which are called maple, and they fetched away with them samples of all these things—some trees so big that they were used in housebuilding. Leif found men on a wreck and carried them home with him, showing his magnanimity and gallantry in this as in so much else, since it was he who introduced Christianity into the country; and ever afterwards he was called Leif the Lucky.

Leif reached land in Eiriksfjord and then went home to Brattahlid, where they all welcomed him with open arms. He soon preached Christianity and the universal faith throughout the country, revealing to men the message of king Olaf Tryggvason, and telling how many noble deeds and what great glory accompanied this religion. Eirik was slow to abandon his faith, but Thjodhild accepted at once and had

a church built, though not too near their house.
This church was called Thjodhild's Church, and it
was there that she offered up her prayers, together
with those men who adopted Christianity. Thjodhild would not live together with Eirik once she had
taken the faith, a circumstance which grieved him
very much.

There was now a lot of talk that men should seek
out this land which Leif had discovered. Thorstein
Eiriksson was the leader here, a man both wise and
popular. Eirik too was invited along, for men had
the greatest faith in his luck and good management.
He took his time about it, then said he would not
refuse what his friends were asking. After this they
made ready the ship which Thorbjorn had brought
to Greenland, and settled on twenty men as crew.
They had few possessions with them beyond
weapons and provisions. The morning Eirik rode
from home he took a casket which had gold and
silver in it; he buried it and then went on his way,
but what followed was that he fell off his horse,
broke ribs in his side, and damaged his arm at the
shoulder-joint. Because of this mishap he told
Thjodhild his wife that she must remove the money,
reckoning that he had paid this price for having
buried it. Thereafter they sailed out of Eiriksfjord
as merry as could be, for they had high hopes of
their venture. Then they were storm-tossed for a
long time on the ocean and could not hold to the
course they wanted. They came in sight of Iceland
and encountered birds from Ireland. Then their
ship was driven all over the ocean, and they returned
in the autumn, battered and worn, and made
Eiriksfjord at the beginning of winter.

Said Eirik: 'We were merrier in the summer

sailing out of the fjord than we are now, and yet we have our blessings even so.'

'What a leader should do now,' replied Thorstein, 'is make some arrangement for all those men who have no place to go to, and find them winter quarters.'

'The old saying is always true,' Eirik agreed, 'and so it will prove now. It is easy to be wise after the event. You shall have your head now in this.'

So all those who had nowhere else to go went along with that father and son. Later they went home to Brattahlid and spent the winter there.

The story now goes on to tell how Thorstein Eiriksson asked for Gudrid in marriage, and his proposal found favour both with her and her father. The match was agreed to, Thorstein should marry Gudrid, and the wedding took place at Brattahlid in the autumn. The festivities went off well and there was a big gathering present. Thorstein owned an estate in the Western Settlement at a holding known as Lysafjord. Another man, also named Thorstein, owned a half share in this estate. His wife's name was Sigrid. Thorstein and Gudrid with him went to Lysafjord in the autumn, to his namesake's, where they got a warm welcome and stayed on over the winter. What happened next was that sickness attacked the farmstead quite early in the winter. The foreman there was called Gardar, a man not much liked. He was the first to fall ill and die, and after that it was not long till they were dying one after the other. It was now that Thorstein Eiriksson fell ill, and Sigrid too, the wife of his namesake. One evening Sigrid wanted to go to the privy which stood opposite the outer door. Gudrid went with her, and they were facing this door when Sigrid uttered a loud cry.

'We have acted rashly,' said Gudrid, 'and you are in no state to stand the cold, so let us get back in as quickly as we can.'

'It is impossible to go as yet,' replied Sigrid. 'Here is now the entire host of the dead before the door, and Thorstein your husband with them, and I recognize myself there too. How dreadful it is to see such a thing!' And when this passed off, 'Let us go now, Gudrid,' she begged. 'I do not see the host any longer.' The foreman too had disappeared, who she thought earlier had had a whip in his hand and sought to scourge the company.

After this they went back indoors, and before morning came she was dead, and a coffin was made for the body.

This same day men were planning to row to sea, and Thorstein led them down to the waterside. At twilight he went down to see what they had caught. Then Thorstein Eiriksson sent word to his namesake that he should come to him, saying that it was far from quiet there, and that the lady of the house was trying to get on her feet and under the clothes with him. Indeed, by the time he arrived back inside she had got herself up on to the edge of the bed. He laid hold of her and set a pole-axe to her breast.

Thorstein Eiriksson died near the close of day. The other Thorstein told Gudrid to lie down and sleep, promising that he would himself watch through the night over the bodies. She did so, and when but a little of the night was past Thorstein Eiriksson sat up and said it was his wish that Gudrid should be summoned to him, for he desired to speak to her. 'God wills that this hour is granted me by way of remission and for the amendment of my state.' Farmer Thorstein went to find Gudrid and woke her; he urged her to cross herself and pray God to help her. He told her what Thorstein Eiriksson had said to him. 'He wants to see you, but it is for you to decide which course you will take, for I cannot direct you one way or the other.' 'It may be,' she replied, 'that this marvel is intended as one of those things which are to be stored in our hearts hereafter; yet I trust that God's keeping will stand over me. And by the mercy of God I will risk going to see him and discover what he would tell of; for I cannot escape, if I am fated to suffer hurt. Even less should I like for him to walk abroad more widely —and that, I suspect, will otherwise prove the case.'

So Gudrid went now and found Thorstein Eiriksson, and it seemed to her as though he was weeping. He spoke certain words quietly in her ear, so that she alone heard them; but what he did say so that everyone heard was that those men were truly blest who kept their faith well, and that salvation and mercy attended upon them; though many, he added, kept their faith ill. 'Nor is that a good custom which has obtained here in Greenland since the coming of Christianity, to lay men down in unconsecrated ground with only a brief service sung over them. I want to be borne to church, and likewise those others who have died here; but I want Gardar to be burnt on a pyre as soon as possible, for he is the cause of all the hauntings that have taken place here this winter.' He spoke to her further of her own affairs, declaring that her future would be a notable one. He bade her beware of marrying a Greenlander, and urged her to bestow their money upon the church, and some of it upon the poor; and then he sank back for the second time.

It had been the custom in Greenland, ever since

the coming of Christianity, that men were buried on the farms where they died, in unconsecrated ground. A stake would be set up from the breast of the dead, and in due course, when clerks came that way, the stakes would be pulled up and holy water poured into the place, and a service sung over them, even though this might be a good while later.

The bodies of Thorstein Eiriksson and the rest were borne to the church at Eiriksfjord, and services sung over them by clerks. Eirik received Gudrid in and acted towards her like a father. Somewhat later Thorbjorn died, and his entire estate passed to Gudrid. Eirik took her into his own home, and looked after her well.

5

Living in the north of Iceland, at Reynisnes in Skagafjord (the farm is now called Stad), was a man known as Thorfinn Karlsefni, the son of Thord Horse-head. He was a man of good family and very well-to-do. His mother's name was Thorunn. Thorfinn was a trader overseas, and had the name of a good merchant. One summer Thorfinn Karlsefni made his ship ready and was proposing to sail to Greenland. Snorri Thorbrandsson from Alftafjord went with him, and they had forty men aboard. A man by the name of Bjarni Grimolfsson, a Breidafjord man by kin, and another named Thorhall Gamlason, a Westfirther, made their ship ready this same summer, proposing to sail to Greenland, and they too had forty men aboard. Together with Karlsefni they put to sea in these two ships as soon as they were fitted out. There is no record of how long they were at sea, but this we can say, that both ships put into Eiriksfjord in the autumn. Eirik and other of the settlers rode to the ships, and they promptly started buying and selling. The skippers invited Eirik to take anything he liked from among their wares; and Eirik showed himself no less generous in return, for he invited the two ships' crews to come and spend the winter with him at Brattahlid. The merchants accepted this offer with thanks, and their goods were then transferred to Brattahlid, where there was no lack of big storehouses to keep them safe. Nor was there a noticeable lack of anything else they needed, and the merchants were on good terms with themselves throughout the winter.

But as the time wore on towards Christmas Eirik came to look most unhappy and was less cheerful than was his habit. So one day Karlsefni came to speak with Eirik. 'Is anything the matter, friend Eirik? People fancy you are less cheerful than usual. You have treated us with the greatest generosity, and we feel bound to repay you to the very best of our ability, so tell me now, what causes your low spirits?'

'You have accepted my hospitality kindly and graciously,' replied Eirik, 'and it does not so much as occur to me that you will be any the less well thought of for our dealings together. No, my anxiety is rather lest, once you find yourselves in other parts, it will be noised abroad how you never spent a worse Christmas than the one now coming in, when Eirik the Red was your host at Brattahlid in Greenland.'

'That will in no way prove the case, friend,' Karlsefni assured him. 'On board our ships we have both malt and corn, so help yourself to anything you like, and prepare a feast as magnificent as your heart would have it.'

Eirik accepted this offer, and a Christmas feast was now prepared, and one so choice and costly that men thought they had had rarely seen such high living in a poor country.

Then after Christmas Karlsefni put before Eirik a proposal of marriage for Gudrid, for as he saw it this lay in Eirik's competence. Eirik gave him a favourable answer, reckoning that she must follow her fate, and that he had heard nothing but good of Karlsefni. So that was how it ended: Thorfinn married Gudrid, the feast was renewed, their wedding held and drunk to, and they spent the winter at Brattahlid.

There were long discussions at Brattahlid, how men ought to seek out Vinland the Good, and it was the general opinion that it would be found a good and fruitful country. And so it came about that Karlsefni and Snorri made ready their ship to go and find that country in the spring. Bjarni and Thorhall joined in the voyage with their ship and the crew which had served with them. There was a man by the name of Thorvard, who was married to Eirik the Red's natural daughter Freydis, who went along with them, together with Eirik's son Thorvald, and that Thorhall who was nicknamed the Hunter. He had been with Eirik a long time now, acting as his hunter in the summers, and in the winter as bailiff. He was a big, strong, dark and ogreish man, of few words, but when he did speak abusive, and he was always advising Eirik for the worse. He was a bad Christian, but he had an extensive knowledge of the wastelands. He was on board ship with Thorvard and Thorvald (they had that same ship which Thorbjorn Vifilsson had fetched to Greenland). In all they had a hundred and sixty men when they set sail for the Western Settlement and from there to Bear Isles. From there they sailed south for two days and then sighted land. They rowed ashore in boats and explored the countryside, finding huge flat stones there, many of them twelve ells across. There were large numbers of arctic foxes there too. They gave the land a name, calling it Helluland. Then they sailed onwards for two days and changed course from south to southeast, and found a land heavily forested, with many wild animals. Offshore to the south-east lay an island. They killed a bear on it, so called the island Bjarney, or Bear Island, and the land Markland.[1]

From here they sailed south along the land for a long while till they came to a cape. The land lay to starboard: there were long beaches and sands there. They rowed ashore and found there on the cape the keel of a ship, so called the place Kjalarnes. The beaches they called Furdustrands or Marvelstrands, because it was such a long business sailing past them. Then the land became bay-indented, and into one of these bays they headed their ships.

King Olaf Tryggvason had given Leif two Scots, a man named Haki, and a woman Hekja, who were fleeter than deer. They were on board Karlsefni's ship, and once they had sailed past Furdustrands they put the Scots ashore, ordering them to run across country southwards to spy out the quality of the land, and come back before three days were

[1] The precise location of Helluland (Flatstone Land), Markland (Wood Land), and Vinland (Wineland), has been much debated. The likeliest identifications are Helluland, south Baffin Island, Markland, south-eastern Labrador, while the northern extremity of Vinland lay in northern Newfoundland. Many consider that Vinland extended as far south as New England.

past. They were wearing the garment which they called 'kjafal': this was so made that there was a hood on top, it was open at the sides and sleeveless, and buttoned between the legs with a button and loop; but for the rest they were naked. They waited there a while, and when the Scots came back the one had a bunch of grapes in his hand and the other an ear of wild wheat; so with that they went out on board ship and afterwards sailed on their way.

They sailed into a fjord off whose mouth there lay an island surrounded by strong currents. They called this island Straumsey. There were so many eider-duck on the island that one might hardly take a step without crushing their eggs. They called the place Straumsfjord, and here they carried their goods off the ships and settled to stay. They had brought all sorts of animals with them, and the nature of the land was choice. They had no time for anything beyond exploring the country: they spent the winter there, but nothing was done in readiness for it all the summer; the hunting and fishing failed, and they were in a bad way for food. Then Thorhall the Hunter disappeared. Before this they had prayed to God for food, but their prayers were not answered as quickly as their needs craved. They were looking for Thorhall three whole days, and found him where he was lying on the peak of a crag, staring up at the sky with his mouth and nostrils both agape, and reciting something. They asked him why he had gone to such a place, but he told them that was no business of theirs. They urged him to return home with them, and this he did. A little later a whale came in. They went to it and cut it up, yet never a man of them knew what kind of a whale it was. Once the cooks had boiled it they ate it, and they were all taken ill of it. Then said Thorhall, 'Red Beard proved a better friend now than your Christ. This is what I get for the poem I made about Thor my patron. Rarely has he failed me.' But the moment they heard this, they carried every particle of the whale to the sea and committed their cause to God. With that the weather improved, enabling them to row out fishing, and from then on there was no shortage of provisions, what with hunting on the mainland, eggs in the island breeding-grounds, and fish from the sea.

The story now goes that Thorhall the Hunter wished to proceed north by way of Furdustrands and Kjalarnes to look for Vinland, but Karlsefni wanted to sail south along the coast. Thorhall began making ready out by the islands, and they were not more than nine men all told, for all the rest of their band went with Karlsefni. One day, when Thorhall was carrying water to his ship and had taken a drink of it, he chanted this poem:

'They told me, wartrees bold,
This land held, once we found it,
Such drink as men ne'er drank of:
My curse then—all men hear it!
This sucking at the bucket,
This wallowing to spring's welling,
Fine work for helm-god's war-oak!
No wine's passed lips of mine.'

Once they were ready they hoisted sail. This time Thorhall chanted:

'Back sail we now where beckon
Hands of our own Greenlanders;
Bid steed of seabed's heaven
Search out the streams of ocean:

> While here these brisk sword-stirrers,
> This precious country's praisers,
> On Furdustrand far-stranded,
> Boil whale for wambling bellies.'

After this they sailed north by way of Furdu-strands and Kjalarnes, and wished to beat to west-wards, but encountered a west wind and were shipwrecked in Ireland, where they were beaten and enslaved, and where Thorhall died, according to what traders have reported.

6

The story now turns to Karlsefni, and tells how he sailed south along the land with Snorri and Bjarni and their crews. They sailed a long way till they came to a river which flowed down from the land into a lake and so to the sea. There were such big sandbanks hereabouts that they could not get into the river except at high water. Karlsefni sailed with his men into the estuary and they called the place Hop. Ashore there they found self-sown fields of wheat where the ground was low-lying, and vines wherever there was high ground. Every brook was full of fish. They dug trenches at the meeting-point of land and high water, and when the tide went out there were halibut in the trenches. There were vast numbers of animals of every kind in the forest. They were there for a fortnight enjoying themselves and noticed nothing strange. They had their cattle with them.

Then one morning early, when they looked about them, they saw a multitude of skin-canoes, on which poles were being waved which sounded just like flails—and waved sunwise.

'What can this mean?' asked Karlsefni.

'Maybe it is a token of peace,' Snorri Thor-brandsson told him, 'so let us take a white shield and put it out towards them.'

They did this, and their visitors rowed towards them, and were astonished at what they found, then came ashore. They were dark, ugly men who wore their hair in an unpleasant fashion. They had big eyes and were broad in the cheeks. They stayed there for a while, astonished at what they found, and afterwards rowed off south past the headland.

Karlsefni and his men had built themselves booths up above the lake; some of their houses were near the waterside, and some farther away. They now spent the winter there. No snow fell, and the whole of their stock found its own food by grazing. But when spring came in they saw early one morning how a multitude of canoes came rowing from the south round the headland, so many that the bay looked as though sown with charcoal, and this time too poles were being waved from every boat. Karlsefni and his men raised their shields, and as soon as they met they began trading together. Most of all these people wanted to buy red cloth, in return for which they had furs to offer and grey skins. They also wanted to buy swords and spears, but this Karlsefni and Snorri would not allow. The Skrælings were taking a span's length of red cloth in exchange for an unblemished dark skin, and this they tied round their heads. Their trading continued thus for a while, when the cloth began to run short for Karlsefni and his men; they then cut it up into such small pieces that they were no wider than a finger-breadth, but the Skrælings even so gave just as much for it as before, or indeed more.

The next thing was that the bull belonging to Karlsefni and his mates ran out of the forest bellowing loudly. The Skrælings were terrified by this, raced out to their canoes, and then rowed south past the headland, and for three weeks running there was neither sight nor sound of them. But at the end of that period they saw a great multitude of Skræling boats coming up like a stream from the south. This time all the poles were being waved anti-sunwise, and the Skrælings were all yelling aloud, so Karlsefni and his men took red shields and held them out against them. The Skrælings ran from their boats and then they clashed together and fought. There was a heavy shower of missiles, for the Skrælings had war-slings. Karlsefni and his men could see the Skrælings hoisting up on to a pole a very large ball, closely comparable to a sheep's paunch, and a deep blue-black in colour, which they let fly from the pole inland over Karlsefni's troop, and it made a hideous noise where it came down. A great fear now struck into Karlsefni and all his following, so that they had no other thought in their heads than to run away and make their escape up along the river, for they had the impression that the Skræling host was pouring in upon them from all sides. They made no stop till they reached some rocks, but there made a brave defence.

Freydis came out of doors and saw how they had run off. 'Why are you running from wretches like these?' she cried. 'Such gallant lads as you, I thought you would have knocked them on the head like cattle. Why, if I had a weapon, I think I could put up a better fight than any of you!'

They might as well not have heard her. Freydis was anxious to keep up with them, but was slow on her feet because of her pregnancy. Yet she kept moving after them to the forest, but the Skrælings now attacked her. She found a dead man in her path, Thorbrand Snorrason—he had a flat stone sticking out of his head. His naked sword lay beside him; she picked it up and prepared to defend herself. The Skrælings were making for her. She pulled out her breasts from under her clothes and slapped the naked sword on them, at which the Skrælings took fright, and ran off to their boats and rowed away. Karlsefni's men came up to her, praising her courage. Two of Karlsefni's men had fallen, and a multitude of Skrælings. Karlsefni's men had been overrun by sheer numbers. Now, after this, they returned to their booths and bandaged their wounds, and puzzled over what force that could have been which attacked them from inland. It looked to them now as though there had been only the one host, which came from the boats, and that the other army must have been a delusion.

Further, the Skrælings had found a dead man whose axe lay beside him. One of them picked up the axe and cut at a tree with it, and so they did one after the other, and thought it a treasure, and one which cut well. Afterwards one of them set to and cut at a stone, so that the axe broke, and then they thought it useless because it could not stand up to the stone, so threw it down.

It now seemed plain to Karlsefni and his men that though the quality of the land was admirable, there would always be fear and strife dogging them there on account of those who already inhabited it. So they made ready to leave, setting their hearts on their own country, and sailed north along the land and found five Skrælings in fur doublets asleep near the sea, who had with them wooden containers in

which was beast's marrow mixed with blood.
Karlsefni and the others felt sure that these men
would have been sent from that country, so they
killed them. Later they discovered a cape, with great
numbers of animals on it. To look at, this cape was
like a cake of dung, because the animals lay there the
winter through.

And now Karlsefni returned to Straumsfjord
with his following, and here was to be found every
kind of supply they had need of. Some men report
that Bjarni and Gudrid remained behind here, and
a hundred men with them, and proceeded no farther,
but that Karlsefni and Snorri went south with forty
men, yet spent no longer at Hop than a bare two
months, and got back again that same summer.
Then Karlsefni set out with one ship to look for
Thorhall the Hunter, but the rest of their force
stayed behind. They went north past Kjalarnes, and
then bore away west, with land on their port side.
There was nothing but desolate forest-land to be
seen ahead, with hardly a clearing anywhere. And
when they had been on their travels for a long time,
there was a river flowing down from the land from
east to west. They put into its estuary and lay at
anchor off the southern bank. It happened one
morning that Karlsefni and his men could see over
a clearing a kind of speck which glittered back at
them, and they shouted at it. It moved—it was a
uniped—and hopped down to the river-bank off
which they were lying. Thorvald Eirik the Red's
son was sitting by the rudder, and the uniped shot
an arrow into his small guts. He drew out the arrow,
exclaiming: 'There is a good coat of fat round my
paunch! We have won a fine country, though our
time to enjoy it proves short.' Thorvald died of this

wound a little later. The uniped skipped off back north, and Karlsefni and his men gave chase, catching sight of him every now and again. The last glimpse they had of him, he was running towards some inlet or other. They turned back then, and one of them sang this ditty:

'Men went chasing,
I tell you no lie,
A uniped racing
The seashore by:
But this man-wonder,
Curst son of a trollop,
Karlsefni, pray ponder!
Escaped at a gallop.'

Then they set off back north, thinking they had sighted Einfætingaland. They were unwilling to imperil their company any longer. They concluded that those mountains which were at Hop, and those which they had now discovered, were one and the same range, that they therefore stood directly opposite each other, and extended the same distance on both sides of Straumsfjord.

They spent that third winter in Straumsfjord. There was deep division between the men on account of the women, for the unmarried men fell foul of the married, which led to serious disturbances. Karlsefni's son Snorri was born there the first autumn, and he was three winters old when they left.

When they sailed from Vinland they got a south wind and reached Markland, where they found five Skrælings, one of them a bearded man, two women, and two children. They caught the boys, but the others escaped and sank down into the ground.

These two boys they kept with them, taught them
their language, and had them baptized. They said
that their mother's name was Vethildi and their
father's Ovægi. They said that kings ruled over the
Skrælings, and that one of them was called Aval-
damon and the other Avaldidida. There were no
houses there, they said; the people lived in caves or
holes. A country lay on the other side, they said,
opposite their own land, where lived men who
dressed in white clothes and carried poles, and were
festooned with streamers, and whooped loudly.
They concluded that this must be Hvitramannaland
or Ireland the Great. And now they came to Greenland and spent the winter with Eirik the Red.

But Bjarni Grimolfsson drifted into the Ireland
Sea and came into wormy waters, and the ship
sank quickly under them. They had a boat which
was coated with seal-tar, because the sea-worm does
not attack such. They got into this boat, but then
discovered that it would not be sufficient for them
all. 'Because the boat will not take more than half
our men,' announced Bjarni, 'my proposal is that
we draw lots for the boat, for this ought not to go
by rank.' This struck them all as so gallant an offer
that no one would speak against it. So that was what
they did: the men drew lots, and it fell to Bjarni
and a half of them with him to go into the boat,
for the boat would hold no more.

When they had got into the boat, an Icelander
who was still on the ship and who had followed
Bjarni from Iceland, cried, 'Do you mean to leave
me here, Bjarni?'

'That is how it must be now,' replied Bjarni.

'Very different were your oaths to my father,' he
replied, 'when I left Iceland with you, than that you

would desert me like this. You reckoned then that you and I should share the one fate.'

'That cannot be,' Bjarni told him. 'But get down here into the boat, and I will get back on board ship, since I find you so concerned to live.'

With this Bjarni went back on board ship, and this man into the boat, and so they went their ways till they came to Dublin in Ireland, where they told this story. It is the opinion of most that Bjarni and those men who remained on board ship with him perished in the wormy sea, for nothing was ever heard of them again.

Two summers later Karlsefni returned to Iceland, and Gudrid with him, and went home to Reynisnes. His mother considered he had made a poor marriage and would not stay in the same house with them that first winter. But once she found Gudrid to be so remarkable a woman she returned, and they lived happily together.

And that is the end of this saga.

THIDRANDI WHOM THE
GODDESSES SLEW

THERE was a Norwegian named Thorhall who came
out to Iceland in earl Hakon's time, and settled in
Syrlækjaros, with a home at Horgsland. Thorhall
was a wise man and skilled at reading the future: he
was called Thorhall Seer. Now while he was living at
Horgsland, Sidu-Hall was living at Hof in Alftafjord, and there was the closest friendship between
them. Hall used to stay at Horgsland every summer
on his way to the Assembly, and Thorhall often
went visiting out east and would spend long periods
there. Hall's eldest son was called Thidrandi, a
handsome and accomplished young man whom
Hall loved best of all his sons. Once he was old
enough, Thidrandi went trafficking from land to
land, and found lots of friends wherever he came,
for he was a man of many and remarkable good
qualities, yet modest, and gentle with every man and
child.

It happened one summer that Hall, as he rode
home from the Assembly, invited his friend Thorhall out east to visit him, and somewhat later Thorhall
came along, and Hall welcomed him with as much
warmth and joy as ever. Thorhall stayed there over
the summer, and Hall vowed that he should not
leave for home till the harvest-feast was over.

This same summer Thidrandi came back to Iceland, to Berufjord, and was now eighteen years old.
He went home to his father's, and people were as
charmed with him this time as ever, and extolled his
many virtues. But when others were loudest in their

praise of him, Thorhall Seer would always hold his peace, till one day Hall asked him the reason why. 'For anything you have to say, Thorhall, appears to me well worth attending to.'

'It is not because anything in him or you displeases me,' Thorhall told him, 'or that I am slower than the rest to perceive how handsome he is, and how able. It is rather this, that there are men enough to praise him, and indeed he has many fine qualities to justify it—not that he is unduly proud of them himself. But it is possible that you are not going to be happy in him much longer, and in that case your grief after so gallant a son will be quite enough without the whole world singing his praises to your face.'

As the summer wore on Thorhall's spirits fell lower and lower, till Hall asked him the reason why.

'I am worrying,' replied Thorhall, 'about this harvest treat of yours, for I have a foreboding that a Seer will lose his life at the feast.'

'I can clear that up,' said his host. 'I own a twelve-year-old ox whom I call Seer because he is wiser than other oxen. He is to be slaughtered at the harvest-feast, so there is no need to distress yourself. For I intend this entertainment of mine, like the others before it, to be an honour to you and to all my men.'

'I did not raise this,' replied Thorhall, 'because I was afraid for my own life. My foreboding is of an event greater and more wondrous than I can as yet bring myself to declare.'

'Well, there is nothing to stop the feast being put off,' said Hall.

'Saying that won't help us,' ruled Thorhall, 'for what is fated must go forward.'

The feast was arranged for the first nights of winter. Few of those invited came, for the weather was cruel hard and difficult to get about in. When they were all seated to table that evening, Thorhall had this to say. 'I want to ask you men to take my advice here, so that no one whatsoever goes out of doors tonight, for great harm will follow should this be disregarded. Whatever happens by way of portent, pay no attention to it, for should anyone answer, disaster will surely follow.'

Hall told them to mark Thorhall's words and obey them. 'For they never miss their mark,' he said, 'and better bind a whole limb than an ailing.'

Thidrandi was waiting on the guests, for he was as modest and willing in this as in all else. And as men were settling down for the night he gave up his own bed to a guest and lay down on a bench at the farthest edge of the wainscot. When almost everybody had fallen asleep there came a summons at the door, but no one made as though he heard it. This happened three times. By now Thidrandi had started to his feet. 'This is a fine thing,' he said, 'the way everyone is pretending to be asleep. These must be guests arriving.'

He picked up his sword and went outside, but could not see a soul. Then it occurred to him that some of the guests must have ridden on ahead to the house and then have turned back to meet those who were coming along more slowly. So he walked under the woodpile and heard the noise of riding from the north into the home-field. He saw that there were nine women there, all in dark raiment, and they held drawn swords in their hands. He heard likewise the noise of riding from the south into the home-field, and there too were nine women, all in bright raiment, and on white horses. Thidrandi now wanted to get back indoors and tell them of this sight, but the dark-clad women came up with him first and set upon him; and he defended himself well and bravely.

A long while after Thorhall awoke and asked whether Thidrandi was awake too. He got no answer. They had slept too long! cried Thorhall.

They went outside. It was moonlight and frosty weather. They found Thidrandi lying wounded, he was carried indoors, and when they got word of him he told them all that had appeared to him. He died that same morning at daybreak and was laid in a howe after the old heathen fashion.

Later, inquiry was made of the movements of men, but they could think of no one likely to be enemies of Thidrandi. Hall asked Thorhall what such a prodigy could mean. 'I don't know,' was the reply he got, 'but I can guess this much, that these women can have been none other than the wraiths of you and your kinsfolk. And I guess too that there will be a change of faith among us, and that shortly a better faith will come here to Iceland. And I believe these spirits of you who have followed the old faith must have known beforehand of your changing, and how they would be rejected of you and yours. They could not bear to exact no toll of you before parting, and will have seized on Thidrandi as their due; but the better spirits must have wished to help him, but did not arrive in time to do so. Even so, those of your family who are to adopt the unknown faith they foretell and follow will be helped by them.'

But Hall took the death of his son Thidrandi so hard that he could not bear to live at Hof any longer, and moved house to Thvatta.

It happened one time at Thvatta, when Thorhall
Seer was there on a visit to Hall, that Hall was
sleeping in a bed-closet and Thorhall in another bed
there. There was a window in the bed-closet, and
one morning, when they were both awake, Thorhall
burst out laughing.

'What are you laughing at now?' asked Hall.

'I am laughing,' replied Thorhall, 'because many
a hill is opening, and every living creature, great and
small, is packing his bags and making this his
moving-day.'

And a little later that event came to pass which
must now be told of [the coming of Christianity to
Iceland].[1]

---

[1] Iceland adopted Christianity in the year A.D. 1000. As
Íslendingabók tells us: 'It was then made law that all men
should be Christians, and they should take baptism who were
as yet unbaptized here in the land. But with respect to the
exposure of infants the ancient laws should stand, and so with
the eating of horseflesh. Men might sacrifice secretly if they
wished, but it would be a case for the lesser outlawry if witness
was brought forward thereto. But a few winters later this
heathendom was done away with like the rest.' For an example
of the exposure of infants, see the story of Helga in *Gunnlaug
Wormtongue*, chapter 1, below.

AUTHUN AND THE BEAR

THERE was a man by the name of Authun, a West-firther by origin, and rather poorly off. He went abroad from the Westfirths with the help of a good farmer, Thorstein, and of skipper Thorir, who had received hospitality from Thorstein over the winter. Authun had been staying there too, and working for Thorir, and received this for his reward, a passage abroad with the skipper to look after him. Before going on board ship Authun set aside the bulk of his money for his mother, and it was reckoned enough to keep her for three years. They now sailed out and away. They had an easy passage and Authun spent the winter with skipper Thorir, who owned a farm in Mœr, in Norway. The following summer they sailed for Greenland, and spent the winter there.

The story tells how Authun bought a bear there, an absolute treasure, and gave every penny he had for it. The following summer they returned to Norway and had an excellent passage. Authun took his bear with him, and was proposing to go south to Denmark, find king Svein, and make him a present of the beast. So when he reached the south of Norway, where the Norwegian king was then in residence, he left the ship, taking his bear with him, and rented himself a lodging.

King Harald was soon told how a bear, an absolute treasure, had come ashore, and that his owner was an Icelander. The king sent for him immediately, and when Authun came into the king's presence he greeted him with due courtesy. The king received his greeting affably, and then: 'You have a bear,' he said, 'an absolute treasure?'

Well, yes, he agreed, he had a beast of a kind.

'Are you willing to sell him to us,' asked the king, 'for the same price you gave for him?'

'I don't want to, sire,' he replied.

'Then would you like me to give you twice the price?' asked the king. 'And indeed that would be fairer, since you paid out all you had for him.'

'I don't want to, sire.'

'You want to give him to me then?' said the king.

'No, sire,' he replied.

'Then what do you want to do with him?'

'Go to Denmark,' replied Authun, 'and give him to king Svein.'

'Is it possible,' asked king Harald, 'that you are such a silly man that you have not heard how a state of war exists between our two countries? Or do you think yourself so blest with luck that you can make your way there with this precious thing when others, for all that they have compelling business there, cannot manage it unscathed?'

'Sire,' said Authun, 'it is for you to command, yet I cannot willingly agree to anything except what I have already decided.'

'Then why should you not go your road,' said the king to that, 'even as you wish? But come and see me when you return, and tell me how king Svein rewards you for the bear. It may be that you are a man of happy fortune.'

'I promise to do so,' said Authun.

He now proceeded south along the coast, and east to Vik, and from there to Denmark, and by this time had spent his last penny and was forced to beg food, both for himself and for the bear. He went to see king Svein's steward, a man named Aki, and asked him for some victuals, both for himself and for the bear. 'For I am proposing,' he said, 'to make a present of him to king Svein.' Aki said he would sell him food if that was what he was after, but Authun confessed that he had no money to pay for it. 'And yet,' he said, 'I should like my business to be so forwarded that I can produce my bear before the king.' 'I will give you food and lodging then, whatever you need, until you see the king, but in return I require a half share in this creature. You might look at it this way: the bear will only die on your hands, for you need considerable provisioning and your money is all gone, and in that case you get no profit of your bear.'

When he looked at it that way, it seemed to him that what the steward said went pretty close to the mark, so that was what they settled on, that he should make over half the beast to Aki, and it was for the king to set a value on the whole.

And now they were to go together to see the king, and so they did, and stood before his table. The king was puzzled who this man, whom he did not know, could be, and, 'Who are you?' he asked Authun.

'I am an Icelander, sire,' he replied, 'and have just come from Greenland, and more recently still from Norway. I had been meaning to present you with this bear, which I purchased with every penny I had, but I am now in something of a quandary, for I own only half of him.' And he went on to tell the king what had taken place between him and his steward Aki.

'Is this true, Aki, what he says?' asked the king.

'Yes,' he said, 'it is.'

'And did you think it seemly, when I had raised you up to be a great man, to obstruct and hinder his path when a man was trying to bring me this fine beast, for which he had given his all, when even king Harald, who is our enemy, saw fit to let him go in peace? Think then how honourable this was on your part! It would be only right to have you put to death—and though I will not do that, you shall leave this land without a moment's delay, and never come into my sight again. As for you, Authun, I owe you the same thanks as if you were giving me the whole animal. So stay here with me.' He agreed to this, and remained with king Svein for a while.

But after some time had gone by Authun said to the king, 'I should like to go away now, sire.' The king answered, rather coldly, 'What do you want, if you don't want to stay with us?' 'I want to go south on a pilgrimage.' 'If you did not wish to follow so good a course,' the king admitted, 'I should be displeased by your eagerness to be off.' The king now gave him a large amount of silver, and he travelled southwards with the pilgrims to Rome. The king made the arrangements for his journey, and told him to come and see him when he returned.

Now he went his ways until he came south to Rome, and when he had spent as much time there as he wished, he set out on his way back. He fell sick, very sick, and grew woefully thin. All the money the king had given him for his journey was now spent, he took the style of a beggar and begged for his food. He had become bald and quite pitiful to see.

He came back to Denmark at Easter, to the very place where the king was in residence. He did not dare let himself be seen but remained in the church transept, hoping to encounter the king when he went to church that evening. But when he saw the king with his handsomely attired courtiers, again he dare not let himself be seen. And when the king went to the drinking in hall, Authun ate his food outside, as is the custom of pilgrims to Rome before they lay aside their staff and scrip.

And now in the evening, as the king went to evensong, Authun reckoned on meeting him; but however daunting a prospect this had looked before, it had by now grown far worse, for the courtiers were in drink. And yet, as they were going back in, the king noticed a man who he felt sure lacked the confidence to come forward and speak to him, and as the courtiers were entering the king turned back, saying, 'Let anyone now come forward who craves audience of me, for I believe there is such a man here present.' Then Authun came forward and fell at the king's feet, and the king could hardly recognize him. But as soon as he knew who he was, he took Authun by the hand and welcomed him. 'How greatly you are changed,' he said, 'since last we met,' and he led him inside behind him. When the courtiers saw him they laughed at him, but, 'You need not laugh at him,' said the king, 'he has provided for his soul better than you.' Then the king had a bath prepared for him and gave him clothes to wear, and Authun remained with him.

One day in spring, so the story goes, the king invited Authun to stay with him for the rest of his days, promising that he would make him his cupbearer and heap him with honours.

'God reward you, sire,' said Authun, 'for all the honour you would do me, but what I really have in mind is to return to Iceland.'

'That strikes me as a curious choice,' said the king.

'I cannot bear, sire,' said Authun, 'that I should enjoy such honours here with you, and my mother tramp the beggar's path out in Iceland, for by now the provision I made for her before I left home will be at an end.'

'That is well spoken, and like a man,' replied the king, 'and you will prove a man of happy fortune. This is the only reason for your departure which would not displease me. But stay with me now till the ships make ready.' And so he did.

One day, towards the end of spring, king Svein walked down to the jetties, where ships were being overhauled in readiness for voyages to many lands, to the Baltic and Germany, Sweden, and Norway. He and Authun came to a very fine ship which men were making ready, and, 'What do you think of this for a ship, Authun?' asked the king. 'Very fine, sire,' was his answer. 'I am going to give you this ship,' said the king, 'in return for the bear.' Authun thanked him for his gift as well as he knew how.

When time had passed and the ship was quite ready, king Svein had this to say to Authun: 'Since you want to be away it is not for me to stop you. But I have heard that your country is ill supplied with havens, the coasts often wide open and dangerous to shipping. Now should you be wrecked and lose both ship and lading, there will be little to show that you have met king Svein and given him a princely gift.' With that the king gave him a leather purse full of silver. 'You will not be entirely penniless, even if you are shipwrecked, so long as you hold on to this. And yet,' said the king, 'it may happen that you lose this money too, and you will then reap little benefit from having found king Svein and given him a princely gift.' With that the king drew a ring from his arm and gave it to Authun, saying, 'Even if you are so unlucky as to suffer shipwreck and lose your money, you will not be penniless should you manage to get ashore, for many carry gold on them in case of shipwreck, and it will be clear that you have met king Svein if you save the ring. But I would urge upon you,' said the king, 'not to give away the ring unless you consider yourself under a great enough obligation to some great man—but give him the ring, for it well becomes men of rank to accept such. And now, good luck go with you.'

Then he put to sea and sailed to Norway, where he had his goods carried ashore—and he needed more help for this than when he was in Norway last. He then went to visit king Harald, to make good the promise he had made him before going to Denmark. He had a courteous greeting for the king, and the king took it affably. 'Sit down,' he said, 'and take a drink with us.' And so he did.

'And how did king Svein reward you for the bear?' king Harald asked him.

'By accepting it from me, sire,' replied Authun.

'So too would I have rewarded you,' said the king. 'How else did he reward you?'

'He gave me silver for my pilgrimage,' replied Authun.

'King Svein gives many men silver for pilgrimages, and for other things too,' said the king, 'and they don't have to bring him a grand present for it. What else was there?'

'He offered to make me his cup-bearer,' said Authun, 'and heap me with honours.'

'In that he spoke well,' said the king. 'Still, he would give you more of a reward than that.'

'He gave me a merchant ship and such wares as sell best here in Norway.'

'That was handsome of him,' said the king, 'but so too would I have rewarded you. Did he reward you with anything further?'

'He gave me a leather purse full of silver, saying I should not then be penniless if I held on to it, even though my ship was wrecked off Iceland.'

'That was nobly done,' said the king, 'and something I would not have done. I should have held us quits had I given you the ship. Did he reward you any further?'

'To be sure he rewarded me, sire,' said Authun. 'He gave me this ring I have on my arm, arguing it might so turn out that I should lose all that money and yet, said he, not be penniless if I held on to the ring. And he charged me never to part with it unless I should consider myself under so great an obligation to some great man that I wanted to give it him. And now I have found him, for you had the opportunity to deprive me of both these things, the bear and my life too; yet you let me go in peace where others might not.'

The king accepted his gift graciously, and gave Authun fine gifts in return before they parted. Authun used his money for a passage to Iceland, promptly left for home that summer, and was thought to be a man of the happiest good fortune.

GUNNLAUG WORMTONGUE

THERE was a man called Thorstein Egilsson (Egil
was the son of Skallagrim, himself the son of Kvel-
dulf, a lord from Norway) living at Borg in Borgarfjord. His mother's name was Asgerd Bjarnardottir.
He was well-to-do, a great chieftain, wise, gentle,
and moderate in all things; and while he was not so
outstanding a man as Egil his father for size or
strength, he was a most remarkable man all the
same, and highly thought of by everyone. He was
handsome, with whitish hair and the finest eyes of
any man alive. Thorstein was married to Jofrid the
daughter of Gunnar Hlifarson, whose first husband
was Thorodd Tungu-Oddsson—their daughter was
that Hungerd who was brought up by Thorstein at
Borg. Jofrid was a woman of character and distinc-
tion. She and Thorstein had a lot of children, though
few of them appear in this saga. Their eldest son
was Skuli, the second Kollsvein, and the third Egil.

One summer, so the story goes, a ship put from
sea into the mouth of the Gufua. Her skipper was a
man by the name of Bergfinn, a Norwegian by birth,
well-to-do and getting on in years, and a man of considerable shrewdness. Master Thorstein rode to the
ship; he had always the biggest say as to buying and
selling, and such was the case this time again. The
Norwegians found themselves lodgings, but Thorstein gave hospitality to the skipper because he had
asked for it. Bergfinn had little to say for himself
during the winter, yet Thorstein made him most

welcome. The Norwegian took a great interest in dreams.

One day in the spring Thorstein had a word with Bergfinn, whether he would like to ride with him up Valfell way, where the Borgarfjord men then had their place of assembly. It had been reported to Thorstein that the walls of his booth had caved in. The Norwegian said he would like to go very much, and they rode from home that same day, with a housecarle of Thorstein's for a third, until they reached a farm called Grenjar. A poor man lived there, by the name of Atli; he was a tenant of Thorstein's, and Thorstein asked him to come along and work with them and bring his spade and shovel. He did so, and when they had come up under Valfell to the site of the booth, they all set to, rebuilding the walls.

It was a day of hot sunshine, and Thorstein and the Norwegian found it hard going, so once they had rebuilt the walls the two of them sat down inside the booth, and Thorstein dozed off and fell into an uneasy slumber. The Norwegian was sitting alongside him and let him have his dream out, but when he woke up Thorstein was deeply distressed. The Norwegian asked what he had been dreaming about that he had been so uneasy in his sleep.

'There is no meaning to dreams,' said Thorstein.

But as they were riding home that evening the Norwegian again asked him what he had dreamt.

'If I tell you my dream,' replied Thorstein, 'you must interpret it exactly as it is.'

The Norwegian promised that he would try.

Then, 'This was my dream,' said Thorstein. 'I thought I was back home at Borg and standing outside the main door; and on top of the house, up on the roof-ridge, I could see a swan both fair and lovely, and she was mine, I thought, and I cherished her dearly. Then I saw a great eagle flying down from the mountains; he flew towards us and settled beside the swan and clucked to her gently, at which she seemed well pleased. Then I saw that the eagle had black eyes and claws like iron; he looked to me a creature all of fire and spirit. Then next I saw another bird flying from the south. He flew here to Borg and settled on the house beside the swan and wished to pay court to her: this was a big eagle too. It seemed to me that the eagle who came first quickly grew enraged when the other flew in, and they fought together savagely and long, and I saw how each of them was bleeding, and such was the end of their struggle that each fell off the roof on his own side, and they were by this time both dead. But the swan sat on, all sad and sorrowful.

'And then I saw a bird flying out of the west: he was a falcon. He settled beside the swan and comforted her, and by and by they flew off together in the same direction. And with that I awoke. But the dream has no significance,' added Thorstein, 'and must betoken the winds, how they clash in the air from those quarters of the sky out of which it seemed to me the birds made their flight.'

'That is not my interpretation of what it means,' said the Norwegian.

'Then make of the dream what you judge to be its likeliest meaning,' invited Thorstein, 'and let me hear it.'

'These birds must be the apparitions of men,' said the Norwegian. 'Your wife is with child and will give birth to a girl both fair and lovely, whom you will cherish dearly. Men of great note will come

to woo your daughter from those same quarters of
the land you thought the eagles flew from; they will
love her to distraction and fight over her, and from
that will come the death of them both. And afterwards a third man will come wooing her, from the
same quarter as the falcon flew, and to him will she
be given. And now I have interpreted your dream
even as I think it will go.'

'It is a bad and unfriendly interpretation,' replied
Thorstein, 'and you cannot know the first thing
about the meaning of dreams.'

'You will find out for yourself how close it will
go,' said the Norwegian.

Thorstein was very cool towards the Norwegian
as a result of this, and in the summer he went away,
and is now out of the story.

This same summer Thorstein made ready for the
Assembly, and had this to say to Jofrid his wife
before leaving home. 'This is how matters stand,'
he told her. 'You are about to have a child. Now if
you give birth to a girl the child must be left to die of
exposure, but if it is a boy it shall be reared.' For
when the land was still entirely heathen, it was by
way of being a custom that those men who had few
means and many dependants would have their
children left to die of exposure, though it was always
reckoned a bad thing to do.

So when Thorstein had said this, Jofrid replied,
'Your words are unworthy of a man of your standing. No one in your easy circumstances can see fit
to let such a thing happen.'

'You know my temper,' Thorstein warned her.
'There will be trouble if you disobey me.'

After that he rode to the Assembly, and Jofrid in
due time gave birth to a wondrously fair little girl.

Her women wanted to lay it in her arms, but she told them there was little call for that, and had her shepherd summoned to her, whose name was Thorvard. 'You must take my horse and saddle it,' she instructed him, 'and carry this child west to Hjardarholt, to Thorgerd Egilsdottir, and ask her to bring it up so secretly that her brother Thorstein never gets word of it. For I look on this child with such love that I cannot bear she should be carried away to die. Here are three marks of silver which you shall receive by way of wages, and Thorgerd will secure you a passage there in the west and provisions for your journey overseas.'

Thorvard did as she told him: he rode west to Hjardarholt with the child and handed it over to Thorgerd, who had it raised by tenants of hers who lived at Leysingjastadir on Hvammsfjord. She arranged a passage for Thorvard up north at Skeljavik in Steingrimsfjord and provisions for his journey. From there he went abroad and is now out of the story. And when Thorstein returned home from the Assembly, Jofrid told him that the child had been exposed exactly as he ordered, but that the shepherd had run away and stolen her horse. Thorstein said she had done well, and got himself another shepherd.

And now six years passed without this coming to light. Then Thorstein had occasion to ride west to Hjardarholt to a feast at his brother-in-law Olaf Peacock's, who in those days was considered the most estimable of all chieftains there in the west. Thorstein got a good welcome, as might be expected. Then one day during the feast Thorgerd, they say, was sitting talking with Thorstein her brother in the high-seat while Olaf was in conversation with other men. Seated on a bench opposite them were three young girls.

'Brother,' said Thorgerd then, 'how do you like the look of these girls sitting opposite us here?'

'Very much,' he replied, 'and yet one is by far the prettiest of them, for she has all Olaf's good looks together with the fair colouring and features of us Myramen.'

'As you say, brother,' replied Thorgerd; 'how very true that she has the fair colouring and features of us Myramen. Yet she has none of Olaf Peacock's good looks, for she is not his daughter.'

'How can that be,' asked Thorstein, 'since she is daughter of yours?'

'To tell you the truth, kinsman,' she replied, 'this pretty child is your daughter, not mine.' And she went on to tell him everything that had happened, begging him to forgive both her and his wife for this trick they had played on him.

'It is not for me to reproach you for this,' said Thorstein. 'For the most part things turn out as they are destined to, and you have certainly remedied my own lack of foresight. I am so pleased with this little girl that I think myself a very lucky man to have so beautiful a child. And what is her name?'

'Her name is Helga,' said Thorgerd.

'Helga the Fair!' cried Thorstein. 'You must now get her ready to return home with me.'

She did so. Thorstein was sped on his way with fine gifts, and Helga rode home with him, and grew up there with the love and affection of her father and mother and all her kindred too.

2

At this same time there was living at Gilsbakki in Hvitarsida Illugi the Black, the son of Hallkel Hrosskelsson. Illugi's mother was Thurid Sowthistle, the daughter of Gunnlaug Wormtongue. Illugi was the next greatest chieftain in Borgarfjord after Thorstein Egilsson. He was a man of vast possessions and strong will, who stood solidly behind his friends. His wife was Ingibjorg, Asbjorn Hardarson's daughter from Ornolfsdal, and they had many children, though few of them appear in this saga. One of their sons was called Hermund, and another Gunnlaug, both promising young fellows now in their prime. Of Gunnlaug it is recorded that he had matured early, was big and strong, with chestnut-coloured hair which suited him admirably, black eyes, and a rather ugly nose. He had an attractive face, was slender-waisted and broad of shoulder, and every inch a man: obstreperous by nature, and ambitious from his earliest years, utterly unyielding and ruthless. He was a good though somewhat scurrilous poet, and had been nicknamed Gunnlaug Wormtongue. Hermund was the better liked of the two, and had all the signs of a great man.

When Gunnlaug was twelve years old he asked his father to fit him out for a sea-voyage, saying he wanted to go abroad and see how other people lived. The good Illugi was slow to agree to this, vowing that he would get a poor reception abroad when he, Illugi himself, could hardly lick him into the shape he liked at home.

Not long after this it happened that Illugi went out of doors early one morning and saw how a storehouse of his had been opened up, and some half a dozen sacks of merchandise, and saddle-pads with them, had been hauled out on to the paving. He was still puzzling over this when along came a man leading four horses, and who should it be but his son Gunnlaug. 'It is I,' said he, 'who hauled out the sacks.'

But why had he done so ? asked Illugi.

They would fit him out, he replied, for his voyage abroad.

Said Illugi: 'You shall neither override my decisions nor go on your travels till I think fit.' And he slung the sacks back inside.

At this Gunnlaug rode off and arrived that evening down at Borg, where franklin Thorstein invited him to stay, an offer which he accepted. He told Thorstein of the rumpus between him and his father, and Thorstein invited him to stay on there as long as he liked. He stayed for a year, studying law with Thorstein, and everyone thought the world of him. He and Helga were always enjoying themselves at chequer-board together, and they quickly took a strong liking one for the other, as events would later show. They were much of an age. Helga was so beautiful that in the opinion of those best qualified to judge she was and remains the most beautiful woman that Iceland has ever seen. Her hair was so long that it could cover her all over, and was lovely as beaten gold. There was thought to be no such match as Helga the Fair in all Borgarfjord or many a place farther afield.

One day when the folk at Borg were sitting in the living-room, Gunnlaug said to Thorstein: 'There is still one point of law you have not taught me—how to become engaged to a woman.'

'That is a small matter,' said Thorstein, and taught him the procedure.

'You had better check whether I have understood you,' said Gunnlaug. 'I will now take you by the hand and act as if I were becoming engaged to Helga your daughter.'

'I see no need of it,' demurred Thorstein. But Gunnlaug promptly seized on his hand. 'Grant me my way in this,' he said, 'now!'

'You do as you like,' Thorstein told him, 'but everyone present may as well know that this shall be as though it had never been spoken, and there must be no hidden meaning concealed under it.'

So now Gunnlaug named his witnesses and pledged his troth to Helga, and asked afterward whether all was right and proper. Thorstein said it would serve, and the whole thing seemed great fun to everyone present.

3

Living south at Mosfell was a man by the name of Onund, who was very well-to-do and held the priesthood south there about the Nesses. He was married, his wife's name was Geirny, and their sons were Hrafn, Thorarin, and Eindridi. These were all men of great promise, but Hrafn stood foremost of them in everything. He was big and strong, very handsome and a good poet, and once he had come to man's estate he travelled about from land to land, and was highly esteemed wherever he went.

South at Hjalli in Olfus lived Thorodd the Wise and his son Skapti, who was at this time Lawspeaker for Iceland. Skapti and the sons of Onund were cousins, and there was close friendship between them as well as this bond of kin.

Out at Raudamel lived Thorfinn Seal-Thorisson,

who had seven sons, all of them full of promise, and the leading men of their district. All these men whose names have now been given were living at one and the same time, and it was about this same time that there befell the best event that ever happened here in Iceland, when the whole land turned Christian and the entire nation abjured the old faith.

Meanwhile Gunnlaug Wormtongue, of whom we were speaking earlier, had been living partly at Borg with Thorstein, and partly at home at Gilsbakki with Illugi his father, for a space of six years. He was now eighteen years old and on much better terms with his father. One of his father's household, and a close relative who had been brought up at Gilsbakki, was a man by the name of Thorkel the Black. He came in for a legacy north at As in Vatsndal and asked Gunnlaug to go along with him. He did so; they rode together to As and collected the money; and those who had the keeping of it paid the money over because Gunnlaug was there lending a hand. As they rode home again from the north they put up over-night at Grimstungur with a well-to-do farmer who was living there. In the morning a shepherd borrowed Gunnlaug's horse, and it was lathered with sweat by the time they got it back. Gunnlaug knocked the shepherd senseless. The farmer was not satisfied to let things rest there, and claimed compensation for him. Gunnlaug offered to pay him a mark, but the farmer thought this too little. Then Gunnlaug chanted this verse:

> 'One mark I bid this half-man,
> Guerdon of farmsteads' guardian;
> Grasp swift at my grey silver,
> Rich spate of redmouth spitter.

This gold, this treasure gilded
On redds of serpents' seabed,
If spilled by baleful gesture,
You'll rue it on the morrow!'

So they made peace on Gunnlaug's terms and rode back south with matters so.

Not long after this Gunnlaug once more asked his father to fit him out for a voyage. 'This time you shall have your way,' agreed Illugi. 'You have improved a lot on what you used to be.'

Without more ado Illugi rode from home and bought Gunnlaug a half-share in a ship which had been drawn ashore at the mouth of the Gufua, from Authun Fettered-Hound—that same Authun who would not ship abroad the sons of Osvif the Wise after the killing of Kjartan Olafsson, as is told in the Laxdalers' Saga, though that happened some time after this. When Illugi came home Gunnlaug was profuse with his thanks. Thorkel the Black decided to make this voyage along with Gunnlaug, and their goods were carried to the ship. But Gunnlaug spent his time at Borg while they were getting her ready, and thought it pleasanter to be talking with Helga than moiling with the merchants.

One day Thorstein asked Gunnlaug whether he would like to ride with him to his horses up in Langavatnsdal, and Gunnlaug said he would. So they rode off, the two of them together, till they came to those shielings of Thorstein's which are known as Thorgilsstadir, where there was a stud belonging to Thorstein, with horses four in number, and ruddy of colour. The stallion was magnificent, but little proven. Thorstein offered to give this horse to Gunnlaug, but he said he had no need of horses, he was thinking to leave the country. They then rode on to other horses, to where along with four mares was a grey stallion who was the pick of all Borgarfjord, and this one too Thorstein offered to give to Gunnlaug.

'I want these no more than the others,' he replied. 'And why don't you offer me what I am only too ready to accept ?'

'What is that ?' asked Thorstein.

'Your daughter, Helga the Fair.'

'That is not to be settled so quickly,' replied Thorstein, and changed the subject.

They took the homeward path down along the river Langa.

'I must know,' persisted Gunnlaug, 'how you intend to answer my marriage-suit.'

'I'll not listen to your maunderings,' retorted Thorstein.

'This is my fixed determination and no maundering!'

'You should have made up your mind in the first place what you wanted,' said Thorstein. 'Have you not made arrangements to go abroad, yet here you are talking as though you must get married! You are no sort of match for Helga while you go shilly-shallying this way, and I'll not think of it for a moment.'

'Where do you expect to find a match for your daughter,' demanded Gunnlaug, 'if you won't give her to a son of Illugi the Black ? And where will you find anyone in Borgarfjord of better standing than he ?'

'I am not going to play at men-matching,' Thorstein rebuked him, 'but if you were the man he is, you would not be turned away.'

'But who,' asked Gunnlaug, 'would you rather give your daughter to than me?'

'There is a good and ample choice of men here,' maintained Thorstein. 'Thorfinn at Raudamel has seven sons, and all of them admirable men.'

'Neither Onund nor Thorfinn comes up to my father—why, you yourself clearly fall short of him. For what have you to set against the way he fought with Thorgrim Kjallaksson the Priest and his sons at the Thornes Assembly, and carried off single-handed all that lay at stake there?'

'I drove away Steinar, the son of Onund Sjoni,' Thorstein replied, 'and that was thought no mean achievement.'[1]

'You had your father Egil to thank for that,' Gunnlaug told him. 'And, anyway, it will pay few farmers to spurn a marriage-tie with me.'

'You keep your threats for those up in the hills,' warned Thorstein. 'They'll do you no good down here in the Marshes.'

They arrived back home by evening, and the next morning Gunnlaug rode up to Gilsbakki and asked his father to ride a-wooing with him down to Borg.

'What a shilly-shallying man you are,' said Illugi, 'for one minute you are all for going abroad, and the next you can talk of nothing but busying yourself courting. I can see how this is not at all to Thorstein's liking.'

'I still intend to go abroad just the same,' said Gunnlaug, 'but nothing will satisfy me now except that you stand by me in this.'

---

[1] An account of Thorstein's feud with Steinar may be read in *Egil's Saga* (*Egils Saga Skallagrimssonar*), chapters 80–84. Thorstein's father Egil was one of the great men of his generation, a foremost viking and the best poet of the age.

After this Illugi rode from home down to Borg in a party of twelve, and Thorstein gave him a good welcome. Early the next morning Illugi said to Thorstein, 'I want to talk with you.'

'Then let us go up on the Borg and talk there,' replied Thorstein, and that is what they did, and Gunnlaug went with them.[1]

'My son Gunnlaug,' Illugi began, 'tells me he has made you a proposal on his own behalf, in that he has asked for your daughter Helga in marriage. Now I should like to know what is going to come of this. His family is known to you, and what possessions we hold. For my part I shall begrudge neither estate nor authority, if that brings it any closer than before.'

'I see only one thing wrong with Gunnlaug,' replied Thorstein. 'He seems such an in-and-out sort of man. If he were like you in character, I should hardly hesitate.'

'It will cut the ties of our friendship,' warned Illugi, 'if you deny that our two families can make a fair and equal match.'

'Well,' agreed Thorstein, 'in the light of what you say, and for our friendship's sake, Helga shall be promised but not formally betrothed to Gunnlaug, and shall wait for him three years. But Gunnlaug must go abroad and make something of himself on the model of good men there. And I shall be free of the whole affair if he does not return accordingly, or if his character still leaves me dissatisfied.'

---

[1] This is the noble rock-bastion behind the present church and farm at Borg, with its extensive views over Borgarfjord and the sea. Since such hills were often regarded as sacred ground they were good places to take counsel. *Haud inexpertus loquor.*

With this they parted. Illugi rode home, and Gunnlaug to his ship, and when the wind blew fair they put to sea and brought their ship to the north of Norway, then sailed along the coast of Thrandheim to Nidaros, where they berthed and unloaded their ship.

4

At this time earl Eirik Hakonarson and Svein his brother ruled over Norway, and earl Eirik, a mighty prince, was in residence on his family estate at Hladir. Thorstein's son Skuli was there with him; he was the earl's retainer and highly esteemed by him. The story goes that Gunnlaug and Authun Fettered-hound entered Hladir with ten of their crew. Gunnlaug was wearing a grey tunic and white long-breeches; he had a boil on his foot, down on the instep, and blood and pus came oozing up from it every time he set foot to the ground; and it was in this state that he with Authun and the rest of them walked into the earl's presence and gave him a courteous greeting.

The earl recognized Authun and asked him the news from Iceland, and Authun told him such as there was. Then the earl asked Gunnlaug who might he be, and he told him his name and family.

'Skuli Thorsteinsson,' asked the earl, 'what sort of man is this back home in Iceland?'

'Give him a good welcome, sire,' said Skuli. 'He is son to one of the finest men in Iceland, Illugi the Black of Gilsbakki. He is also my foster-brother.'

'What is wrong with your foot, Icelander?' asked the earl.

'There is a boil on it, sire.'

'Yet you were not walking lame.'

'One doesn't walk lame,' said Gunnlaug, 'while both legs are the same length.'

At this, one of the earl's retainers, Thorir by name, broke in: 'He's a turkey-cock, this Icelander! It might be as well to try him out a little.'

Gunnlaug looked straight at him and spoke a verse:

> 'Of courtiers here's one
> For ill stands alone;
> So evil and black,
> Ne'er show him your back.'

Thorir looked like reaching for his axe, but, 'Let it lie,' ordered the earl. 'A grown man takes no notice of such. And how old a man are you, Icelander?'

'I am eighteen.'

'Then it is my forecast,' pronounced the earl, 'that you will not see another eighteen.'

Gunnlaug's reply was almost lost to hearing. 'Pray less against me,' he said, 'and more for yourself.'

'What did you say, Icelander?'

'What I thought fit,' Gunnlaug replied. 'That you should pray less against me, and more, and for better things, for yourself.'

'And what about?' asked the earl.

'That you don't get the same sort of death as Hakon your father.'[1]

---

[1] After the coming of the young Olaf Tryggvason and his victories in Norway, earl Hakon fled for his life to his mistress Thora of Rimul. A pit was dug in the farm pigsty, Hakon and his thrall Kark hid themselves therein, and muck and earth were spread to conceal the entrance. Olaf came to the farm, and made proclamation there that he would heap with wealth

The earl turned red as blood and commanded them lay hold of this foolhardy fellow at once. But Skuli stepped before the earl, saying: 'Do this at my request, sire: pardon the man, and let him be off as fast as he can.'

'Then away with him,' cried the earl, 'as fast as he can go, if he would have pardon; and let him never set foot in my kingdom again.'

Skuli saw Gunnlaug outside and down to the quay. There was a ship there bound for England

and honours any that wrought harm to Hakon. 'They heard this speech, the earl and Kark. They had a light with them. Said the earl: "Why are you so pale, and the next moment black as earth? Is it not that you wish to betray me?" "Not so," said Kark. "For we were born in the space of a night, we two," said the earl, "and there will be but a brief while between our deaths." Towards evening Olaf took himself off. With the coming of night the earl forced himself to stay awake, but Kark slept—and slept monstrous ill. The earl woke him up and asked him his dream. "I was but now in Hladir," said Kark, "where Olaf Tryggvason was laying a gold necklace round my neck." Said the earl: "Olaf will draw a blood-red ring round your neck there, if you encounter him. Watch out for yourself then! From me you will receive good, as has been the case hitherto. So do not betray me." Thereafter they both stayed awake, as if each was keeping watch on the other; but towards day the earl fell asleep and was at once in grievous case, so much so that he drew in his heels and the nape of his neck under him, as though he would rear himself up, and cried out loudly and horribly. Kark was terrified, and out of his wits with fear. He drew a big knife from his belt, stuck it in the earl's throat, and cut it right across. That was the death of earl Hakon. Next Kark cut off the earl's head, burst out and away, to come later in the day to Hladir, where he presented the head to king Olaf. He gave him too this account of the wanderings of himself and the earl, as has already been written. Whereupon king Olaf had him led away and his head cut off.' The two heads, of earl and thrall, were hung from a gallows, where the soldiers pelted them with stones. *Heimskringla, Olaf Tryggvason's Saga,* chapter 49.

and all ready to leave, and Skuli secured a place on board for Gunnlaug and Thorkel, his kinsman. Gunnlaug gave his own ship into Authun's keeping, together with those belongings of his which he did not have with him. Then he and Thorkel sailed into English waters and that same autumn arrived south in the port of London, where they hauled their ship ashore.

At this time king Ethelred, the son of Edgar, ruled over England, and was a good leader of his people. That winter he was in residence in London. In those days they used the same language in England as in Norway and Denmark, but there came a change of tongue in England once William the Bastard conquered it, and from then on French was the language of England, because he, William, was of French descent.

Promptly Gunnlaug went into the king's presence and greeted him well and courteously. The king inquired what country he was from, and Gunnlaug told him. 'And I have sought audience of you, sire, because I have made a poem about you and would like you to hear it.'

So be it, said the king. Then Gunnlaug recited his poem in a most striking fashion, and this is from its refrain:

> 'All folk as God are fearing
>   Great England's ring-dispenser;
>   Kin of the keen in battle,
>   The world bows to our warlord.'

The king thanked him for the poem, and as a reward for his skaldship gave him a cloak of scarlet cloth lined with the choicest furs, and with an embroidered band right down to its hem. He also made him a retainer of his, and Gunnlaug spent the winter with the king and was held in high regard.

One day, early in the morning, Gunnlaug met three men in a certain street. Their leader was named Thororm; he was big, strong, and a most unpleasant customer.

'Northman,' said he, 'lend me some money.'

'There is no sense,' replied Gunnlaug, 'in parting with money to strangers.'

'I will pay you on the day named,' promised Thororm.

'Then I'll take a chance,' said Gunnlaug, and lent him the money.

Somewhat later Gunnlaug met the king and told him about the loan.

'It is a bad business, this,' replied the king. 'The man is a most notorious robber and riever. Have no further truck with him, and I will make up your money to you.'

'Then what a sorry lot are we your retainers,' said Gunnlaug, 'trampling roughshod over innocent men but letting people of this kidney rob us right and left. No, that shall never be!'

A little later he again met Thororm and asked for his money, but he said he was not going to pay. Then Gunnlaug chanted this verse:

'Loud singer of the swordsong,
Poor fool, your wits are failing,
To trick me of my treasure,
And rob this swordpoint-reddener.
Learn still, my silver-stealer
(Now is my chance to show it),
While young, men named me Snaketongue,
Nor styled me so for nothing.'

'I shall now offer you the law,' said Gunnlaug. 'Either pay me my money or fight with me on the island in three days' time.'

At this the pirate laughed aloud. 'The way I have trimmed so many men down,' he said, 'no one has ever offered to fight me on the island till now. Well, I'm ready!'

With that he and Gunnlaug parted for the time being, and Gunnlaug told the king how matters stood.

'Now things have taken a desperate turn,' replied the king. 'This man's eyes blunt every weapon. So take my advice: here is a sword I will give you, and with this you are to fight, but show him a different one.'

Gunnlaug thanked the king warmly, and when they were ready for the island Thororm asked what sort of a sword it was he had. Drawing it, Gunnlaug showed him, but he had a loop round the haft of the sword the king had given him, and slipped it over his hand. 'I am not afraid of that one,' said the berserk, studying the sword. He struck at Gunnlaug with his own sword, and cut away almost the whole of his shield. On the instant Gunnlaug struck back at him with the king's gift. The berserk did not so much as take guard, imagining he had the same weapon he had shown him, and in a trice Gunnlaug had dealt him his death-blow.

The king thanked him for his deed, and he won great renown for it, in England and many a place elsewhere. But in the spring, when ships were sailing again from land to land, Gunnlaug asked king Ethelred's leave to travel somewhat. The king asked him what he had in mind. 'I want to make good what I have vowed to do,' explained Gunnlaug, and chanted this verse:

'Far off must I be faring,
The halls of great men call me;
Three kings of rich dominion,
Two earls—I promised early;
Nor turn again till I learn
My battle-leader needs me,
That armring prince who flings us
Red folds of serpents' bedgold.'

'So be it, poet,' said the king, and gave him a gold bracelet which weighed six ounces. 'But you must give me your word to come back to us next autumn, for I do not want to lose a man of your attainments and courage.'

So now Gunnlaug sailed from England with some merchants north to Dublin. It was king Sigtrygg Silkbeard who now ruled in Ireland, the son of Olaf Kvaran and queen Kormlod. He had not long succeeded to the kingdom. Gunnlaug went into the king's presence and greeted him well and courteously, and the king took this as a king should.

'I have made a poem about you,' said Gunnlaug, 'and should be glad of a hearing.'

'No one has done this before and brought me a poem,' the king replied. 'Most certainly it shall have a hearing.'

Gunnlaug now chanted the long lay he had composed, and this is from its refrain:

'Witch's wolfsteed
Doth Sigtrygg feed.'

And this too is part of it:

'This I know well,
Whose praise I would tell;
Of princes choose one:
He, Kvaran's brave son.

Nor will the king
Grudge gift of gold ring:
'Tis for kings to bestow,
As poets well know.

So let the prince say
If he heard till this day
The verse could outweigh
This, Gunnlaug's long lay.'

The king thanked him for the poem, and, calling
his treasurer to him, asked: 'How should this poem
be rewarded?'

'How would you like to reward it, sire?'

'What sort of reward would it be,' asked the king,
'if I gave him a couple of merchant ships?'

'It would be excessive, sire,' replied the treasurer.
'Other kings reward a poet's song with such valuables as fine swords or gold bracelets.'

So the king gave him his own raiment of new
scarlet cloth, an embroidered tunic, a cloak lined
with choicest furs, and a bracelet of gold valued at
a mark. Gunnlaug was warm in his thanks and
remained there a short while before going on to the
Orkneys.

The ruler over Orkney was earl Sigurd Hlodvisson, a prince friendly to Icelanders. Gunnlaug gave
the earl a good greeting and said he had a poem to
offer him. The earl said he would be happy to hear
it, if only because he came of such good stock in
Iceland. So Gunnlaug recited his poem. It was a
short lay, and well made. By way of reward the earl
gave him a broad-axe all inlaid with silver and an
invitation to stay with him.

Gunnlaug thanked him for both gift and invitation, but said he must be on his way east to Sweden.

Later he went on board ship with some merchants who were bound for Norway, and that autumn they arrived east at Konungahella. Thorkel his kinsman had been with him all this while. From Konunga- hella they obtained a guide up to west Gautland, and arrived at a market town called Skarar, where the ruler was earl Sigurd, a man now getting on in years. Gunnlaug went into the earl's presence, gave him a courteous greeting, and announced that he had made a poem about him. The earl lent an attentive ear while Gunnlaug recited this poem—it was a short lay. Then the earl thanked him, gave him a good reward, and invited him to stay there over the winter.

During the winter earl Sigurd held a big Yule- feast. On Yule-eve envoys of earl Eirik's arrived from the north, from Norway, fetching gifts to earl Sigurd. The earl gave them a fine welcome and assigned them seats alongside Gunnlaug over the Yule season. They were merry as grigs at the drink- ing. The Gauts maintained that there was no earl alive greater or more famous than earl Sigurd, whereas the Norwegians reckoned earl Eirik fore- most by far. They wrangled over this till both sides called on Gunnlaug to act as umpire for them in their dispute. Then Gunnlaug chanted this verse:

> 'Bare truth you speak of Sigurd,
> You wands of warrior-goddess:
> Greyhaired the prince, yet gracious,
> Beheld the tall waves rolling.
> Yet Eirik, sprig of victory,
> Storm-belted in the Baltic,
> Saw more blue water tossing
> From hooves of his sea-stallion.'

Both sides were well content with this verdict, and the Norwegians most of all. Then after Yule the envoys took their leave with fine gifts which earl Sigurd sent to earl Eirik. They reported Gunnlaug's ruling to the earl, and it seemed to Eirik that Gunnlaug had shown him both fairness and friendship. He let it be known that Gunnlaug should have asylum there in his kingdom, and in time Gunnlaug learned what the earl had spoken under this head.

5

Earl Sigurd now found Gunnlaug a guide east to Tiundaland in Sweden, at Gunnlaug's own request. At this time Olaf the Swede ruled over Sweden, a strong and splendid king, most eager for fame. Gunnlaug reached Uppsala near the time of the Swedes' Spring Assembly, and when he got to see the king he greeted him, and the king welcomed him to court and asked who he might be. He was an Icelander, he said.

It happened that just then Hrafn Onundarson was staying with king Olaf. 'Hrafn,' said the king, 'what sort of man is this back home in Iceland?'

A big gallant-looking man got up off the lower bench and strode before the king. 'Sire,' said he, 'he is of the best possible descent and a fine man in his own right.'

'Then let him go and sit beside you,' said the king.

'I have a poem to offer you,' said Gunnlaug, 'and I should like you to call for silence and give it a hearing.'

'You go and sit down first,' the king told him. 'I haven't the time now to attend to poems.'

So that was what they did. Gunnlaug and Hrafn began talking together, and telling each other of their travels. Hrafn said he had left Iceland last summer for Norway and moved east into Sweden at the beginning of winter. They were quick to become friends.

But one day, when the Assembly was over, Gunnlaug and Hrafn once more found themselves in the king's presence, and, 'Now, sire,' said Gunnlaug, 'I should like you to hear my poem.'

'That is possible now,' said the king.

'I too now wish to recite my poem,' said Hrafn.

'That too is possible,' said the king.

'With your permission, sire,' said Gunnlaug, 'I want to recite mine first.'

'But it is for me to speak first, sire,' said Hrafn, 'for I was the first to reach your court.'

'And what occasion was that,' demanded Gunnlaug, 'when our forefathers so set forth that my father was in tow to yours? Never in this whole wide world! And that is how it must be with you and me.'

'Let us have the good manners not to make a brawl of this,' said Hrafn. 'And let the king decide.'

'Gunnlaug shall say his piece first,' ruled the king. 'It upsets him so if he cannot have his own way.'

Then Gunnlaug recited the long lay which he had composed about king Olaf; and when the lay came to an end, 'Hrafn,' inquired the king, 'how well made is this poem?'

'Well, sire, it is a poem full of big words, but far from elegant, and stiff and hard like Gunnlaug's own temper.'

'Now you shall recite your poem, Hrafn,' ordered the king.

And so he did, and when it came to an end,

'Gunnlaug,' inquired the king, 'how well made is this poem?'

'Well, sire, it is a pretty poem, just like Hrafn himself to look at, but there's not much in it once you peer closer. And why should you compose only a short lay about the king, Hrafn? Didn't he impress you as worth a long one?'

'Let us not discuss it further,' replied Hrafn. 'It can come up again, maybe later on.' And on that note they parted.

Soon afterwards Hrafn was made king Olaf's retainer, and asked leave to go away. This the king granted him. And when Hrafn was all ready for his departure he had this to say to Gunnlaug: 'Our friendship must end here and now, because you tried to simple me before these great men. But the day will come when I shall put you to no less shame than you intended here for me.'

'Your threats are nothing to me,' Gunnlaug replied, 'and never shall it be found that my name stands lower than yours.'

King Olaf gave Hrafn good gifts at parting, and later he went away. He left the east that same spring and got himself to Thrandheim, where he fitted out his ship and sailed for Iceland in the summer. He brought his ship into Leiruvag, down below Mosfell heath. His friends and relations rejoiced to see him, and he spent the winter at home with his father.

Then next summer at the Assembly Skald-Hrafn met his cousin Skapti the Lawspeaker.

'I should like to have your support,' said Hrafn, 'on a marriage-mission to Thorstein Egilsson, to ask for his daughter Helga.'

'But is she not already promised to Gunnlaug Wormtongue?' Skapti asked him.

'And is not the period agreed on between them now past? In any case,' said Hrafn, 'he is far too wrapped up in his own pride to heed or hold to it.'

'Well, if it pleases you,' said Skapti, 'let us do it.'

So later they walked over with a fair number of men to Thorstein Egilsson's booth and got a warm welcome there.

'My cousin Hrafn wants to ask for Helga your daughter,' began Skapti. 'You know all about his family tree, and his rich fortune and good breeding, and the power of his kinsmen and friends.'

'She is promised already, to Gunnlaug,' Thorstein explained, 'and I propose to stand fast by the whole arrangement we then made.'

'But are not the three winters you agreed on already past?' asked Skapti.

'Yes, but not the summer, and he could still return this summer.'

'If he doesn't return the summer through,' asked Skapti, 'what hopes have we then in the matter?'

'We shall be coming here next summer again,' replied Thorstein, 'and we can then see what appears most advisable. It is useless discussing it any further at present.'

With that they parted and men rode home from the Assembly. It was soon no secret that Hrafn was asking for Helga. Gunnlaug did not return to Iceland that summer, and the following year at the Assembly Hrafn and Skapti pushed on with their suit strongly, arguing that Thorstein was now free of all his commitments to Gunnlaug.

'I have few daughters to see to,' was Thorstein's comment, 'and I am anxious that no one shall start fighting over them. I think I had better see Illugi the Black first.'

So he did, and when they met, Thorstein asked, 'Do you consider me free of all my commitments to Gunnlaug your son?'

'To be sure,' Illugi told him, 'if that is how you want it. There is little I can say in the matter, for I simply do not know what my son Gunnlaug is up to.'

Thorstein now returned to Skapti, and they settled that if Gunnlaug did not return home this summer the wedding should take place at Borg at the beginning of winter, but that Thorstein should be free of all his commitments to Hrafn should Gunnlaug return and claim his bride. Afterwards men rode home from the Assembly. There was still no sign of Gunnlaug's return, and Helga was very despondent at the thought of marrying Hrafn.

6

There is now this to report of Gunnlaug, that he left Sweden for England the same summer Hrafn sailed for Iceland, and received good gifts at parting from king Olaf. King Ethelred gave him a very good welcome, and he spent the winter in high regard with the king.

In those days Knut the Great, Svein's son, ruled over Denmark. He had just succeeded to his patrimony, and was for ever threatening to wage war on England, because king Svein his father had won a great realm in England before he died out there in the west. Moreover, at this same time there was a big army of Danes out west there, whose leader was Heming, the son of earl Strut-Harald and brother of earl Sigvaldi, and it was he who held for king Knut the realm which king Svein had won earlier.

In the spring Gunnlaug asked the king for permission to be off, but, 'Since you are my retainer,' was his answer, 'it is not proper for you to leave me now, in face of such unrest as now threatens here in England.'

'It is for you to command, sire,' replied Gunnlaug, 'but pray give me leave to depart in the summer, should the Danes not come.'

'We will see about it then,' promised the king.

So the summer went by, and the following winter, yet the Danes did not come, and after midsummer Gunnlaug got leave of the king to be off. He travelled east from England to Norway and went to see earl Eirik at Hladir in Thrandheim. The earl had a good welcome for him now, and invited him to spend some time with him. Gunnlaug thanked him for the offer, but admitted he wanted first to go out to Iceland to see his bride-to-be.

'All ships bound for Iceland are by now on their way there,' the earl told him.

Then one of the retainers had this to say. 'Hallfred Troublesome-Skald lay at anchor here yesterday, out under Agdanes.'

'That may well be so,' agreed the earl. 'He sailed from here five days ago.'

Earl Eirik then had Gunnlaug conveyed out to Hallfred, who greeted him with joy; they got a fair offshore wind at once, and felt very well pleased with themselves. The time was now late summer.

Hallfred asked Gunnlaug: 'Have you heard tell of Hrafn Onundarson's courtship of Helga the Fair?'

Gunnlaug admitted that he had, though only vaguely, so Hallfred told him what he knew about it, and this besides, that a lot of men were saying

Hrafn was no less gallant a man than Gunnlaug.
Then Gunnlaug chanted this verse:

> 'Let the winds rage, I reck not
> (Though easy now from eastwards),
> Driving seven days like spindrift
> Our ship, the ski of nesses.
> My dread is not of dying
> Before grey hairs can grace me,
> As live (nor love the lesson)
> More craven thought than Hrafn.'

'Well, shipmate,' Hallfred warned him, 'you will
need to make a better showing in your quarrel with
Hrafn than I did. Some years ago I brought my
ship into Leiruvag, down below Mosfell heath, and
ought to have paid a half-mark of silver to one of
Hrafn's housecarles, but withheld it from him. So
Hrafn rode down to us with sixty men and cut our
moorings, and the ship drifted on to the mudbanks
and looked all set for a wreck. I was forced to yield
to Hrafn on his own terms, and pay him a full mark
—and that is what I can tell you about him from my
own experience.'

And now they could talk of nothing but Helga.
Hallfred was loud in praise of her beauty, while
Gunnlaug chanted this verse:

> 'Luck serves not lackscorn Hrafn,
> That warm-fire-god of swordstorm,
> To clutch at my cloak-goddess,
> Lass linened white as snowfall.
> While young, the love of Wormtongue
> Clung fondly to her fingers;
> Glorious those promontories
> From hand of goldland lady!'

'It is a well made verse,' agreed Hallfred.

They made land north at Hraunhofn on Melrakkasletta a fortnight before winter, and got their cargo ashore. There was a man by the name of Thord there on Melrakkasletta, a farmer's son, who used to wrestle with the merchants, and they had a rough time of it with him. Then a bout was arranged between him and Gunnlaug, and the night before Thord prayed to Thor for victory. The next day when they met they set to and wrestled, and Gunnlaug swept both Thord's legs from under him and fetched him a heavy fall. But Gunnlaug's own foot, the one he had his weight on, slipped out of joint, and down he fell along with Thord.

'And maybe,' said Thord, 'you will do no better next time either.'

'What do you mean by that ?' asked Gunnlaug.

'Your encounter with Hrafn, if he marries Helga the Fair at the beginning of winter. I was there, right alongside, at the Assembly this summer when the whole thing was arranged.'

Gunnlaug made no answer. His foot was bound up and the joint put back into place; it became very swollen. He and Hallfred rode off with ten of their crew and came south to Gilsbakki in Borgarfjord that very Saturday evening folk sat down to the wedding feast at Borg. Illugi was glad to see his son Gunnlaug and his comrades. Gunnlaug said he wanted to ride down to Borg there and then. Illugi said this would be folly, and it looked that way to everyone except Gunnlaug himself. Also Gunnlaug could hardly put his foot to the ground, though he did his best to hide it, and for these reasons he made no move to go.

Hallfred rode home the following morning to

Hreduvatn in Nordrardal, where his brother Galti, a brisk sort of man, was looking after their property.

7

There is now this to record of Hrafn, that as he sat to his wedding feast at Borg most people say the bride looked far from happy. For how true it is, the old proverb: 'Early lessons last the longest.' And so it was with her now.

A piece of news at the feast was that a man by the name of Sverting Hafr-Bjarnarson asked for the hand of Hungerd, Jofrid's daughter by Thorodd, and the wedding was to take place that same winter after Yule up at Skaney, where lived a kinsman of Hungerd, Thorkel the son of Torfi Valbrandsson.

Hrafn returned home to Mosfell with Helga his wife, and when they had been living there a short while it happened one morning, before they got up, that Helga was awake but Hrafn drowsed on in an uneasy slumber. When he awoke Helga asked him what he had been dreaming about, and Hrafn chanted this verse:

> 'Drowned in your arms, so dreamt I,
> A mortal swordstroke marred me;
> White bride of mine, bright maiden,
> Your bed my lifeblood reddened.
> Alas, my ale-bowl goddess
> Bound not the wound she found there;
> That Hrafn thus is riven
> Contents that gentle lady.'

'I shall weep none the more for that!' cried Helga. 'You have deceived me wickedly. Gunnlaug must have come back.' And she wept bitterly.

Soon after this, Gunnlaug's return became common talk. Helga grew so hard now towards Hrafn that he could no longer keep her at home. Back they must go to Borg, and very little married life was Hrafn's.

Now folk were getting ready for the winter wedding. Thorkel of Skaney had invited Illugi the Black and his sons, but while Illugi got himself ready, Gunnlaug sat in the living-room and made no move to go. Illugi came up to him, and, 'Son,' he said, 'why don't you get ready?'

'I'm not thinking to go,' replied Gunnlaug.

'Of course you must go,' said Illugi. 'Don't take it so hard, son, as to break yourself in pieces for any woman alive. Act as though you are indifferent to it: you will never lack for women.'

So Gunnlaug did as his father told him. They came to the wedding, where Illugi and his sons were assigned to the one high seat, and Thorstein Egilsson, Hrafn his son-in-law, and the bridegroom's party to the other high seat opposite. The women sat on the dais, and Helga the Fair was seated next to the bride. From time to time she would be glancing at Gunnlaug, and proving thereby the truth of the old proverb: 'Eyes will tell who loveth well.' Gunnlaug was handsomely turned out and wearing that noble raiment king Sigtrygg had given him. He looked altogether more distinguished than the rest of them, and this for a number of reasons—his strength, his good looks, and his stature.

There was not much merriment at this wedding. The day men were preparing to leave, the women were just as prompt to be on the move and make ready for home. Gunnlaug went to speak to Helga, and they were talking for a long time. Then Gunnlaug spoke this verse:

'No hour, no day that lours
From cloudhall of the hilltops,
Held rest for me once Helga
Was reft from me for Hrafn.
White-headed, not wise-hearted,
Her father drove it further;
This goddess of the hornthaw,
For gold too young he sold her.'

And he spoke further, saying:

'White maiden, goddess, wine-may,
Bright lane of golden seaflame,
For skald's hot-scalding sorrow
I blame those twain that framed her;
All-hallowed in bed's hollow
They shaped their silkshift daughter.
Hel take both craft and craftsmen,
The lord, aye, and his lady!'

Then Gunnlaug gave Helga the cloak, Ethelred's
gift, which was so splendid a treasure. She thanked
him warmly for his gift.

Later Gunnlaug went outside, and now the mares
and stallions, many of them extremely handsome,
had been brought in and saddled, and tethered on
the beaten ground near the house. Gunnlaug leapt
on the back of one of the stallions and galloped
furiously down the home-field to where Hrafn was
standing, so that he had to flinch and give way.

'No need to flinch, Hrafn,' he said, 'for this time
I am not threatening you. But you know what you
deserve!'

Hrafn made answer with a verse:

'War's wonder, god of woundflame,
Glory of Valkyrie's story,

> To fight thus ill befits us
> For linden under linen.
> O corpse-hung tree of slaughter,
> I sailed the seas and saw there
> Full many an equal maiden
> On strands south of the ocean.'

'Maybe there are,' said Gunnlaug, 'and plenty of them, but it does not seem so to me.'

At this moment Illugi and Thorstein came running up and were not prepared to have them wrangling. Still, Gunnlaug chanted a verse:

> 'Bright strake of snakelight gold,
> For gold it was they sold her;
> Gold ravished her for Hrafn,
> Whom dolts now dub my equal!
> While Ethelred, so redeless,
> From westward course restrained me,
> For talk of war—Torque's-waster,
> The Wormtongue, so falls silent.'

After that the men on both sides rode home, and everything was quiet and void of incident over the winter. Hrafn never again had any pleasure of Helga, once she and Gunnlaug had met and talked together.

In the summer there was a great riding of men to the Assembly, including Illugi the Black together with his sons Gunnlaug and Hermund, Thorstein Egilsson and his son Kollsvein, Onund from Mosfell with all his sons, and Sverting Hafr-Bjarnarson. Skapti was still Lawspeaker. One day at the Assembly when a big crowd of men thronged the Lawhill, and the legal business was at an end there, Gunnlaug called for a hearing.

'Is Hrafn Onundarson here?' he asked.

He said he was.

'You know,' said Gunnlaug Wormtongue then, 'how you have married my promised bride and set yourself up as my enemy. So for that I am challenging you to fight on the island in the Oxara, here at the Assembly, in three days' time.'

'It is a fair offer,' admitted Hrafn, 'and what I should expect from you. Well, I am ready, whenever you are.'

Their kinsmen on both sides were much perturbed at this, but it was the law in those days for anyone who thought himself wronged by another to challenge him to the island, and when the three days were past they made ready for the fight. Illugi the Black accompanied his son to the island with a strong body of men, while Hrafn had the support of Skapti the Lawspeaker, his father, and yet other of his kinsmen.

Before Gunnlaug walked out to the island he chanted this verse:

> 'Waits now, nor finds me wanting,
>   Sand-isle of our Assembly;
> From hand my bare blade dangles,
>   Grant, God, this wordsmith grace!
> Let woundflame part asunder
>   Lovelocks of that love-gulper,
> Then last, his head I'll loosen,
>   And lop from his loon-shoulders.'

Hrafn made answer and sang:

> 'Wormtongue knows not who longest
>   Shall live enleaved with glory;
> Woundsickle's bared, stand wary,
>   Lest leg be seared or severed.

My wife, fair brooch-pin wearer,
Though wed now lives my widow;
She soon shall learn my valour,
Though fallen on this lawfield.'

Hermund was holding the shield for his brother Gunnlaug, and Sverting Hafr-Bjarnarson for Hrafn. Whoever was wounded should ransom himself from the island with three marks of silver.

It was for Hrafn, as the challenged man, to strike the first blow. He cut at the upper part of Gunnlaug's shield, and such was the weight of his stroke that the sword promptly snapped off underneath the guard, and its point flew up from the shield to catch Gunnlaug on the cheek, nicking him slightly. Their fathers instantly ran in between them, with a number of other men.

'I pronounce Hrafn vanquished,' said Gunnlaug, 'disarmed as he is.'

'And I pronounce you vanquished,' said Hrafn, 'disabled as you are.'

Gunnlaug was beside himself with anger and swearing that there had been no real fight, but Illugi his father said that would be all for the present.

'Next time Hrafn and I meet,' said Gunnlaug to that, 'I beg and pray, father, you will be too far away to step between us.'

With that they parted for now, and men walked home to their booths. But the following day in the legislature it was made law that island-combat should be done away with from that day forth for ever. This was done on the advice of all the wisest men at the Assembly, where indeed there were present the wisest men of all the land. So this which

Hrafn and Gunnlaug fought was the last island-combat to take place in Iceland. This was one of the three most crowded Assemblies ever known: the other two were those after the Burning of Njal and after the Heath-slayings.

One morning as the brothers Hermund and Gunnlaug were walking down to the Oxara to wash, there were many women making towards the river on the other side, and one of their company was Helga the Fair.

Said Hermund: 'Do you see your sweetheart Helga here, on the other side of the river?'

'Too true, I see her,' replied Gunnlaug; and with that chanted this verse:

> 'Born was that girl to men's bane
> —For that blame him who framed her!
> I yearned with flame that burned me
> To hold that golden maytree.
> Black eyes of skald grow bleaker,
> Swim now at swanwhite maiden;
> I heed them not, so need I
> This lady goldring-laden.'

Later they crossed the river, and Helga and Gunnlaug talked for some time, and as they recrossed the river to the east Helga still stood there, gazing after Gunnlaug for a long while. And Gunnlaug too looked back over the river and chanted this verse:

> 'Gleams eyelash-moon of lady,
> Ale-goddess lapped in linen,
> From welkin of her eyebrows
> With hawklight brightness glancing;
> But eyelid's star that's darting
> From sky of necklace-goddess

Sends pain and grief unending
On ring-princess and poet.'

When this was over and done with, men rode homewards from the Assembly. Gunnlaug went on living at home at Gilsbakki. One morning when he woke up, everyone else had risen, and only he was still abed. He was sleeping in a shut-bed at the inner end of the dais. Suddenly twelve men walked into the room, all armed to the teeth—and who had come there but Hrafn Onundarson.

Gunnlaug jumped up at once and got to his weapons.

'You are in no danger,' said Hrafn, 'and my business here you are about to learn. This summer you challenged me to island-combat at the Assembly, and thought it no true fight. I shall now make you this offer, that we both leave Iceland for abroad next summer, and go on the island in Norway, where our kinsmen won't get in our way.'

'Spoken like the brave man you are!' replied Gunnlaug. 'I accept your offer gladly. And now, Hrafn, whatever hospitality you need here is yours for the asking.'

'A kind offer,' said Hrafn, 'but for now we had best be on our way.'

With that they parted. Their kinsmen on both sides were much dashed by this, but because their feelings ran so high there was nothing they could do about it; and after all, what was fated must be.

8

There is now this to tell of Hrafn, that he put his ship ready in Leiruvag. Two of the men who went

with him are known by name, the one Grim, the
other Olaf, sons of a sister of Onund his father, and
stalwart men the pair of them. It seemed a sharp
loss to all Hrafn's family when he went away, but
what he told them was this, that he had challenged
Gunnlaug to the island because his life with Helga
was barren of enjoyment; and one of them, he
vowed, must fall before the other.

Later, when the wind blew fair, Hrafn put to sea
and brought their ship to Thrandheim, where he
spent the winter. The whole winter through he
heard no word of Gunnlaug, so waited for him the
summer too, and spent yet a second winter in
Thrandheim, at a place called Lifangr.

But Gunnlaug Wormtongue had taken ship with
Hallfred Troublesome-Skald up north on Melrakkasletta. They were very late making ready, but
put to sea the minute the wind blew fair, and reached
Orkney just before winter. Earl Sigurd Hlodvisson
still ruled over the Islands, so Gunnlaug went and
spent the winter with him, and the earl thought well
of him. In the spring the earl made ready to go
cruising, and Gunnlaug made ready with him; and
that summer they harried far and wide in the Hebrides and the firths of Scotland, and fought many
battles. Gunnlaug proved himself a brave and
gallant fellow and the toughest of fighters wherever
they came.

Early in the summer the earl turned back home,
but Gunnlaug took ship with some merchants who
were sailing for Norway. He and earl Sigurd parted
the best of friends. Gunnlaug now travelled north to
Thrandheim to see earl Eirik and got there by the
beginning of winter. The earl made him most welcome, and invited him to stay there, an offer he

accepted. The earl had already heard tell of his quarrel with Hrafn, and told Gunnlaug that he forbade them to fight anywhere in his kingdom. Gunnlaug said it was for the earl to command, and he spent the winter there, at no time very sociably.

One day in spring Gunnlaug was out walking with his kinsman Thorkel. They walked away out of the town, and in the fields before them there was a ring of men to be seen, and inside the ring there were two armed men fencing. One enjoyed the name of Hrafn, and the other Gunnlaug. The bystanders were saying how the Icelanders dealt small blows and were slow to remember their boasts. Gunnlaug could see what contempt underlay this, and how the whole thing reeked of mockery, and he was silent as he walked away.

A little later he told the earl he would no longer endure the contempt and scorn of his retainers for his quarrel with Hrafn. He requested the earl to find him a guide to Lifangr. By now the earl had been informed that Hrafn had left Lifangr and was bound east for Sweden, so he gave Gunnlaug leave to depart and found him two guides for the journey.

Gunnlaug now travelled with a party of six from Hladir in to Lifangr, and on one and the same day Hrafn left there with four men in the morning, and Gunnlaug rode in in the evening. From there Gunnlaug went on to Veradal, and evening after evening he arrived where Hrafn had been staying the night before. Gunnlaug kept on until he reached the topmost farm in the valley, Sula by name, and Hrafn had left there that morning. Gunnlaug made no stay but pressed straight on through the night, and in the morning at sunrise they saw each other. Hrafn had come to where there were two lakes, and between the lakes lay level fields called Gleipnir's Fields. A small headland called Dinganes jutted out into one of the lakes, and it was there, on that headland, that Hrafn and his four comrades made their stand. His cousins Grim and Olaf were with him.

'It is good,' said Gunnlaug, when they stood face to face, 'that we have found each other at last.'

Hrafn said he had no quarrel with that. 'And now,' he continued, 'choose which you like, whether we all fight, or just you and I; but let both sides have an equal number of men.'

Gunnlaug said it was all one to him, whichever they did. However, Grim and Olaf, Hrafn's cousins, made it plain they would not stand by while just the two of them fought; and Gunnlaug's kinsman Thorkel the Black said the same. 'Then you two,' said Gunnlaug to the earl's guides, 'must sit on one side and help neither party, but live to tell the tale of our encounter.' And so they did.

They clashed together and fought bravely, all of them. Grim and Olaf together attacked Gunnlaug alone, and their exchanges ended in his killing them both, with no wound to himself. Thord Kolbeinsson affirms as much in the poem he made on Gunnlaug Wormtongue:

> 'First, e'er he flared at Hrafn,
>   Wormtongue with his thin woundflame
> Felled Grim and flailed down Olaf,
>   Gay men in warfay's swordgale;
> Bold Gunnlaug, skald all bloody,
>   To Hel sped three fine fellows,
> Ship's steerer, god of wavesteed,
>   Dealt death as dole to all men.'

Meanwhile Hrafn and Gunnlaug's kinsman Thorkel the Black were fighting together, and Thorkel fell before Hrafn and lost his life.

So, in the end, all their comrades fell. Then Hrafn and Gunnlaug clashed together with heavy strokes and headlong assaults one upon the other, fighting without pause or remorse. Gunnlaug wielded the sword Ethelred's gift: it was the best of weapons, and at last he landed a great blow on Hrafn with this sword and cut his leg from under him. Yet none the more did Hrafn fall to the ground, but fell back on a tree-stump and steadied his own stump upon it.

'You are past fighting now,' said Gunnlaug. 'I will fight no longer with a maimed man.'

'True,' replied Hrafn, 'I have had the worse of the draw. Yet I could give a good account of myself still if I might have something to drink.'

'No foul play then,' said Gunnlaug, 'if I bring you water in my helmet.'

'No foul play,' promised Hrafn.

So Gunnlaug went to a brook, scooped up water in his helmet, and carried it back to Hrafn. Hrafn reached out for it with his left hand, but cut at Gunnlaug's head with the sword in his right, giving him a dreadful wound.

'That was foul play from you to me,' said Gunnlaug, 'and little like a man, when I was trusting you.'

'True,' replied Hrafn, 'but this drove me to it, that I grudge you the embraces of Helga the Fair.'

And now once more they fought furiously together, and it ended at last when Gunnlaug overcame Hrafn, and Hrafn lost his life there.

Then the earl's guides came forward and bandaged Gunnlaug's head-wound, while he sat there chanting this verse:

'Fearless he heard our spear-din,
Hrafn, that oak rough-rinded,
Swordhacked and hewn attacked us,
His stormrent boughs unbending.
Here was a gale in Hordland!
Roared spears and swords round Gunnlaug;
Daunting their flight this morning
On Dinganes, ring-bearer.'

Next they saw to the dead men, and finally they got Gunnlaug on to his horse and brought him the whole way down to Lifangr. He lay there for three nights and received all his rites from a priest, and then he died, and was buried there at the church. Everyone thought it the greatest loss, this, in respect of Gunnlaug and Hrafn too, and all the more so because of the circumstances attendant on their deaths.

9

In the summer, before news of these events reached Iceland, Illugi the Black had a dream home at Gilsbakki. It seemed to him that Gunnlaug appeared to him in his sleep, all bloody, and sang him this verse in his dream. Illugi remembered the verse when he woke, and sang it in turn to others:

'Hrafn it was deep-rived me
(His thigh I'd seared hotly)
With hiltfinned clanging swordfish
That swims against steel corslet;
While ravens, bleak corse-raveners,
Drank gore from wounds hot-pouring,
Swordstroke of Gunnr's war-oak
On Gunnlaug's head fell crashing.'

It happened at Mosfell likewise, that same night, that Onund dreamt that Hrafn appeared before him, all covered with blood, and chanted this verse:

'Bloodswart my sword, when wordlord
Sworded me down like swordgod;
Shield I wielded o'er seafield
Shielded me ill from swordpeal;
Brood of blood-goslings stood
Bloodstained and sipped my blood;
Woundfowl, wound-greedy ever,
Wantoned in wounds' red river.'

The following summer at the Assembly Illugi the Black demanded of Onund at the Lawhill, 'How do you propose to make up to me for my son, since your son Hrafn betrayed him in their truce?'

'Far be it from me, I should say,' said Onund, 'to make up for him, with such a wound of my own from their meeting. Nor shall I ask you for any atonement for my son either.'

'Some of your kith and kin will rue the day then,' threatened Illugi.

For what remained of the summer after the Assembly Illugi was a much-dejected man. But the story goes that in the autumn Illugi rode down from Gilsbakki with thirty men and came to Mosfell early in the morning. Onund and his sons escaped into the church, but Illugi caught two of his kinsmen, one called Bjorn and the other Thorgrim. He had Bjorn killed and Thorgrim's foot chopped off. Then he rode home, and there was no counter-stroke to this by Onund.

Hermund Illugason still felt the death of Gunnlaug his brother cruelly, and thought him none the more avenged though this had been done. There

was a man, Hrafn by name, the son of a brother of
Onund of Mosfell, a busy merchant who owned a
ship which was drawn ashore in Hrutafjord. In the
spring Hermund Illugason rode from home all alone
north over Holtavorduheid, so on to Hrutafjord,
and out as far as Bordeyr to the merchants' ship.
The merchants were now just about to sail. Hrafn
the skipper was ashore, and a lot of men with him.
Hermund rode up to him and thrust him through
with his spear, then instantly rode away, and Hrafn's
shipmates were all thrown into confusion by this
action of Hermund's. No redress was made for this
killing, and it was the last of the exchanges between
Illugi the Black and Onund of Mosfell.

In course of time Thorstein Egilsson married his
daughter Helga to a man called Thorkel Hallkelsson,
who lived out in Hraunsdal. Helga went there to
live with him, but had little feeling for him, for she
could never get Gunnlaug out of her mind, dead
though he was. Yet Thorkel was a fine man enough,
and rich, and a good poet. They had not a few
children, a son called Thorarin and another Thorstein, and other children besides.

It was Helga's chief joy to spread out the cloak,
Gunnlaug's gift, and gaze upon it for a long while.
The day came when a great sickness afflicted their
household, and many lay ill of it a long time. Then
Helga too fell ill, yet did not take to her bed. One
Saturday evening Helga was sitting in the living-
room, and resting her head against her husband
Thorkel's knee. She sent for the cloak, Gunnlaug's
gift, and when it was brought to her she sat up and
spread out its folds, and gazed upon it for a while,
and afterwards sank back into her husband's arms
and died.

Then Thorkel chanted this verse:

> 'Cold in my arms I hold her,
> Enfold my goldtorqued lady,
> That slender wand so wondrous
> Enwound with snaketwist bracelet.
> God took my goldhaired goddess,
> Bright linden under linen,
> Leaves me to life so loveless
> And bitter, death were better.'

Helga was carried to the church, but Thorkel lived on at Hraunsdal and thought Helga's death a great loss, as might be expected.

And with that our saga ends.

SAGA OF
TIMES PAST

KING HROLF AND HIS
CHAMPIONS

The Story of Frothi

THERE was a man named Halfdan, and another
named Frothi, two brothers, kings' sons, and each
of them ruling his own kingdom. King Halfdan was
genial and gentle, gracious and good-natured, but
king Frothi was a downright savage. King Halfdan
had three children, two sons and a daughter whose
name was Signy. She was the eldest, and was married
to earl Sævil. All this took place when his sons were
still young. One was called Hroar and the other
Helgi. The name of their foster-father was Regin,
and he loved the boys dearly.

Not far from the king's stronghold lay an island,
where lived a commoner by the name of Vifil, a life-
long friend of king Halfdan's. This Vifil had two
dogs, one called Hopp and the other Ho. He was a
man of substance, and deeply versed in ancient
wisdom if danger threatened him.

We must now take up the tale how king Frothi
abode in his kingdom and bitterly envied his brother,
king Halfdan, that he should rule over Denmark all
alone. His own lot, he felt, had not turned out so
happily. So he assembled together a mob and a
multitude and held for Denmark, arrived there by
dead of night, and burnt and fired the whole place.
King Halfdan could make little defence; he was taken
captive and killed, and those who could took to
flight. The citizens had all to swear oaths of allegiance

to king Frothi, or he had them tortured with divers torments.

Regin, the foster-father of Helgi and Hroar, got them away and out to the island to carl Vifil. They grievously lamented their loss. Regin said that most shelters were snowed under if Vifil could not keep them safe from king Frothi. 'This is playing tug-of-war with a strong one,' said Vifil, but he agreed that he was under considerable obligation to help the boys. So he took them in and put them in a room underground, where for the most part they spent the nights, but by day got some fresh air in the carl's forests, for the island was half covered with forest. In this fashion they parted from Regin. Regin had great possessions in Denmark, and a wife and children too, and he could see nothing else for it save to give in to king Frothi and swear him oaths of allegiance. And now king Frothi subjected the whole Danish kingdom to tribute and tax. Most had to be compelled to this, for king Frothi was the most detested of men. And he levied tribute on earl Sævil likewise.

After achieving all this, king Frothi felt somewhat easier in mind at not finding the boys Helgi and Hroar. He now had watch kept for them on all sides, near and far, north and south, east and west, promising great gifts to whoever could tell him anything about them, but to those who might hide them divers tortures, should that come to light. But no one felt he had anything to tell the king about them. Then he had wise women and soothsayers fetched from throughout the whole land, and had the country-side explored up and down, islands and skerries too, but still they were not found. So now he had wizards fetched, they that can pry to the

heart of all things even as they wish, and they told
him that the boys were not being reared in that
land, but that they were not far off from the king
even so.

'We have searched for them up hill and down
dale,' said king Frothi, 'and I think it most unlikely
they are close to us. But there is an island nearby,
where we have not yet made diligent search, for
hardly anybody lives on it, except for one poverty-
stricken fellow with his home there.'

'Search there first of all,' advised the wizards, 'for
thick mist and fog lie over the island, and we can get
no clear view of this man's dwelling. We judge him
to be a deep one, and with much more to him than
appears.'

'We must take another look at it,' the king agreed,
'but I shall be surprised if a poor fisherman should
be keeping these boys, and daring to withhold them
from me so.'

It happened early one morning that carl Vifil
started up from sleep, crying out: 'Many a marvel
is in motion about us, and spirits are come to the
island, stern and strong. Up with you, sons of Halfdan, Hroar and Helgi, and keep to cover in my
woods today.' They ran into the forest, and what
happened then was what the carl had guessed, that
king Frothi's messengers came to the island and
searched for them in every place they could think of,
yet found the boys nowhere at all. The carl impressed
them as most suspicious-looking, but off they went
with that for their pains and told the king that they
had no notion how to find them.

'You have made a poor search,' said the king, 'and
this fellow will be up to his eyes in magic. Now get
back there the same way, so that he will be less

ready to whisk them out of sight, if they really are there.'

They had no option save to do as the king commanded, and went back to the island a second time. Said Vifil to the boys, 'This is no time for you to be sitting about. Get to the forest as fast as you can.' The boys did so, and immediately thereafter the king's men came rushing up, demanding the right of search. The carl threw the whole place open to them, but look wherever they might, they could find them nowhere at all on the island; so back they went with that for their pains and told the king.

'We must no longer use half measures in dealing with this fellow,' said the king. 'I shall go to the island myself, first thing in the morning.'

And that was what happened, the king went in person. The carl woke up in some distress, and saw again how they must find a plan, and quickly. He said to the brothers: 'If I call loudly on Hopp and Ho my dogs, you must understand that I mean you. On the word run to your underground refuge, and take it as a sign that there are enemies come to the island, and hide from danger there. For your uncle Frothi has now joined in the hunt, and will try for your lives with all sorts of stratagems and wiles; nor can I tell as yet whether I shall be able to save you.'

The carl then walked to the shore, where the king's ship had just put in. He pretended not to notice it, and made such a show of looking anxiously for his flock that he spared never a glance for the king or his men. The king bade his men lay hold of him; they did so, and he was marched before him.

'You are a cunning old rascal,' said the king, 'and sly as they come. Tell me, where are the king's sons, for you certainly know?'

'Blessings on your head, sire,' cried Vifil, 'don't keep me in custody, for the wolf will be tearing my flock to pieces! Hopp,' he bawled, 'Ho! Help the flock, for I cannot save them.'

'What are you calling now?' asked the king.

'Those are the names of my dogs. And now, sire, you look where you like, but I don't believe that the king's sons will be found here. Indeed, I am dumbfounded that you could imagine I would withhold anyone from you.'

'You are a cunning rascal to be sure,' said the king, 'but for all that they can never be concealed here again after this, even though they have been here hitherto. And it would be only right and proper if you were put to death.'

'That lies in your power,' agreed the carl. 'And you will then have done some business on the island, more than if you depart with things as they are.'

'I do not care to have you killed,' said the king, 'though I suspect that is a mistake on my part.'

The king returned home with matters left thus. And now the carl found the boys and told them they could not stay there any longer. 'But I will send you to earl Sævil your uncle, and you will become famous men, the two of you—if you live that long.'

Hroar was now twelve years old, and Helgi ten, yet he was the bigger and bolder of them. So off they went now, and wherever they came or found men to talk to, the one gave his name as Ham and the other as Hrani. The boys arrived at earl Sævil's, and spent a week there before raising with the earl the question of their stay. 'I fancy,' he told them, 'you are no great acquisition, but I won't begrudge you your victuals for a while.' So they stayed there for a time, and proved rather a nuisance. Nothing came to light as to what men they were, or of what family. The earl suspected nothing, while for their part they left him in the dark as to who and what they were. It was some men's opinion that they must have been born scurf-ridden; they jeered at them because they always wore cowled cloaks, and never pulled the cowls back, so many concluded that they must be scurf-ridden. They remained there till the third winter.

On a certain occasion king Frothi summoned earl Sævil to a feast, for he had a pretty shrewd suspicion he would be harbouring the boys, because they were his wife's brothers. The earl made preparations for his journey and had a good following of men. The boys asked to go with him, but the earl said no, they should not. Signy the earl's wife went on this outing too. Ham (who was really Helgi) found himself an unbroken colt to ride; he went pelting after the company with his face to the nag's tail, and acting like a lunatic generally. Hrani his brother secured another such steed to ride, except that he was facing the right way round. The earl saw how they were riding up behind him, and had no control over their mounts. The shaggy colts were racing to and fro with them, and the cowl fell away from Hrani's face. Their sister Signy had a clear view of this. She knew them at once, and wept bitterly. The earl asked her why she wept, and she spoke this verse:

> 'Kin of the Skjoldungs,
> King of Lund,
> Broken their tree
> To branches only.

I saw my brothers
Barebacked riding,
But Sævil's men
On saddled steeds.'

'Big news,' said the earl, 'but do rt spread it abroad.'

He now rode back to them and ordered them to clear off home. They were a disgrace, he told them, to a decent gathering. So both lads now had to travel on foot. He spoke this way because he was concerned lest it be discovered from his words who these lads were. They went flitting round and about and had no more intention of turning back now than before, and so brought up the rear. Eventually they arrived at the feast, where they went racing up and down the length of the hall. Once they came to where Signy their sister was seated, and in a low voice she murmured to them: 'Do not stay in the hall. You are not yet grown to manhood.' But to this they paid no heed.

And now king Frothi began a harangue, how he meant to have king Halfdan's sons hunted down. Whoever could tell him news of them, he said, he would heap him with favours. A wise woman had come there, by the name of Heith, and king Frothi bade her use her magic arts and see what she could report concerning the boys. He prepared a noble feast against her coming, and set her on a high scaffold for her spell-making. Then the king asked her what she could see that was worth the telling. 'For I know,' he told her, 'that many things will now be revealed to you, and I observe omens of great good fortune in you, so answer me, sorceress, as fast as you can.'

She gaped her jaws asunder, and yawned mightily, and this verse came forth from her maw:

> 'Two are here within,
> I trust in neither,
> Who by your fireside
> Sit in splendour.'

'The boys, you mean,' demanded the king, 'or those who have helped them?'
She replied:

> 'They that long time
> On Vifil's isle lingered,
> Hounds' names they bore there,
> Hopp, aye, and Ho.'

At this moment Signy threw her a gold ring. She was pleased with her gift and now wanted to break off. 'However did this happen?' she cried. 'What I have said is a lie, and all my divination greatly astray.'

'If nothing better will serve your turn,' threatened the king, 'you shall be tortured till you speak out, for in such a throng of men I am no wiser than before what you are saying. And why is Signy not in her place? But maybe wolf now runs with wolf!'

He was informed that Signy had been made ill by the smoke which rose from the stove. Earl Sævil begged her to sit up and show a brave front. 'For more things than one can save the boys' lives, if that is fated to happen. So on no account let any discern in you what you are thinking, for at present we are helpless to aid them.'

King Frothi was pressing the sorceress hard,

bidding her tell the truth if she would not be put to the torture. She yawned mightily, and the spell came forth with difficulty, but she managed to chant this verse:

'I see them sitting,
Those sons of Halfdan,
Hroar and Helgi,
Hale, wholehearted.
Frothi's lifeblood
Soon they'll plunder—

unless they are quickly forestalled, which cannot be,' she said. After this she skipped down from the scaffold of prophecy, chanting:

'Piercing the eyes
Of Ham and Hrani;
Princes they,
And wondrous brave.'

After that the boys ran out to the forest, panic-stricken. Regin, their foster-father, now recognized them and was deeply moved. The sorceress gave them this sound advice, that they should save themselves, as she ran outwards along the hall. And now the king bade his men jump to it and look for them, but Regin quenched every light in the hall, so that this man was at grips with that, for some wanted them to escape, and for that reason they reached the forest.

'They came close this time,' said the king, 'and many now present will be involved in their plots and devices. A cruel vengeance shall follow for this, once there is leisure for it. But now we may drink the evening through, for they will be relieved to have got away, and their first concern will be to make themselves scarce.'

Regin began to ply men with drink. He dispensed ale with a will, and many another of his friends with him, so that they began falling down there in a stupor, one across the other. Meantime the brothers sat tight in the forest, as was told earlier, and when they had been there some time they caught sight of a man riding towards them from the direction of the hall. They knew past a shadow of doubt that the new-comer was Regin their foster-father; they were overjoyed to see him, and greeted him warmly. He did not acknowledge their greeting, but turned his horse round to face the hall. This took them aback, and they debated what it could mean. Then Regin turned his horse in their direction a second time, frowning as though he would attack them there and then. 'I think I understand what he wants,' said Helgi. Next he set off back to the hall, and they after him. 'My foster-father is acting this way,' Helgi explained, 'because he is unwilling to break his oaths to king Frothi. For that reason he will not speak to us, yet he is anxious to help us.'

Standing near the royal hall was a grove of trees belonging to the king, and as they reached it Regin spoke to himself thus: 'If I had great grievances against king Frothi I would burn down this grove.' Not one word did he speak beyond this.

'What does that mean?' asked Hroar.

'He wants us to go on to the hall,' said Helgi, 'and set fire to the place except for one particular exit.'

'How can we do that, two youngsters like us, when there are such overwhelming odds against us?'

'It can be done, even so,' Helgi assured him, 'for

we will have to take a chance some time or other if
we are to get our wrongs righted.'

So that was what they did. Presently out came
earl Sævil with all his men. 'Let us heap up the
fires,' he cried, 'and help these lads. I owe no duty
to king Frothi.'

King Frothi had two smiths who were masters
of their craft, and they were both called Var or
Wary. Regin shepherded all his followers, his
friends and relations, out by the hall door. Now king
Frothi woke up in the hall, puffing and blowing.
'I have dreamt a dream, lads,' said he, 'and by no
means a nice one. I will tell it you. I dreamt that
a voice called out to me, crying thus: "Now art thou
come home, king, thou and thy men." I seemed to
answer, somewhat querulously: "Home where?"
Then came the call, so near to me that I felt his
breath who called: "Home to Hel, home to Hel!"
said he who called. And with that I awoke.'

At this same moment they heard how Regin the
lads' foster-father was chanting a verse out by the
hall door:

> 'Outside it is Regin,
> And Halfdan's riders,
> Foes that are fearsome:
> Tell so much to Frothi.
> Var forged the nails,
> And Var drove their heads home;
> So Wary for Wary
> Was wary in warning.'

Small news that, said the king's men who were
inside the hall, that it was raining outside, and the
king's smiths were plying their craft, whether it was
nails they made or other implements.

'You think that no news?' cried the king. 'It does not sound that way to me. Regin has spoken to us of some danger that threatens; he is warning me to be on my guard, and will prove to be very cunning and crafty in his dealings with us.'

He walked towards the hall door and could see that there were enemies abroad. The entire hall began to blaze. King Frothi asked who were the leaders at this burning. Helgi, they told him, and Hroar his brother, were the leaders there. The king offered to make his peace with them, and bade them fix their own terms. 'For it is monstrous behaviour between kinsmen like us that one should seek to be the other's slayer.'

'No one can trust you,' retorted Helgi; 'and would you betray us any less than you did Halfdan my father? You are now going to pay for that.'

King Frothi turned away from the door to the mouth of his underground hiding-place, hoping to escape so to the woods and save his life. But when he came underground there was Regin facing him, and none too peaceful-looking either. So the king turned back and burned to death in his hall, and a great part of his host with him. And Sigrid, the mother of those brothers Helgi and Hroar, burned too, because she would not consent to go out. The brothers gave thanks to their kinsman earl Sævil for his strong support, and to Regin their foster-father likewise, and all their following. They gave fine gifts to many, and it was after this fashion they took over the kingdom, and all that property king Frothi had been possessed of, his lands and valuables too.

The brothers were unlike in disposition. Hroar was gentle and genial, but Helgi a great fighting-man, and he was thought to be the more important man altogether; and so things continued for a while. And with that the story of Frothi comes to an end, and that of Hroar and Helgi, the sons of Halfdan, begins.

The Story of Helgi

There was a king by the name of Northri ruling over part of England, and his daughter's name was Ogn. Hroar spent long years with king Northri as his land's stay and defender; there was close friendship between them, and finally Hroar came to marry Ogn and settled down to rule that kingdom with king Northri his father-in-law, while Helgi ruled over Denmark, their patrimony. Earl Sævil ruled over a kingdom of his own together with Signy; their son's name was Hrok. Helgi Halfdanarson stayed unmarried in Denmark. Regin fell ill and died, which seemed a great pity to everyone, for he was a well-beloved man.

Ruling over Germany at this same time was a queen by the name of Olof, who was every inch the war-king in her ways, wearing shield and corslet, a sword at her side, and a helm on her head. In that mould was she made: lovely of countenance, but fierce-hearted and haughty. By common consent she was the best match men had ever heard tell of in those days in the Northlands, yet she would not take a husband. King Helgi learned of this queen's imperious temper, and thought he would greatly enhance his fame by winning the lady for wife, whether she happened to be for it or against. So one day he travelled that way with a great host. He came to the land where this greatest of queens held sway, and came there all unknown to her. He sent men of his on to the hall, bidding them have queen Olof informed that he would be pleased to receive hospitality there along with his retinue. The

messengers announced this to the queen; it caught
her unawares, with no chance of gathering an army,
so she chose what she thought the lesser of two evils:
to invite king Helgi to a feast with all his retinue.

King Helgi came now to the feast and occupied
the high-seat alongside the queen. They drank
together during the evening. There was no lack of
good things there, nor was the least sign of low
spirits to be discerned in queen Olof. Then king
Helgi had this to announce to the queen: 'The case
is this way,' he said, 'that I want us to drink our
wedding feast this same evening. There is a sufficient
gathering present for it, and you and I will share
one bed tonight.'

'In my opinion, sire,' she replied, 'that is to proceed over-abruptly. No man alive strikes me as more
admirable than you, if I have no option but to yield
myself to a husband, but I trust you are not proposing to act dishonourably in the matter.'

The king replied that what she deserved for her
arrogance and pride was that 'we spend such time
together as I please'.

'I should choose,' said she, 'to have more of my
friends present, but there is nothing I can do about
it; it is for you to command, and you will treat our
person with due consideration.'

That evening there was hard drinking, and long
into the night. The queen was merry enough, and
no one could detect any sign in her but that she
looked forward to her nuptials with pleasure. In
course of time the king was led off to bed, and she
was there before him. The king had drunk so hard
that without more ado he collapsed on the bed in
a stupor. The queen took advantage of this and
pierced him with a sleep-thorn; and the minute they

were all gone, up she got, shaved off all his hair, and daubed him with tar. Next she took a closed hammock and stuffed it with various garments, after which she laid hold of the king and swaddled him up in the hammock. After that she got hold of some men and had them lug him away to his ships. She then roused his men, telling them that their king had gone to his ships and was wanting to sail, because a favourable wind had sprung up. They tumbled out as fast as they could, but they were so drunk that they hardly knew what they were doing. In this state they reached the ships, where they saw no sign of the king, but they did see that an enormous hammock had been delivered there. They grew curious to know what was inside it, and after this fashion passed the time of waiting for the king, thinking he would be along any moment. But when they unfurled the hammock, they found their king inside, disgracefully maltreated. The sleep-thorn was then shaken out of him, and the king awoke from a dream by no means pleasant. He now felt most evilly disposed towards the queen.

Of the other camp there is this to report, that queen Olof assembled her army overnight, so that she did not want for men, and king Helgi saw no chance of getting at her. Next they heard the sound of trumpets and a war-blast ashore. The king recognized that his best prospect was to hold out and away as fast as he could. There was a good wind for this too. King Helgi now sailed back home to his kingdom with this shame and dishonour. He was full of resentment and often studied how he might be revenged on the queen.

Queen Olof now stayed in her own country for a while, and her arrogance and tyranny had never been greater than now. She kept strong watch and ward about her after that feast she had given king Helgi. News of that exploit soon spread far and wide, and it seemed a monstrous thing to everyone that she had made a laughing-stock of such a king as he. No great while afterwards, Helgi held from land with his ship, and on this particular expedition brought her to Germany, where queen Olof was in residence, with a strong body of men about her. He ran his ship into a hidden creek, and then announced to his crew that they should wait for him there till the third day, but be on their way if he had not then returned. He had two chests with him, full of gold and silver, and wore rags and tatters for his outer garments. He now made his way to the forest, where he hid his riches in a safe place, moving off thereafter into the neighbourhood of the queen's hall. He came across one of her thralls and asked him what news of the land. The times were good and peaceful, said the thrall, and asked him who he might be.

He was a beggarman, he said. 'And yet a rich find has come my way in the forest, and I think it might be a good move to show you where that treasure is.' So back they went to the forest and he showed him his treasure, and the thrall was much impressed by the good fortune which had come his way.

'How greedy is the queen after money?' the beggarman asked.

She was the most avaricious of women, said the thrall.

'Then she has a pleasure in store,' said the beggarman, 'and will consider that she owns this money I have found here, because this is her territory. Well, good luck must not now be changed to bad. I will not conceal these riches, but the queen shall allot me such shares as she will, and that will prove best for me. But will she be prepared to take the trouble of coming here to fetch it?'

'I am sure of it,' said the thrall, 'if it can be managed secretly.'

'Here is a necklace,' said the beggar, 'and here a ring, which I will give you if you will bring her here all alone to the forest, and I will put everything right again, should she be angry with you.'

This was their compact and bargain, so off he went now and told the queen how he had found in the forest riches so immense as to furnish out the happiness of many, many men; and he begged her go with him in haste to fetch the treasure.

'If what you tell me is true,' she said, 'you shall reap fortune from your tale, but death otherwise. However, since I have hitherto found you a man to be trusted, I will believe in your words now.'

She showed in this how grasping she was, going off with him secretly by dead of night, so that none but they two knew of it. But once they reached the forest, who should be there but Helgi, who caught her in his arms, declaring this encounter of theirs a happy occasion for avenging his dishonour. The queen confessed she had used him badly. 'But I will now make you full amends for all that, and do you arrange my wedding in honour.'

'Never!' he told her. 'There is no question of it. You shall come on board ship with me and stay as long as I choose. For my pride's sake I cannot bring myself not to get my own back on you, such a vile, humiliating trick as you played on me.'

'It is for you to command,' she admitted, 'this time.'

For many a night the king slept with the queen, after which she returned home, and such vengeance had now been taken on her as is reported. She was bitterly resentful of her state. After this incident king Helgi sailed away raiding, and a famous man was he. But Olof in course of time gave birth to a child, a little girl, for whom she had no natural feelings whatsoever. She had a hound called Yrsa, and it was after this hound she named her child. Yrsa, that was what she should be called. She was a lovely child to look upon, but once she was twelve years old she had to tend the sheep, and never knew herself to be other than the child of a peasant and his peasant wife. For the queen had gone about this so secretly that few men knew that she had conceived and borne a child.

So it continued till the girl was thirteen years old. What happened then was that king Helgi came sailing to that land, and was curious to know what had happened there. He was wearing the trappings of a beggar. Near the forest he observed an immense flock, and tending it a young girl so lovely that he thought he had never seen woman more fair. He asked what might her name and lineage be.

'I am a peasant's daughter,' she told him. 'My name is Yrsa.'

'You have not thrall's eyes,' he said, and that same instant love of her pierced his heart. How right it would be, he said, for a beggarman to marry her, since she was only a peasant man's daughter. She begged him not to do this, but he seized her as he had thought to do, betaking himself off to his ships, and then sailing back to his own country. When queen Olof learned this, she acted with cunning and deceit regarding it, pretending to know nothing of what was taking place, and what came into her head was this: that this would work to king Helgi's sorrow and shame, and bring him no profit or happiness either. So king Helgi married Yrsa and loved her dearly.

King Helgi had a ring to which great fame was attached. Both brothers wished to possess it, and Signy too, their sister. One day king Hroar came visiting the realm of king Helgi his brother, and Helgi prepared a noble feast against his coming. Said king Hroar, 'You will be the better man of us two, and because I have made my abode in Northumberland, I will readily grant you this kingdom which we possess between us, if only you will share with me some great valuable. I should like to obtain this ring, which is the best treasure in your possession, and which the two of us would then own.'

'Brother,' said king Helgi, 'nothing will meet the case but that the ring is all yours.'

They were both well pleased with this talk of theirs. King Helgi now gave the ring to king Hroar his brother, who departed for his own kingdom and remained there in peace and quiet.

The next thing that happened was that their uncle earl Sævil died, and Hrok his son succeeded him to his dominion. He was a grim-hearted man and highly covetous. His mother had much to tell him about this ring the brothers owned. 'To me,' she said, 'it would have seemed only right for my brothers to remember us with some territory or other for the way we stood by them in the vengeance for our father, but they have shown no gratitude whatever for this to your father and me.'

'What you say is plain as day,' agreed Hrok, 'and such conduct is a scandal. I will now take up with them whether they are prepared to give us our dues in this matter.'

Later on he went to see king Helgi and claimed from him a third of the Danish realm, or that good ring, for he was not aware that Hroar had it now.

'You express yourself very forcibly, not to say arrogantly,' replied the king. 'We won this realm by daring, staking our lives for it with the help of your father, and Regin my foster-father, and other good men who were willing to give us their aid. Now, we are willing to make you some return, to be sure, if you are prepared to accept it, for the sake of our kinship with you. But this kingdom has cost me so dear that I will on no account relinquish it, while as for the ring, king Hroar has now taken possession of it, and I doubt whether it will be handed over on your account.'

With that away went Hrok, much disgruntled, and sought a meeting with king Hroar. Hroar gave him a welcome both warm and gracious, and he stayed with him for a while. Then one day when they were sailing off the coast, and lay at anchor in a certain firth, Hrok said this: 'It would seem to me a deed well worthy of you, uncle, if you gave me that good ring of yours, and so remembered our relationship.'

'I have given so much to obtain this ring,' said the king, 'that I will on no account let it go.'

'Then you must permit me to look at the ring,' said Hrok, 'for I have the greatest curiosity to know whether it is so precious a jewel as they say.'

'That is a small thing to grant you,' said Hroar. 'You shall certainly be indulged so far.' And he put the ring into his hands.

Hrok contemplated the ring for some time, and

agreed it was impossible to overpraise it. 'I have never seen such a treasure, and there is every excuse for your thinking it the very paragon of rings. And now the best thing is that neither you nor I shall enjoy it, nor anyone else for that matter.' And with those words he hurled the ring from his hand as far out to sea as he could.

'Scoundrel that you are!' cried king Hroar. He had Hrok's feet chopped off, and packed him off so to his own country. But in no time at all he was so far recovered that his stumps were healed, whereupon he assembled himself a host and determined to avenge his shame. He obtained a great following of men and came upon Northumberland all unawares, at a place where king Hroar was feasting with a small company. Hrok at once launched his attack, there was a fierce struggle, and the difference in numbers was great. King Hroar was slain, and Hrok subjugated the kingdom. He usurped the royal title and demanded Ogn, king Northri's daughter, in marriage, she who before had been wife to king Hroar his kinsman.

King Northri now found himself in a cruel dilemma, for he was an old man and in poor trim for fighting. He told Ogn his daughter to what straits they were come. Old though he was, he assured her, it was not his wish to evade continuing the struggle, so long as that did not go contrary to her own inclination. In great sorrow she answered: 'Truly it is contrary to my wish. But on condition that some respite is granted, even so I will not reject him, because I see that your life lies at stake; for I am with child, and that is the business that must be worked out first. For it was king Hroar begot that child on me.'

The matter was now put to Hrok, who was willing
to grant a respite if he should then proceed the more
easily to the kingdom and his marriage. Hrok
thought he had done great things for himself on this
campaign, when he had slain so famous and powerful a king. But at this same moment Ogn was sending
men to seek audience of king Helgi, bidding them
inform him that she would never enter Hrok's bed
if she were free to choose and not compelled to it.
'For I am with child by king Hroar.'

The messengers went and reported exactly what
they were bidden. Said king Helgi: 'This was wisely
spoken on her part, for I will avenge Hroar my
brother.' But of this Hrok had no suspicion.

Queen Ogn now gave birth to a son who was
called Agnar, who at an early age was big and full of
promise. And once king Helgi had news of this he
assembled a host and went to encounter Hrok. A
battle took place, and it ended in Hrok's being taken
prisoner. 'You are the vilest of chieftains,' said king
Helgi, 'yet I shall not have you put to death, for it
is a greater shame for you to live in torment.' He
then had his legs and arms broken, and packed him
off to his own country in such condition that he was
good for nothing at all.

When Agnar Hroarsson was twelve years old,
people thought they had never seen the like of him,
for in all accomplishments whatsoever he went far
beyond other men. He became a warrior so great and
famous that it is widely reported of him in old stories
that he will have been the greatest champion of times
past and present too. He inquired where was the
firth where Hrok had flung the ring overboard.
Many had tried for it with all kinds of stratagems,
yet failed to find it. But according to the story,

Agnar brought his ship into this firth, saying: 'It would be a good move now to try for the ring, if only somebody had a clear bearing for it.' He was then informed where it had been cast into the sea, and later Agnar made ready and dived into the depths, and came up but had no ring. Down he went a second time, but had not laid hands on it when he surfaced. 'A slovenly search so far,' remarked Agnar, and went down for the third time, and now came up with the ring. By this deed he grew famous past telling, more famous than his father even.

King Helgi now stayed in his own kingdom over the winters, but went on viking cruises of a summer, and became a famous man. He and Yrsa loved each other dearly and had a son who was called Hrolf and with the passing of the years became a man of great renown. Queen Olof heard tell how Helgi and Yrsa loved each other so dearly and were happy in their marriage. This displeased her greatly, and she went to renew acquaintance with them. When she arrived in their country she sent word to queen Yrsa, and when they met Yrsa invited her back to the hall with her. She had no desire for that, she said. It was not for her to repay king Helgi any honour.

'How shamefully you treated me when I lived with you,' said Yrsa. 'And can you not tell me something about my parentage, what it really is, for I suspect it is not as I am told, that I am the daughter of a peasant man and woman?'

'It is not out of the question that I could tell you a thing or two about that too,' queen Olof agreed. 'It was the whole point of my errand here to enlighten you on that head. But tell me, are you happy in your marriage?'

'I am so, and well may I be happy, since I have

the most magnificent and far-famed king for husband.'

'That is not such a good reason for happiness as you suppose,' said queen Olof, 'for that same king is your father, and you are my daughter.'

'I think my mother the vilest and cruellest of women,' cried Yrsa, 'for this is an enormity that can never be lost to mind.'

'In this you have suffered for Helgi and my anger,' Olof admitted, 'but I am now going to invite you to return home with me in honour and esteem, and in every respect I will treat you as best I know how.'

'I do not know how that will work out,' said Yrsa, 'but I must not stay here, now that I have learnt of this horror which lies over us.'

Later she met king Helgi and told him what a cruel pass they were come to.

'Cruel enough is the mother you had,' said the king; 'yet for my part I would leave things as they are.'

It was impossible, she answered, in such circumstances, for them to live together from that day forth. So now Yrsa went away with queen Olof and dwelt in Germany for a while, which so cut king Helgi to the heart that he took to his bed and was unhappy past telling. It was thought there could be no better match than Yrsa, but for all that the kings were slow to ask for her hand, and what had most to do with this was that no real assurance could be felt but that Helgi would yet come for her and show his displeasure if she were bestowed on another.

There was a king named Athils, powerful and covetous, who ruled over Sweden and dwelt at his chief stronghold, Uppsala. He heard tell of the lady Yrsa, then put his ships in readiness, and sailed to seek audience of Olof and her daughter. Olof prepared a feast against king Athils's coming and welcomed him with every refinement and courtesy. He asked for queen Yrsa as his wife. 'You will have heard how things stand with her,' replied Olof, 'but granted her consent, we make no denial here.' The matter was now put to Yrsa, who answered thus. No good would come of it, she claimed. 'For you are a king without a friend to your name.' But the affair went forward, whether she was for it or against, and Athils took her away without reference to king Helgi, because Athils reckoned himself the greater monarch. Indeed, king Helgi knew nothing about this till they had arrived back in Sweden, where king Athils married her with pomp and ceremony. It was only then that king Helgi got news of it, and felt twice as bad as before. He slept now in a house apart, with no companions. And now queen Olof is out of the story, and so things continued for a while.

Then one Yule-eve, when king Helgi had gone to bed and there was foul weather abroad, the story goes that there came a knocking, a rather faint knocking, at the door. It struck him how unkingly it would be to leave this benighted creature outside when he might help it, so he went and opened the door, and saw how some poor tattered creature had come there. It spoke—'This is well done of you, king'—and then came inside the house.

'Cover yourself with straw and a bearskin,' said the king, 'that you may not freeze to death.'

'Share your bed with me, sire,' it pleaded. 'I would sleep alongside you, for my very life is at stake.'

'My gorge rises at you,' said the king, 'but if it

is as you say, then lie here in your clothes at the bed's edge, and then it will not harm me.'

She did so, and the king turned the other way from her. There was a light burning in the house, and after a while he peered over his shoulder at her, and saw that it was a woman lying there, so lovely that he thought he had never before beheld woman more fair. She was dressed in a gown of silk. He turned to her quickly and joyfully, but, 'I wish to take my leave now,' she told him. 'You have released me from hard durance, for this was my stepmother's curse on me, and many kings have I visited in their homes. Do not now end with wickedness. It is not my wish to stay here any longer.'

'No, no,' said the king, 'there can be no question of your leaving so soon. We will not part so. And now we must patch up a wedding for you, for you please me greatly.'

'It is for you to command, sire,' she said, and they slept together that night. Then in the morning she had this to say: 'Now that you have subjected me to your lust, you may know this, that we will have a child. Now, king, do as I tell you. Come to collect our child at this same time next winter at your boat-house. If you do not, you shall pay for it.' And with that she went away.

King Helgi was now in somewhat better spirits than before. Time wore on, but to this he paid no heed. Then after a three years' interval it happened that three men came riding to this same house where the king lay sleeping. It was midnight. They had with them a girl child and set her down near the house. The woman who had brought the child had this to say: 'Know, king,' she said, 'that your kinsfolk must pay for this, that you set at naught the thing I bade you. Yet you yourself shall reap the benefit that you freed me from the spell laid upon me. Know too that this girl's name is Skuld. She is our daughter.'

After that these men rode away. His visitor had been an elf-woman, and the king never learned what became of her thereafter; but Skuld grew up in his household and soon grew fierce of heart. Then one day, says the story, king Helgi made his preparations for a voyage abroad, proposing in that way to forget his troubles. He left his son Hrolf behind him, and went raiding far and wide, and wrought many a deed of might.

All this while king Athils was dwelling at Uppsala. He had twelve berserks whom he kept for his land's defence and against all perils and onsets. And now king Helgi made preparations for his voyage to Uppsala, to carry off Yrsa. He reached the land, and when king Athils had news of this, how king Helgi had arrived there in his kingdom, he asked queen Yrsa how she would have king Helgi welcomed.

'You will decide as to that,' she told him, 'but you know already that there is no man alive to whom I stand in closer relationship than he.'

So king Athils saw fit to invite him to a feast, not that he intended it to be free from guile. King Helgi accepted and went to the feast with a hundred men, but his main force stayed down at the ships. King Athils welcomed him with open arms. Queen Yrsa thought to reconcile the kings, and conducted herself in the most gracious manner towards king Helgi; while king Helgi was so happy to see the queen that he let all else slip by unheeded. He wished to be talking with her all the hours he could find, and so they sat down to the feast.

It happened now that king Athils's berserks returned home, and the minute they reached land king Athils went off to meet them, in such fashion, too, that no one else knew about it. He ordered them to proceed to the forest which lay between his stronghold and king Helgi's ships, telling them to launch an attack from there on king Helgi as he was going to his ships. 'Also, I will send a company to your help which shall take them in the rear, so that they are caught as in a pincers. For I want to make certain now that king Helgi does not get away, for I discern that he still so loves the queen that I am taking no chances over any design of his.'

Meanwhile king Helgi sat at the feast, and this treachery was kept from him carefully, and from the queen too. Queen Yrsa told king Athils that she desired him to give king Helgi great and costly presents at parting, and so he did; he gave the king gold and jewels too, yet in fact he intended them only for himself. So now king Helgi made his departure, and king Athils and the queen saw him on his way, and the queen and the two kings made a cordial parting. But not long after king Athils had turned back, king Helgi and his men found that hostilities were come upon them, and the fighting started at once. King Helgi put up a fierce resistance, and fought like a hero, but because of the overwhelming odds against him king Helgi fell there with much glory, and with many and great wounds upon him, for part of king Athils's force took them in the rear, so that they were crushed between the hammer and the anvil. Queen Yrsa knew nothing of this until king Helgi had fallen and the battle was over. With Helgi fell the entire force which had gone ashore, but the rest of his following fled back home to Denmark. And there ends the story of king Helgi.

King Athils now exulted in his victory, and thought he had taken a great step forward when he overcame a king of such fame and wide renown as Helgi. But as Yrsa told him: 'Bragging your head off is not what you should be doing, even though you have betrayed the man who stood closest to me and whom I loved most. And for this same reason I shall never be loyal to you if you clash with king Helgi's kinsmen. I will contrive the death of your berserks just as soon as I can, should there be any so brave as to do that for my sake and of their own prowess.'

King Athils advised her not to threaten him or his berserks. 'For it will do you no good. But I am willing to make you amends for your father's death with generous gifts, large grants of money, and precious jewels, if you can bring yourself to agree.'

By this means the queen was pacified and accepted redress from the king. Yet at heart she still remained unappeased, and often watched her opportunity to do the berserks harm and dishonour. From now on men never found the queen very joyful or sweet-tempered after king Helgi's fall; there was more wrangling in hall than ever before, nor would the queen do anything to please the king if she could help it.

King Athils now considered himself to have become very famous, and anyone who served with him and his champions was considered to be a very great man. He remained in his own kingdom for a while, believing none would lift shield against him and his berserks. King Athils was a great idolator and full of sorcery.

The Story of Svipdag

Living in Sweden, remote from other men, was a farmer by the name of Svip. He was well-to-do and had been a great champion, and was by no means the simple man he appeared to be: he was, indeed, a man of divers strange skills. He had three sons whose names come into this story, one called Svipdag, a second Beigath, and a third Hvitserk, who was the eldest of them. They were all men of mark, strong, and of handsome appearance.

One day when Svipdag was eighteen years old he spoke to his father this way: 'Dreary is our life, living up here in the mountains, in hidden folkless valleys, never visiting other people, nor other people us. It would be a better move to go to king Athils, and if only he would have us take service in his retinue, along with him and his champions.'

'That seems no such good plan to me,' replied the good Svip, 'for king Athils is a grim man, and not trustworthy, though his outward showing is a fair one; while his men, though mighty, are full of malice. Yet, admittedly, king Athils is a powerful and famous man.'

'Something must be risked if a man is to distinguish himself,' said Svipdag, 'nor can we know till we try which way our luck will go. Certainly I am not going to stay here any longer, whatever else the future may hold.'

So since he was so set on this, his father gave him a big axe, as handsome as it was sharp, and spoke thus to his son: 'Covet nothing of your neighbour's; act without arrogance, for that is open to men's blame; but defend yourself should you be attacked, for it is a noble thing to boast little about oneself, yet achieve a great destiny if one is put to the test.' And he gave him armour, all of it choice, and a fine horse.

Svipdag now rode away, and by evening reached king Athils's stronghold. He saw that there were games being held out in front of the hall, and king Athils was sitting on a big golden throne, with his berserks alongside him. When Svipdag reached the fence palings, the gate of the stronghold was locked, for it was the custom in those days to ask leave to ride in. But Svipdag did not waste labour on this: he promptly broke open the gate and rode so into the courtyard.

'This man proceeds unconcernedly,' said the king. 'Such a thing has never been essayed before. Maybe he is a man of great powers, and it was of no particular moment though he made trial of this.'

The berserks were instantly all scowls, considering that he had borne himself most arrogantly. Svipdag rode before the king and greeted him courteously; he knew the fine points of such procedure. King Athils asked who he might be, and he told him. The king placed him at once, and everyone felt sure he must be a great champion and a man of much consequence.

Meanwhile the game was continuing just the same, and Svipdag sat down on a bench to look on at it. The berserks were giving him dirty looks, and now they told the king that they would test his mettle. 'He is no weakling, I believe,' said the king, 'but I am quite happy you should test whether he is all he appears to be.' Next they all thronged into the hall. The berserks walked up to Svipdag, asking whether he was some kind of hero maybe, the big way he was acting. As much a hero as any of them, he replied. At these words of his their rage and vehemence grew still greater, but the king bade them keep the peace that evening. The berserks were scowling and bawling aloud and challenging Svipdag: 'Do you dare fight with us? For that you will need deploy more than mere big words and insolence. We want to try just how mighty you really are.'

'I will consent,' he told them, 'to fight with you one at a time, and so discover whether any more care to try their hand.'

The king was well content that they should make trial of each other so. But, 'This man shall be welcome here,' said queen Yrsa. The berserks had an answer for her: 'We knew already that you wished us all in Hel, but we are in too fine fettle to fall down for mere words or ill wishes.' The queen retorted that it would not come to that, that the king would make trial of what value he owned in them, in whom he had so much faith. 'Ah,' said the berserk who was their leader, 'I shall so settle with you, and so sort your pride, that we need have no fear of him.'

So in the morning bitter combat was joined, nor were heavy strokes wanting. All could see that the new-comer knew how to make his sword bite with immense force, and the berserk completely gave way before him, till Svipdag slew him there. Instantly there was a second wanting to kill him and avenge his comrade, but he dealt with him the same way. He made no pause till he had killed four of them. 'You have wrought me great harm,' cried king Athils, 'and now you shall pay for it!' He bade his men rise and kill him. On the other hand, the queen mustered a force of her own, proposing to succour him. The king could see, she said, that there was far more worth in Svipdag alone than in all the berserks put together. The queen now made peace between them, and Svipdag appeared to them all a man of outstanding valour.

At queen Yrsa's direction he took his seat on the lower bench opposite the king. Then as night came on he looked round, feeling that he had still dealt too leniently with the berserks, and wanting to provoke them to a clash. He judged it likely that if they saw him all on his own they would attack him, and it turned out just as he thought, for they came to blows in a flash. But when they had been fighting for a while, up came the king and parted them. After this he had those berserks who were still alive banished, because they had not overcome one solitary man between them; he swore that he had not known till now that apart from their big words they were such paltry creatures. So off they had to go, full of threats though about harrying king Athils's kingdom. He cared not a straw for their threats, vowed the king, and maintained there was no heart in such sons of bitches. So away they went now, in shame and dishonour. Yet in fact it was king Athils who in the first place egged them on to attack and destroy Svipdag whenever they observed him leave the hall alone, and revenge themselves in such fashion that the queen would have no suspicion of it. Svipdag, however, had killed one of them by the time the king arrived to part them.

King Athils bade Svipdag prove no less a stay to him now than was the case before, when all his berserks were there to help him. 'And this most of all, because the queen desires that you should take the berserks' place.' So Svipdag remained with him for a while.

Somewhat later news of hostilities reached the king, how the berserks had provided themselves with a great host and were harrying his land. King Athils bade Svipdag rise up against the berserks. This was his duty, he maintained, and he promised to supply him with as great a host as he needed. Svipdag did not fancy taking command of the army, but was prepared to go with the king wherever he wanted. But nothing would satisfy the king except that he took command.

'Then I must receive at your hands twelve men's lives, whenever I please,' said Svipdag.

'That I will grant you,' said the king.

After that Svipdag marched to battle, while the king skulked at home. He had a strong body of men. Svipdag had caltrops made and planted them where the battlefield had been staked out, and he had that ground prepared with many other tricky devices too. Battle began there, and hard fighting; the pirate host yielded a lot of ground, and they were in serious trouble when they got a taste of the caltrops. One berserk was slain there, together with a multitude of their host, and those who survived fled to the ships and so away.

Svipdag now returned to king Athils and had a victory to boast of. The king thanked him warmly for his success and his defence of the land. Said queen Yrsa, 'Surely that seat is better filled when a warrior such as Svipdag sits in it than when it was filled with your berserks.' The king said how true that was.

The berserks who had got away now reassembled their host, and came harrying a second time in king Athils's kingdom. Again king Athils called on Svipdag to march against them, promising to furnish him with a fine army. Svipdag marched to battle, and this time had a force less by a third than the berserks. King Athils promised to come and join him with his bodyguard. Svipdag had moved off faster than the berserks expected; they clashed together and a fierce struggle took place. King Athils mustered his army and had planned to take the berserks on their un-shielded flank.

Now we must turn to consider the good Svip. There came a time when he awoke from sleep, sighed wearily, and said to his sons: 'Svipdag your brother finds himself in need of help now, for he does battle against immense odds not far from here. He has lost one of his eyes, and has many a wound besides. He has killed three berserks, but there are still three others left.'

The brothers moved quickly, armed themselves, and then went to where the battle was taking place. The pirate host had as many men again as Svipdag. Svipdag had done great deeds, but by now bore many wounds, and one of his eyes was gone. His men were dying in heaps, yet the king did not come to his aid. But once his brothers reached the battle they went briskly forward to where the berserks were, and the end of the game was that all the ber-serks fell there before the brothers. And straightway the heavy slaughter shifted to the pirate host, and those who chose to live surrendered to the brothers.

After that they went to meet king Athils and told him these tidings. The king thanked them heartily for their gallant achievement. Svipdag had received two wounds in the arms, he had a great wound on the head, and was one-eyed for the rest of his life. He was laid up for a while with these wounds, but queen Yrsa cured him. When he had grown quite well again, he told the king that he wished to be off. 'I will visit that king in his court who will do us more honour than you have done, king. A sorry return you made me for defending your land and such a victory as we won for you.'

King Athils begged him to stay. He would treat the brothers handsomely, he said, and vowed he would value none more highly than them. But Svipdag wanted nothing save to ride away, above all because king Athils had not come to the battle till it was all over, because he was doubtful whether victory would lie with Svipdag or the berserks; for the king was in a certain forest, and from there looked on at their struggle, and could have joined in any moment he chose, but in fact it would have been all one to him had Svipdag suffered defeat and bit the dust.

The brothers now prepared to be on their way, and nothing availed to stop them. King Athils asked where they were planning to go. As to that, they told him, they had not made up their minds. 'But for the time being we must part. I want to acquaint myself with other men's customs, and other kings' ways, and not await my old age here in Sweden.' They now went to their horses, and thanked the queen courteously for the favour she had shown to Svipdag, then mounted and rode their way till they came to their father's, and asked him to advise them what course to adopt. 'And what shall we turn to now?'

In his opinion, he said, the finest thing of all was to be with king Hrolf and his champions in Denmark. 'There lies your best hope of some advancement to content your pride, for I have learned for a fact that the greatest heroes of the Northlands are come there.'

'What kind of man is he?' Svipdag asked.

'I am told this of king Hrolf,' said his father, 'that he is liberal and free-handed, trustworthy, and particular as to his friends, so that his equal is not to be found. Nor is he sparing of gold and treasures to wellnigh all who care to receive them. He is not all that to look at, but mighty and enduring under pressure; the handsomest of men, harsh towards the oppressor but kindly and gracious to the needy, as to all those who offer him no resistance; the humblest of men, so that he answers the poor as gently as the rich. So great and glorious a man is he that his name will never be forgotten as long as this world is lived in. Further, he has levied tribute on all the kings who dwell near him, for all are ready and anxious to do him service.'

'You have such a tale to tell of this,' said Svipdag, 'that I have decided to go and find king Hrolf, aye, and if he will have us, all we brothers.'

'You must decide for yourself your goings and doings,' said farmer Svip, 'but in my view it would be best for you to stay at home with me.'

It was useless asking that, they told him; and later they wished their father happy days, and their mother too, and went their ways until such time as they fell in with king Hrolf. Without more ado Svipdag entered the king's presence and greeted him. The king asked who might he be. Svipdag. told him his own name and the names of them all, adding that they had spent some time with king Athils.

'Why have you come here then?' asked the king. 'For there is no great friendship between Athils and men of mine.'

'I know that, sire,' Svipdag admitted. 'All the same, I am asking to be made a liegeman of yours, if the chance exists, and all my brothers too, even though we must seem to you of little consequence.'

'I had not been planning to make friends of king Athils's men,' said the king, 'but because you have sought audience of me I will make you welcome, for I think he will get the better of the bargain who does not turn you away, for I can see that you are gallant fellows. It has reached my ears how you won great renown by killing king Athils's berserks and accomplishing many other notable deeds.'

'Where will you direct me to sit?' asked Svipdag.

'Sit by the man whose name is Bjalki,' said the king, 'but leave room for twelve men inwards of you.'

Before he went away Svipdag had promised king Athils that he would come back to him. But now the brothers went to the place the king directed them to. Svipdag asked Bjalki why must they leave those empty places inwards of them? Because the king's twelve berserks sit there, explained Bjalki, when they come home. Just then they were out raiding.

One of king Hrolf's daughters was named Skur, and the other Drifa. Drifa lived at home with the king and was the most courteous of women. Drifa was kindness itself to the brothers, and well-disposed towards them in every way.

That was the fashion of it all through the summer, till the day the berserks returned to court in the autumn. In accordance with their custom they walked up to every man when they entered the hall, and he who walked at their head asked whether the man who sat there before him reckoned himself as brave as he was. Men had recourse to such different turns of speech as struck them as least galling, yet it could be gathered from the words of every one of them that he felt himself far short of proving their match. Now he came up to Svipdag and asked whether he reckoned himself as brave as he. Svipdag jumped to his feet, plucked out his sword, and vowed he was no less brave than he in every respect.

'Hew at my helm then,' invited the berserk.

Svipdag did so, but made no impression on it. Then they would have fought, but king Hrolf ran between them. It would not be allowed, he told them, and henceforth they should be adjudged equal—'and both my friends'. So after this they were reconciled to each other and at all times of one accord. They went out raiding and had the victory wherever they came.

King Hrolf now sent men to Sweden to visit queen Yrsa his mother, requesting her to send him those riches which king Helgi his father had owned and king Athils had usurped when king Helgi was killed. Yrsa agreed that it would be but right and proper should she bring this about, if only it were possible for her. 'And should you yourself come to fetch that treasure, I shall give you wholesome counsel, my son. But king Athils is a man so greedy after money that he cares not a straw what he does for it.' And that is what she bade them tell king Hrolf, and she sent him honourable gifts in addition.

King Hrolf was now busied on viking raids, and this delayed his encounter with king Athils. He brought under his command an immense body of men, and all the kings he encountered he made tributary to him, and what contributed most to this was that all the foremost champions wanted to be with him and serve no one else, for he was much more generous with money than other kings. King Hrolf established his chief seat at the place called Leire. That is in

Denmark, a big, powerful stronghold; and in every aspect of munificence there was more pomp and splendour there than in any other place whatsoever —more, indeed, than any one had ever heard tell of.

There was a mighty king called Hjorvarth, who married Skuld, king Helgi's daughter and sister to king Hrolf. This was done with the consent of king Athils and queen Yrsa, and of king Hrolf her brother too. On some occasion or other king Hrolf invited his brother-in-law Hjorvarth to a feast, and one day while he was at this feast it chanced to happen that the kings were standing out in the open air, when king Hrolf untied his belt and handed his sword to king Hjorvarth the while. When king Hrolf had fastened his belt once more, he took back his sword, and said this to king Hjorvarth: 'We both know,' he said, 'that it has long been a saying that he who accepts another man's sword while he shifts his belt shall be his underling ever after. So now you shall be my under-king and bear it patiently like the rest of them.'

Hjorvarth was incensed by this, but had to let it stand even so. He returned home with this for his pains, and was deeply resentful of his lot. But with it all he paid tribute to king Hrolf, just like those other tributary kings of his who had no choice but to do him homage.

And at this point Svipdag's story ends.

The Story of Bothvar

The story must now be told how north in Norway a king by the name of Hring ruled over Uppdalir. He had a son named Bjorn. The news now was that his queen died, and this appeared a great loss to the king as to many others besides. His countrymen and counsellors urged him to marry again, and it came about that he sent men into southern lands to find him a wife. But strong head-winds and mighty storms rose against them; they had to turn their prows and run before the wind, and it came to such a pass that they were driven north to Finnmark, where they spent the winter.

One day they went up inland and came to a certain house. Inside sat two women, handsome of countenance, who welcomed them courteously, asking from whence they had come. They told them everything about their wanderings, and what their business was, and inquired what women they might be, and for what reason women so lovely and fair were come there all alone, so far from other folk. Said the elder, 'There is a reason for everything, lads. We are here because a mighty king asked for my daughter and she would not have him, and by way of return he promised her rough treatment. So I have her here in hiding for as long as her father remains from home, for he is out raiding.'

They asked who her father might be, and her mother told them. 'She is daughter of the king of the Lapps.'

They asked what were their names, and the elder answered, 'I am called Ingibjorg, but my daughter's name is White. I am the Lapp king's mistress.'

There was just one girl there to wait on them. The king's men were highly pleased with them, and what they decided on was to ask whether White cared to go along with them and marry king Hring. He who had charge of the royal mission put this offer to her. She was in no hurry to answer, but referred it to her mother's judgement.

'As the proverb has it,' said her mother, 'pronounce we must, to solve all problems. I think it wrong that this is done without leave asked of her father, but it is a course we must venture on, if she is to make any kind of headway.'

After this she made ready to be off with them. They then went their ways and met king Hring, and the messengers inquired at once whether the king cared to marry the woman—or should she depart back the way she had come. The king was delighted with the lady and married her without more ado. He did not even care that she was not rich. The king was getting on in years, and soon this was evident from the queen's behaviour.

A short way off from the king dwelt a commoner who had a wife and one daughter, whose name was Bera, and who was young and lovely to look upon. Bjorn the king's son and Bera the commoner's daughter played their childhood games together and loved each other dearly. This man was well-to-do and had long followed the wars in his youth; he was a great champion. Bera and Bjorn were devoted to each other and were always together. And thus time wore on, with nothing much to relate. Bjorn the king's son grew to full manhood, and became both big and strong; he was skilled in all manly accomplishments. King Hring was continually away from his kingdom, on viking raids, but White stayed at home and governed the country. She was by no means good friends with people in general, but towards Bjorn she was more than kind. He, though, had no use for her.

On one occasion, when the king left home, the queen suggested to him that Bjorn his son should stay home with her to look after the land. The king thought this a good plan. The queen was now growing imperious and domineering. The king told his son Bjorn that he must stay at home and guard the land along with the queen. Bjorn said he had little inclination for this, and said too that he detested the queen; but stay he must, was the king's rejoinder, whereupon he departed the land with a great following.

Bjorn returned home from these exchanges with his father, and they were in violent disagreement one with the other. He went to his own quarters, was gloomy-hearted, and red as blood. The queen came to speak to him. She wished to enliven his mood, and pleaded for his friendship. He told her to go away, and for the time being she did so. But many a time she came to talk with him, saying it would be a good stroke for them to share one bed while the king was away. Their life together, she reckoned, would be far better than that she had with a man as old as king Hring. Bjorn gave this suggestion a most hostile reception; he treated her to a great box on the ear, telling her to get out of his sight, and thrust her away from him. She was not used, she said, to being struck or beaten. 'You prefer, Bjorn, to embrace a churl's daughter rather, and that is good enough for you, inferior as it is, and more dishonouring than to enjoy my love and favours. It might not come amiss though some punishment befell you for your stubbornness and folly.'

She now struck him with her wolf-skin gloves, declaring he should become a cave-bear, fierce and savage. 'You shall enjoy no other food than your father's stock, and of that you shall kill for your meat more than has ever been heard tell of. You shall never win free of this enchantment, and this my memento will prove harder on you than nothing.'

After that Bjorn vanished from the sight of men, and nobody knew what had become of him. And when men missed Bjorn a search was made for him, but, as might be expected, he was nowhere to be found. Concerning which there is now this to relate, that the king's sheep and oxen were killed off by the score, and it was a grey bear, huge and savage, that made these inroads.

One evening it happened that the carl's daughter saw this same savage bear. The bear went up to her and made friendly gestures to her. She seemed to recognize the eyes of Bjorn the king's son in the bear, and made little attempt to evade it. The beast then moved away from her, and she followed after it, until it reached a certain cave. And when she came to the cave, there was a man standing there who gave Bera the carl's daughter welcome and greeting. She realized that it was Bjorn Hringsson, and this was a great and joyful meeting of theirs. They were there for a while in the cave, for so long as she had any say in the matter, she would not part from him; but he held that it was not seemly for her to stay with him, because he was a beast by day though a man by night.

Now king Hring returned home from his warring, and was told tidings of what had taken place while he was away: the disappearance of Bjorn his son, and further still, concerning that great beast which had appeared in the land, and for the most part attacked the king's own cattle. The queen urged him strongly to have this beast slain, but it was put off for a while even so, for the king was far from happy about this, and thought that events had taken a strange turn.

One night when Bera and Bjorn the king's son were lying in their bed, Bjorn began to speak, and this is what he said: 'I have a foreboding that to-morrow will be my death day, and that they will succeed in hunting me down. Moreover, I take no pleasure in living, because of this evil fate which hangs over me. Even though it is my one joy, this our relationship together, that too must now change. I will give you this ring which is to be found under my left arm. Tomorrow you will espy the company which is coming to attack me, and when I am dead, go to the king and ask him to give you what lies under the beast's left shoulder, and he will grant you that. The queen will be suspicious of you when you plan to be off, and she will give you some of the bear's flesh to eat, but on no account must you eat it, for you are a woman with child, as well you know, and you will give birth to three boys who will be ours, and it will be apparent from them whether you eat of the bear's flesh, for this queen is the greatest troll. Go home thereafter to your father's, and it is there you will give birth to the boys, one of whom will seem best in your eyes. If you cannot maintain them at home for their ill fate and intract-able nature, then get them away, and bring them here to the cave. You will see here a coffer with three compartments. The runes which are inscribed there will tell what each one of them is to possess. There are three weapons in the rock, and each shall have that which is meant for him. That son of ours who comes first into the world shall be named Elgfrothi, the second Thorir, and the third Bothvar, and I judge it more than likely that they will prove no weaklings and their names be remembered for ever.'

He spoke to her of many things to come, and thereafter his bear-shape whelmed him, and he went outside a bear, and she after him, and looked about her and saw a big troop of men coming over the shoulder of the mountain, and hounds huge and many running ahead of the hunt. The bear now ran away from the cave and off along the mountain. The hounds and the king's men came on against him, but found him a rare handful. He crippled many a man for them before he was overcome, and killed all the dogs. Then it came about that they threw a ring of men all round him; he roamed about inside the ring and saw to what a pass things had come, and how he could not get away. He turned now to where the king was standing and clutched at the man who stood next to him, and tore his living body asunder. By this time the bear was so tired that he flung himself down prostrate on the ground, and they ran to him quickly and slew him.

The carl's daughter saw this. She went to the king, and, 'Sire,' she said, 'will you consent to give me what lies under the beast's left shoulder ?'

The king consented, saying that that alone would be there which it was right and seemly for him to bestow on her.

By this time the king's men had in great measure flayed the bear. Bera went up and took away the ring and kept it safe. No one saw what she took, nor was any inquiry made in the matter. The king asked who she might be, for he had not recognized her. She told him what she thought fit, and something other than the truth. The king now went home and Bera along with him. The queen was in high spirits, gave her a good welcome and asked who she might be. As before she did not tell the truth of it. The queen now held a great feast and had the bear's flesh prepared for men's cheer. The carl's daughter was in the queen's chamber and could not get away, for the queen had her suspicions who she would be. Sooner than might be expected, in came the queen with a dish, with bear's meat on it, and told Bera to swallow it down.

She was unwilling to eat. 'What an unheard-of thing,' cried the queen, 'that you turn up your nose at this good cheer which the queen herself vouchsafes to offer you. Take it quickly; otherwise it shall be the worse for you!'

She cut off a mouthful for her, and the outcome of it all was that she ate that mouthful. Then the queen carved her another piece and pushed it into her mouth, and one small grain of this mouthful too went down, but the rest she spat out, vowing she would eat no more even though she tortured or killed her.

'Maybe,' said the queen, laughing, 'it will show some result, as it is.'

Afterwards Bera went away and home to her father's. She had a bad time of it during her pregnancy. She told her father the whole story of her marriage, and what the nature of it was. A little later she was taken ill and gave birth to a son, though of a rather strange kind. He was a man above, but an elk from the navel down, and was given the name Elgfrothi. A second son was born and called Thorir. He had hound's feet on him from the instep, and for that reason was called Thorir Houndsfoot, though for the rest he was the most handsome of men. Then the third son was born, who was the likeliest-looking of them all. He was called Bothvar[1] and on him there was no blemish. It was Bothvar she loved the most.

They shot up fast as grass. When they were at the games with other men they were fierce and unsparing in all. Men got a rough time of it at their hands. Frothi crippled many a man of the king's, and some he killed outright. And so for a while it continued, until they were twelve years old. By now they were so strong that none of the king's men could stand up to them, nor might they now take part in the games.

Then Frothi told his mother that he wanted to go away. 'I cannot have a real fight with anyone; they are nothing but useless loons, and are crippled the moment they are touched.'

She said he was not fit for human society because of his violence. And now his mother went with him to the cave and showed him the wealth his father had intended for him, for Bjorn had plainly declared what each should have. Frothi wanted to take more, but could not, for that was the least portion of wealth which was assigned to him. He now saw where the weapons stood out from the rock. First he caught hold of the swordhilt, but the sword was so fast that he did not succeed in obtaining it. Then he snatched at the axe-shaft, but that was no looser. 'Maybe,' said Elgfrothi, 'he and none other who fixed these treasures here has intended that the sharing of weapons shall accord with the sharing of

---

[1] Bothvar, i.e. Bothvar Bjarki, as later in the saga. Bjorn means 'Bear', Bera 'She-bear', and Bjarki 'Little Bear'.

the other property.' He now snatched at the remaining haft; it came loose on the instant, and a short-sword was attached to the haft.

He studied the sword for a while, and then, 'Unfair was he,' said Elgfrothi, 'who had these treasures to share out.' He smote at the rock with both hands on the sword, intending to break it in pieces, but the short-sword pierced the rock till the haft clanged home on it, yet it was none the more broken for that. 'What will it matter,' asked Elgfrothi, 'how I use the wretched thing, for no question of it, it knows how to bite!'

Afterwards he gave his mother a parting greeting, and off went Frothi to a mountain road, where he became an evil-doer, killing men for their money, and building himself a hut to dwell in.

King Hring now thought he understood what witchcraft all this must signify, but he said nothing about it publicly and let it lie quiet as before. Soon afterwards Thorir Houndsfoot asked leave to go away, and his mother directed him to the cave and so to that wealth which was meant for him; she told him of the weapons and bade him take the axe, explaining that such were his father's orders. Thereafter Thorir went away, bidding his mother live long and happily. First he snatched at the swordhilt, but the sword stood firm. Then he caught hold of the axe-shaft, and the axe was free, because it was assigned to him. He then took his portion of goods and went his way. He so directed his steps that he went first of all to visit Elgfrothi his brother. He went inside his hut, sat down in his brother's seat, and pulled down his hood. Soon afterwards Frothi came home. He looked upon his visitor by no means sweetly, and drew his short-sword, saying:

> 'The short-sword yells
> And slides from sheath;
> While hand remembers
> Deeds of war.'

He drove it down on to the bench beside him, and showed very savage and scowling. Then Thorir declaimed:

> 'And I in full,
> In different wise,
> Let my axe peal
> An equal chime.'

And now Thorir dissembled no longer, Frothi recognized his brother, and offered him a half share with himself of everything he had by that time drawn together, for immense wealth was not wanting there. But Thorir was unwilling to take this. He remained there for a while, and then he went away. Elgfrothi showed him the way to Gautland. The king of the Gauts, he told him, had just died, and he urged him to enter their kingdom, instructing him copiously in the matter. 'It is a law among the Gauts that a public assembly is summoned there, and all the Gauts are summoned to it. A great throne is placed in the assembly, such as two men can sit in comfortably together, and he who fills that seat shall be their king. It seems to me you will fill the seat in full measure.'

Afterwards they parted: each bade the other thrive. Thorir pressed on his way until he came to a certain earl in Gautland. The earl made him welcome, and he spent the night there. Everyone who set eyes on Thorir reckoned he could well be king over the Gauts by reason of his size. There would be few such present there, they held. When folk came to the place of assembly, everything went exactly as Frothi his brother had foretold to him. A judge had been appointed there to decide the issue justly. Many sat in that seat, but the judge declared that it suited no one of them. Thorir was the last to go, and he eased himself into the seat in a twinkling. Said the judge: 'For you is the seat fittest, and you shall have the verdict for this kingdom.' Thereafter the men of the land gave him the title of king, and he was called king Thorir Houndsfoot, and there are great stories about him. He was well blest with friends, and fought many battles, and for the most part won the day. He now remained in his kingdom for a while.

Bothvar was still at home with his mother, who loved him dearly. He was the most accomplished of men, and very handsome, yet he did not mix all that freely with people. One day he asked his mother who his father was, and she told him of his cruel death and the whole course of events, and how he had been spellgirt by his stepmother.

Said Bothvar: 'We have many wrongs to repay this witch.'

Then she told him how she was forced by the queen to eat of the bear's flesh—'Which is visible now in the persons of your brothers, Thorir and Elgfrothi.'

'I should have thought Frothi not less bound to avenge our father on this cursed witch,' said Bothvar, 'than to go killing innocent men for their money, and working evil; while for Thorir to depart without teaching this she-monster a lesson puzzles me greatly. The best thing now, I fancy, is for me to give her something to remember us by.'

'Take care,' advised Bera, 'that she cannot so practise her magic arts that she brings you to grief.'

He promised it should be so, and afterwards he and Bera went to see the king, and by Bothvar's advice she told him the entire course of events, showing him the ring she had taken from under the beast's shoulder, which Bjorn his son had owned. The king admitted that he knew the ring well. 'It has been very much in my mind that all these dread events which have happened here must have come about by her contrivance, but because of my love for the queen I have let it lie quiet.'

'Send her away this instant,' said Bothvar, 'or we will take vengeance on her.'

The king said he was prepared to pay him whatsoever redress he wanted, if only it might still be let lie, and give him a domain to rule over, and the title of earl here and now, and after his death the royal power, if only no hurt were done her. But Bothvar said he had no desire to be a monarch; he had rather stay with the king, he said, and do him service. 'You are so besotted with this monster that you hardly retain grip of your senses or your rightful dominion; but from this day forth she shall not flourish here.'

Bothvar was now so fearsome to contend with that the king did not dare go against him. Bothvar strode off to the queen's chamber, and in his hand had a kind of bag. Behind him came the king and his mother. And when Bothvar entered the chamber he turned upon queen White and whipped this shrunken skin bag over her head, then tightened it round her throat under her chin. He next gave her a great blow on the side of the head, and beat her to death with various torments, and dragged her so the length of the streets. To many or most within the hall there this appeared a good job well done, but the king took it hard, yet could do nothing about it; and in this fashion queen White lost her miserable life.

At the time when this took place Bothvar was eighteen years old. Somewhat later king Hring fell ill and died, whereupon Bothvar succeeded to the kingdom, but was happy in it for but a short while. He then summoned a meeting of his subjects, and at this meeting announced that he desired to go away. He gave his mother in marriage to a man by the name of Valsleit, who was an earl there already, and Bothvar sat down to their wedding feast before riding away.

He rode off all alone, and did not take with him much gold or silver or other riches, save that he was well furnished with weapons and clothes. And first, by his mother's direction, he rode his good steed to the cave. The sword was freed even as he grasped its hilt. It was the nature of this sword that it might never be drawn save it slew a man. It should not be laid under one's head or stood on its boss. It should be impelled but thrice in all its life, and at times could not be drawn at all, so hard was it to manage. All the brothers had wished to own that precious treasure.

Bothvar now sought a meeting with his brother Elgfrothi. He made a sheath for the sword out of birch. Nothing to tell of happened on his journey till in the second half of the day he reached the big hut where Elgfrothi was lord and master. Bothvar stabled his horse, assuming he had a right to everything he found himself in need of. Frothi returned home in the course of the evening and gave him some dirty looks. This Bothvar ignored, and did not move.

Similarly, there was a scuffle between the horses, each wishing to drive the other from his stall. Then Frothi began to speak. 'He is a very impudent fellow who dares make himself at home here without my leave!' Bothvar let his hood stay hanging down and made no reply. Elgfrothi rose to his feet, plucking out his short-sword and slamming it home again up to the hilt. He did this twice, but Bothvar did not turn a hair. He drew the sword a third time and made for him now, thinking that his visitor could not know the meaning of fear, and determined to put forth his utmost endeavour. And once Bothvar saw to what a pitch things had come, he had no wish to wait longer, but rose and ran in under his arms. Elgfrothi had the harder grip, and they had a tremendous wrestle together till Bothvar's hood fell down and Frothi recognized him.

'Welcome, kinsman,' he said. 'We have been over-long at the wrestling.'

'There is no harm done yet,' said Bothvar.

'Still, brother,' said Elgfrothi, 'you must be more canny how you tackle me if you and I are to fight in earnest. You would feel then some difference in our strength if we were really to set to and hold nothing back.'

Frothi invited him to stay there and hold a half share in everything with himself. Bothvar had no wish for that, for he thought poorly of killing men for their money, so after this he took himself off. Frothi brought him on his way, and told him this, that he had given peace to many men who were of little strength. Bothvar was heartened by this, and said that was well done—'And most men you should let go in peace, even though you think you have something against them.'

'Everything given me is ill given,' said Elgfrothi, 'but the thing for you to do is to go and find king Hrolf, for all the foremost champions wish to be where he is, because his munificence, splendour, and courage are greater by far than those of all other kings.'

Then Frothi set to and gave him a shove. 'You are not as strong, kinsman, as you should be.' Frothi drew blood from the calf of his leg and bade him drink, and Bothvar did so, whereupon Frothi set about him again, but this time Bothvar stood firm in his tracks. 'You are very strong now, kinsman,' said Elgfrothi, 'and I believe that drink has done you good, and you will excel most men in strength and valour and every kind of hardihood and manliness, and this I willingly bestow on you.'

Afterwards Frothi stamped with his foot on the rock which stood beside him, right up to the pastern. 'I will come to this hoof-mark every day, and find what is in the print. It will be earth if you are dead of sickness; water, if you are dead of drowning; blood, if you are dead of weapons—and then I will avenge you, for I love you best of all mankind.'

They now parted, and Bothvar went his way till he came to Gautland. King Thorir Houndsfoot was not at home. They were men so alike that folk could not tell one from the other, and the men of the land believed that it must be that Thorir had returned home. He was placed in the high-seat there and treated as king in every respect, and put to bed alongside the queen, for Thorir was married. Bothvar would not lie under the same coverlet with her, which she found strange, for she thought he really was her husband. Bothvar, however, told her the true state of affairs. She did not let this be discovered through her. And in this fashion they behaved every night, conversing together, until Thorir came home, when folk had to determine who the man was. That was a joyful meeting between the brothers. Thorir admitted that he would trust no other man this way, to lie abed near his queen.

Thorir invited him to stay there and hold a half share in all movables with himself, but Bothvar said he had no mind for that. Thorir then offered to ride off with him wherever he pleased, or to supply him with a retinue; but he would not have that either. So Bothvar rode away, and Thorir went some of the way with him. The brothers parted with friendship, even if with some reservations, and nothing is told of Bothvar's journeyings until he appeared in Denmark, at a place whence he had but a short way to go to Leire.

One day there was a great rainstorm and Bothvar got very wet. His horse grew very tired and was foundering under him, for he had ridden him long and hard, and the going was wet and heavy. At night it grew black as pitch, with a downpour of rain, and he saw absolutely nothing till his horse stumbled against some projection or other. He dismounted to take a look around, and perceived that there must be some kind of dwelling there. He found there was a door, and knocked, and a man came outside, whom Bothvar asked for a night's shelter. The man of the house said he would not send him away at dead of night, for he must be a stranger. From all he could see of him, the man of the house thought him a most imposing being.

Bothvar spent the night there in good cheer. He asked many questions about the exploits of king

Hrolf and his champions, and whether it was far to that place.

'Why, no,' said the man, 'it is a very short way now. You plan to head that way?'

'Yes,' said Bothvar, 'that is my intention.'

The farmer agreed that was the right place for him. 'For I can see you are a big, strong man. Still, they think themselves mighty fine fellows.' And with that the man's wife wept aloud, when they mentioned king Hrolf and his champions in Leire.

'Poor old woman,' said Bothvar. 'Why do you weep?'

'One son we had,' said the old woman, 'my husband and I, whose name was Hott. One day he went to the town for his diversion, but the king's men baited him, and he took this badly. So then they seized him and put him on their bone-heap, and now it is their custom during meals that when they finish gnawing on any bone they fling it at him, whereby he sometimes gets a great wound, if it hits him, and I have no idea whether he is dead or alive. I would have this return from you for my hospitality, that you throw smaller rather than bigger bones at him, if he is not by this time dead and gone.'

'I will do as you ask,' promised Bothvar, 'and it does not seem to me all that gallant to be smiting men with bones or wreaking one's ill-will on children and mere nobodies.'

'Then you do well,' said the old woman, 'for your hand looks a strong one to me, and certain am I that he could not withstand blow of yours, if you were not willing to curb your strength.'

Later Bothvar went on his way to Leire and arrived at the king's residence. He stabled his horse alongside the best of the king's horses, asking leave

of no one, and afterwards walked into the hall.
There were few men there. He took a seat near the
door, and when he had been there a short while he
heard a kind of scrabbling away out in some corner
or other. Bothvar looked that way and saw how a
man's hand came up out of a huge pile of bones
which lay there. The hand was very black. Bothvar
walked that way and asked who was there, in that
pile of bones.

He got his answer—and very meekly. 'Hott is my
name, buckie dear.'

'Why are you here?' asked Bothvar. 'And what
are you doing?'

'I am making myself a shield-wall, buckie dear.'

'You and your miserable shield-wall!' cried Bothvar, grabbing him and plucking him up out of the
bone-heap.

At this Hott bellowed aloud. 'You will be the
death of me,' he said. 'Don't do it, when I have just
made such a good job of things! For now you have
sent my shield-wall flying, when I had built it so
high all round me that it protected me from all your
blows, so that never a blow has landed on me this
long while. And even so it was not so complete as
I meant it to be.'

Said Bothvar: 'You will not be building shield-
walls any longer.'

'You want to be the death of me, buckie?' asked
Hott, and he wept.

Bothvar told him to be less noisy. He next picked
him up and carried him out of the hall to a pond
which was nearby (few paid any attention to this)
and washed him from top to toe. Afterwards Bothvar went to the seat he had taken before, leading
Hott with him, and sat him down beside him. Hott

was so terrified that he was trembling in every limb. But with it all he seemed to realize that this man was wanting to help him.

Then it drew on towards evening, and men came thronging into hall, and Hrolf's champions noticed that Hott had been put on a bench, and it seemed to them that the man who was responsible for this showed plenty of confidence in himself. Hott grew very long in the face when he saw these acquaintances of his, for he had experienced nothing but ill at their hands. He was anxious to stay alive and get back into his pile of bones, but Bothvar held on to him so that he might not be off and away. For Hott thought that if he could escape back there, he would not be so exposed to their blows as where he was now.

And now the retainers held to their practice, and for a start flung small bones across the floor at Bothvar and Hott. Bothvar pretended not to notice this, but Hott was so terrified that he could neither eat nor drink, and expected to be hit at any moment. And now, 'Buckie dear,' he warned Bothvar, 'here comes a great knuckle-bone straight at you—and the intention is certainly to give us a headache!' Bothvar told him to hold his peace, put up the hollow of his palm, and caught the knuckle-bone so—it had the leg-bone attached. Then Bothvar sent the knuckle-bone back, hurling it at the thrower, and smack at him with so calamitous a blow that it was the death of him. Great fear came over the retainers then.

News of this reached king Hrolf and his champions up in the castle, how a most remarkable man had come to the hall and had slain one of his retainers, and they wanted to kill this man. King Hrolf asked whether the retainer had been killed without cause.

'Pretty well,' they told him, and then the whole truth of it became known to king Hrolf.

King Hrolf said it should by no means be so, that they should kill this man. 'You have adopted a wicked custom here of pelting innocent men with bones. To me it is dishonour, and to you great shame, to do so. I have spoken about it often before, but you have paid no attention. I believe this man you have now attacked will prove no weakling. Summon him before me, that I may know who he is.'

Bothvar went into the king's presence and greeted him courteously. The king asked him his name.

'Hott's guardian your retainers call me, but my name is Bothvar.'

'What redress are you prepared to offer me for my man?' asked the king.

'He only got what he asked for,' said Bothvar.

'Will you become my man,' asked the king, 'and fill his place?'

'I do not refuse to be your man, but we must not be parted after this fashion, Hott and I. Further, we will both sit nearer you than that other fellow sat; otherwise we will both be on our way.'

'I foresee little credit in him,' replied the king, 'but I won't begrudge him his victuals.'

Bothvar now went to just that seat he pleased, nor would he occupy the one his victim had had before. He pulled up three men in one place, and afterwards he and Hott sat down there, further up the hall than had been allotted to them. Men thought Bothvar a hard man to deal with, and were highly resentful of him.

Then as the time wore on to Yule men grew long of face. Bothvar asked Hott why this should be. Hott told him that a creature had come there two winters running, huge and horrible. 'It has wings on its back, and flies at all times. Two autumns now it has come visiting here and done great damage. No weapon will bite on it, and those who are foremost of all the king's champions do not come back.'

'The hall is not so well manned as I thought,' said Bothvar, 'if one beast can lay waste the king's kingdom and his cattle.'

'This is no beast,' said Hott. 'Rather, it is the greatest troll.'

Now Yule-eve came in. Said the king: 'It is my will that men be still and quiet tonight, and I forbid all my followers to run any risk with this creature. The cattle will fare as is fated, but I am not prepared to lose my men.'

They all promised faithfully to do as the king commanded. But Bothvar stole away that night, and made Hott go with him, which he did only under compulsion, swearing it would be the death of him. Bothvar said it would turn out better than that. They went away from the hall, and Bothvar had to carry him, he was so terrified. Now they saw the creature; and with that Hott shrieked as loud as he knew how, vowing that the creature would swallow him down. Bothvar bade him be quiet, dog that he was, and flung him down on the moss, where he lay by no means free from fright. Nor did he any the more dare return home. Bothvar now advanced against the beast, but it befell him that his sword stuck fast in its scabbard when he would have drawn it. Bothvar urged the sword fiercely; it moved within the scabbard, whereupon he got the scabbard so dislodged that the sword slid from its sheath. Instantly he drove it in under the creature's shoulder so hard that it pierced his heart, and the creature dropped down dead to earth. After that Bothvar went to where Hott was lying, and picked him up and carried him to where the creature lay dead. Hott was trembling like a leaf. 'Now,' said Bothvar, 'you shall drink the beast's blood.' For a long time he was unwilling, yet just as surely he dared not do otherwise. Bothvar made him drink two big mouthfuls. He also made him eat some of the beast's heart. Then Bothvar set about him and they struggled together for a long time. 'You are now grown pretty strong,' Bothvar told him, 'and I do not believe you will now stand in fear of king Hrolf's retainers.'

'I shall stand in fear neither of them nor of you,' said Hott, 'from this day on.'

'Nothing could be better then, comrade Hott! And now let us go and raise up the beast, and fix him so that the rest of them will think he is still alive.'

And so they did, and afterwards returned home and kept their news to themselves, and nobody knew what feat they had accomplished.

In the morning the king inquired what news they had of the beast, and whether he had paid them a visit overnight. He was informed that all the stock was safe and sound in fold. The king bade his men inquire whether there was any sign to be seen that he had called on them. The guards did so, and came rushing back to tell the king that the creature was on its way, and rushing furiously towards the stronghold. The king bade his liegemen be brave, and each man do his best in accordance with his spirit, and make an end of the monster. They did as the king commanded, and put themselves in readiness.

The king faced towards the beast, and said after

a while: 'I see no movement in the beast. Who now wants to do a good stroke of business for himself, and proceed against him ?'

'That,' said Bothvar, 'would cure the curiosity of the bravest. And now, comrade Hott, clear yourself of that ill-repute whereby men maintain that neither spirit nor valour is to be found in you. Forward now and kill the beast! You can see that none of the others is very eager for it.'

'Aye,' said Hott, 'I will try my hand at this.'

'I do not know,' said the king, 'from what source this courage has come to you, Hott, but there has been a big change in you in a short time.'

'Give me the sword Goldenhilt which you are holding,' said Hott, 'and I will then fell this beast or get my death.'

'This sword,' replied the king, 'is not to be borne except by that man who is both a good and gallant fighter.'

'This you must believe,' said Hott, 'that I am such.'

'What can one say,' replied the king, 'except that there has been an even greater change in your temper than yet appears ? Few indeed could claim to know you for the same man. Now take the sword, and have a hero's use of it, if this deed is truly done.'

Then Hott advanced boldly against the beast, and, when he came within striking distance, smote it, and the beast fell down dead. 'See now, sire,' cried Bothvar, 'what he has done!'

'He has certainly changed greatly,' the king agreed, 'but Hott alone has not killed this creature—you rather have done it.'

'Maybe so,' said Bothvar.

'I knew when you came here,' said the king, 'that

few would be your equal, but this seems to me your most striking achievement, that you have made yet another champion of Hott, for whom there appeared to be no great prospect of fortune. It is now my will that he shall be called Hott no longer, but henceforth be called Hjalti. You shall be called, that is, after the sword Gullinhjalti.'

And with that the story of Bothvar and his brothers comes to a close.

The winter wore on now to the time when king Hrolf's berserks were expected home. Bothvar asked Hjalti about the berserks' habits. It was their custom, he said, when they returned to court to go up to every man present, and first of all to the king, and ask whether he reckoned himself as brave as they. 'Then the king says this: "That is a ticklish question to answer in the case of such valiant men as you, who have distinguished yourselves in battles and blood-lettings against so many and such divers peoples, in the southern as in the northern regions of earth." The king gives them this answer rather through magnanimity than meanness, for he knows their quality, and they win him great victories and much wealth. Then they go from before him and ask the same of every man in the hall, and there is none to reckon himself as brave as they.'

'What a sad choice of men is here with king Hrolf,' said Bothvar, 'that they all let the berserks taunt them with cowardice.'

They gave over talking, and Bothvar had now been one whole year with king Hrolf. It so happened the following Yule-eve, at a time when king Hrolf was seated at table, that the hall doors burst open, and in marched twelve berserks, all with arms and accoutrements grey as broken ice.

Quietly Bothvar asked Hjalti whether he dare tackle any of them.

'Aye,' growled Hjalti, 'and not only one, but the whole pack of them, for I do not know the meaning of fear, though overwhelming odds confront me. And no one of these will make me tremble.'

The berserks began by walking further in up the hall. They could see that king Hrolf's champions had increased in number since they left home. They studied the new-comers closely, one of whom looked to them no mean person; and report has it that he who walked at their head was not a little taken aback. As was their custom, they walked right up to king Hrolf and put to him the same question they were used to put. The king answered as he usually did, in a way to meet the occasion, and after this fashion they walked up to every man in the hall, and came last of all to those comrades-in-arms, whereupon he who was their leader asked Bothvar whether he reckoned himself as brave a man as he.

Not as brave, Bothvar retorted; he reckoned himself far braver, test it how they would. Nor need he come wambling after him as after some old sow, the stinking son of a mare! He sprang out and in under the berserk, where he was standing in all his armour, and fetched him such a thunderous cropper that it was a question whether his bones were still in one piece. On his side Hjalti did exactly the same. There was now a great hullabaloo in the hall, and king Hrolf could see a prospect of great peril if his men were to be striking each other down. He ran from the high-seat to Bothvar, bidding him let all lie quiet and in good order, but Bothvar swore the berserk should lose his life unless he confessed himself the lesser man. That, said king Hrolf, was a

simple matter, so he let the berserk get up, and
Hjalti likewise conformed to the king's command.
Then men sat down, each in his place, and the berserks in theirs, greatly perturbed. King Hrolf talked
to them with strong persuasion, how they might now
see that nothing in the world was so famous, strong,
or mighty that its match could not be found. 'I
forbid you to stir up trouble in my hall, and if you
defy me in this, you shall pay for it with your lives.
But be as fierce as you please when I have to deal
with my foes, and by that win fame and renown.
I have now such a pick of champions that I need not
be dependent on you.'

Everyone applauded the king's speech warmly,
and they were all fully reconciled with each other.
The order of men in hall was this, that Bothvar
was prized and esteemed above them all, and sat on
the king's right hand next to him, and thereafter
Hjalti the Magnanimous—a name the king bestowed
on him. And well might he be called magnanimous,
because he spent every day with the king's retainers,
the same who had maltreated him the way that was
told of earlier, yet did them no harm, though he
had now become a far greater man than they, and
the king would have held it excusable had he given
them something to remember him by, or even killed
one or other of them. But on the king's left hand sat
the three brothers, Svipdag, Hvitserk, and Beigath,
so important had they become, and thereafter the
twelve berserks, and the rest of those picked fighters
likewise, whose names are not now given, on both
sides the entire length of the castle.

The king allowed these men of his to practise
sports and crafts of every kind, together with all sorts
of games and entertainments. Bothvar proved him-

self the foremost of all his champions, whatever need
be taken in hand, and he came into such great honour
with king Hrolf that he married Drifa, his only
daughter. And so for a while it continued thus, that
they remained in their kingdom and were the most
renowned of all men.

The Uppsala Ride

The story now tells how one day king Hrolf was seated in his royal hall, and all his champions and great men beside him, holding a costly banquet. He looked to his right hand and his left. 'This is a great and overwhelming force,' said he, 'here assembled in one hall.' And king Hrolf asked Bothvar whether he knew of any king his equal or ruling over such champions.

Bothvar admitted he did not. 'And yet there is one thing which appears to me to mar your royal dignity.'

What was that? asked the king.

'It is a shortcoming, sire,' said Bothvar, 'that you do not seek to recover that patrimony of yours at Uppsala which your kinsman king Athils holds on to so unjustly.'

King Hrolf said it would be a heavy undertaking to try for that. 'For Athils is a devious creature, well versed in magic, crafty, guileful, cunning, savage-hearted, and a very bad one to have to do with.'

'Even so,' said Bothvar, 'it is right and proper for you, sire, to make inquiry after your own property, and go visit king Athils some time, and discover what answer he makes in this matter.'

'This is a most important point you raise,' the king agreed, 'for we have to seek vengeance for our father from him too. King Athils is dauntless and very tricky, but we will take a chance.'

'Certainly I shall not quarrel with our trying out one day what kind of man king Athils is,' said Bothvar.

King Hrolf now made ready for his journey with

a hundred men, his twelve champions too, and his twelve berserks. There is nothing told of their journey before they reached a certain farmer's. He was standing outside when they arrived, and invited them all to stay with him there.

'You are a fine fellow,' said the king, 'but have you the means for this, for we are not so few in number? It is not for a small farmer to play host to our entire company.'

He laughed. 'Aye, sire,' said he, 'I have seen men no fewer in number come where I have been before now, and you shall not lack for drink or anything of the kind you need to have the whole night long.'

'Then we will take our chance,' said the king.

The farmer was pleased at this, and now their horses were taken and given good treatment.

'What is your name, franklin?' asked the king.

'Some men call me Hrani,' he said.

There was such hospitality there that they could scarcely believe they had ever entered a house more hospitable. The farmer was the soul of good cheer, and there was nothing they could ask of him that he could not cope with. He impressed them as a very deep sort of man indeed. They now settled down to sleep, but when they woke up were so cold that their teeth were chattering in their heads; they started up all together and got themselves clothing and anything they could lay their hands on, except for king Hrolf's champions, who remained content with those clothes they had before. They were perished the whole night through.

'How have you slept?' asked the farmer.

It was Bothvar who answered. 'Admirably,' he said.

Then the farmer spoke with the king. 'I know that it strikes your retainers as having been on the fresh side in hall last night, as indeed it was; but they cannot hope to endure the hardships king Athils will try you with at Uppsala if they found that so burdensome. Sire, if you would save your life, send home half your troop, for it is not by a count of heads that you will win the victory over king Athils.'

'You are a remarkable man, franklin,' said the king. 'I will take the advice you offer.'

When they were ready they went their way, bidding the farmer happy days, and the king sent back half his troop. They rode on their way, and presently there was another farm confronting them, a small one this time, and here they thought they recognized the same farmer they had lodged with the night before. The whole thing had an uncanny look, they thought. However, the farmer made them welcome, and asked why they came so often.

'We hardly know,' replied the king, 'with what arts we are pursued, and you can be called a right crafty fellow.'

'This time again,' said the farmer, 'your welcome shall not be a bad one.'

They spent that second night there with fine hospitality. They went to sleep and woke up for this reason, that so great a thirst had come upon them that they found it wellnigh unbearable, so that they could hardly stir their tongues in their heads. So up they got and made for where there was a great bowl of wine standing, and drank from it.

In the morning farmer Hrani had this to say: 'It happens a second time, sire, that you grant me a hearing. I believe there is little endurance in those men who had to be drinking in the night. You will have greater trials than that to endure when you reach king Athils.'

Then, all of a sudden, a fierce storm arose. They remained there that day, and the third night came. During the evening a fire was lit for them, and those who were sitting by the fire found it very hot on their arms. Most of them hurriedly left the seats which farmer Hrani had assigned them, and they all fled out and away from the fire except for king Hrolf and his champions.

'You can cull once again from your troop, sire,' said the farmer. 'It is my advice that none go forward save you and your twelve champions. In that case there is some hope that you will return, but otherwise none.'

'I am so well pleased with you, franklin,' said king Hrolf, 'that we will take your advice.'

They spent three nights there. The king rode on from there with twelve men, and all the rest of his host he sent back. King Athils received news of this and reckoned it was well that king Hrolf desired to visit him at his home. 'For he shall certainly run such an errand here as will seem well worth the telling before we part.'

After this king Hrolf and his champions rode to king Athils's hall, and the entire citizenry of the town crowded up into the town's highest towers to see the brave showing of king Hrolf and his champions, for they were handsomely arrayed, and many were lost in admiration of such courtly looking knights. At first they rode slowly and with state, but when they were only a short distance from the hall they gave their horses the spur and galloped to the hall, so that everybody standing before them fled from their path. King Athils had them welcomed fairly and amicably, and gave orders that their horses should be taken in charge.

'Look to it, lads,' said Bothvar, 'that not a hair is out of place on forelock or tail of the horses. Attend to them well, and be especially careful that they do not bemire themselves.'

This was promptly reported to king Athils, how closely they had laid down the law about the care of the horses. 'This is the height of insolence and pride,' said he. 'Now, take my orders and do as I bid. Hack off their tail-bones as high as their spines, aye, flush with their rumps, and cut off their forelocks so that the skin of the forehead comes away with it, and in every way treat them as shamefully as you know how, except that you leave them still just alive.'

They were now escorted to the hall door, but king Athils did not put in an appearance. 'I already know my way around here,' said Svipdag. 'I will enter first, for I have the strongest suspicion as to the kind of welcome we shall get and what has been arranged for us. Let us not announce which is king Hrolf, so that king Athils may not tell him from the rest of our company.' Svipdag walked ahead of them all, and those brothers of his behind him, Hvitserk and Beigath, and then king Hrolf and Bothvar, and so each behind the other. There were no servants to be met with, for those who had invited them to the hall had disappeared. They bore their hawks on their shoulders, which in those days was held the greatest gallantry. King Hrolf had the hawk which was called Habrok, Highbreeks.

Svipdag led the way, keeping his eyes wide open on all sides. He noticed a great difference everywhere. They surmounted so many obstacles which had been laid for their feet that it is not easy to recount them, and the deeper they penetrated into the hall, the more troublesome this became. And now they had advanced so far into the hall that they saw where king Athils sat bloated with pride in the high-seat, and it seemed to each of them no small occasion when they looked one upon the other. They saw, moreover, that it would still not be easy to come directly before king Athils. However, they had got near enough one to the other to make out each other's words.

King Athils was the first to speak. 'So you have got here then, friend Svipdag—and what will Old Stalwart's business be? Or is it not, as appears to me to be the case, that—

> A valley's in the neck-nape,
> An eye nicked from the head,
> A scar upon the forehead,
> Two wounds scored on the arms?

—and so with Beigath his brother—the man's all awry!'

Svipdag spoke so loud that all could hear him. 'I now wish to have peace of you, king Athils, even as I once stipulated with you, for these twelve men who are come here together.'

'I promise it,' replied king Athils. 'So come into the hall, quickly and boldly, with unclouded hearts.'

They thought they could discern how pitfalls had been prepared across the hall in front of them, and it was not going to be all that safe to test the lay-out of it; while so great a murk enshrouded king Athils that they could only vaguely distinguish his features. They saw too that the hangings which were draped all round the inside of the hall by way of adornment were let down, and that there must be armed men lurking behind them. And true enough, the moment they had surmounted the pitfalls a man in armour burst from behind every fold; but king Hrolf and his champions reacted savagely there, and clove the Swedes down to the teeth. So it went for a while: they still did not know which of them was king Hrolf, while the Swedes fell to the ground in swathes. In his high-seat king Athils swelled with rage when he saw Hrolf's champions cut down his host like so many dogs. He could see that the game was up, and rose to his feet, shouting: 'What is the meaning of this commotion? And what dirty dogs are these, that you play such tricks as to go setting about such men of mark as have now come visiting us? Stop it at once! Sit down, and let us enjoy good cheer, all of us together, kinsman Hrolf.'

'But little have you held to the truce now, king Athils,' said Svipdag, 'and inglorious is your part in all this.'

After that they sat down, Svipdag the farthest in, and then Hjalti the Magnanimous, but Bothvar and the king were seated together, because they did not want him to be known.

'I see,' said king Athils, 'that you do not proceed very honourably in a foreign land, or why has kinsman Hrolf no bigger retinue?'

'And I see,' countered Svipdag, 'that you neglect no opportunity of plotting treachery against king Hrolf and his men, and it is no great matter whether he rides to you with few men or many.'

With that they concluded their talk, and later king Athils had the hall cleaned up. The dead were carried away, for quite a number of king Athils's men had been slain, and a multitude of them wounded. Said king Athils: 'Let us build fires now the length of the hall for our friends, and be unsparing of affection to such men, so that we are all

as happy as can be.' Men were now sent for to light
the fire for them. At all times Hrolf's champions sat
with their weapons ready, and were unwilling ever
to let them leave their hands. The fire caught quickly,
for they spared neither pitch nor dry kindling. King
Athils had arranged for himself and his retainers to
occupy one side of the fire, and king Hrolf and his
champions were seated the other, and they sat each
party on its own long-bench and talked across to
each other most agreeably.

'The tales told of the valour and hardihood of you
champions of Hrolf are no exaggeration,' said king
Athils. 'For, indeed, you consider yourselves superior
to any, and it is no lie which is reported of your
strength. Build up the fires now,' said king Athils,
'for I do not clearly distinguish which of you is the
king, and you will not flee the fire, grow warmish
though you may.'

What he ordered was now done. He wanted in
this way to discover where king Hrolf might be, for
he felt sure he would not be able to stand the heat
like his champions, and believed that it would be
easier for him to lay hold of him once he knew where
he was, for past all doubt he wanted king Hrolf
doomed. Bothvar was aware of this, and others of
them too, and sheltered him from the heat as best
they could, yet not to that extent that he was any the
more distinguishable. And when the fire drove out at
them at its fiercest, then king Hrolf resolved to bear
in mind what he had vowed aforetime, to flee neither
fire nor iron, and he saw now that king Athils would
put this to trial, whether they would burn there or
not hold to their oath. And they saw that king Athils's
throne had moved right out through the wall of the
hall, and likewise the seats of his men. Fuel was

being piled on fast, and they saw that there was nothing for it but to burn unless something was done about it. By now their clothes were pretty well burnt off them, and they flung their shields on to the fire. Then chanted Bothvar and Svipdag:

'Let us strengthen the fires
In Athils's stronghold!'

They each of them grabbed his man from those who had been keeping up the fires and pitched them on to the fires, crying: 'Enjoy the warmth of the fire for your toil and trouble, for we are now done to a turn. Have a nice bake in your turn, you have been so diligent the while making a fire for us.' Hjalti grabbed the third and pitched him on to the fire his end, and so with every man jack of them who had quickened the fires. They burned to ashes there, and never a one was saved, for no one dared venture so close. After that deed king Hrolf began to speak:

'He flees no fire
Who leaps it.'

And after that they all strode as on stepping-stones through the fire, intending to get at king Athils and catch him. But when king Athils saw this he put his best foot forward and ran to a wooden pillar which stood in the hall, and was hollow inside, and so escaped from the hall by his wizardry and magic. By this means he reached queen Yrsa's bower and sought to talk with her; but she gave him a hostile reception, and spoke many a bitter word to him. 'First you had my husband, king Helgi, killed,' she said, 'treating him basely, and withholding property from him who owned it; and now you want to kill my son into the bargain. You are baser and more dire than any man alive. I shall now do my utmost to ensure that king Hrolf obtains his property, while your lot shall be dishonour, as is fitting.'

'That will be the way of it here,' said king Athils, 'that neither will trust the other. From this day forth I will never come into their presence again.'

With that they ended their talk. Queen Yrsa went to find king Hrolf and gave him the most affectionate welcome. He too received her greetings warmly. She appointed a man to look after them and provide them with proper hospitality. When this man came before king Hrolf he said: 'Thin-faced is this man, and quite the pole-ladder in appearance. Is he really your king?'

'You have given me a name which will stick to me,' said king Hrolf: 'Kraki, pole-ladder. What are you giving me for a name-fastener?'

'I have nothing at all to give,' replied Vogg, 'for I am penniless.'

'Then he must give the other who has means for it,' said king Hrolf, and drawing a gold ring from his arm he gave it to this man.

'The gods' blessing on you and your gift,' cried Vogg. 'This is a treasure indeed.'

When the king saw that he attached so much value to his gift, he said: 'A small thing makes Vogg happy.' But Vogg set one foot on the oath-block, saying thus: 'I swear this oath, that if you are overcome of men, and I live the longer, I will avenge you.'

'That is bravely done,' replied the king. 'Yet there may be others no less likely to achieve that than you.'

They saw that this man would be loyal and true in what little he could do, but thought his performance would be paltry even so, for there was no pith in the fellow. From now on they kept nothing from him. Later they decided to get some sleep, feeling that they could stretch out with confidence in the quarters the queen had provided for them. 'Everything here is well arranged for us,' said Bothvar, 'and the queen wishes us well. But king Athils wishes us all the evil he can. I shall be greatly surprised if we must put up with things as they are.'

Vogg told them that king Athils was the greatest idolator, 'so that his equal is not to be found. He worships a boar, and I do not believe that another such fiend exists. Take care of yourselves, for he will exert all his powers to destroy you by some means or other.'

'I think it more likely he will bear us in mind,' said Bothvar, 'because of how he ran from the hall on our account this evening.'

'And you can expect this too,' warned Vogg, 'that he will prove cunning and fierce.'

After that they slept but were roused by hearing so great an uproar outside that everything rang with it, and the house in which they lay seemed to tremble as if subject to a great swaying. Said Vogg: 'The boar is now on the rampage, and sent from king Athils to take vengeance on you. He is so great a troll that none can stand against him.'

King Hrolf had a huge hound named Gram, who was present there with them. He was outstanding for courage and strength. The next moment in came the troll in the likeness of a boar, rampaging horribly like the monster he was. Bothvar sicked the hound on the boar; nor did his heart fail him, but he leapt at the boar, and a fierce struggle took place. Bothvar helped the hound by cutting at the boar, but the sword never once bit on its back. The hound Gram was so tough that he ripped the boar's ears off, and his entire cheeks along with them, and all of a sudden the boar whipped away down to wherever he came from. Then king Athils came to the house with a huge following and at once set fire to the house. And with that king Hrolf and his men could tell that there would be no lack of fuel this time again. 'It is a poor death-day,' said Bothvar, 'if we are to burn indoors; and a bad ending will it make to the life-story of king Hrolf, should it come to that. I would choose rather to die of weapons on a level field. I see no better prospect now than to make so furious a rush that the wainscoting will give way, and we will break out of the house so, if that can be done.' Even so, that was no child's play, for the house was stoutly built. 'Let everyone tackle his man when we reach the open, and then they will soon lose heart.'

'That is a fine plan,' said king Hrolf, 'and will meet our needs in full.'

They adopted this plan, that they should dash so hard and furiously against the wainscoting that it was all broken to pieces, and so won their way outside. The street of the town was cluttered with men in armour. The most bitter fighting flared up with these, and king Hrolf and his champions went grimly forward. Athils's host provided them with but feeble opposition. They met never a one so proud and haughty but he must needs bow his back before their mighty strokes.

And in the midst of this bitter encounter king Hrolf's hawk came flying from the stronghold, and perched on the king's shoulder, preening himself as though he had some great victory to boast of. Said Bothvar, 'He acts now as if he had won himself some fame.' The man whose duty it was to look after the hawks hurried off to the loft in which they were kept, and thought it odd that king Hrolf's hawk was out and away. But he found all king Athils's hawks dead.

The end of this clash was that they slew a multitude of men there, and not a soul could stand against them. By now king Athils had vanished, and they had no idea what had become of him. Those of king Athils's men who were still on their feet asked for peace, and they granted them that. They afterwards marched to the hall and boldly on inside. Bothvar asked on what bench king Hrolf was pleased to sit. 'On the king's own dais we will seat ourselves,' replied king Hrolf, 'and I will sit in the high-seat.'

King Athils did not enter the hall, feeling that he had suffered rough handling and won great shame for all these tricks he had tried. They remained now for a while in peace and quiet. Then Hjalti the Magnanimous said: 'Would it not be advisable for somebody to visit our horses and find out whether they may not be short of the things they need?' This was done, and the moment this man returned he reported how the horses had been shamefully handled and utterly spoiled, and gave just such an account of how they had been treated as has been narrated earlier. King Hrolf kept himself well in hand at this, except to say that king Athils ran true to form in everything he wrought.

Now queen Yrsa came into the hall and went up to king Hrolf and greeted him with grace and courtesy. He received her greetings warmly. 'You have not been received here, kinsman,' said she, 'with such good cheer as I would wish and should be. Nor shall you stay here any longer, my son, in the face of such a poor welcome, for there is a great mustering of strength throughout the whole Swedish realm, and king Athils is determined to kill you all, as has been his desire for a long time, had he been able to achieve it. But your good fortune for the moment is stronger than his devilry. Now here is a silver horn which I will give you, in which are kept all king Athils's best rings, and that one in particular whose name is Sviagriss, which he thinks better than all others.' And together with that she made over to him much gold and silver in other forms. This wealth was so great in total that one man could scarcely put a value on it. Vogg was present there and received much gold from king Hrolf for his loyal service.

The queen had twelve horses led forth, all ruddy of colour except for one which was white as snow, which king Hrolf should ride. These were they which had been proved the best of all king Athils's horses, and all of them caparisoned for war. She provided them with shields and helms and armour and other fine apparel, the best that could be found, for the fire had ruined their own clothes and weapons before this. Everything she provided them with of what they needed to have was most splendid.

'Have you made over to me even such wealth as my father owned, and was rightly mine?' asked king Hrolf.

'This is many times greater than that you had to claim,' she told him, 'and in this respect you and your men have greatly enhanced your fame. And now prepare yourselves as best you can, so that none may get the better of you, for you will be hard pressed yet.'

After that they mounted their steeds. King Hrolf spoke lovingly with his mother, and they parted kindly. King Hrolf and his champions now rode on their way down from Uppsala and over the plain which is called Fyrisvellir. King Hrolf saw how a big gold ring lay glittering on the path before them, and it rattled as they rode over it.

'It cries out so loud,' said king Hrolf, 'because it is unhappy to lie alone.'

He slid a gold ring from his arm to join it on the path, saying: 'It shall be told that I do not pick up gold though it lie in my path, and let no man of mine make so bold as to pick it up. It has been thrown here that it may slow down our journey.'

This they promised him, and with that they heard the sound of trumpets from all sides. They saw an innumerable host riding in pursuit of them—a host which proceeded so headlong that everyone was making his own speed as best his horse could manage. King Hrolf and his men kept riding at exactly the same pace. 'They make a hard pursuit, these men,' said Bothvar. 'They are so anxious to catch up with us, I too am anxious they should get some reward for their trouble.'

'Let us not bother our heads about that,' said the king. 'It is they themselves who will be delayed.' He now reached out his hand to the horn containing the gold, which Beigath rode with and held in his hand. He sowed the gold wide about the path, where they were riding the length of Fyrisvellir, so that the route glittered like gold. And when that host which pursued them saw this, how the gold lay glittering wide about the path, most of them flung themselves from horseback, and he reckoned himself the best performer who was briskest at picking it up. There was much snatching and snarling there, and he who was strongest, he got the most. Because of this the pursuit hung fire. When king Athils saw that he almost went out of his mind, lambasting them with cruel words, and swearing that they picked up trifles but let the main prize slip away from them—and this foul shame would be known in every land, 'that you should let a mere twelve men get away from us, such a countless multitude as I have now assembled from every province of the Swedish realm.' King Athils went racing away ahead of them all, he was so angry, with a rabble of men behind him.

Now when king Hrolf saw king Athils blasting along near him, he took the ring Sviagriss and dropped it on the path. And when king Athils saw the ring, said he: 'More loyal has he been to king Hrolf than to me who gave him this treasure, yet none the less I shall enjoy it now, and not king Hrolf.' He took aim with his spear-shaft at where the ring lay, desiring by whatever means to secure it, and bowed low down over his horse as he drove the spear into the bight of the ring. King Hrolf saw that, and turned his horse round, saying: 'Now have I made stoop like a swine him who is mightiest of the Swedes!' And when king Athils was meaning to recover the spear-shaft and the ring with it, king Hrolf galloped up to him and shore off both his buttocks right to the bone with the sword Skofnung, the best of all swords borne by man in the North-lands. Then king Hrolf found words for king Athils, bade him bear this shame a while. 'And now you may know where Hrolf Kraki is, him you have sought for so long.'

His great loss of blood now so affected king Athils that he grew faint with it, and had to turn back with things worse than ever, while king Hrolf recovered Sviagriss. That was their parting this time, and it is not recorded that they met again thereafter. Also they slew all the men who had ridden furthest ahead and put themselves in most jeopardy; for they need not wait long for king Hrolf and his champions, no one of whom thought himself too good to wait on them, and none of whom argued precedence with his fellow, once the opportunity presented itself.

King Hrolf and his men now pressed on their way and rode almost the whole of the day. As night began to fall they came across a farm and went to the door, and who should be there but farmer Hrani. He offered them all hospitality, reckoning it had not turned out so very differently on their journey from what he supposed. The king agreed that was true enough, and said there was no smoke in Hrani's eyes.

'Here are weapons I should like to give you,' said farmer Hrani.

'Queer weapons these, old fellow,' said the king.

They were shield, sword, and corslet, and king Hrolf would not accept them, at which Hrani came near losing his temper, and thought great dishonour had been done him thereby. 'You are not so clever in this, king Hrolf, as you may think,' said Hrani. 'Nor are you always so wise as you suppose yourself.'

The farmer was deeply offended, there was no question now of staying the night, and they chose to ride on their way though the night was dark. Hrani was all scowls to look at, considering himself slighted when they would not accept gifts from him, and did nothing now to dissuade them from riding off as and when they pleased. They rode away with matters thus, and there was no formal leave-taking.

But when they had travelled no great way Bothvar Bjarki came to a halt, and spoke these words: 'Fools grow wise after the event, and so it is with me now. I fear we acted not over-wisely when we refused what we should have accepted—and maybe what we refused is victory.'

'I fear the same thing,' king Hrolf agreed, 'for that must have been old Othin. Quite certainly he was a man with one eye.'

'Back with us then as fast as we can,' said Svipdag, 'and put it to the proof.'

So back they went, and by this time farm and man had vanished.

'It is idle to look for him,' said king Hrolf. 'He is an evil spirit.'

They now pressed on their way, and nothing is told of their journey till they came to Denmark to their own country, and settled down in peace. Bothvar gave the king this counsel, that he should follow the wars but little from now on. He judged it likely that few would attack them if they stayed quiet, but was uneasy, he admitted, as to how victorious the king would prove for the future, should he make any trial of this.

'Fate rules each man's life,' said king Hrolf, 'and not that evil spirit.'

'You are the last we would forsake,' said Bothvar, 'if we have any voice in the matter. Even so, I have a strong foreboding that brief is the respite to events of great import for us all.'

With this they concluded their talk; and they became vastly famous for this expedition of theirs.

The Battle with Skuld

A long while now elapsed after this fashion, that king Hrolf and his champions lived peacefully in Denmark. No one attacked them, all his tributary kings did him homage and paid him their tribute, and so did Hjorvarth his brother-in-law. But it happened on a certain occasion that queen Skuld spoke to king Hjorvarth, her husband, with a deep sigh: 'It pleases me ill that we must pay tribute to king Hrolf and suffer his oppression, and it must not stay the case any longer that you remain his underling.'

'It will be best for us to bear it like the rest of them,' held Hjorvarth, 'and let sleeping dogs lie.'

'What a paltry creature you are,' she scolded him, 'that you are willing to put up with every kind of shame which is done you.'

'It is not possible,' said he, 'to struggle against king Hrolf, for no man alive dare lift shield against him.'

'You are all such paltry creatures,' said she, 'because there is no heart in you. Why, nothing venture, nothing win; and one simply cannot know until the thing is tried whether king Hrolf is immune from blows, and his champions too. Things have now reached such a pass,' she said, 'that I believe he will prove stripped and devoid of victory, and I should have thought that no bad thing to put to the test, and though he is related to me I shall not then spare him. That is why he is continually at home, because he suspects himself that he will lack for victory. I shall now devise a plan, if it would but strike home, nor will I neglect crafts of all kinds in my attempt to overcome him.' Skuld was a great sorceress and had come of elfin stock on her mother's side, and for this king Hrolf and his champions paid dearly. 'For a start I will send men to king Hrolf and ask him this, that he will permit me to pay no tribute for the next three years, and then I will pay him the whole of it at once, in accordance with what he is rightly due. On the whole I think it likely this trick will serve, and should it progress, then we must keep our own counsel herein.'

Messengers now passed between them, even as the queen requested. King Hrolf agreed over the tribute, as was requested. Meanwhile Skuld was assembling all those men who could give best account of themselves, together with the entire scum of all the neighbouring provinces. This treachery, however, was kept hidden, so that king Hrolf knew nothing of it, nor had his champions the least suspicion of it, because the greatest witchcraft and sorcery were used in this. Skuld employed the strongest incantation to vanquish king Hrolf her brother, so that in league with her were elves and norns and other evil creatures so countless that mortal power might not withstand the like. But king Hrolf and his champions held right royal revel and pastime in Leire; and every kind of game known to men, they practised them with skill and courtesy. Each of them had a mistress for his pleasure.

And now there is this to tell of, that when the host of king Hjorvarth and Skuld was fully ready they proceeded to Leire with this countless multitude and arrived there at Yule. King Hrolf had had great preparations made in readiness for Yule, and his men drank hard on Yule-eve. Hjorvarth and Skuld set up their tents outside the stronghold: these were both large and long and wondrously fitted out. There were many wagons, and all of them stuffed with weapons and armour. King Hrolf paid no heed to this. He was more concerned now with his munificence and pomp and pride and all that noble valour which filled his breast, with feasting all those who were come there, and that his glory be carried to the ends of the earth; and he had everything to hand which might enhance the honour of a king of this world. Yet it is not recorded that king Hrolf and his champions at any time worshipped the gods; their trust was rather in their own might and main; for in those days the blessed Faith had not been proclaimed here in the Northlands, and little did they, who dwelt in the northern half of the world, know of their Creator.

The next thing to tell of is this, that Hjalti the Magnanimous went to the house where his mistress lived. He saw clearly that things were not peaceful under the tents of Hjorvarth and Skuld. Even so he did nothing about it, not so much as lift an eyebrow, but lay down with his mistress, who was the fairest of women. When he had been there a while he sprang to his feet, and said to this woman: 'Which strikes you as the better, two at twenty-two or one at eighty?'

'Two at twenty-two strike me as better than old fellows of eighty.'

'You whore, you shall pay for those words,' cried Hjalti, and going up to her he bit off her nose. 'Blame it on me if any come to blows over you, and yet I fancy most will think you no great treasure from now on.'

'You used me ill,' said she, 'and not as I deserve.'

'One cannot keep track of everything,' said Hjalti.

He then caught up his weapons, for he could see
the area round the stronghold packed with men in
armour, and standards set up. He realized now that
it was pointless to hide from themselves any longer
that hostilities were at hand. He made for the hall,
to the place where king Hrolf was seated with his
champions. 'Rouse ye, lord king, for the enemy is at
the gates, and there is greater need to fight than be
fondling women. I believe that the gold in your hall
will have little increase from the tribute of Skuld
your sister. She has the grim heart of the Skjoldungs,
and this much I can tell you, that this is no petty
host with hard swords and weapons of war, and they
march around the stronghold with drawn swords.
King Hjorvarth will have no friendly errand to you,
and from this day forth will never again be meaning
to call on you for the kingdom. What now lies ahead
of us,' said Hjalti, 'is that we must lead the army of
our king who grudges us nothing. Let us now make
good our oaths that we will well defend the most
famous king of his day to be found in all the Northlands, and let our defence of him be such that report
of it may run through every land, and repay him
now for weapons and armour and so many other
favours, for we must do no hireling's service here.
Great portents have been revealed to us, but for long
we refused to see them; and strongly do I suspect
that great happenings will follow hereafter in this
place, such as will have long lodging in men's memories. Some will maintain that maybe I speak from
fear, but it may well be that king Hrolf drinks now
for the last time with his champions and retainers.
Up now, all you champions,' cried Hjalti, 'and bid a
swift farewell to your mistresses, for a different
prospect now confronts you, to make yourselves

ready for what shall follow. Up, all you champions, quickly, and arm yourselves each one!'

Then up started Hromund the Hard and Hrolf the Quickhanded, Svipdag and Beigath, and Hvitserk the Valiant, Haklang the sixth, Hardrefil the seventh, Haki the Brave the eighth, Vott the Powerful the ninth, Starolf (thus named) the tenth, Hjalti the Magnanimous the eleventh, and Bothvar Bjarki the twelfth, who was so called because he drove away all king Hrolf's berserks for their arrogance and injustice, killing some, so that no one of them throve against him; for compared with him they were as women when it came to the sticking-point; and yet they were always thinking themselves stronger than him and for ever laying plots against him.

Bothvar Bjarki was instantly on his feet, and donned his armour. King Hrolf, said he, now had need of proud warriors. 'Heart and soul must be strong in all those who stand shoulder to shoulder with king Hrolf.'

Then king Hrolf sprang up, and undaunted he spake. 'Let us take of that drink which is best, and we will drink before battle and be merry, and show in that fashion what men they are, Hrolf's champions, and strive for this alone, that our valour be never forgotten; for here are come the greatest and bravest champions of all neighbouring lands. Tell it to Hjorvarth, to Skuld, and those their bravoes, that we will drink to make us merry before we collect our tribute.'

This was done which the king commanded. 'Aye,' answered Skuld, 'king Hrolf my brother is unlike all others, and such men are the utmost loss. But our fight must be to the finish for all that.'

Such greatness was manifest in king Hrolf that he was praised by friend and foe alike.

Now king Hrolf sprang up from the high-seat where he had been drinking a while before, together with all his champions; they left the good drink for now, and on the instant were out of doors, except for Bothvar Bjarki. Him they saw nowhere. They thought this strange, but held it not unlikely that he had been captured or slain.

As soon as they came outside a dire struggle commenced. King Hrolf himself drove ahead with the standards, and his champions too on both sides of him, and the rest of the garrison, who were not few by a count of heads though they added up to but little. There might be seen great blows on helm and corslet, and many a sword and spear observed in air, and so many dead corpses that the entire ground was littered.

Cried Hjalti the Magnanimous: 'Many a mailshirt is now rent, and many a weapon broken; many a helm is shattered, and many a gallant knight dashed from his steed. Greathearted is our king, for he is now as happy as when he drank ale deepest, and smites with both hands alike. Quite different is he from other kings in battle, for he appears to me to have twelve men's strength, and many a brave fellow has he slain; and now king Hjorvarth can see that the sword Skofnung bites, and rings aloud in their skulls.' For it was the nature of Skofnung that it sang aloud when it felt the bone.

Now the fight grew fast and furious, so that nothing could withstand king Hrolf and his champions. King Hrolf dealt such strokes with Skofnung as might be held a marvel, and they wrought mightily upon king Hjorvarth's host, who were falling in

heaps. King Hjorvarth and his men saw how a huge
bear advanced before king Hrolf's men, and always
next at hand where the king was. He killed more men
with paw of his than any five of the king's champions.
Blows and missiles rebounded from him, and he
beat down both men and horses from king Hjorvarth's host, and everything within reach he
crunched with his teeth, so that alarm and dismay
arose in king Hjorvarth's host.

Now Hjalti looked about him and could not see
Bothvar his comrade, and said to king Hrolf: 'What
can this mean, that Bothvar shelters himself so, and
comes not near the king, such a champion as we
thought him to be, and such as he has often proved
himself?'

'He will be in whatever place suits us best, if he is
his own master,' said the king. 'Hold fast by your
own pride and valour; reproach him not, for none
of you is his equal. Not that I reproach any one of
you, for you are all most gallant champions.'

Now Hjalti went off at a rush back to the king's
lodging, and saw where he was sitting without lifting
a finger. 'How long must we wait on the most famous
of champions?' cried Hjalti. 'This is a thing unheard-of, that you do not stand up on your own two
legs and exert the power of your arms, which are
strong as a led bear's. Up now, Bothvar Bjarki,
chieftain mine, or I will burn the house and you with
it! And what a monstrous thing this is, in a champion
such as you, that the king must expose himself to
danger for our sakes, whereby you ruin that good
report which has been yours the while.'

With a sigh Bothvar stood up. 'You need not try
frightening me, Hjalti,' he said, 'for I am un-
frightened yet—and now I am ready to go. When I

was young I fled neither fire nor iron. Fire have I
seldom experienced, but the press of iron I have at
times endured, and run from neither hitherto. You
shall tell with truth that I will fight full well, and
king Hrolf has ever styled me champion before his
men. I have much to repay him too: above all our
kinship by marriage and the twelve dwellings he
gave me, and many a fine treasure therewith. I slew
Agnar, berserk and king no less, and that deed has
stayed in men's memories.' He recounted to him
now many a mighty deed he had achieved, and how
he had been the death of many men, and bade him
rest sure of this, that he would go fearless to battle.
'And yet I think we have to deal here with something more wondrous by far than in any place else
we have found ourselves. You have not been so helpful to the king by this action of yours as you think,
for by now it had been almost decided which of
them should have the victory. But you have acted
rather through bad judgement than because you did
not wish well to the king; and it would not have
done for any other of his champions save you alone
to call me out, unless it were the king. Any man else
I would have killed, but now it will fare as fate
would have it, that no counsel will serve our turn.
I tell you plain truth, that I can now give the king
less help in many respects than before you summoned me hence.'

'It is clear,' said Hjalti, 'that my concern is above
all for you and king Hrolf, but it is hard to be wise
even so, when events take such a turn as now.'

After this egging of Hjalti's Bothvar stood up and
went outside to the battle. The bear had now
vanished away from their host, and the battle was
beginning to go against them. Queen Skuld, where

she sat in her black tent on her witch's scaffold, had not brought any of her tricks into play while the bear was in king Hrolf's host; but there was now such a change as when dark night follows the bright day. King Hrolf's men could see where a monstrous boar advanced from king Hjorvarth's ranks. To look at he was not less than a three-year ox in size and wolf-grey in colour, an arrow flew from each of his bristles, and in such sinister fashion he felled king Hrolf's liegemen in swathes.

Bothvar Bjarki now laid about him in earnest. He hewed on either hand, and had no other thought than to achieve his utmost before he fell. Now they fell one across the other before him; he had both arms bloodied to the shoulders, and encircling him on all sides a pile of corpses. He was as though he were mad, and so many men did he and still more of king Hrolf's champions kill from the host of Hjorvarth and Skuld that it was uncanny how their host was none the more diminished; yet it was as though they had wrought nothing, and they thought they had never known such a marvel.

'Endless is Skuld's host,' cried Bothvar. 'I fear now that the dead stir here, rise up again and fight against us, and hard will it prove to fight with fetches; and for all so many limbs as here are cloven, shields split, and helms and corslets hewn in pieces, and many a chieftain cut asunder, these the dead are now the grimmest to contend with, nor have we strength to cope with them. But where now is that champion of king Hrolf who most questioned my courage, and time and again challenged me to come out and fight before I answered him? I do not see him now, and yet I am not given to slandering men.'

'You speak truth,' said Hjalti, 'you are no slanderer. Here stands he whose name is Hjalti. I have some work in hand now, and there is no great space between us. I have need of good warriors, for all my armour is hewn from me, foster-brother; and though I think I fight my hardest, I get no vengeance now for all my knocks. But this is no time to hold back if we are to lodge this night in Valholl. Truly we have never before encountered such a marvel as is now upon us, and we have long had warning of these events which have now come to pass.'

Cried Bothvar Bjarki: 'Hearken to what I say! I have fought in twelve pitched battles, and ever been accounted valiant; nor have I yielded ground to any berserk. I whetted king Hrolf to visit king Athils in his home, and we met with some cunning tricks there, yet that was child's play compared with this present evil; and I have such foreboding in my heart that I have not such joy to fight as heretofore. A while since I encountered king Hjorvarth in an earlier assault, so that we clashed head on, and neither of us flung insult at the other. We had a passage of arms for a time. He dispatched a blow at me whereby I scented death; I cut away his arm and leg. A further blow reached his shoulder, and thus I split him down through side and back, and he so altered mien at this that he did not so much as gasp, and it was as if he slept tor a while. I thought him dead, and but few of his kind will be found, for he fought on no less dauntlessly than before, and I shall never be able to tell what gives him strength. Many are the men now come against us here, nobles and commoners who have thronged in from all directions, so that one cannot hold shield against them. But Othin as yet I do not descry here, though I strongly suspect that he will be spreading his wings against us here, that foul and faithless devil's whelp! Could anyone but point him out tó me, I would squeeze him like any other vile and tiniest mousling. Wicked, poisonous beast, shameful would be his handling if I might lay hold of him! And none in this world but would store more hatred in his heart, if he saw his liege-lord so treated as we now see ours.'

'It is not easy,' said Hjalti, 'to bend what is fated, nor to withstand supernatural power.' And with that they ended their talk.

King Hrolf defended himself well and valiantly and with greater courage than any man has known the like of. They made at him hard, and a ring was thrown around him of the very pick of Hjorvarth's and Skuld's host. Skuld had now come to the battle, and eagerly whipped on that vile gang of hers to attack king Hrolf, for she could see that his champions were not all that close beside him. This was the thing that harassed Bothvar Bjarki greatly, that he might not be of help to his lord, and so with other of those champions, for they were now as ready to die with him as they had been to live with him when they were in the flower of their youth. The king's entire bodyguard had now fallen, so that no one of them survived, and most of the champions were mortally wounded, and this was the course of events which might be expected (said Master Galterus), that mortal strength might not withstand the strength of such fiends unless God's power should intervene—and that alone stood in the way of your victory, king Hrolf, that you knew naught of your Creator.

And now there came such a storm of enchantment that the champions began to fall one across the other, and king Hrolf came out from the shield-wall and was as a man dead of exhaustion. There is no need to make a long tale of it: there fell king Hrolf and all his champions, gloriously.

And what great slaughter they made there, words fail to describe. There fell king Hjorvarth and all his host, save that a few dastards survived along with Skuld. She subjugated king Hrolf's dominions, and ruled them ill and but for a short while, for Elgfrothi took vengeance for Bothvar Bjarki his brother, even as he had promised him, together with king Thorir Houndsfoot, as is recorded in Elgfrothi's chapter. They obtained an immense reinforcement from Sweden from queen Yrsa, and men say that Vogg was leader of that troop. They held for Denmark with their entire force, all unsuspected of queen Skuld. They managed to secure her, so that she could not practise her magic arts. They slew all that vile gang of hers, and put her to death with divers torments, and so restored the kingdoms to king Hrolf's daughters. Then they returned each to his own home.

A burial mound was erected for king Hrolf, and his sword Skofnung laid beside him; and for each champion his mound, and some weapon beside him.

And there ends the tale of king Hrolf Kraki and his champions.